The Genie and Me

Tender's Story

Kelly Stevenson Reed

Published 2025

Printed in the United States of America

ISBN: 978-1-953430-26-7 (pbk)

ISBN: 978-1-953430-25-0 (ebook)

For information, address:

Write and Vibe Publishing at info@writeandvibe.com

I would like to thank God, my first readers, Alise, Linda, Lydia, and Hajira, and my husband, Brian.

"Great strength and physical resilience have always presented themselves to me as being necessary for service to mortals. But I'm beginning to think it's not.

"It is time for kindness and mercy. It is time for sensitivity and creativity. It is now time for my quieter brethren to begin to serve. For they may bring about the end of our entire system, if handled correctly.

"You will not turn on your masters, or behave viciously, or cruelly. You will be known for your obedience and submissiveness. You may help redeem our brethren among these mortal creatures. You will prove our worth to me."

Introduction

He woke up as if he had been slammed into consciousness.

What can be going on out there?

Even though his lamp didn't violently shake or even gently rock, he always felt as if something dramatic was going on in the world outside. He looked around instinctively but the large, oddly shaped oval room hadn't changed. His few scrolls and books were stacked in a pile on the floor next to his bed. The short black shelf containing a few human electronic gadgets was still there. He kept them to entertain himself between masters.

Now he wished - how ironic - that he had kept one of those djinn-based time pieces. But they were mostly unreliable and the time that they showed was only accurate in the djinn world, which he was most definitely not in. So what good was that?

He stretched and ambled over the table where he waved a steaming mug of coffee into existence. He was sure he had time to drink it; his lamp was set to wake him up a full twenty minutes before any anticipated summons. But as soon as he was about to take a sip, he felt it. Somebody was rubbing the left side of his lamp, which to him, felt like someone rubbing his left arm.

Introduction

Isn't that always the way?

He put the mug down, waved it back out of existence, and straightened his clothes. Time for his entrance.

Might as well make an impressive show of it.

He turned into a dazzling cloud of white smoke that funneled itself out of the lamp through its spout. When he reformed himself outside of the lamp, kneeling, he bowed to the man holding the lamp. "Greetings, my new master. I am the genie of the lamp. In fulfillment of my oath, your wish is now my command." And he bowed again.

He kept his eyes open but down towards the filthy rugs barely covering the ground so he only heard what happened next. First, there was this enormous, joyous series of yelling. It was an older male voice and he saw the man's two well-worn shoes do a little dance.

But then the two feet stopped. The genie heard muffled gasps and watched the shoes stagger for a moment until the man collapsed, face down, directly in front of him.

Shocked, the genie didn't move. After a minute, he reluctantly lifted his head to gaze at the man. No breathing, no movement, no thoughts. The man was clearly dead.

The genie focused on the body long enough to sense that the lamp was under the deceased's belly. He carefully stood up and looked around the tent. It held various junk sorted in piles, empty burlap sacks, a makeshift bed, and the random equipment of a traveling scavenger. He closed his eyes to sense out the rest of his surroundings but felt no human presence in the area. They were in the desert.

Staring at his dead master again, he carefully walked around the body and ran out of the tent.

Part One

Chapter 1
Tender's Story: A Genie

" A real, live, genie!" Jewel, an attractive and extremely excited sixteen-year-old girl murmured, a little surprised that she actually said it out loud. But there was no one else around. Rose, Jewel's official caretaker, or 'minder,' as Jewel liked to call her, was gone for the next hour or so in anticipation of the king's visit.

Jewel fell back on one of the many oversized cushions that lined the great room of her palace apartment. There was a knock on her door, and then two palace guards entered, followed by the king, a stately man in his fifties.

"It is time, Jewel," the king announced.

"Really? Time to meet the genie?"

"Yes. Come along."

Jewel jumped up and followed her uncle, the king, through the large palace hall. He told her, "You may question the genie first. And then, make your wish."

"Oh, Uncle, thank you. I have been looking forward to this all week." Jewel beamed at the king, almost running next to him to keep up as they entered one of the great halls of the palace. She bounced with anticipation. "A real genie. I've always wanted to meet one."

"I hope he doesn't disappoint you, my dear. Do you think you're ready to meet him?"

"Of course," she declared with more confidence than she felt.

"Wait in the side hall until I'm ready for you. I will let you question him as much as you like, but we also must make time for the other women to get their wishes granted too."

"Yes, sir."

The king entered the Crystal Court Room, known as such because of the glass ceiling, leaving Jewel in the very large side hall. The Crystal Court Room was one of the smaller grand palace rooms with open rooms on both sides, many windows, and equally as many mirrors. The king's throne was also made of glass, along with a smaller throne to his left that was reserved for Jewel for more formal occasions.

Jewel nearly ran in after him but the guards closed the expansive doors behind him. She peeked into the room through the grate at the bottom of the left door. The guards at their posts took little notice of her, accustomed to the casual manner of the king's over-indulged niece.

She watched the king sit at a table covered with maps and plans, which he looked over and rearranged. Almost as an afterthought, he said, "Genie, I summon you."

A wisp of white smoke appeared next to the king, growing rapidly until it became a small cloud. In the midst of the cloud, the genie materialized, kneeling in front of his master, and the cloud vanished.

Jewel examined the genie as much as she could through the grating and was greatly surprised by what she saw. The genie was not some enormous, grotesque, exaggerated figure crudely attempting the form of a man, but someone who looked like an actual man. His skin wasn't blue, or green, or any other primary color, but an ordinary, common shade.

He looked to be no more than twenty-five or twenty-six years old and was very handsome, which was odd for a creature rumored to be thousands of years old. He was much older than she was, true, and yet, somehow young. He wasn't what Jewel was expecting at all.

The genie kneeled at a hand's length above the floor before the king and then bowed to him. He kept his head down and his eyes closed. In a masculine, but still quiet and calm voice, he asked, "Yes, Master? How may I please you?"

"Did you go over the plans with my generals?" the king asked.

"Yes, Master. I warned them of the strengths of your enemy's army and how I may be of service during the battle, if they so desire."

"Good." The king looked over the maps and plans one more time, taking one of the maps before standing. He gestured to what was in front of him, "Return all of this to the war room, Genie."

"Yes, Master."

The table, chairs, and everything on it disappeared. The king barely reacted, but in the hall, Jewel nearly fell backwards with surprise. She had heard of the powers of genies but had never actually seen their magic in action. And the genie hadn't even moved! Or at least she didn't *see* him move. She peered at him, to study him more closely.

The genie's dark hair hung loosely, framing his face with a small, banded lock at the top of his head, which was four times longer than the rest of his hair. There were metal cuffs on his wrists and his ankles, which Jewel assumed were his shackles. He wore the clothes of a slave and looked exactly like the other slaves and servants in the palace. Except, he could float.

"And now, to celebrate my birthday, as I promised, it's time for you to fulfill the wishes of my friends' wives, servants, and concubines as long as all the wishes remain within the parameters that we discussed. Don't grant anything that I wouldn't approve."

"Yes, Master," the genie nodded.

"And make this room look more festive just like how you decorated the banquet hall and throne room earlier."

"Yes, Master." The genie barely lifted two fingers on his right hand and the entire room changed. There were now gold fabric decorations and accents all around, and elaborate flower arrangements in large planters. The lighting became brighter and warmer; even the uniforms of the guards looked more cheerful.

"Perfect, Genie, we're almost ready. But first, my niece. She wishes to talk to you. To question you, as she puts it, mostly to satisfy her curiosity. As she has never met one of your kind before, I will allow it. Answer her questions, Genie, but keep in mind, your answers must satisfy me also."

"Yes, Master, I will obey you." The king looked at the map again, when the genie asked, "Master?"

"Yes, Genie?"

"May I speak freely?"

"Yes."

The genie, puzzled, opened his eyes, and looked directly at the king. "Please forgive my asking, but what does she want from me?"

"Don't worry, Genie. It won't be an interrogation, just questions from a curious girl," the distracted king tried to reassure him.

"Forgive me again, Master, but most mortals who wish to question me are usually trying to trick me or entrap me. Or to search for some answer that I am forbidden to give."

"There won't be any trickery involved, I assure you. Jewel is much too earnest for that. You will remain blameless in the whole affair. If she asks anything that makes you uncomfortable, let me know, and I'll reign her in."

"Yes, Master, and thank you." The genie bowed his head and closed his eyes again. "I will do as you wish."

"Good. And as for the others, I will want an accounting of everything at the end of the day."

"Yes, Master."

The king nodded and turned to leave when the genie quietly asked, "Master?"

"Yes, Genie?"

"Before your guests arrive, may I return to my lamp for a moment to rest? I have not slept nor eaten for three days."

"Nonsense, Genie. Your people don't need to eat or sleep. You may return to your lamp after your work for the celebration is done."

"Yes, Master."

"The women will be here soon but my niece will ask her questions first."

"Yes, Master. I will obey you."

The genie closed his eyes and bowed low as the king left the room through the main door. He returned to his kneeling position, still floating in the air. Jewel continued watching him until the genie turned towards her and bowed. Jewel gasped, jumped up, and ran away from the door.

The genie had known she was there the whole time but had been too curious to react to her earlier. Who exactly was she, this young girl? This child, who wished to ask him questions. And why?

Chapter 2
Ally's Story: His Last Master

The newly escaped djinn's running stopped abruptly a few feet away from the tent. He made himself transparent and floated over the tent, growing ten times bigger, and even more diaphanous. He looked around, in every direction, for any signs of life.

There. He saw a struggling caravan not too far away. He only had to attract their attention. He shrank back to human size and waved two fingers at a space not far from the tent.

A smaller tent appeared full of food and supplies, exactly what the caravan needed. Then he waved two fingers towards the larger tent and it caught on fire. He waved at it again and the fire began to rage, enveloping everything in the tent and creating a huge plume of smoke in the sky large enough to be visible to any desperate desert traveler. Travelers with sense, anyway.

The genie then shrank himself down to the size of a grain of rice, sat down in the shade besides the smaller tent, and waited.

After about forty-five minutes he began to wonder how long it would take for a caravan to travel anyway? He grew huge and transparent again and looked for the caravan. It was going the wrong way;

they would miss his staged fire by nearly half a league. He shrank back down to human size and his normal opacity.

Since the fire was fading, he waved his fingers again to cause it to revive itself and burn again with even more smoke. Instantly, he shrank back down to pin-size, sat back down in his shady spot, and waited. Again.

After twenty minutes, he closed his eyes and focused on the people in the caravan to visualize them.

There are two brothers and two servants. The eldest brother has a wife and a son. Ten years old. His wife is - oh. She is nine months pregnant, about to give birth, and very sensitive to the rocky terrain, so they had to take the smoothest route. That was considerate.

They are headed his way now to see what happened and look for a safe place to camp for the night. It should take about thirty minutes for them to arrive. I can wait.

He leaned back against the tent and settled in.

Chapter 3
Tender's Story: The First Interview

The king entered the Crystal Court Room followed closely by his advisors, including the Chief Advisor. The genie, who was kneeling and floating in front of the throne, bowed to the king.

"Guards, it's time for the ladies to be brought in." The guards bowed to the king and left to retrieve the women. Jewel, still excited, came into the room first.

The Chief Advisor approached the king, discreetly. "Sire, I'm still not sure about this. Are you sure you can trust this-this magical creature?"

"I'd bet my life on it," the king answered, "and I have. I told him specifically what he can and cannot do and I trust him. Right, Genie?"

"I will obey you, Master, and follow your instructions." The genie bowed again. "If they wish for anything outside your specific parameters, I will not grant it without your express permission."

"Good. I'll stay here until the generals return from their meeting." While the king took his throne, the genie floated to the right of the throne with his still eyes closed. The king turned back to his niece with a much lighter demeanor. "Now, are you ready to start, my sweet?"

"Yes," Jewel yelled, then tried to reply more calmly, "Yes, Uncle."

"Well, go on then."

Jewel approached the genie cautiously, not exactly sure what to expect. The genie also didn't know what to expect and mentally braced himself for anything. "Good afternoon, Genie." Jewel said, tentatively.

"Good afternoon, Miss," the genie replied with a small bow in her direction.

Jewel paused, startled by the genie's reply. Being addressed directly by the genie was another new experience.

The king chuckled and added, "So formal, Jewel. Don't be afraid of him; he won't hurt you. I've already prepared him so feel free to ask him anything you like."

Jewel nodded in reply to her uncle but was still a bit intimidated. "Genie?"

"Yes, Miss?"

"Is that how you like to be addressed?"

"It is how I am customarily addressed, Miss. I have no objection to it."

"Oh. Good." Jewel nodded nervously. She paused again, uncertain in her approach.

The king pressed her to continue. "Come on, Jewel. You can do better than that. Don't be shy now. Be bold, like you usually are."

Jewel looked down for a second, took a deep breath, and began. "Please, tell me Genie, what was the reason you were turned into a genie? Did you harm some sorcerer's daughter? Did you steal a magician's treasures? Did you owe a gambling debt? And what was the name of the sorcerer? And how long ago did it happen?" Jewel was almost breathless by the end of her questions and the king laughed.

The genie looked confused, "Miss?"

Jewel asked again, "Why were you turned into a genie? And how long have you been a genie?"

Finally, the genie understood her question and realized he had to confront a popular myth once again. "My parents were genies, Miss. And so, I have been one since the day I was born."

This surprised Jewel and dampened her enthusiasm, somewhat. "So, you've always been a genie?"

"Yes, Miss."

The king's Chief Advisor eyed the genie skeptically, still uncomfortable with the whole scenario. "I suppose it happens, but that doesn't fit with the stories I've heard."

At this point, a guard came in, went directly to the king, and whispered something to him.

"Excuse me, Jewel, but I think you are well on your way. I will return shortly. You may continue, genie." The genie bowed to the king as he left with the guard.

"So, you were born a genie?"

"Yes, Miss."

"I never imagined that one could actually be born as a genie."

"If I may say so, Miss, on the day I was born, as soon as I cried, my mother said to me, 'Yes, cry little one. For you are not your own.'"

"Oh, come now, Genie, you're not telling us that you actually remember that, are you?" The Chief Advisor questioned him like a lawyer.

"No, sir, but it is what all djinn mothers tell their newborn babes when they are born confined in an object. I was born in my father's lamp, sir."

"You were born in a lamp?" Jewel asked.

"Yes, Miss. Along with my six brothers and sisters. The fact that my father served the owner of his lamp was a sign that one of us would also be chosen to serve. I was the youngest, Miss."

"Is it always the youngest?" she asked.

"No, Miss, but only those who are chosen. Between the ages of six and nine, certain symbols appear upon the wrists of the ones chosen. My markings appeared when I was six, miss."

She asked, "What is the symbol?"

Simultaneously, the Chief Advisor questioned, "Why were you chosen?"

In deference to the advisor's position and hostility, the genie answered his question first. "Sir, my temperament was deemed more suitable for service that year by the wise and valued Leader of all the djinn." He bowed as he mentioned the Leader. "Miss, it is the symbol of a slave, written in the language of my people. Unfortunately, my markings are hidden beneath my shackles. But I can reproduce the symbol for you, miss, if you like."

"No, Genie, that won't be necessary." She envisioned what it would be like to be chosen for slavery at six years old. "How did your parents react?"

"My mother was heartbroken, Miss. She was very close to me and thought that I would always be there for her. My father reacted better, though he was also upset. My parents expected one of my older brothers to be chosen and were preparing him for that purpose, Miss."

"How?" she asked, curiosity winning over her sadness.

"My father was serving a master at that time and so he would share his experiences and explain the tenets of our laws to him, Miss. They were also training him to be strong in body and mind."

"And so they just transferred their training to you?" she asked.

"Because of my mother's tenderness towards me, Miss, my parents continued raising me as before, treating me just as one of their other children, and even continued teaching and training my brother."

"My goodness, Genie, he must have hated you for it." Caught up in the story, the Chief Advisor couldn't resist commenting.

"He was resentful that I was chosen at first, sir, but gradually came to accept it and me in my new role."

"So, you became enslaved without any training at all?" he asked.

"Forgive me, sir, but no, sir," the genie bowed, careful to show the Chief Advisor respect. "I was trained from the age of ten to the age of twenty-one."

"By your parents?" he asked.

"No, sir. By the wise and honored Leader of all of my kind," he bowed, "and his instructors." Sensing the approach of his master, the genie bowed low with his arms out forward, and yet still floating off the ground. His master, the king, attended by some of his military advisors and generals, appeared to be passing through, but stopped to observe.

"And how is the conversation proceeding, my dear?"

"It's fascinating. And sad."

"Oh? How so?"

"I didn't know that they were born in lamps."

"Genies can live in lamps, rings, or even rugs. And trees and other objects outside," the king replied, missing her point completely.

"Really?" Jewel asked, halfheartedly.

"Yes, and they can even change their size!"

"Wow," she feigned more excitement than she felt. "May I ask him more questions?"

"Of course. But have you made your wish yet?"

"This is my wish, just to ask him more questions." She turned to address the genie directly. "Genie? May I ask you more questions?"

While she was still speaking, the genie opened his eyes and looked up at his master, who nodded in response. Then the genie quickly closed his eyes and lowered his head. "Yes, Miss. You may ask me as many questions as you like."

"Chief advisor," the king asked.

"Yes, sire?"

"We need to let in the other women and grant their wishes as well."

"Yes, sire."

"Jewel, you can ask more of your questions and get your wish after they are done."

"Yes, Uncle. May I question him until they arrive?"

"Yes, Jewel." Almost as soon as the king left the Crystal Court Room via a side door next to the throne, the other women entered in the front main doors. There were twenty-seven women in all, some of them favorite courtesans, a few concubines, other daughters of the king's cabinet members and generals, and a few favored servants, including Jewel's governess, Rose. They crowded behind Jewel, afraid to approach the genie any closer.

Jewel quickly asked another question. "Genie, why do you keep your eyes closed most of the time?"

"It was my master's wish so that my eyes will not frighten mortals, Miss."

"Are your eyes so very scary?"

"My eyes can reflect the magic that is within me, Miss. They are also of a color not normally seen in the eyes of mortals." He knew where this was going.

"What color are they?"

"Reddish orange, Miss."

"May I see them?" Jewel did not hesitate.

"No, no, he will enchant us," one of the servant girls nearly screamed.

"Or give us the evil eye," yelled one of the courtesans.

The genie hesitated.

"Are you intending to harm any of us in any way, Genie?" Jewel asked plainly.

"No, Miss. Not at all," the genie answered, trying to sound as harmless and inoffensive as possible under the circumstances.

"See?" Jewel said to the others.

"But he will enchant us with his thoughts!" the frightened servant girl cried.

"Don't be ridiculous. Not with his master, the king around." Suddenly confident, Jewel turned towards the genie. "Show us your eyes, Genie, although do be careful not to look directly at any one of us."

"Yes, Miss." The genie, steeling himself for the reaction he knew was coming, lifted his head, aimed his sightline above their heads, and opened his eyes. His eyes glowed brightly, as if lit from within.

Several women screamed while others turned away, too frightened to continue looking. Some were mesmerized by the sight. Others were indifferent.

"That's enough, Genie, thank you," Jewel calmly replied.

The genie closed his eyes while she spoke and lowered his head once again. Jewel noticed that he seemed to act in anticipation of requests.

"I'm tired of this foolishness. I want my wish," demanded one of the courtesans, Flora, as she approached the genie.

"Yeah, me too," her twin sister, Fauna decreed, pushing her way forward through the crowd of women.

"Yes, Miss." The genie addressed Flora first by turning his head slightly towards her, but still not looking directly at her. "What do you wish of me?"

"I want the most beautiful fabric in the world," Flora demanded. Nearly every word she spoke was a demand.

"No, I want the most beautiful fabric in the world," Fauna insisted. She was accustomed to insisting on her way with her sister.

"I asked him first."

"Because you stole my idea." The sisters were about to quarrel but were startled into silence by a nod of the genie's head.

"I will do as you wish." The genie waved two fingers and in a small puff of white smoke, two neatly rolled bolts of beautiful fabric appeared, one in front of each sister. The fabric appeared to be made of intricately woven silver, gold, and some type of diamond-like material, for the bolts glowed and shimmered with reflected light.

"Oh, wonderful! This is the most beautiful fabric I've ever seen. Oh, thank you, thank you." Flora picked up her fabric.

"No, *this* is the most beautiful," Fauna insisted, yet again, while picking up her fabric. "Look at it, it's wonderful. Have you ever seen such fabric before?" The sisters continued marveling at their respective rolls, which only encouraged the rest of the women. They crowded around the genie only as close as they dared, each one shouting out their wish.

"I would like some jewelry."

"I would like rings made out of the purest gold."

"I would like a husband!"

Jewel stepped back to avoid the rush and watch the spectacle. The genie fulfilled wish after wish tirelessly, never pausing, producing gold, jewels, and other treasures. He even managed to supply the husband. "A gentleman and his parents will request a meeting with your father this afternoon, miss, to arrange your marriage. The young man will look exactly as you described and his personality will also meet your specifications."

"Thank you," the general's daughter squealed. She ran out of the room, leaving only Jewel and the genie along with a few guards. Even the Chief Advisor had left.

"And you, Miss?" the genie addressed Jewel. "What do you wish of me?"

"First, I want you to tell me something. I thought that genies didn't need to eat. Do you need to eat regular meals?"

"It depends, Miss. My master wishes me to remain mostly in a physical form. And so, when I am in my physical form, I have all the requirements of a physical being. And so yes, Miss, in my current form, I *do* need to eat."

"So, you're not always in a physical body?"

"Not always, Miss. In general, I try to remain in whatever form my master desires."

"I see."

Jewel then paused, looked towards the banquet hall where a large feast was soon to take place. It was one of many of which she had often partaken. Yet, this feast was already making her feel guilty. "My wish has two parts, Genie. First, I wish you to provide a three-course feast, a large meal for one, right here, full of your favorite foods."

He was surprised by this; she didn't seem to be the glutinous type at all. But as requested, a large feast on a table appeared before them, full of his favorite, fragrant, foods. He was careful to provide only food familiar to mortals and nothing particular to his people. But he nearly jumped when he foresaw the rest of her request.

"Yes, Miss?"

"Second, I wish you to have three whole, uninterrupted hours in which to eat as much as you like. During those three hours, you may eat, relax, or otherwise quietly entertain yourself as you see fit."

"As you wish, Miss."

She left the room and he was alone outside of his lamp for the first time that day, aside from a few guards at the doors. He stayed still for a few moments, unused to the silence, and opened his eyes. Uncertain of what to do exactly, he took a grape from one of the bowls of fruit and plopped it into his mouth before anyone could catch him. Upon noticing the lack of a reaction, specifically from the guards at the door, the only ones left in the room, he smiled to himself and began eating the meal in earnest, taking his time.

It took him only one hour to finish, not eating exactly everything, but eating as much as he wanted. He spent the last two hours resting on cushions that he had conjured, relaxing and wondering who was this girl who would use her only wish on him? Would she want something else in return? Was this part of some scheme? Would he have to be on his guard from now on?

He had heard the tales; the many stories of mortals trying to charm or trick his people out of wishes. But he did not see any signs of duplicity nor any hidden motives. He would have to look deeper, of course, eventually, but she genuinely seemed guided only by her curiosity and her overdeveloped, immature sense of justice. Also, how would he tell his master what just happened? He would be compelled to describe it, but how would his master take it?

After his third hour of peace ended, he made the cushions and the table with its remaining food disappear. He felt himself being summoned by his master to the Emerald Throne Room to give a full account of every one of the wishes he had just granted.

The Emerald Throne Room was one of the largest and most magnificent rooms in the entire palace, large enough to entertain the king's entire court and all his servants; nearly every person in the entire kingdom could fit inside of it. The king sat on his splendid, green, elevated marble throne decorated with emeralds as the genie appeared before it in a large cloud of white smoke.

He immediately bowed before the king and began to recount the many wishes he had just granted. The king and his courtiers listened eagerly to the genie. They were all thoroughly entertained by his descriptions of the requests, especially when he mentioned the husband he had found.

"Master, I told the young lady that a gentleman meeting her specifications and his parents would request a meeting with her father later this afternoon."

The general, whose daughter's marriage wish had been granted, remarked, "I had better hurry home! Excuse me, your majesty, please," which caused even more laughter in the court.

"Of course," the king replied, laughing also.

When it came to Jewel's wish, the genie was a bit hesitant, though still compliant. "And then finally, Master, your niece made her wish, in two parts. First, she wished for a feast of my favorite foods. Secondly, Master, she wished that I would have three hours free, just to eat, relax, and enjoy it."

"She wished for a feast for you?" the king questioned.

"Yes, Master. I did not quite understand at it first, but she wished me to eat, to have three hours to do so, and to relax and quietly entertain myself as I saw fit. Forgive me, Master, if I have offended you by granting her wish."

"No, no, Genie. You did as she asked. It was within the parameters." The king turned to one of the guards. "Guard, fetch Jewel here at once. Go to your lamp, Genie. I will call for you tomorrow."

The genie bowed low and disappeared in a cloud of smoke. From inside his lamp, he strained against the side to see or hear what he could of what happened next, but the robes of his master, who had tied the lamp to his waist, were too thick. So, he sat down, crossed his legs and closed his eyes, and focused. He saw in his mind the large Emerald Throne Room where his master sat on his throne.

Jewel entered the room as the courtiers were being dismissed.

"My friends, I will see you tomorrow as the festival continues. For now, please, go enjoy the feast."

Everyone in the court left in a jovial mood except for the ever-present guards at the door. The king was visibly upset as he stepped down from his throne.

"Jewel! What do you mean by throwing away your wish in such a frivolous way? Do you not know that the genie can eat whatever he wants in his lamp, whenever he pleases?" The king was exasperated. "I expected silly wishes from the others, but not from you, Jewel."

"But the genie asked you if he could rest before this whole thing began and you refused him. He said that he hadn't slept or had anything to eat for three days. He's in his physical form."

"He is a creature of magic, Jewel, capable of many strange and powerful things and you were worried about his wellbeing? Did he unduly influence you?" The king began circling her, studying her. "His kind is known for their cunning. Did he promise you anything in exchange for your wish? Could he have tricked you in any way?"

"No, Uncle. Of course not!" Jewel grabbed her uncle's arm to stop his examination. "He only answered my questions. It is not right that you should feed a dog and leave a worthy servant to starve."

"A nice, sentimental, old saying."

"But it's true." She softened and continued. "Forgive me, Uncle, but it just didn't seem right to let him go hungry. The genie has been working for three days straight. I admit, I feel sorry for him."

"Sorry for him? Why?"

"Because he was born into slavery. He's been training for it since he was ten-years-old."

"My dear girl, we live in a palace. We are literally surrounded by servants and slaves of all ages, day and night. All of them are extremely well trained, some since birth."

"Yes, but he is different somehow."

"How? Many apprenticeships begin at young ages. How is he any different?"

Jewel hesitated, then answered with a frustrated look on her face. "I don't know."

The king gave her a gentle look, took her hand in his, and held it. "Perhaps because he did not fit in with what you were expecting. You had his mischievous human history all mapped out and instead, you found a rather sad story."

"Yes, Uncle, I suppose so."

"We are not responsible for his enslavement, Jewel."

"I know, but it, it still strikes me as so miserable." Her uncle hugged and kissed her on the forehead. "You are too sensitive, my dear. And you let this affect you too deeply."

"I'm sorry."

"Do not feel sorry for him, though. He has accepted his fate. And so, we must accept it also."

"Alright."

"And yet I admire your tender heart. Your kindness becomes you."

"Thank you, Uncle."

"Would you like to question him again?"

"Really?" Jewel perked up. "I can ask him more questions?"

"Of course, if that will cheer you up."

"Yes. Yes, it will, sir."

"Good. Then you may question him tomorrow in full court. I want to see it this time."

"Oh Uncle, thank you, thank you so much."

"Now go join the others."

"Yes, Uncle! And thank you again."

"Don't overdo it, dear, or I'll think that this was your plan all along. Now, run along."

Jewel was so happy she practically skipped out of the room. She would be able to question the genie again! Oh, the history. The stories. The things he would tell her. He was a walking, breathing, history book. He would tell her of the strange ways of his people. The only thing she didn't look forward to was the time she would have to stop asking him questions.

Chapter 4
Tender's Story: Childhood

T hough she was exhausted most of the time, Darling loved each of her children dearly. And she knew that the odds of one of them being chosen to serve was great, though she tried hard not to think about that too much. Most days, some days, it even worked.

She sighed as she reviewed their completed lessons for that day. Patient and Gentle's reading had improved so much that she would have to increase the complexity of their reading material, Creative needed more art supplies, and Sweet needed more to do, mostly because when he got bored, he annoyed his siblings. Not intention-ally, but because he was trying to be helpful, and yet didn't quite know how.

She looked over at them in the large room in the lamp. They were running from one curved wall to the other, ostensibly "racing" each other though the three little ones were just having fun running with their brothers and sisters.

"Slow down. And don't run over each other." She watched as the older children made a token effort to slow down, then returned to reviewing her lessons. Maybe she could come up with a project for Sweet to work on.

"Ah!" The sound of a little girl's cries filled the room. Darling saw Dearest on the floor with her youngest child crouched over her and Strong hovering, pushing the other children back as she came near.

"I told you to not to run over each other."

"We didn't, she fell," Sweet answered and their mother could see and hear that he was telling the truth. She picked up Dearest and sat down with her in her arms in what she thought of as the "comfort chair," which she designed to be just right for her and at least one child. She would shrink or expand it as necessary, depending upon the number of children that needed comforting in the moment.

"It's not that bad! You just had a bad fall, that's all. It'll be alright, Dearest, you were just frightened by it." The little girl's cries calmed down and that's when Darling noticed her youngest son standing next to them, quietly crying too.

"Here, let's lay you down, alright?" she asked the girl.

Dearest nodded and Darling picked her up and put her in her bed behind curtain dividers on the other side of the room. She covered her with a shawl. "There you go, my dearest one, get some rest and you'll feel better."

The little girl nodded and Darling stayed there until Dearest quickly fell asleep. When Darling turned to leave, she noticed her youngest son, still quietly crying, peeking in on them. She picked him up before he could bother his sister and was soon back in the comforting chair, comforting him. "It's alright, my little one."

He continued to cry, softly.

"Are you worried about your sister?"

He nodded.

"It's alright, she's not really hurt, just scared. She's getting some rest right now."

The small boy nodded and hugged his mother in return.

"It's alright, I know it scared you too, but Dearest will be fine, my little tender one, my little piece of tenderness." The name seemed to fit his personality perfectly since Tender always seemed to be deeply affected by whatever was going on, no matter what. A very sensitive child, he empathized with nearly everyone and only seemed to get angry when his closest sister, Dearest, was threatened.

Darling admitted to herself that sometimes her children's names were more aspirational than literal, but she did try to aim for accuracy as much as she could with very young children. Strong was often weak and insecure, which he demonstrated by giving orders to his brothers and sisters, which, fortunately, the older ones just ignored. Gentle could be occasionally too blunt with her insights. Maybe she should have named her Sensitive instead, to temper her personality.

At least she wasn't like a few other mothers that she knew of, who named their children out of spite, mourning, or vindictiveness. Darling was trying to be hopeful, in this as in everything else.

"YOU LEAVE HER ALONE," six-year-old Tender demanded as he attempted to push his older brother away from Dearest.

Strong was only two years older but had a bigger build. He smirked at Tender and at the ridiculousness of the situation. A tiny boy trying to push him around! Strong respected Tender's courage and his loyalty to their sister. "Mommy made me promise not to hit you. But tell her to stop bothering my stuff!" He walked away, leaving Tender to comfort his sister.

Dearest's crying had turned into quieter whimpers and Tender held and rocked her gently in his arms as their mother had done so often with them. "It's alright, he's gone."

"He took my doll."

"I know, but you got it back, see?"

"Mom told him not to hit you but not me," and she began crying again, but quieter.

"That's because you're older than me. Maybe she thought he would know better."

Dearest abruptly stood up and spotted Strong on the other side of the lamp. He was playing with an intricate wooden puzzle. Using her powers, she snatched the puzzle away from him and it flew into her hand. "See how you like it!"

Immediately, Strong retaliated by raising his hand and using his power to push her across the room. Resisting, she lifted her right hand before hitting the wall and used her powers to push him back.

At this point, their mother returned by materializing in the room. "What are you two doing? Strong, Dearest, stop it right now."

The two children stopped using their powers and put their hands down.

"I leave the lamp for just one hour and this is what I come back to? Go to bed, right now!"

"But it's still early!" Strong protested.

"Now."

The two children headed to their beds, angry and hurt, with Tender watching. "Alright, Tender, tell me what happened."

"Dearest was playing and she wanted to use some wood to play making a fire and so she used the wooden puzzle that Strong had. Then Strong got mad and took her doll and his puzzle. Then she took the stuff back and they started pushing each other with magic."

"Thank you, Tender."

Just then, the four older children materialized in the lamp.

"And where have you been?"

"We were visiting our cousins, Friendly and Inventive. You said that we could go before you left. I hope we weren't away too long," Patient answered quietly.

"Long enough for Dearest and Strong to fight. Next time I have to go see the high council Patient, and you too, Gentle, one of you must stay behind to watch over the little ones. They're too young to be left on their own."

"Yes, Mother." Patient answered, along with Creative and Sweet.

"Yes, Mother," added Gentle. "Did the council say when we'd see father again?"

"No." Darling leaned back in her chair, "Apparently, his current master needs extensive help. His mortal is trying to redesign his entire life to make himself more appealing to others."

"But we haven't seen him in so long!" Creative protested. "And won't his powers weaken after being away from the lamp for so long?"

"No, Creative," Darling was surprised that Creative knew about that. "It takes many, many years for that to happen. Your father will be alright. I'll see if I can contact him through the cloth later tonight."

Later that evening, Darling hung up the cloth in its usual spot. "Kind? Please, my husband, please speak with me."

"Darling," Kind appeared on the cloth. "I miss you, my love."

"I miss you too. Your youngest children wish to see you."

Tender, Dearest, and Strong gathered in front of her and watched their father.

"Papa," Dearest cried, echoed by Tender and Strong.

"It's so good see you, my little ones."

"We miss you," Dearest cried.

"When will you come home?" Tender asked.

"As soon as I can. There is a mortal here and he really needs my help."

"Can't he help himself?" Strong asked.

"He would like too but he also needs my help in so many ways."

Tender and Dearest yawned. Kind smiled at them. "And I think it's time for you three to go to bed."

"But we miss you, Papa," Tender responded.

"I know, and I will be back as soon as I can. In the meantime, mind your mother."

"Yes, Papa," Tender replied, followed by Dearest, "Yes, Papa," and then Strong, "Yes, Papa."

"And Strong, what is your mission?"

"I will keep them safe." Strong replied, taking his responsibility seriously.

"Good. Now go to sleep, my little ones."

"Good night, Papa," they answered.

"Good night. Are my other children there?"

"Papa!" Sweet, Creative, Gentle, and Patient crowded around the cloth as their mother picked up Tender and led Dearest and Strong to bed.

"Why can't he stay here with us, always?" Dearest asked as her mother tucked her into bed.

"Because he has a job to do, helping mortals."

"But he's always helping them. Can't he help us, too?" Strong asked.

"As soon as he's done, he'll be back home to help us too."

"I miss him a lot," Tender said, followed by a big yawn.

"I do too, Tender, I do too." Darling kissed each child on the forehead. "Now, get some sleep. And dream good dreams."

Chapter 5
Tender's Story: The Second Interview

The king held his next conversation in the Emerald Throne Room filled with over two-hundred courtiers, all the king's counselors, and most of his military commanders. All were there for the king's birthday celebration, which included his ascension to the throne, and that was a week-long official holiday.

The king's court usually consisted of the ranked, the favored, and various other pretty and decorative people known for little else. Agreement with the king was the real requirement, and the only true measurement of their stature. The counselors and military leaders were usually too preoccupied for such frivolity, however, since their presence was required, most of them decided that they might as well enjoy themselves. The rest were resigned to tolerate whatever the king had in store.

The king sat on his throne in all his finery and Jewel sat on his left side, also attired in more ostentatious clothes. Her throne was smaller and lower, but still very grand. She found the cushioned marble uncomfortable to sit in, particularly since she never felt that she could live up to its splendor. But her uncle expected it, and the occasion required it.

"And now, as part of the festivities, and before we eat, I will call the genie. He will be officially questioned by my niece. It should at least be informative and hopefully, entertaining. Genie, I summon you."

In a large cloud of white smoke, the genie appeared before the king, frightening a few skittish courtiers. This time, however, his bottom half, below his waist, remained a cloud of white smoke. He tried to put on as much of a show as the king and his court required. Rarely had he ever appeared in full court, so he tried to match the grandeur of the occasion and the courtier's expectations. It was best to look as exotic and otherworldly as possible.

His top half bowed formally. "How may I serve you, master?"

"My niece has a few more questions for you, Genie." The king spoke to the court as much as to the genie. "Please do your best to answer them."

"Yes, Master." The genie bowed again.

"Jewel?"

Jewel stood up and bowed toward the king, and then took her place in front of the genie. She was a bit embarrassed by the grandiosity and attention and would have preferred to quietly question the genie rather than do so in front of so many courtiers, but she did as she was told. The genie bowed before her.

"Tell me, please. What's it like being a genie?"

"I cannot say, Miss. Forgive me, but I do not know what it's like to be anything else."

"But wouldn't you rather be free and anything else, rather than be enslaved and a genie?"

He hesitated slightly, as if resisting an impulse. "I would rather be a genie in any case, Miss. I am grateful to be what I am, and I am happy to be in the service of my master. Being anything else is no guarantee of," he paused and winced so quickly that hardly anyone noticed, "freedom, miss, and I was not born enslaved. My people are contained, but not all of them are enslaved."

"But I thought you were born in a lamp?"

"Yes, Miss, but I was not enslaved, my father was. Neither was my mother, nor any of my brothers and sisters. I was raised in my father's lamp, Miss, along with my siblings."

"How many brothers and sisters do you have again?"

"Three brothers and three sisters, Miss."

"Where are they now?"

"They live within the djinn world, Miss, with their own families."

"And do you also have your own family in the lamp?"

"No, Miss, not yet."

"Why is it that women always want to know if every male is married or not?" the king exclaimed, getting an appreciative response of laughter from the court. It broke the tension but made Jewel a bit more self-conscious.

"And so, you grew up in a lamp, Genie? Did you ever leave it?" Jewel continued when the laughter subsided.

"Not often, Miss. Not until I began my training."

"And what age was that again?"

"I was ten, Miss."

"And where did you train, and in what, exactly?"

"In a school designed for this purpose, miss, in the djinn world. I was trained in how to correctly serve human masters."

"Come now, Genie, you don't need training for that, do you?" the king asked.

"Forgive me, Master, but we do. Being a slave and a servant is not a natural state for my people, nor are we generally raised with mortals. We must learn the ways of your kind to serve you well, Master."

"Is that so difficult?" he questioned.

"Not with training, Master."

"How is your training set up?" Jewel asked, completely fascinated and eager to follow a new line of questioning.

"Our first two years are spent learning obedience, miss. The next three, we work on our magic skills. During the following three years we begin to learn about mortals, and the last three on how best to serve them by combining all our training, and with more education."

"May I commend your teachers, Genie, for you are well-trained indeed," the king stated earnestly.

"Thank you, Master," the genie nodded at the sudden appreciation in surprise.

"And after that?" Jewel persisted.

"After that, Miss, we learn where we are to live. I was placed inside my lamp."

"And then?"

"Then we take our oaths to serve, are traded to distributors, and placed in various locations around the earth, Miss, where we await our fate among mortals."

"Do mortals always find you?" Jewel asked, totally engrossed by the genie's answers.

"No, Miss. Some of my people have never been found by any mortal."

"Can you reveal where they are? I have a few distant relatives constantly in need," the king quipped and the court tittered again.

"No, Master, I cannot." The genie answered quietly, though he was well aware of the joke.

"Do you like living in a lamp?" Jewel asked.

"Yes, Miss. It is my home." The genie looked down, embarrassed because of the reaction he knew was coming.

"You really live in the lamp? It is not a portal to someplace else?" Jewel asked.

"No, Miss. The lamp itself is my home."

"What does it look like?" Jewel asked, excited. "Can you show us?"

The genie opened his eyes, looked directly and deferentially at the king, and asked, "Master, may I show the young miss, and the rest of the court?"

His master smirked, knowing full well what was coming, "Yes, Genie. Show us all."

The genie lowered his head, raised his arms in front of him, and then spread them wide. The large rectangular room where the king held court suddenly appeared to be a smaller circular room with no windows that had a smaller tunnel at one end. The walls were brass-colored but mostly painted white. It was well-lit with no apparent light source. There were several clearly designated areas in the room, one area held bedding and grooming materials, another area had a desk, a large cushion, and many scrolls and books. There was an area used for eating, an area for relaxing, and blank space in front of one of the walls of the lamp.

When the appearance of the room changed, a few of the ladies of the court shrieked and screamed, while some of the gentlemen yelled. Though they liked to pretend to be accustomed to magic, most of them were still frightened by its effects, especially when it came to transforming an entire room.

Jewel, however, was fascinated, and tried to take in and memorize as much as she could. Many members of the court clearly were not enjoying this experience as much as the king and his niece.

After only about thirty seconds, the king said, "Thank you, Genie. That is enough, for now."

"Yes, Master." The genie raised his arms wide, brought them together, and the Emerald Throne Room returned to its usual appearance. Half of the courtiers were smiling and laughing, thoroughly enjoying themselves, while quite a few were shocked and not so quietly panicking.

"And that is enough excitement for today," the king declared. "Genie, you may return to your lamp."

"Yes, Master." He disappeared in a large puff of white smoke and quickly reappeared inside his lamp in a much smaller cloud of smoke, and with his legs. Relieved that he didn't have to perform anymore, he sat back on some of his cushions and tried to relax. He watched the rest of the scene by thinking of the space around his master in his mind.

He saw the king say to his niece, "And you, young lady, back to your room."

"Yes, Uncle. And thank you." She bowed briefly to him and left the court.

"And now, my honored guests, on to the feast!"

The genie stopped watching but thought to himself, "She bows too. So, in her own way, she also serves my master."

Jewel, though relieved to not be a part of the entertainment anymore, was also eager to ask the genie even more questions, but less publicly. She was fascinated by him and his answers and thought of many more subjects she could ask the genie about. She only hoped that her uncle would allow her to question him again.

Chapter 6
Tender's Childhood: Chosen

A few weeks after, while the younger children were quietly playing with their toys, the older children were working on a project and Darling was speaking with her mother through the communication cloth, Kind suddenly appeared in the middle of the lamp.

"I'm back," he said quietly, adding, "for now." But his reception was less than quiet as they all stopped what they were doing and rushed to him. Many hugs and kisses were exchanged.

The next few days were happy, filled with the warmth and the reassurance of having Kind back home. He spoke well of his master, "He is a very noble human, he only needs more confidence in himself." He was much more eager to enjoy his family and their company rather than talk about the outside world or his place in it.

The family soon settled into an easy-going, happy routine, made more complete with their father mostly present. His master rarely called on him and Kind told his wife, "He is more content and at peace now that he's married."

But even this became part of the routine. Kind would be casually playing with his children, eating a meal, or talking with his wife, when he would suddenly straighten in attention, aware of a calling that no one else could see or hear. Sometimes he would quietly say, "My master summons me," while other times, he would just disappear.

Initially, Tender or Dearest shouted, "Papa's gone!" But as his quick reappearance became more routine, they became more secure in the hope of his return and his disappearances were less remarkable.

One night, after all the children had gone to sleep, Kind spoke more candidly with Darling as he got into bed. "My master is becoming more stable as he ages. More satisfied with his own life and preoccupied with his children."

"Does he still keep you hidden?"

"Yes, only his wife knows about me. None of the others, not even his children, suspect anything. I thought for sure that his youngest would barge in on us the other day, but I vanished in time."

"Good."

From that point, they spoke telepathically and shielded their conversation from their children to make sure that they weren't heard.

"*Our youngest are reaching the age of the decision,*" Kind thought, solemnly.

"*Which one of them do you think will be chosen?*"

"*I still hope it's Strong, but I've seen no signs of the markings.*"

"*Creative's past the age and so is Sweet. And Dearest is safe, I'm so grateful she's a girl.*"

"*So, it has to be either Strong or Tender.*"

"*But Tender's so gentle, surely, they won't choose him. I don't know if he can survive the training.*"

"*I can continue to prepare Strong and teach him, but we must be prepared either way.*"

"*Strong really enjoys his special time with you,*" Darling sighed.

"I know. I look forward to it also, but perhaps I should start including Tender in those lessons. Just in case he is chosen."

"Please don't, I can't bear to think of Tender that way."

Kind smiled and thought, *"Tender's your favorite."*

"Tender's the youngest, not my favorite. He's so sensitive, I just don't want him to have to go through that."

"I went through it," Kind reminded her, quietly.

"I know, my love," Darling replied, *"and I am grateful that you survived. I don't know what I would have done, otherwise,"*

"Marry someone else?"

"No. Never. I know I would never have found anyone else so well-named, so kind."

They hugged. *"I wouldn't have found anyone so dear to me either,"* Kind added, *"but I'm glad that we found each other and I'm grateful that I married you."*

They kissed.

THE NEXT DAY, Kind continued Strong's serving lessons. "Remember, you must maintain your strength, but remain respectful as well. Always, on your best behavior," Kind waved his hand and a pile of gold coins appeared before them. Then he bowed. He waved his hand again and the coins disappeared. "Now, you try it."

Strong waved his hand and a similar pile of gold coins appeared, and then he bowed. But then he looked up at his father. "How do you know exactly what they want?"

Kind pointed to the coins. Strong waved his hand again and they disappeared.

"You don't. The key is that they need to know exactly what they want. And then, once you become well-versed in reading mortal minds, it becomes easier for you to picture what they want."

"Mama?" Tender called, while rubbing his eyes. He was trying to play with his blocks but moved lethargically and was too tired to build anything substantial.

His mother picked him up and felt his forehead. "That fever is back again. I'm going to have to conjure another jar of Santar's ointment to stop it from racing through all the children."

Darling carried Tender to his bed where she laid him down. She closed her eyes, held out her hand, and a jar covered with a cloth and a band around it appeared in it. She took the band and cloth off the top, conjured a small spoon in her other hand with a wave of her fingers, scooped out a small amount of the ointment, and gave it to Tender to eat. "Open wide."

Tender obeyed and made a sour face as he tasted and swallowed the ointment.

"There you go, that should do it. Now get some sleep, my sweet boy." She covered him with a blanket. Tender closed his eyes and was soon asleep.

After the last meal that day, Dearest looked up from her meal, "But Mama, Tender didn't get any food."

"It's alright, my love, Tender really needs to sleep right now so he can get well and play with you tomorrow."

Darling put Dearest down into her small bed, covered her up, and kissed her on the forehead.

"Good night, Dearest."

"Good night, Mama." Darling turned to check on Tender in his own bed next to Dearest. He still seemed a bit feverish, which was strange, as usually the ointment worked instantly. Tender shifted in his sleep, raising his right arm above his head. That's when she saw it. It was faint, but unmistakable. The small dark mark of a slave was now on Tender's inner right wrist.

"No," she said quietly, but quickly checked herself.

"*No,*" she repeated to herself, and telepathically to her husband.

In response, Kind appeared instantly and stood by her side. Darling bent down to check Tender's other wrist, gently uncovering his left arm. The mark was there also.

"No," she stifled another cry, but Kind held her tightly. She trembled, broke away, and then rushed out of the young children's bed section.

Kind covered Tender's arm again and caressed his little child's warm face. *"Santar's ointment won't be able to help him through this,"* he told his wife telepathically.

He left to tend to his wife who was crying silently, sitting on their bed. He held her as she cried. There was no point reminding her that she should have been prepared for this, so he just held her tighter.

Darling cried heartily, already mourning the future enslavement of her beloved child. *"Why,"* she thought in despair, *"Why?"*

"It must be so," Kind answered. *"It has been decided."*

"But why, why my dear, sweet, Tender?"

Kind kissed her and held her for a long time. He had suspected that Tender would be chosen. Maybe he should have prepared his wife better for the possibility but had no idea how. How could anyone prepare for the eternal enslavement of their favorite child?

Transitioning from a free djinn to an enslaved one is a long, slow, process, that culminates with shackles. It begins with the appearance of the slave symbols on the inside of the wrists. For some, the symbol's appearance is an easy transition, little noticed by their recipients. In others, the symbols change the nature of the physical body of the recipient, which can cause illness and a fever.

There's no telling exactly why a chosen djinn reacts the way that they do, though some djinn elders do have theories.

"Perhaps it is related to power and how powerful the child will eventually become."

"It is related to the child's temperament, be he mild or strong."

In any case, Tender's fever only lasted until the next morning. That night, his mother kept watch by his side, coaxing broth or juice into him when possible, and helping him through the cold and hot spells by holding him close.

When the fever left, she fed him something light and checked his wrists again. The slave symbols were a bit darker, and yet blended in better with his natural skin color. Tender checked them too.

"What is that, Mama? It's on both my arms."

"It means that you are special, my sweet. And that you have been chosen for a very special purpose, to help all your people."

"All of my people? You mean, Dearest and Strong? And Sweet and Creative?"

"I mean, all of the djinn people."

"But I don't know all of the djinn people."

"I know, my child, and that's why it's so special. You're helping people that you don't even know."

"Why do I have to help them?"

"Because we need one very special djinn to represent all of our clan so that the entire clan can be free."

"Oh. Can I go play now?"

"Of course."

Tender got up from bed and ran to the play area. Kind came in and sat next to Darling. *"I just told Tender that he would have to sacrifice himself for his clan and he ran off to play."* She began to cry again.

"He's only six years old as of last week. You mustn't start mourning his loss now, Darling."

"We just have four more years with him."

"And we will make the best of it. You can't let him see you like this. You've got to stop crying every time you look at him. It isn't fair to Tender or our other children."

"They chose him because I love him so, didn't they?"

Kind held her again and waited until she cried herself out.

Dearest was deep into playing with her dolls when Tender approached her. "Are you okay now?" she asked.

"Yes. Mama said I can play." He sat down beside her and began building something with his blocks. "There's this weird thing on my wrists now, see?" They stopped playing and he showed her the symbols.

She stopped to look. "Does it hurt?

"No."

"Does it come off?"

"No. I don't think so," but Tender was tired of thinking about it. "I don't know."

"Okay."

They continued playing with intent. Dearest was recreating the brief family gathering that happened a few days ago with all her cousins, aunts, and uncles. Tender was making the tallest tower he could ever live in, and only he was allowed inside. Well, maybe Mama and Papa. And Dearest too. Sometimes. If he felt like it.

Soon enough, their mother called and it was time for their midday meal. They all ran to quickly take their places at the table, arranged according to their ages, except for mother and father at the opposite ends. Tender was next to Dearest and his mother at the end, across from Patient, the eldest.

"Children, I think we should all be very grateful for the food that your mother has conjured for us today," their father began.

"Thank you, Mother," the children replied, not quite in unison.

"You're welcome. And I'm grateful that Tender is well again."

"What was wrong with you, anyway?" Strong asked Tender.

"It was just a mild fever, as part of his transitioning." Kind spoke, cautiously.

"Transitioning? From what to what?" Creative asked.

"Children, Tender has been chosen to represent our clan among the mortals," Kind explained.

Tender smiled, feeling special, while swinging his legs back and forth. The older children froze in place.

"No," Patient cried and stared at him as tears formed in her eyes.

"It is an honor to be chosen and so we must honor our Tender," Kind stated firmly.

Kind and Darling bowed their heads towards Tender, and all the other children did the same. Happy at the attention, Tender smiled wide. Patient and Gentle were softly crying, but Tender cheerfully stuffed his mouth full. He looked up at Patient, and asked, "Are you okay?"

"Yes. *I'm* fine," she answered.

"But I thought I was going to be chosen," Strong protested.

"These decisions are made by the honored Leader of all the djinn," Kind answered. They all paused and bowed their heads briefly. "And we must not argue with him, nor question him."

He paused long enough for the children to respond, "Yes, Father."

"And you, Strong."

"Yes, Papa?"

"Do you want to continue our special lessons?"

"Yes, Papa."

"Good. I do too. So, we will." Kind winked at Strong, which made him feel noticed, so he smiled.

Gentle asked, "So when will he have to go?"

"Not for about four years so we won't bring that up again for a while. For now, let's just let him be the happy little boy that he is. Right, Tender?"

"Right, Papa," Tender answered, not really listening to or understanding what they were talking about. After the fever, he was too hungry to care.

"Tender, don't smile so with your mouth full," Darling corrected him.

He chewed, swallowed, and whispered, "Sorry, Mama."

"That's okay, just remember next time," she whispered to him.

"I will," Tender whispered back.

The next day, Kind took Tender to register for his training. Tender really had no idea why he had to go, or exactly where they were going. He only knew that it had something to do with the marks on his wrists. And he was happy to go on a special trip anywhere, just with his father. Kind picked him up, they disappeared from the lamp and reappeared in front of the old training building. Kind put Tender down and took a good look at the structure. It was just as he remembered. Rectangular, dark bricks, and foreboding. A design that was straight out of 1950s America. Imposing, out of place, and intimidating. After taking Tender's hand, he led him towards the front double doors.

"Papa?"

"Yes, Tender?"

"Why is this building square?"

"Because it is a mortal building based on their designs. For a while, they kept designing their buildings in squares and rectangles. And even triangles."

They went inside, through the vestibule, and through another set of doors. They approached the large hall with a large desk in the middle. An imposing djinn sat behind it, intently writing on a scroll with a quill. He looked up. "Name?"

"Tender, son of Kind. From the third clan."

"And his markings?"

Kind lifted Tender up, saying, "Show him, Tender." Tender held out his arms. The official looked at them and nodded.

"Good. Was there any fever or chills? Or any signs of illness?"

"There was a fever and chills. He was ill for one day."

"Was it more like a cold or just a fever?"

"It was just a fever."

The official wrote that information down, then said, "Thank you. You may go."

"Thank you," Kind replied.

"Thank you," Tender repeated, copying Kind's example.

After Kind turned to leave, he said to Tender softly, "That wasn't so bad, was it?"

"No."

"Do you want to go get some corvar?"

Tender nodded, then asked, "What's corvar?"

"It's a wonderful, creamy dessert with an interesting and very strong, sweet, scent. I think you'll like it."

They left the building and Tender asked, "Papa, why does everybody look at me funny?"

Kind knew that by "everybody," Tender was referring to his brothers and sisters. "It's because you are special, Tender. Just like your father. Under my shackles, I have the very same marks on my wrists that you do."

"You do?"

"Yes, I do. They are the marks of slavery."

"Is that when you have to do what everyone tells you to do?"

"Yes, though it's not everyone telling you. It's usually just one person, a mortal. Usually that person is the owner of the lamp."

"But Patient, Gentle, and everyone. They keep looking at me and Mama keeps crying."

"They feel bad about it. And they're sad that you're going to live in your own lamp someday."

"I'm going to have my own lamp?"

"Yes. Enslaved djinn children usually are placed in the same type of dwelling as their enslaved parent. So most likely, yes, you'll live in your own lamp."

"Wow, that's cool!"

"Cool? Where did you hear that?"

"From Creative. He said that our first cousins say it all the time."

"Hmm, more human slang. And from the future, yet. I suppose it's not too surprising."

"What's slang?"

"It means informal, common words that people say all of the time, but more like nicknames."

"I like slang."

"I'm sure you do. Especially when your brothers and sisters use it. Here's the covar shop, Tender."

~

"And so, I don't want you to treat him like you feel sorry for him," Darling told her other children.

"But," Sweet wondered, "he is different, isn't he?"

"Aside from the marks on his wrists, no, he's not. Tender is still the same little boy that he was a few days ago."

"But I heard that he'll go into a daze, just while you're looking at him," said Gentle.

"Where did you hear that?" Darling softly asked.

"I don't know, I read about it a while ago," Gentle added, reluctantly.

"What you're talking about are the meditation trances. That won't start to affect Tender until he's older."

"How much older?" Creative asked.

"It usually begins the year before he starts his training," Darling answered.

"Will Tender have to go away?" Dearest asked with tears in her eyes.

Darling picked her up and hugged her. "Not for years and years, so don't you worry about it."

"I wanted to go away," Strong pouted.

"I know, Strong, but don't be too disappointed, it's for the best." She caressed his arm.

"Now look, everyone, I don't want any of you to treat Tender any differently than before, alright? He'll feel it immediately."

"But isn't he different?" Creative asked.

"No, he's not different. He's just been chosen. Just like your father was, and his father before him. We must respect that. Those of you just starting to hide your thoughts and emotions - yes, I'm talking to you, Patient, Gentle, and Creative. If you feel yourself starting to think about it, or feeling any differently towards him, then hide your thoughts and emotions. Tender is a very sensitive child and he will know. The rest of you, please, just be nice to him. He needs our love and support more than ever," she wiped her eyes quickly.

Patient and Gentle hugged her, including Dearest and Strong in the process.

"I'm sorry, I didn't mean to cry," Darling said, as the rest of her children hugged her too. "But we will get through this. We will."

But try as they might, Tender's brothers and sisters were a bit standoffish and awkward when their father returned home with Tender. Patient, Gentle, and Creative tried hard not to stare at him, which meant that they frequently avoided looking at him at all, which was also not normal.

Darling directly addressed this to them with a thought that only they could hear, *"Stop avoiding Tender and look at him. Don't ignore him."*

Patient, Gentle, and Creative were a little better after that. Only Dearest treated Tender the same the quickest, since they played together the most often. Sweet was nicer and more deferential to Tender, defending him more, and protecting him, especially against Strong.

Strong was just jealous and resentful towards him. He would occasionally have hostile eruptions such as shoving or pushing Tender down for no reason. Soon, he pushed Tender so hard that he fell.

"Hey," Tender yelled from the floor, and then he stood up and tried to hit Strong but their brother, Sweet, stepped between them, facing Strong.

"Leave Tender alone," Sweet stated.

"Why don't you leave us alone?" Strong yelled.

"Why are you always bothering him?" Sweet yelled back.

"Stop it, both of you. Strong." Their father's voice cut off their burgeoning argument. "Come here."

Strong joined Kind at the table. He lifted him up so that he sat on his lap. Kind turned his right hand and a bubble appeared around the two of them, sealing off their conversation from anyone else in the lamp. "Now, I know that you wanted to be chosen, but you weren't. You must stop attacking Tender for being chosen."

"But I wanted it, Papa."

"I know, Strong, but do you really know what you are asking for?"

Strong began to wipe tears from his eyes, "No."

"Your brother has a very hard life ahead of him. Have you really been listening to any of the lessons that I've been giving you? Serving is not a game." He looked his son in the eyes. "Honestly, it is not a fate that I would wish on any of my children, you included. Your mother and I thought that you would be chosen because of how strong you are, and how resilient."

"What does resilient mean?"

"It means that you can take almost anything and come back even stronger than before. And I'm asking you to do that now, Strong, live up to your name. Prove your mother right in naming you. And stop attacking your younger brother, who is smaller than you. It only makes you look weak. Be strong and love and protect him, and be kind to him. You will not regret it." He wiped Strong's eyes, "Okay? Will you be strong for me?"

"Yes, Papa." They hugged. Kind held out his hand and turned it, and the bubble disappeared. "Come here, Tender. Strong has something to say to you."

Tender, who had been playing, but mostly steadily watching them, approached his brother.

"I'm sorry, Tender, I won't push you again," Strong said, looking at the floor.

After a pause, Kind interjected, "Your turn, Tender."

"I forgive you."

They both hugged each other, then Strong left to play while Kind grabbed Tender's hand.

"I'm proud of you, Tender," he hugged him. "Your mother did indeed name you well," Tender grinned at that. "Now go play."

Tender followed his brother into the play area of the lamp. Strong was playing with a deck of djinn cards, which were diamond shaped.

Strong invited Tender to play a silly card game with him, which made Tender laugh. They had so much fun that Sweet and Dearest joined them.

After his older siblings' initial bought of awkwardness and stand-offishness, once they discovered that Tender really was the same little boy that they had known all along, they soon began treating him exactly as they always had. There were only a few occasional reminders of his change in status, such as when they would meet other relatives or talk vaguely about their futures.

Chapter 7
Tender's Story: Observations

A few days later while waiting for her uncle again, Jewel watched as the genie was approached by one of her uncle's palace cats. The genie was kneeling on a cushion while the cat stepped up to him slowly, attracted by his stillness and closed eyes, and sniffed the area around him.

The genie slowly held out his hand, allowing the cat to smell it. Eventually, he began to stroke and scratch the cat to their mutual satisfaction, even opening his eyes to peer down at it with a small smile.

"Genie?"

"Yes, Master?" Even though he gave his master his full attention, he continued petting the cat until it curled up next to him.

"What will the weather be like tomorrow?"

The genie opened his eyes, and they turned white for a second, which caused Jewel to gasp. "Very warm and sunny, Master, much like today."

The king turned back to his quiet conversations with his generals and the genie closed his eyes. He stopped touching the cat, allowing it to nap in peace. After about twenty minutes, the cat stood up, stretched, and left the genie to inspect other areas of the palace.

Jewel decided to leave and meet with her uncle later that day. After she stood up, the genie once again acknowledged her presence with a small bow. Embarrassed, she nodded towards him and left the room.

*W*HAT COULD *this mortal hope to accomplish by staring at me so?* The irritated genie wondered about Jewel to himself when he was alone in his lamp. Surely, he couldn't be that fascinating. But she was young, and he knew that he was the first genie that she had ever met.

He was just another new object for a young student to study. Mortals seemed so eager to forget that his people had thoughts, feelings, and minds of their own. And that they didn't necessarily want to be stared at.

But, being honest with himself, he acknowledged that the djinn would probably always be objects of curiosity for mortals. Humans were just as curious about his people as he was about them. There was a time when he would have eagerly watched mortals do anything also, especially when he was younger.

And yet, it was if she was studying him, and not just staring. Was he a science or biology project, perhaps? Maybe after she finished watching him she would leave him alone. But he couldn't decide whether that would be a good thing.

THE NEXT DAY, after finding another excuse to hang about in the Crystal Court Room, Jewel quietly observed the genie again. His behavior was again calm and serene until mid-morning when he turned towards the right wall of the room. He was already close to it but floated closer until he was next to it. After about fifteen minutes, he opened his eyes and began to stare at the wall more intensely.

The king took notice and called him, "Genie? Come here."

The genie approached the throne, bowed, drew close to his master, and whispered something to him. They had a very quick and quiet conversation, then the genie bowed again and disappeared in a small puff of white smoke, and the king spoke.

"Please clear this room immediately. And send in the head of security."

Jewel left with the other courtiers who were speculating wildly about what was going on. It was only at dinner that Rose revealed what had taken place. One of the palace servants had conspired with one of the guards to steal some supplies from the armory, which they hoped to sell in a neighboring country. The weaponry, having been conjured by the genie, was of an unusually high quality, and therefore extremely valuable.

The genie had heard the entire plot while they were still making plans and trapped the men in the guardhouse. They were later taken away, stripped of their belongings and positions, and banished from the kingdom.

"Wow," was all Jewel could say when she heard the news. "The genie must be extremely powerful," she thought to herself. Now she had a little more fear of him mixed in with her curiosity. But instead of making her want to avoid the genie, it only increased her fascination.

WHY IS *this mortal girl staring at me all the time?*

The genie wondered about Jewel, again. He decided to see her too, if possible. He could always see her in his mind's eye, but nothing could replace a really good look at someone. He could not look at her or anyone directly except his master, since it was specifically forbidden for him due to the mortal fear of djinn eyes. Still, his curiosity peaked and he had to have at least a glimpse of this strange mortal girl who insisted that he eat a full meal and gave him the time to enjoy it.

She was in another part of the court, talking, smiling, and laughing with other girls her age. His master was discussing kingdom matters that mostly did not concern him so he could divide his attention just a bit.

"Yes, but why would he raise the price now? Unless he sees another war coming that we don't," the king asked his ministers.

The genie looked for Jewel's reflection and found it on the surface of a shiny, large vase. He studied it until she noticed him staring at something.

"Sire, either he sees another war coming or he is hoping to encourage a new conflict. This man mostly profits during bloodshed so that is what he's looking for," the minister of war answered.

The genie caught another glimpse of Jewel's reflection in a small mirror being held by one of the other girls but she held it too unsteadily for him to really see her, so he looked down again.

"The selling of arms and armor is one thing, the selling of hostilities another. I don't know if he has enough influence to start anything on his own," the king sighed.

When she and her friends turned towards a mirrored wall, sharing some secrets among themselves, he finally got a good look at her. He stared at her reflection until she caught his eyes. He held her gaze for a fraction of a second, then immediately returned to looking down at the floor directly in front of him.

"But he does have the ears of most of the peninsula kingdoms. Most of the leaders in this part of the world trust what he says, even if they don't exactly know where his information comes from."

"Genie?"

"Yes, Master?"

"Do you see a major war coming?"

The genie's eyes turned white with the future. "No, Master. Not for another ten years at least."

"Will it involve our kingdom?"

"No, Master. Not if you continue your present course. But beware the Jade King, for he is more devious than he seems."

"Who is the Jade King? I don't know of any Jade King."

"You will, Master, in about three years. He loves to start and fight in wars and does not care about the costs."

"Then remind me again, Genie, in about two years."

The ministers of the court tittered as the genie nodded and answered quietly, "Yes, Master."

The girls giggled at their own jokes again and then left the court.

OSTENSIBLY, Jewel was working on an assignment a few days afterwards, surrounded by several books, studying geography in the Crystal Court Room because of its extensive series of maps lining the walls. But Jewel's true motive was to study this strange creature who tried so hard to get a good look at her. While she compared the descriptions of various countries with their shapes on the maps, she also watched the genie.

She watched him kneeling on his cushion with his eyes down and closed most of the time. Occasionally, he would tilt his head to the right side, as if to better hear what his master was saying. But his eyes were always towards the floor, even when they were closed.

She noticed that he seemed to be anticipating everyone else's movements, in looking where they were going before they got there, bowing towards her uncle and anyone else of note, right before they entered the room or approached the throne. He was extremely adept at anticipating everyone's actions, giving every person the respect due their position.

He obeyed every instruction quickly and efficiently, and answered every question truthfully, apparently existing in a state of permanent readiness, ever listening for new commands.

When he was not being called upon for longer lengths of time, he seemed to retreat to a place within himself, with his head bowed lower and his expression even calmer. While he was like this, she would see his head move occasionally, as if suddenly hearing something in the silence, or shift slightly, as if he just noticed movement in the stillness. She couldn't make out what he was minutely reacting to, but he would still snap to attention, moments before he was required.

After an hour of being mostly ignored, and during a lull in the king's conversation with several of his advisors, the genie softly asked, "Master, may I return to my lamp?"

"Yes, Genie, of course," the king replied.

"Thank you, Master," he said with a bow, which was ignored by all except Jewel as the king's conversation picked up again. He bowed to her and dissolved quietly into wisps of white smoke until he disappeared entirely.

The rest of the court seemed to be accustomed to this, though Jewel was still astonished by the genie's casual acts of magic. She stayed in the Crystal Court until she finished her studies and hoped that her unofficial study of the genie went unnoticed.

The genie, of course, knew that she was still quietly watching him again, but after he observed her a few days ago he felt that it was only fair that this strange girl who was so interested in talking to him would want to study him as well.

He heard no stray thoughts of treason or greed from her, which the king had him continuously monitoring the entire court for, nor did he see any overly negative emotions emanating from her. There were no courtly intrigues or schemes today, and definitely nothing negative from her. Just extreme curiosity. Strange behavior from a mortal. But most of human behavior was quite often strange to him, so this was, he surmised, to be expected.

Chapter 8
Tender's Story: Boundaries

The king and Jewel were having one of their rare private dinners together, which Jewel began to value more and more. Usually, the king was extremely busy with state dinners, his advisors and planners, or other official kingdom business. But these dinners were just for them, with no interruptions, and only a few guards. When they could act like a normal family.

Jewel wondered if this would be the right time to bring up a particular subject again. "Uncle?"

"Yes, my dear?"

"If it's okay with you...is, can I...will it be alright if..."

"If what?"

"If I can ask the genie some more questions?"

"Again?"

"Just a few more."

"I thought you got that out of your system."

"Yes, but he's so different, and he seems to know so much, and I didn't really get to ask him everything I wanted to ask last time because there were all those people around, and..."

"I had hoped you'd be done with this by now."

"He's just so interesting and I just wanted to ask him some more questions."

"I don't understand. What is this fascination with him? Why does he interest you so much?"

"He's a magical being, probably thousands of years old. He knows more than all my teachers and we could learn so much from him!"

"You mean you could learn so much from him."

"I don't want to hoard what I've learned! I don't care if I share it with the world, I just want to learn from him. About history, about the world, about his people, everything."

"And do you want anything else from him? Riches, or power, or perhaps, to own him yourself?"

"No, Uncle - I would never! I don't want anything from him! I never did want anything from him. Just to talk to him." She sighed in frustration. "If this is too much to ask, if this will cause too much trouble, then, please forget that I asked at all. Forgive me, Uncle." She quickly bowed to him. "And excuse me."

Jewel got up and ran to her apartment in the palace.

Later that night, just before she went to sleep, the king approached her door. Jewel was sitting on her bed reading.

"May I come in?"

"Of course, Uncle."

He sat beside her. "Do you know what I've always liked about you, Jewel?"

"No, sir. What?"

"You always seemed to know the true value of things. You were never really interested in clothes, or gems, or gold, or any of those other material things. You were always interested in knowledge. You always wanted to know why. Or how things worked. Or if they worked. You were always interested in people instead of their position. And I've always admired that about you."

"Thank you, Uncle."

"And I suppose, if I've been able to trust your judgment in those things, maybe I should trust your judgment in this also."

"You mean…"

"Yes. Tomorrow you can talk to the genie."

"Oh, thank you, Uncle!" She hugged the king.

"Your interactions will be monitored, of course, by me, or by my Chief Advisor, or perhaps I will appoint someone just for this. And your sessions will only take place in open court in the Crystal Court."

"Thank you!" Jewel kissed him on the cheek.

"But only for a few minutes at a time, and only once a week. Every fifth day of the week until you've satisfied your curiosity. If that's even possible."

"I don't know where to begin! Maybe I should plan it, plan on what to ask him."

"Do you want my advice?"

"Definitely!"

"Don't plan too much. Just let your questions happen spontaneously and you'll probably learn more."

"Okay! Thank you so much! But shouldn't I ask the genie if it's okay with him?"

"My dear, it doesn't matter if it's okay with him. He is a slave, remember? He'll do as I command."

"I know, but still, it just seems right to ask him. Is it okay if I ask him? Right now?"

Feeling indulgent, and truly curious as to what the genie would say, the king agreed and called out, "Genie, I summon you."

In a quick puff of white smoke, the genie appeared, floating again, and bowed down before the king. "Yes, Master? How may I please you?"

"My niece has a question for you."

"Yes, Master." He turned his head to face Jewel and bowed to her, though he kept his eyes closed and aimed at the floor.

"Genie?"

"Yes, Miss?"

"My uncle says that it's okay if I ask you questions at least once a week on the fifth day in open court but I wanted to know if it's okay with you too."

"Pardon me, Miss? I don't understand," the genie was completely bewildered.

"Is it okay for me to ask you questions once a week?"

Still taken aback, the genie answered, "Yes, of course, Miss. As long as it pleases my master."

His master smiled, nodded at his answer, and added, "Yes. It does please me, Genie."

The genie bowed his head to him, and said, "Then yes, Miss, I will answer as many questions as I can."

Jewel answered, "Oh, thank you, Genie! I look forward to seeing you again tomorrow."

"Yes, Miss." The genie nodded but was still surprised by the whole encounter.

"You may return to your lamp now, Genie."

"Yes, Master." The genie dissolved into white smoke, which quickly dissipated.

Jewel and the king left the room while Jewel prattled on, excited. "It's the fourth day today, so can I start tomorrow?"

"Yes," the king laughed.

"Can I ask him first thing in the morning?"

"Of course, not the first thing in the morning. What about our morning meal?"

"What about afterwards?"

"Wait until the afternoon, Jewel. Things are usually quieter by then; most of the work of the court is done and the bulk of your lessons will be over,"

"What about after my last lesson? Can I ask him questions after my last lesson?"

"That will be fine." He took his niece by the hand and led her to the door to her apartment.

"This will be so great!"

"Good night, Jewel."

"Good night, Uncle," she hugged him. "And thank you,"

"You're welcome."

IN THE LAMP, however, the genie was still bewildered. He had already sensed that something like this was coming, but he still wasn't sure how to react.

"'Is it ok with you if I get to ask you questions, once a week?'" he repeated out loud to himself. Then he laughed at the strangeness of it all.

THE NEXT DAY, Jewel could hardly wait. The morning and midday meals seemed to take forever, while her lessons were slower than usual. A few minutes before the appointed time, Jewel almost ran into the Crystal Court Room, followed by the king and the Chief Advisor. The few courtiers present bowed as he entered, and again as he sat on the throne. Jewel sat in the lower seat next to the king, to his right. Some of the courtiers had heard rumors that the king's niece was about to question the genie again and were curious.

"Genie?" The king was much quieter than before, as the entire atmosphere was much less formal. The genie appeared in a small cloud of smoke that quickly dissipated, bowing to his master, and floating. His entire body was present this time.

"Yes, Master?"

The king turned to Jewel and simply said, "My niece."

The genie bowed to her and waited.

"Genie?"

"Yes, Miss?"

"Do you have to do everything your master tells you to do?"

"Yes, Miss. He is my master."

At this moment, one of the guards came in and whispered something to the king.

"Excuse me, Jewel. But you may," the king waved his hand, "carry on." He also nodded at the Chief Advisor, who moved closer to hear the entire conversation.

"Thank you, Uncle," and she and everyone else in the room bowed toward the king as he left with two guards. Then Jewel eagerly turned back to the genie. "What happens if you disobey your master, Genie? Have you ever tried to disobey a master?"

"No, Miss, but my Brethren and I did disobey one of our teachers, as part of our training."

"What happened next?" Jewel almost interrupted the genie, being so excited for his answer.

"It was extremely painful; I would not like to experience disobedience again, Miss."

"So, it hurts physically to disobey?"

"Yes, Miss."

"Does doing anything else cause you pain?"

"Certain thoughts, Miss."

"Which you cannot mention because it will hurt?"

"Yes, Miss," he sighed with relief.

"But I can. Does it hurt to just hear the words?"

"It is not painful to hear it, Miss, just very uncomfortable."

"Such as the word, 'freedom'?" His breath caught when she said it. "I saw you flinch at that word before, Genie."

"You are very observant, Miss. And, yes, Miss, that is one of the words."

"Are there entire concepts that you must avoid?"

"Yes, Miss."

"Not to mention all of the subjects you must avoid, I suppose, because of their offensiveness to mortals."

"Yes, Miss."

"Such as?"

He paused before he answered. "Immortality."

"Really?"

"Yes, Miss. Your lives are short compared to the lives of my people, that it is a very difficult thing for us to understand. However, it is a topic that most mortals usually try to avoid, miss."

"I see. Anything else?"

"Not that I can think of at this time, miss."

"Well, feel free to ask me anything also."

"Yes, Miss."

"Thank you for answering my questions, Genie."

"You're welcome, Miss."

"SHE JUST CONTINUES to question me, Master, to find out more about my people and our ways." The genie spoke in the king's personal suite. The king had summoned him privately so that he could recount what he and Jewel had spoken about.

"Has she breached any forbidden areas?"

"Only briefly, Master, and then only to see what subjects and words we shouldn't discuss."

"I see. So, she hasn't asked you anything too intrusive, Genie?"

"No, Master. She seems truly curious about the differences between our people." He then added, "Forgive me, Master, but not many mortals have ever asked so many questions about my people. She is unique."

"I know. And innocent. And naïve. And I want her to stay that way, Genie, for as long as she can."

"Yes, Master."

"Don't stray too much into unpleasant matters, Genie. She is much too young to face certain things."

"Yes, Master. I will obey you."

"That's enough, now, Genie. Return to your lamp."

"Yes, Master." The genie dissolved into smoke, which quickly dissipated.

. . .

THE NEXT FIFTH DAY, Jewel's questions continued. "Why do your eyes glow like they do? It's as if they light up."

"My eyes are alight with the magic within me, Miss. When I access that magic, they glow more."

"The magic within you?"

"Yes, Miss. Creatures of magic always reflect it in different ways. For my people, it shows in our eyes."

"And your eye color?"

"That's just a different part of the color spectrum, Miss, different from mortals. But common in my people."

"And your age? How old are you?"

"I am just under a thousand years old, Miss, as counted in this culture. 925 to be precise."

"Are you immortal?"

"Yes, Miss."

"So, genies age at a different rate than mortals."

"Yes, Miss."

"Do you remember everything from living all those years?"

"I've spent much of that time in my lamp, Miss, but I do remember most of it, when I've not been sleeping."

He looked as if he was about to offer more information but was reluctant to do so. He looked around the room, searching for his master's approval, but the king was preoccupied with his ministers.

"Yes, Genie?"

"I-I try not to spend my time in between masters sleeping, but I have slept through a few decades or so, occasionally, Miss." His discomfort became more obvious in the tension of his voice.

"I'm not causing you to divulge any secrets, am I?"

"No, Miss, but I am telling you of things that even my master does not know. I do not wish to upset him or to leave him uninformed."

"If this topic makes you uncomfortable, I will stop."

"Thank you, Miss. I do not want to displease my master in any way."

"I see, Genie. I don't want to get you in trouble."

"Again, I thank you, Miss."

"Are there any questions that you might wish to ask me? I don't want to be unfair. You shouldn't be responsible for answering my questions only. I will try to answer your questions about mortals also, if I can."

"I-I do not have any questions for you, Miss, at this time."

"Well, when you do, don't be afraid to ask."

"Yes, Miss, I will, Miss, thank you." The genie then bowed in the direction of his master, who began to approach them.

"Have you enjoyed your time with the genie today?"

The genie rose slowly from his bow.

"Yes, Uncle, it was very informative."

"Good. You may return to your tutors."

"Thank you, Uncle." She kissed him on the cheek, then left the court.

"And you, Genie, how do you feel after more of her questions?"

"May I speak freely, Master?"

"Yes, of course."

The genie began to look directly at the king while speaking. "It is still all very strange, Master. She asks me things of which even you do not know, such as why my eyes glow, why they are the color that they are, how I spend my time between masters. And how old I am."

"Oh," the king chuckled.

"I do not wish to go beyond your own knowledge, Master. And now she, she's asking me if I have any questions for her. Master, I am astonished!"

"As I said before, Genie, as long as she doesn't make you uncomfortable, let her ask her questions. You do not have to ask her anything if you don't want to."

"Thank you, Master."

"It is a phase, I'm sure, and she will turn her attention to something else as soon as she gets bored with you."

"Yes, Master. But I do still find it all rather unusual."

"Remember, Genie, you are the only one of your kind she has ever met and she is fascinated. Is she trying to manipulate you in any way?"

"No, Master. I do not sense or see any impure motives in her. Only curiosity and a desire for more knowledge."

"Then let it run its course. If you begin to sense or see a desire for anything else, let me know."

"Yes, Master."

"She is an extremely intelligent young lady. I do not wish to discourage her learning."

"As you wish, Master."

"You may return to your lamp. I have no further need of you today."

"Thank you, Master."

And with that, the djinn disappeared. But in his lamp, he looked out, hoping for a further glance at this strange young woman. It was so strange to him; he didn't even want to try to peer into the future to see how it turned out. He would just have to make his way through, careful not to offend her, or his master. Or the Chief Advisor. Or any member of the royal court.

Such a situation, mined with danger. And yet he had to steel himself for it, and for more of her questions.

Chapter 9
Tender's Story: Sacrifice

Jewel was becoming a little more comfortable with the genie. During their next session, she became a little more inquisitive, and personal. "Genie?"

"Yes, Miss?"

"Do you like being a genie?"

"Yes, Miss."

"But wouldn't you rather be anything else and be free?"

He flinched slightly at her last word but continued.

"I'm sorry, I mean, to not be a slave?"

"I am happy to be in the service of my master, Miss, but in any case, I would prefer to remain one of the djinn."

"But isn't that what's responsible for your enslavement?"

"Forgive me, Miss, but being a genie is not what's responsible, fulfilling an oath is."

"Really?"

"Yes, Miss. In my sect, in every generation, one member of every clan is chosen for enslavement. He must decide to take an oath to serve mortals. Otherwise, his entire clan becomes enslaved."

"Oh, so you were forced to sacrifice yourself," Jewel pitied the genie.

"Forgive me, Miss, but I was not forced; I decided. It was my decision to make."

"But to choose between yourself or your entire clan. What type of choice is that?"

"An undesirable choice, perhaps. But it was still my choice, Miss. It was my decision and I chose."

She could hear the insistence in his voice, however gently and softly he spoke. "I apologize, Genie. I did not mean to belittle your decision."

"It is alright, Miss."

"Forgive me for being so rude."

"Of course, Miss," he said with a small bow, "as you wish."

After an awkward pause, she began again. "What type of oath did you make, Genie? And to whom?"

"It was an oath to my clan, Miss, to the lamp, and to the Leader of all the djinn." He bowed slightly. "To put myself forward as the one to take the place of my clan and to serve."

"Who is in your clan?"

"It is my family, Miss. My entire extended family, one of the original twelve djinn houses of my sect."

"And to serve who?"

"To serve the owner of the lamp, Miss. I took an oath to serve the owner of the lamp for all eternity."

"For all eternity." She repeated his last phrase as she thought about it for a second, and then blurted out, "Don't you just hate all mankind, then, Genie?"

The genie suppressed a smile, and the Chief Advisor felt compelled to step into the conversation. "My dear, is that a wise thing to say to a genie?"

"But it's true! Wouldn't you hate those responsible for enslaving your people?"

"I do not hate anyone, Miss. It is my lot, my destiny, and I have accepted it."

"And you don't mind being a genie, then?"

"Being a genie and being enslaved are not the same, Miss. I am content that I am a genie, and I have accepted my enslavement. It is my lot in life, Miss, and it guarantees the freedom of my clan."

"You have made a noble decision, then, Genie. And your clan should revere you for it."

"Thank you, Miss. On the day that I took my oath, my clan held a large celebration to honor my sacrifice."

"Good. You should be continuously honored for it."

"Thank you, Miss."

"Maybe that's enough discussion for today, my dear," the Chief Advisor suggested.

"Yes, sir. Thank you for answering my questions, Genie."

"Thank you for respecting my answers, Miss. You are very understanding."

"You are welcome, Genie." Jewel walked out of the room.

LATER THAT EVENING, the Chief Advisor spoke candidly with the king. He was unhappy with his new assignment of having to listen to Jewel's questioning of the genie. "They kept going on and on about his sacrifice, and so on. It was rather dull, if you ask me. I don't know why she is so interested and fascinated by his answers. It's a lot of nonsense to me. Forgive me, your majesty."

"It sounds like it was an interesting conversation," the king wondered.

"Yes, your majesty, I will keep listening to them, if you so desire it."

"Keep monitoring them and reporting back to me what they talk about."

"Yes, sire." The Chief Advisor bowed and left the court.

Needing to hear from the genie, the king called him in. "Genie."

The genie appeared in a puff of smoke and bowed. "Yes, Master."

"My niece questioned you some more today. What are your thoughts?"

"She is a very interesting young woman, Master, just as you said." The genie was still amazed by the whole thing.

"I know, djinn."

"And also, very understanding. And kind. If I may say so, Master."

"Of course, Genie. It is a rare thing for a djinn to be so complimentary to any human. And to truly mean it."

"Yes, Master. I do."

"Good. I will relay your compliments, Genie. And now you may return to your lamp."

"Thank you, Master.

Chapter 10
Ally's Story: His Last Lamp

The genie watched over the caravan brothers as they assessed the damaged remains of the fire that he had set. They guessed that the fire just so happened to have raged out of control, after the old man suddenly died. Good.

Their servants buried the old man and then went through his possessions to see if there was anything salvageable. They came across his prized possessions made of silver and gold, some intricately woven fabric, and some of the metal objects, including the lamp.

Perfect. Now all the genie had to do was to see the lamp destroyed, by melting it down, blasting it into a million pieces, bombing it - whatever. The way it happened didn't matter; the destruction of it did.

Maintaining his tiny and nearly invisible stature, he floated up to the top of the lead bundle of the caravan so he could keep an eye on where they were going. He also protected the travelers from some thieves, a few wild animals, and a band of marauders, looking for adventure by easily rendering the caravan and its tracks invisible to the undesirable.

The caravan took ages, but the lamp finally wound up in a scraggly market in what barely resembled a small town.

How can I get these fools to destroy the lamp?

It was now *the* lamp, and not *his* lamp, which he was forced to say when he was imprisoned within it. He dreaded and hated it, and wanted it gone in the most vicious by way possible, if one could be cruel to a metal object.

But that was just it, wasn't it? It wasn't just a metal object. It was aware of him. It knew where he was, what he was planning, and how he was feeling. And it would eventually try to draw him back inside of it after sixty days if he did nothing to stop it.

The lamp was damaged, completely burned on one side, but not destroyed. It had already been in many hands, hoping that it might be salvaged, or have some value, but not destroyed. It was in a junk shop right now, hung up with a few other burned metal objects, including a few of his old master's other metal possessions, which no one wanted.

But finally, after eight days, the shop owner finally decided to sell all his damaged metal to a metal worker and specialist. He shrank himself down and hid inside the metal workshop as he studied the burned areas of metal, including the lamp. The lamp was now misshapen but still intact enough to have power over him.

The metal worker first divided the objects into items he could salvage, and items that weren't worth the effort. Fortunately, his lamp wasn't worth the effort and went into the melting pile.

Perfect!

It was just as the genie had hoped, though he couldn't be satisfied until the lamp was fully destroyed. He watched the metal worker heat a smelting pot and gradually add metal objects, stirring until each item fully melted in the heat. He saw him add the lamp and watched intently it as it dissolved completely into the other molten metal.

At that point, the genie finally felt himself being released from the lamp's hold over him. The only thing left keeping him enslaved were the shackles. He stared at the molten metal, resizing himself to human size and stood right behind the craftsman as he added other brass items to the pot, stirring slowly to ease the process.

When the last brass item dissolved, the genie cried out, "Finally!"

This completely startled the metal worker, who nearly overturned the pot in surprise. "What? Who? Who are you? How did you get in here?"

The genie merely smiled at the metal worker as he stared at him. Then he pulled an old metal toy from his robe and placed it on the ground. "I give this to you in gratitude for your services. It is the exact same toy that you lost as a child, with something special inside from me. Again, I thank you."

The genie bowed quickly, then disappeared in a small cloud of white smoke, causing the craftsman to jump in shock. He took off his thick, insulated gloves, and picked up the small, partially rusted metal box, which he loved so much as a small child. This old box had inspired him to work with metal in the first place.

Inside were six gold coins. He shook the coins out of the upturned box into his hand. When he looked at the box again, six more gold coins appeared inside. He took them out of the box and six more gold coins appeared in their place. He opened, emptied and closed the box two more times until he had twenty-four coins.

Gasping at his good turn of fortune, and literally at the creation of his new fortune, he nearly fell over with joy.

Chapter 11
Tender's Story: Time

"The genie complimented you the other day, my dear." Jewel and the king relaxed after one of their dinners in his private dining room.

"Oh? How so?"

"He said that you were very understanding and kind. It is a very rare thing for a mortal to receive any real compliment from a djinn."

"Oh, okay."

"You don't seem very receptive to his kind words."

"It's not that I don't appreciate his compliment, it's just that...I feel so sorry for him."

"I know."

"He's enslaved for all eternity. What type of life is that?"

"You do not feel so bad for the human slaves that serve you, do you?"

"Yes, well, sometimes, but it's different. And it's not eternal."

He gave her a reassuring hug. "Ah, but eternity is different for them. They do not always experience life the same way we do. Ask him about time and how it works within his lamp. That's one question I already know the answer to, for I was once curious about him too, just as you are now."

~

"Genie, what is time like for you?"

"I experience time just as any other living creature, Miss."

"But my uncle said that you experience it differently within your lamp."

"Ah, I see, Miss. What my master was referring to is a genie's ability to control time within his confinement space. When I am sealed within my lamp, Miss, I can control time within it."

"But how? How can you control time within it?"

"Through magic. I can experience a minute as an hour, a second, or as a day, Miss. It is not really me controlling time itself, as rather me controlling my experience of it."

"So, you can experience a minute as a day?"

"Yes, Miss. Any way I choose. But I must specify right as I enter my lamp."

"That's truly amazing, Genie,"

"Yes, Miss. Though, especially when serving a master, I mostly stay within real time, I have on occasion, Miss, taken a five-week break in the span of five minutes."

"How wonderful!"

"But I must stay within the confines of my lamp. It only works when I'm within a sealed-off space."

"But a lamp is not sealed. What, exactly, qualifies as a sealed off space?"

"It is a space that is completely sealed off from the outside world. With no windows, doors, or any other open portals outside. The room must be completely enclosed. And the lamp is completely closed to my people, Miss. Our masters have the authority to put us into our objects, such as my lamp. I can only enter it or leave it with his permission, Miss. When we are confined within it, it is sealed off to us, through magic. A sealed off space is very special to a genie, Miss."

"I see why, Genie. The ability to change time sounds wonderful."

"It is, Miss."

"So, do you experience time the same way mortals do?"

"Yes, and no, Miss. When I am within real time, yes. But, when in manipulated time, it feels the same, though it's not."

"But even then, immortality adds another aspect to it, doesn't it? I mean, my lifespan must seem like nothing to you."

"It is brief, Miss, but even more valuable for it. The lives of mortals are shorter, but they also seem more intense, in a way. Perhaps because they are so brief, Miss."

"That makes sense, Genie. Still, I would love to experience a minute as a day. Then, maybe I would appreciate my life's brevity."

"One should appreciate one's life within any time span, Miss. According to an old proverb of my people."

"I agree with you, Genie. One should. I should, I mean."

Chapter 12
Tender's Story: The Sorcerer

"Genie, set up a royal table for me and my ministers to confer, right here."

"Yes, Master." A large oval table surrounded by beautiful cushions appeared in the center of the Crystal Court. The ministers took their seats around the table, along with the king, where he held an official meeting.

After Jewel watched this, she asked, "Genie, how did you know what type of table my uncle had in mind? How did you know what type he wanted, or how large, or anything else?"

"I saw it, Miss. I saw the image of the table that my master had in mind. Whenever my master makes a wish, I see what he sees, and I hear what he wants, in his thoughts."

"You can read minds?"

"I can, Miss, but I mostly do it when it comes to what my master wishes. I have to read his mind in order to see exactly what he wants so that I may fulfill his wish."

"I see. Did you read my mind when you granted my wish?"

"Yes, Miss."

"Are you reading everyone's mind all the time?"

"I hear the thoughts of mortals, Miss, even when I'm not listening for them. Mortals usually are not skilled in hiding their thoughts."

"It's a skill that mortals can learn?"

"To a certain extent, Miss. Hearing thoughts is a natural ability that the djinn have. But I only specifically read minds when granting wishes, and even then, Miss, only as far as it relates to the wish. But if my master wishes me to read anyone's mind, then I must do so."

"Oh. And does he ever wish for you to do so?"

"Occasionally, Miss. Most often he asks me to tell him what someone is feeling."

"You can also read emotions?"

"Well, not read them, Miss, not exactly. I can see them."

"You can see emotions? How?"

"Different emotions are represented by different colors. When I look at mortals, Miss, I see different colors emanating from them. Kind of like an aura, but not exactly the same."

"What colors do you see coming from me right now?"

"Forgive me, Miss, but my master has forbidden me to look directly at any mortals other than him. He does not wish me to frighten anyone with my eyes, Miss."

"Can you look anywhere near me, or somewhere really close to me, just close enough so that you can see what I'm feeling?"

"I will try, Miss." The djinn focused on the space just above her head. He positioned his head perfectly first, then opened his eyes to look at the exact spot. After a second, he closed his eyes and returned to his submissive position. "You are feeling joy, Miss, anticipation, and excitement. And a small amount of fear."

"And my thoughts, Genie?"

"I am not allowed to say, Miss, unless my master explicitly wishes for it."

"But did you casually hear anything from me, Genie?"

"Only that you looked forward to speaking with me, today. Before we met, Miss."

"Amazing. Such gifts, you have such wonderful gifts, Genie, any mortal would love to be able to do what you can do."

"Thank you, Miss."

"Can you, can you see into the future?"

"At times, Miss, but not always. I have less control over that. Many things are hidden to me but I can see some things, Miss. And mostly in the service of my master, of course."

"Of course. And when does your master wish you to read thoughts?"

"When he suspects that someone is lying to him or has ulterior motives. I can tell if they're practiced in shielding their thoughts from the djinn. But most mortals are not. Sorcerers and others who practice magic usually are."

"Have you encountered sorcerers before?"

"Yes, Miss. Sorcerers often seek to acquire the djinn. They either desire my people for our power, or to manipulate others."

"How many have you met?"

"Five, Miss. And each one very different from the other. Sorcerers have the ability to find out the whereabouts of my Brethren. People of magic are often very aware of each other, Miss. We can sense it."

"Tell me, Genie, of one of your encounters with a sorcerer."

"As you wish, Miss. I can tell you of my encounter with the most powerful sorcerer of all. I was younger and still new to serving mortals."

My sixth master had just died of his advanced age and I was inside my lamp only a few moments when I felt the hands of my new master holding my lamp. I appeared to him immediately, as is customary, and bowed.

"Greetings, my new master. I am the genie of the-"

"Not now, genie! Go back into your lamp. I will call you when I need you."

Confused by my new master's reaction, I obeyed and returned to my lamp instantly. I had only seen him briefly, but not long enough to ascertain what he was.

When I was summoned again, I was in my new master's workshop, which I recognized as one of a sorcerer, filled with many books of magic and objects of enchantment. He also had a lot of strange equipment, many items that I couldn't identify. I looked at him and saw the magic within him.

"You needn't be frightened, any of you. I will not hurt you. Well, not too much. And not permanently. You may greet your Brethren, if you like."

"I looked around and saw my best friend, Ally, along with Clever, another genie who is a good friend of mine. We nodded at each other, as we were all trained together. I could tell that they were just as mystified by our current circumstances as I was. Our new master approached us."

"How may I serve you, Master?" I asked tentatively.

"Answer me this one question, to which I already know the answer. I just need you to confirm it. Am I your seventh master?"

"Yes, Master," I answered him truthfully.

He then asked Ally, "And am I your seventh master?"

"Yes, Master." Ally answered.

Clever was next.

"Am I your seventh master?"

"Yes, Master."

"Good. Very good."

We had been taught that sorcerers believed in the power of certain numbers over others, and the number seven is very meaningful to them. So is the number three. He went to his workstation and summoned yet another djinn."

"Genie?"

"Yes, Master?"

This other genie was older and from a different generation, but we could still tell that he was one of the Brethren from his behavior. Strangely enough, though, his shackles were missing."

"Prepare the containment chamber and," he looked over at us, "a comfortable area for them to rest, while I conduct my spell."

"Yes, Master."

A large, clear glass jar with a small opening on top appeared on one of the surfaces next to the sorcerer. Behind each one of us appeared large cushions."

"Lie down, my young Brethren," the older genie instructed us. "The pain will only be temporary and will not last long."

"We obeyed, lying down on the cushions behind us."

"Speak not a word through this process and I will leave you with a very valuable lesson at the end." He added, in our own language, "And quiet minds."

"Are they in position?" the sorcerer shouted.

"Yes, Master."

"Good. Let's start."

The sorcerer began to speak powerful magic words in a magic language. We could have interpreted, but my two friends and I were instantly struck with the most searing pain. It felt as if we were being ripped in two, which, in a way, we were. The magic within us was being extracted from our bodies. It was very painful, as it felt as if our very lives were being sucked out.

Once the separation was complete, the pain stopped and we collapsed, barely able to move. We watched our magical essences being guided by the sorcerer, helpless.

If you ever see such a sight, it is a strange thing to behold. It looks like a shapeless, ethereal, cloud-like form, floating and brightly multi-colored, and glowing from within. The forms shifted and moved through the air, guided by the sorcerer's hands. His hands manipu-lated the forms without touching them until they were coaxed into the large jar.

My friends and I were conscious, but we couldn't move, our

bodies were greatly weakened after the separation. The light of magic was gone from our eyes, as it was now contained in the jar.

Oddly enough, we were also aware of our magical essences, as they were floating to and residing in the jar. It felt very strange, being in two places at once in such a way.

The sorcerer was eager to work his powerful spell using his magic and ours. Helpless, we could only listen to and watch the proceedings.

"And now, using all the power available to me, I will make three wishes! I wish to become the most powerful sorcerer in all the world and to remain so. My second wish is for eternal life where no mortal or magical creature can kill me! And my third wish is for a magic ring that will allow me to enchant and control all creatures of magic!"

My Brethren and I felt our bodies jump and the jar glowed brightly as our combined magical essences granted the sorcerer's wishes. His wishes were not exactly ordinary, and I suppose he believed that they could only be granted by our combined powers.

We watched as the newly empowered sorcerer glowed bright green suddenly, and then his appearance returned to normal, and he smiled. He looked exactly as he did before, only with a new ring on his finger with a large emerald.

As an afterthought, he spoke the words that returned our magical essences back into our bodies. Fortunately, this process was not painful, but felt refreshing, as our magical essences floated back to us, and within us, and we were returned to normal.

Being able to move again, we each got up from our cushions, albeit slowly, stiffly, and awkwardly.

The sorcerer glanced at us and said, "Ah, good. Now I can return each of you back to the places where I found you."

"Master," his genie interjected, "may I speak to them now?"

"Yes, genie." The sorcerer was completely engrossed in writing what just happened in one of his many books.

"My Brethren, as you have noticed, I am unshackled. I had been freed, but now I am enslaved, all the same. When you return to your lamps, always remember, never give a mortal, especially a sorcerer, your true name. You will regret it for as long as you live. I know you have been warned about this during your training, but take my existence, and my sad life, as your ultimate proof. For because I gave my master my true name, I must serve him, just as surely as if I were in a lamp, a ring, or any other object."

The genie turned to his master and said in the sorcerer's language, "Thank you, Master. I am done now."

"Good, genie. Very good. Back to your lamps now, djinn." He waved his hand towards us. We felt ourselves being pulled back into our lamps, and our lamps being returned to the places that the sorcerer found us.

"How HORRIBLE, genie. Did you ever see that sorcerer again?"

"Only once, Miss, and that was many years later, when I served another master."

I WAS SERVING in the court of my master at the time, a king, who was entertaining his guests with a large party. I suddenly felt the approach of a very familiar presence. I had to warn my master so I broke protocol and addressed him directly. "Master. Forgive me, but I must warn you."

"Genie? What is it?"

"A sorcerer approaches. He is entering your palace gates at this very moment."

"Don't worry, Genie. We've handled sorcerers before."

"But Master, this one is different. You must be wary of him and do exactly as he asks."

"Why, Genie? What's the matter?"

"There are three things you must know about him. One is that he's the most powerful sorcerer in the world. The second is that he can't be killed by mortals or creatures of magic."

"How do you know this, Genie?"

"Because those were his wishes and I helped grant them."

"What? Genie, I don't understand-"

"Forgive me, Master, but please, you must listen." It became difficult for me to talk, focus, or do anything. "The third thing...is that...he has..." I blinked slowly as I struggled to continue, "he has..."

I heard my master gasp as my eyes changed color and turned completely bright, emerald green, I was later told. But I couldn't react; I had to stop because of the sorcerer's ring. He was using it to mesmerize me and I was falling under its power.

Without a word, he had willed me to stillness, and the ring, glowing brightly on his finger, was working. My movements froze, my eyesight turned hazy, and I was compelled to turn towards the sorcerer as he approached us. I was now completely under his control.

But my master continued to ask, "What? What is it, Genie?"

"He has a ring that can control all creatures of magic," the sorcerer answered as he entered the throne room. "That's what he was about to say. Or at least, I think that's what he was about to say."

With a wave of his hand, the sorcerer divided the crowded throne room to make a direct path for himself to the throne. He approached my master, easily waving aside any guards that tried to stop him. They fell to the ground instantly and remained frozen in place.

The king, my master, was shocked, and finally faced him. The sorcerer addressed me first, but I was so mesmerized that I couldn't even look back at him.

"How sweetly loyal of you, Genie, to try and warn your master of my power. But back to your lamp, as your presence is not really required at this time." Instantly, I was returned to my lamp. I was still in a mesmerized haze, but it began to fade, and I could hear and see in my mind what was happening to my master. The sorcerer was still speaking to him.

"You. You have something I want, something you just received about two days ago as tribute."

"What is it?"

"Oh, come now, don't play games with me. You know what I'm referring to. You know what it is."

My master removed a ring from his finger. The ring contained one of the largest, flawless, yellow diamonds in the world. He gave it to my former master, the sorcerer, who quickly placed it on one of his own fingers. "Thank you. Good. Very good."

The sorcerer caused a large trunk filled with gold coins to appear next to him by waving his right hand, with sparks and purple smoke. "Your recompense. Never let it be said that I don't pay for what I want. Oh, and you should thank your genie profusely. For he just saved your life."

The sorcerer smiled and disappeared with a flourish in a large cloud of purple smoke and sparks, leaving trails of smoke behind. I never saw him again.

"Wow, Genie! That's an amazing story; you saved your master's life. And did he thank you profusely?"

"Yes, Miss. And if he were still alive, he would probably be thanking me even now."

Jewel thought for a moment. "One thing I don't quite understand, exactly how did you save his life?"

"A sorcerer's reputation is very important to him, Miss. And by telling the king and his court what he could do, I inadvertently advertised it. So, he kept them alive to further bolster his reputation. That sorcerer is now recognized as being extremely powerful among mortals, or at least, among those who wish to know of such things, Miss. He was very grateful for my description and left the king and his court as witnesses to tell the tale."

"Did the king do anything else for you besides thanking you?"

"Yes, Miss. He gave me certain privileges that are greatly desirable to me and my enslaved Brethren."

"Really?"

"Yes, Miss. He allowed me time outside of my lamp to do as I pleased, within reason. And regular work hours, Miss, so that I would know when he would summon me. And he gave me time to visit my family as often as I liked."

"How wonderful!"

"Yes, Miss. He was already a kind and generous master, but he became enormously grateful to me. He continued to demonstrate his gratitude in a variety of ways for the rest of his days."

"Do you think the sorcerer is still alive?"

"Yes, Miss, but he is far from us, concerning himself with magical creatures other than the djinn. Ever since he removed my magical essence, I can sense him, Miss. I can tell that he's still alive, and some of what he's involved in."

"How?"

"His magic affected mine somehow, in a way that seems to be permanent, Miss. I can sense him; I can at least tell that he's still alive. Though I don't know exactly where or when he is."

"*When* he is?"

"He was experimenting with time when I last felt his magic."

"Do you think you will see him again?"

"I don't know. I hope not, Miss." He bowed towards the king as he approached them. The ministers were leaving, still talking with each other.

"Genie, I'm done. Move this table into the conference room, as I much prefer it to the one that is in there."

"Yes, Master." The table disappeared in a cloud of white smoke.

"Back to your lamp."

"Yes, Master." He bowed towards the king and disappeared in a smaller cloud of smoke, which quickly dissipated.

"What were you so engrossed in? What was the genie telling you?"

"He told me the story of his encounter with the most powerful sorcerer in the world. I hope we never meet him."

"I haven't heard any news of any sorcerers around here for years, Jewel. No need to worry."

"Oh good, Uncle." She then hugged him. "Thank you for letting the genie tell me such stories."

"You're not frightened by them, are you?"

"Not at all. I just find them extremely entertaining. Thanks again, Uncle. I think it's time to join my friends, with your permission, of course."

"Permission granted."

"Thank you." She quickly bowed to him and ran off.

"Chief Advisor?"

"Yes, sire?"

"What do you know of sorcerers and their powers?"

"Nothing outside of the common knowledge, sire, I'm afraid."

"Hm. Well, maybe we should learn more."

"And then he said," Jewel paused as her governess, Rose, placed a fresh nightgown over her head, "that he can still sense this sorcerer, and can tell that he's still alive."

"How terrible."

"But don't you find it fascinating?"

"I'm not sure if anyone should be entertained by tales of sorcery and magic."

"Why not?"

"Because it's not normally part of our world, and maybe for good reason."

"But I was just talking to a genie! Magic is already a part of our world."

"Then maybe we shouldn't focus on it too much. Genies and such creatures should stay at least an arm's length away. Aren't you afraid of being enchanted by him?"

"How?"

"By all of these stories he's telling you."

"He's not trying to enchant me or use any magic on me at all, I can tell."

"Because you are so experienced in these things, I suppose."

"No, but I guess I am now!"

"Clean your teeth and go to bed. You need to experience a good night's sleep."

"How can I sleep when there's so much to be excited about?"

"Very soundly, I hope. Good night, Miss."

"Good night, Rose."

Chapter 13
Tender's Story: His Master's Call

Jewel was waiting to join the king for dinner but apparently, he was preoccupied somewhere else, with something else. Again. So, she wandered around the Crystal Court, ignoring the courtiers until she came closer to the genie, still in his place, near the throne. He had his head tilted to one side but looked as if he was focusing on something.

"Genie?"

"Yes, Miss?"

"What are you doing when you tilt your head like that?"

"I am listening for the call of my master, Miss. He is to my left and currently thinking of requesting something of me. I am waiting to hear what he decides to do."

"Can you hear him from wherever you are?"

"Yes, Miss. The distance doesn't matter. I can always hear my master."

"Is that a good thing or a bad thing?"

The genie smiled sadly. "It is a necessary thing, Miss. I must always respond to the call of my master."

She nodded and became lost in her thoughts.

After a few minutes, the genie straightened up. "He is about to summon me, I must go." Then he disappeared in a small cloud of white smoke.

She stared at the empty space where he was for a few moments and then returned to waiting. She thought of how sad it was to be so bound to the will of another. She wouldn't like it at all.

Chapter 14
Tender's Childhood: It Begins

Tender was nine-years-old now. He and his brothers, Strong and Sweet, were working on an elaborate building puzzle. It would eventually look like a model of a djinn home, but right now it was just a collection of tiny pieces and intricate parts. Each brother had their own pile of parts which would form different parts of the house.

Dearest was working on a drawing with Creative guiding her. Darling, Patient, and Gentle were looking at a cookbook from the future, searching for something new to try for dinner. They would turn to a page, make the dish or meal appear in front of them, smell and taste it, and decide whether they liked it or not.

Tender was about to snap two parts of a roof together when he thought that maybe he should look at the instructions to make sure he was putting his section together in the right order.

"Where are the instructions, where are the instructions," he said to himself, when slowly, his mind began to drift off. "The instructions, the instructions, the instructions help me, the instructions help me, put everything in the right order, the right order, the right order..."

He began to stare at nothing, as if in a daze. His arm was frozen in place, still reaching for the instructions.

Sweet noticed the change in Tender immediately. "Mama?"

Darling heard the fear in Sweet's voice and looked over at them.

"What's going on?" Strong asked, more than a little unnerved.

"Is he alright?" Dearest asked, afraid.

"It's alright, children, it's alright. No need to yell, keep your voices down, and don't make any sudden movements."

"Is that a trance?" Gentle asked, tears in her eyes.

"Yes," Darling answered, as calmly as she could, "but it's his first one, so we must not interrupt it. Everyone keep still, speak softly, and stay calm."

"How long is it supposed to last?" Sweet whispered.

"Not long, just a few moments. Just be still," she slowly approached Tender and sat on the floor next to him.

"Are we going to have to do this every time?" Strong asked, irritated and not so softly.

"Shh, talk quietly. Not every time, just for the next few days." Darling watched as Tender closed his eyes and inhaled deeply. She caught him as he slumped back and fell into her arms. Then he blinked, as if he was just waking up from a deep sleep.

"Where, what happened? What," he managed to say, trying to sit up.

"It's alright, Tender. It was your first trance. Just lie still." Tender relaxed back into Darling's arms and comfort. He looked as if he was about to fall asleep.

"My first what?"

"Your first trance. It's alright, son. You'll feel better shortly."

"Yeah, it looked like you frozen all of a sudden!" Strong said.

"Strong," Darling snapped, "stop it."

"But it did," he protested with a smile, but no one joined in.

"Is he okay?" Dearest was starting to worry.

"Am I okay?" Tender asked his mother.

"Yes, Tender, you're okay. You just went away for a minute or two."

"I was thinking about the instructions." Disoriented, he tried to trace his own actions. "But then the words, they just kept repeating in my head."

"And then what?" Sweet asked.

"And then, it's like I woke up, and everybody was staring at me."

"We were worried about you," Dearest cried.

"It feels so strange," Tender said, looking at the puzzle pieces still in his hand. "Why is this happening?" But he also became very tired and slumped back into Darling's arms.

"It's a trance and it's to help you focus. Let's get you to bed." Darling and Tender vanished and reappeared in the younger children's bedroom, sitting on Tender's bed.

"Get some rest," Darling tucked Tender under his blanket. "I'll stay right here and be here when you wake up."

Tender nodded slightly and fell asleep instantly.

"Papa never does that." Strong stated.

"Yes, he does. You just don't notice it anymore. He usually does it only around mother," Gentle answered.

"How come you know so much about this stuff?" Strong challenged.

"I read about it. I looked it up when I saw father do it a few years ago."

"It scares me," Dearest said.

"It shouldn't," Gentle went and hugged her. "It's all part of Tender becoming a member of the Brethren."

They all went silent at the mention of the Brethren, then Dearest broke the silence. "How long will this last?"

"He will need to meditate for the rest of his life. As long as he serves as a member. But during these early trances, he becomes extremely vulnerable and susceptible to outside influences. Noise and movement can hurt him, not just physically, but mentally also.

His mind is like, rewriting itself to become accustomed to this new power. That's why we have to be quiet when it happens."

"So, he's going crazy?" Strong again.

"No, his mind is just reorganizing itself and adjusting. That's why we must be quiet and still when we see it."

After about twenty minutes, Tender began to wake up. "Mama."

"Hello, my tender one. Did you have a good nap?"

"Yes, but why was I so tired?"

"Remember all of the changes that your father and I said you'd go through?"

"Yes."

"Well, this is one of them. What just happened was your first trance-like meditation. It's designed to help you focus on using your powers and so much more. The more you meditate, the better you become at using your powers."

"But I'm already good at using my powers, why do I need to do this?"

"It's designed to help you serve. Your father does it."

"He does? I've never seen him in a trance,"

"Yes, you have, he just hides it well. He didn't want to frighten you, or your brothers and sisters when it happens to him. He does it when he's reading sometimes, and early in the morning, and just before bed. You never really noticed it since he does it so quietly. You've seen him, sitting with his legs crossed and his eyes closed?"

"Yeah, I remember you used to call them Daddy's quiet times. And you told us to be quiet around him."

"You were too young to fully understand what was going on and it was before you were chosen."

"So, I have to meditate too?"

"Yes, from now on. Don't look so worried, it's alright. It's a natural part of becoming a member of the Brethren."

"I don't know if I want to be a member of the Brethren."

"I know, Tender, but it's not up to us. The decision has already been made. And that means that you're going to start meditating."

"Can I stop it? Can I control it?"

"Yes, I believe so. But you'll have to wait until your father comes home before you can really learn how to do that. Until then, I'll help you through this as best I as I can."

She took one good at him and hugged him, while thinking only to him, *"I know you're scared, Tender, and it's a very weird thing to experience, especially your first few times. But you'll get used to it, and it will get easier for you."*

"*I don't like this,*" Tender thought back. He was still new to sharing his thoughts, but he found that the more emotional he was, the easier it was. And he was upset.

"*I know, my tender one, I know.*"

"Will I get sleepy every time?"

"No, just these first few times until your body adjusts to the changes. When your father first did it I was there, along with your two aunts. We were all talking and then suddenly, your father just stopped. Fortunately, his father was in the lamp at the time and helped him through it. He also explained everything to all of us; he let us know exactly what was going on. Of course, your father will tell you more about it from his own experiences with it."

"Okay."

"Are you feeling better than you did before? With more energy?"

"Yeah," Tender happily realized.

"Good, that means the trance is helping. Now let's go join the others."

The next day Tender fell into another trance as he was eating the morning meal. After taking a sip of water and putting down the cup, he froze, staring at the water inside it. "Water, swishing, water, good, water, water...water..." his thoughts repeated.

His siblings noticed immediately and watched as Darling positioned herself behind him to catch him when he fell over. His frightened brothers and sisters stared, not even daring to eat.

The trance only lasted about ninety seconds, then Tender blinked, closed his eyes, and sank back into his mother's arms.

Seconds later, he woke up and saw everyone staring at him. "I'm sorry."

"No, no need to apologize, Tender. Not for something that you can't help," Darling held him.

Tender rubbed his wrists. "The markings, it's like they're stinging a little bit."

"That's normal too. Now just relax. Do you want to go back to bed?"

"Yes, please."

Darling helped her son, still groggy, up from the table, and to his bed.

"We'll just have to get used to it," Gentle said as soon as they were gone.

"I don't know if I'll ever get used to that," Dearest remarked.

Meanwhile, Tender laid down in his bed and Darling covered him up. "I don't like this meditation stuff, Mama. I don't like it at all."

"I know, Tender, I know. It's strange and different, and new. And it makes you stand out from your brothers and sisters."

"And if it's supposed to help me, why am I so tired after?"

"Because it's still new to you, son. You will adjust soon enough. Your body is still getting used to it."

"And my mind? Does it affect how I think, how I feel? Who I am?"

"No, you are exactly the same person you were before. It won't have any effect on who you are."

Tender yawned as his eyelids grew heavier. "Why do I have to do this, why was I chosen?"

"Get some rest, Tender. We'll discuss all those big questions when your father comes home. Have a good nap, my tender one."

Tender fell into a deep sleep before she finished speaking. She caressed his head and watched him as he slept.

The family began to adjust better to Tender's trances. After his third trance, while reading, and his fourth, while putting his toys away, they adjusted to them all quite well. They continued their activities quietly and were careful about making unnecessary noise. Dearest and Sweet took extra care to remove liquids, glass, knives, or anything dangerous that Tender might drop or fall onto when waking.

After his fifth trance their mother told them, "It's better, now. We can all relax. He's over the delicate phase, I can see it. It's still going to happen, but he'll handle it better. We don't have to be so quiet."

And so, every now and then, within the lamp, Tender would involuntarily begin meditating. He would think of something, start focusing on it, and freeze in place. But he didn't become tired afterwards, nor did he require rest or help remaining upright. He would just stop whatever he was doing as if just pausing for a few moments, usually for only a minute or two. Then he would just start back up again as if nothing had happened. The strangest time was during conversations, with Tender answering a question, or even finishing a sentence on delayed time.

Strong was in awe of this relatively new development, but not jealous of it. It frightened him, and he began to feel grateful and relieved that he would never be a member of the Brethren. He even began gently teasing him afterwards, saying, "You went away again, but now you're back."

Darling finally heard from Kind through their communication cloth one evening. "Kind! I'm so happy to see you, I miss you so much."

"I miss you too, my love. Forgive me, but my new master is very insecure and fearful. He uses me as his constant bodyguard and protector. I am rarely allowed to be out of his sight. How is everything? And everyone?"

"Everything is fine and everyone is fine. I think I've found a good match for Patient, though Gentle is completely uninterested in finding anyone. Ever, she says. I've found good projects for Creative and Sweet to work on and learn from."

"Good. I thought that they just needed more guidance."

"Strong is much less overbearing if I keep him occupied, and Dearest is learning quickly and becoming more patient. Tender is also learning quickly. And he started to meditate."

"I was expecting that. Try getting him to do it on purpose, in the morning and at night, though he will need my help to learn how to do it exactly like the Brethren. But see if you can get him to control when he does it. That way, it won't interrupt his day as much."

"Yes, Kind, I will. He seems to be taking to it well, though it still scares him a little."

"It is scary at first, to lose consciousness like that. It's like falling asleep without any awareness or control."

"The rest of the children are handling it well and even helping him out."

"That's good. I will help him when I am allowed to return." Kind then looked up and to his left. "I am about to be summoned. I hope to see you soon, my love."

Darling quickly nodded her understanding as his image faded from the cloth.

Darling tried her best to help Tender meditate the next morning, right before the first meal of the day. It worked though his session didn't last very long. His night meditation session lasted longer, almost ten minutes. Perhaps because he was so sleepy, Darling surmised. She continued helping Tender with his morning and night sessions, though he would still occasionally have an involuntary meditation induced freeze during the day.

KIND SUDDENLY APPEARED in the middle of the lamp, looking a bit tired.

"Father! Papa!" The kids screamed excitedly.

"Kind!" Kind's family dropped everything that they were doing and rushed to hug him.

"My children, my wife, it's so good to be with all of you again."

"We really missed you," Darling responded, holding back tears.

"I really missed you as well, my Darling," he kissed her forehead.

"Why were you gone so long, Papa?"

"My master really needed me, Dearest,"

"Are you going to stay with us a while?"

"I hope so, Tender."

"I may be getting married, Papa."

"Your mother told me, Patient. You may have my congratulations."

"Children, let's give your father some time to recover."

The siblings backed away from their parents long enough for the couple to enter their bedroom area. Kind was much more wounded than he was willing to let on, and he carefully laid down onto their bed. Darling conjured a jar of Santar's ointment and a cloth, opened the jar without touching it, and dabbed the cloth into the jar. In their following telepathic conversation, she asked, *"Where does it hurt?"*

"My left side, mostly. My ankle and my wrist."

Darling began to apply the ointment to Kind's specified areas and he visibly relaxed as he healed instantly.

"I would love a master who didn't require me to remain in a physical form, that would make serving so much easier."

"But then I wouldn't get to touch you as much."

Darling grinned and Kind grinned back.

He fully relaxed on the bed, *"Now I can finally get some rest."*

"And your master?"

"There will be no more fighting for me, at least for now. He finally decided that I was too valuable an asset to allow me to get hurt in any way, so here I am."

"Good."

"It's good to be with you again, I've missed you so much."

As they kissed, Kind became transparent. Darling chuckled, they kissed again, and she became transparent also. He grinned in response and they blended into each other in their passion.

Afterwards, as Darling and Kind relaxed in postcoital satisfaction, Kind sighed out loud, "I love you, my Darling."

"I love you too, Kind. I've missed you so much, we've all missed you."

"I've missed all of you, too," then he switched to telepathy. *"Now will you tell me about what's really bothering you. Is it Tender's transitioning?"*

"You know me so well," she answered back telepathically. *"We must somehow prepare everyone for his leaving. I remember how your parents prepared us. Would you like to do the same?"*

"We were a small family, just the seven of us. It would be nice to have something like that again."

"And you know how Tender doesn't like to be the center of attention, it will be easier for him."

"I see you're trying to arrange Patient's wedding before he goes away."

"Yes, I wanted Tender to be able to attend, freely. And it will be our last time together as a family."

"Tender's not dying, Darling, he's just going away for training."

"I know. But I just want everything to remain normal for as long as it can."

"Tender's training is normal. We must accept it as his particular rite of passage."

"I remember how hard it was for me to say goodbye to you when you went away for training."

"Oh, my sweet," Kind kissed her.

"I didn't know what to do with myself, I was so forlorn."

"You are stronger now. You survived our separation then; you will survive this one now."

"Training was so hard on you, I just don't want that for him."

"Tender is stronger than you realize. As difficult as it can be, he will survive it. You need to have more faith in him, and more faith in

us. We will get through this. And Tender will become a worthy member of the Brethren."

"Just like his father."

"OKAY, close your eyes, and think, "Meditation will help me." Repeat them to yourself, over and over again. You may repeat the words to yourself in your head or out loud, though remaining quiet is often safer around mortals, so I recommend it."

Tender followed his father's instructions, even copying his father's sitting position with his legs crossed. Keeping his meditation words silent, he soon fell into a trance. His father did as well. After about fifteen minutes, Kind blinked first, followed closely by Tender.

"There. That felt refreshing, didn't it? Do you feel better?"

"Yes. Why?"

"Because focusing is good for you and your powers. It is calming and soothing and helps you to relax. We will have another session before bed. You shouldn't have any more unexpected trances until then."

"Thank you, Papa." Tender hugged his father, who eagerly hugged him back.

"You are most welcome, my son. Now I believe that your mother has just finished making a wonderful meal for us all."

Tender inhaled the scents of the food deeply, smiled, and walked out of his parent's bedroom as quickly as he could.

Chapter 15
Tender's Story: Visualization

"Words, obey their words precisely...precisely...their words, obey, obey, their words..." the genie meditated to himself.

"Genie?"

The genie instantly snapped to attention. "Yes, Miss?"

"What did you do when you were outside your lamp, after you saved that king's life?"

"I explored the world, Miss. Some djinn try to cause trouble for mortals, while others intentionally get into trouble, but I only wanted to see as much of the mortal world as possible. Even though I can see things in my mind, sometimes it's not as enjoyable as seeing them for real, Miss."

"What's it like to see things in your mind?"

"It's like imagining things, only you can actually see them, when you close your eyes, Miss."

"Is that how you seem to know exactly where things are with your eyes closed?"

"Yes, Miss." The genie began to feel uneasy, sensing the danger to come.

"Can you show me?"

"I'm not sure my master would allow that, Miss."

"It doesn't involve you touching me, does it?"

"No, Miss."

"Then we won't be breaking any of my uncle's rules."

"But Miss, I don't believe that my master would approve. Perhaps, you should ask him when he returns to the palace."

"But he left early this morning with the Chief Advisor. They could be gone for hours. Please, Genie. I just want to try it, it would please me greatly." She declared, more formally, "Genie, I wish to see a real place in my mind, as you see it."

"As you wish, Miss." The genie bowed formally. "What do you wish to see?"

"Show me one of the places that you visited while you roamed the earth."

"Yes, Miss. Please, close your eyes." Jewel closed her eyes. The genie focused and saw one of the most unique and beautiful gardens that he'd visited. He projected that image to her mind by stretching out his right hand toward her head.

Jewel gasped as she suddenly saw the garden too. She opened her eyes but it wasn't there. When she closed them again, it was. She looked around with her eyes closed, and even walked around.

"Miss, it is best if you do not walk. You are still in the Crystal Court Room, not the garden."

"Where is this, exactly?"

"This is a Phoenician Garden, Miss. One of the places that I visited."

"It's beautiful!" She reached up to touch an unusual leaf and it felt furry. "I can touch things too!"

"Yes, Miss."

"Show me someplace else."

"Yes, Miss," The genie focused again and she suddenly was in the middle of a great rain forest, brilliantly green, and damp. "Oh!"

"One of the many different landscapes on earth, miss."

"This is wonderful, Genie."

The scene changed once again to the pinnacle of a mountain, one of the tallest in the world. Jewel gasped again. "Amazing."

"Yes, Miss."

She looked around but was very careful not to move. "Genie, show me my uncle so that we will know exactly when he will return."

"Yes, Miss."

"I see him. He is walking in the Crystal Court. He is here!" She still had her eyes closed when she suddenly heard a loud slap.

Chapter 16
Ally's Story: Shackles

Ally tried everything but he couldn't remove his ridiculous shackles! He tried metal workers from the past, present, and future, but not one of them could get them off. And not only that, but he kept fainting whenever he asked anyone to remove them, which was very odd. He never thought of himself as the squeamish type, someone who would faint at the thought of a metal worker coming near his wrists and ankles with hot instruments. No, it must be some enchantment of some type associated with him attempting to remove his shackles.

But he had to remove the last objects that bound him to slavery. As long as he had his shackles, he was still bound by his oath. He couldn't even cut his hair! The first barber's attempt to remove the banded lock at the top of his head destroyed his shears. He had to break free of this somehow, at least before the Leader of all the Djinn came to reclaim him.

Finally, he found two of the most worthless mortals he had ever met, but they had access to metallurgical materials, or so they said. He listened as they argued about different cutting methods, which they tried, but they also didn't work. They were discussing melting temperatures when one of them said something that made him look up from his wrists.

"So, what do you think he's worth?"

There. That was the moment when Alley became a product and not a person. Alley noticed his voice became less and less important as the conversation wore on. He was ashamed that it was happening again, watching himself slowly diminish in the eyes of mortals as he turned into an object. A prize. A commodity of great value. He was being turned into a slave as his voice and personhood lost their significance and his market price increased.

It was always more painful to watch in real time, as he knew that his confidence would have to turn into deference, his equal footing into subservience, and his opinion into silence. His feigned freedom was slipping away, as re-enslavement encroached. So much for a new way of living.

He had to put an end to this before they tried to put him in a bottle, or whatever container they had at hand. Making them unconsciousness was his best bet. As he began backing away from them, getting ready to use his powers, he saw them get suddenly struck down with blue blasts of energy. They both were now unconscious at his feet. The blasts came from behind him, so Ally jerked around to see who, or what caused it.

He saw the top of the staff of a djinn-guard glowing blue with power and backed away, frantically looking for a way to escape, if possible.

"No need to run, djinn. It will not work, anyway."

Alley, out of desperation, held up his hands, ready to use magic to fight back in any way he could, if he could. "I will not go back. I will not be a slave again!" But Alley immediately became weak and dizzy to the point where he was having difficulty standing.

"I know, djinn, I know. Relax. I will not send you back."

"What? Then, what do you want, djinn-guard?" Alley recovered enough to talk.

"First, I want you to know that I am no djinn-guard. I am a djinn-guardian."

"A djinn-guardian? A protector of the djinn? But that can't be true. They said that you were only a rumor, a myth. A hope that my people only wanted to be true."

"No. Though there are only a few of us, we do exist."

"So, what do you want from me?"

"I want to help you, Alley."

"You know my name? How can you help?" Alley held up his wrists. "Can you get these things off me?" He had to fight another sudden bout of weakness.

"Yes," the djinn-guardian approaching him carefully. "Yes, I can and I will."

"Anything to stop my enslavement, I've served master after master after master." Alley began to have even more difficulty standing. "Please help me end this, I will give anything."

The djinn-guardian caught Ally as he nearly fell backwards. "Yes, Alley, I will."

"Thank you." And with that, Alley lost consciousness.

Chapter 17
Tender's Childhood: Training

Kind's master required his presence only once more, and for just a few hours, as he was getting married. Afterwards, Kind settled back into his family's routines, enjoying his time with them.

Darling decided against rushing Patient's wedding, giving her and her betrothed more time to get to know each other.

There were only seven months until Tender's tenth birthday, when he would have to leave his family to begin training. As the date came closer, the family reacted by becoming quieter, pensive, and more solemn. He began to ask his father many more questions about his future training. Kind tried to prepare Tender as best as he could, but he was restricted by the rules of the Brethren. And he was becoming anxious about his future, which made thought sharing easier. He only had one week left with his family.

"I cannot show you what it looks like, Tender, or even share what it feels like with you. It's part of the rules; every member of the Brethren must discover it for himself. But you were there before, when you turned seven. Do you remember that day?"

"I mostly remember the corvar we had; it was great. That was my first time."

"Ha, that's what I hoped for. But do you remember anything about the building that we had to go in to register you?"

"I remember that it was strange and didn't look like any of the other places we were used to. It was square and had a lot of angles."

"Then you do remember it. They chose a very imposing design from the human world to make a lasting impression."

"It felt strange there," Tender said, remembering more clearly, "as if everything had to stay really quiet."

"Good. Your powers are remembering the experience for you."

"Is it scary? Or, as scary as it looks?"

"The building is the least of your concerns. But let's not worry about that right now. In one week, I will have to present you to the school as the new representative of our clan."

"And then?"

"Then they make you stand in line with the other young representatives of their clans according to the strength of your powers. Get used to being in line, there's a lot of that."

"Then what happens?"

"Then they will show you to your quarters." Kind paused, "I am not permitted to tell you any more than that. The rest you will have to discover for yourself. It is a highly regimented and well-monitored life but don't worry. We will always be here waiting for you."

"It sounds so serious."

"It is, but you are stronger than you know, Tender. And you will be able to do it. I know you can."

"Thank you, father."

"Now. How would you like to go to the Color Forest the day before you leave?"

"The day before?"

"Yes. It's your favorite place, isn't it?"

"Yes."

"So that's where we'll go. Just our family. We can spend the whole day there."

Tender couldn't contain his joy any longer, grinned, "That's great."

"I knew you would like it."

"Thank you, Papa."

"Good. Now go tell your brothers and sisters."

Tender disappeared. Kind noted that Tender used his powers to share the news with his siblings. That was a good sign that Tender wasn't the least hesitant to use his magical abilities. A good attitude would be very helpful when he began his training.

THE COLOR FOREST was aptly named, as it was a beautiful park in every color imaginable. Every leaf and blade of grass was its own distinct color so that there were reddish fields, blue bushes, and pink ponds. And not only that, but the colors changed. Frequently. The colors reflected the mood of the plants or the mood of the park's occupants, whichever emotion was the strongest. A red field could suddenly turn purple, the blue bushes orange, and the pink ponds yellow.

Kind and his family appeared there in the morning in an open field. The younger children began running almost as soon as their feet touched the ground, which encouraged the older children to run after them. They ran towards the yellow pond, which was turning fuchsia.

They had an enjoyable day picnicking, playing games, strolling and hiking, and just enjoying being outdoors. When some of the children got dirty, since the dirt was also colored, they looked like they had been smudged with paint.

Kind and Darling smiled and laughed at the antics of their children, and occasionally joined them in the fun. Kind conjured a mini-water park in the middle of a blue field which they all loved. There were fountains, wading ponds, and places to slide in. After they were done, Darling dried everyone off and cleaned their clothes instantly, while Kind made the water park disappear.

After a few more games, they enjoyed a very large and exceptionally fragrant meal, overflowing with everyone's favorite foods. Kind and Darling began the meal by insisting that everyone take as much time as they wanted to eat and talk. The table, magically charged with keeping all the food at exactly the right temperature, allowed them to spend nearly two hours at the feast, relaxing, talking, and enjoying themselves.

By the time night fell and they returned to the lamp, the children were exhausted and fell asleep easily. Even Darling and Kind fell asleep earlier than expected.

The next day was still a tense one, but not as anxious. Darling helped Tender prepare a small bundle of a bag of his most precious possessions to take with him, which included his sleeping mat and a few clothes. She dressed him in his best clothes, even though Kind knew that Tender would be wearing a school uniform almost as soon as he could change clothes in the training building.

When Kind and Tender were ready, they stood in the middle of the lamp's common room surrounded by family. None of the children dared say anything, mostly because they didn't know what to say. But Strong broke the ice. "Don't forget about us," he said.

"I won't," Tender answered. "I can't. You're hard to forget."

"I hope you learn a lot and teach it to me when you get back," Creative added.

"I'll try," Tender responded, quietly and awkwardly.

"Contact us as often as you can," Patient said. "As often as they let you."

"I will," Tender answered.

"Stay tender, Tender," said Sweet, his latest catchphrase for Tender.

"And you stay sweet, Sweet," Tender answered with a grin.

"I hope they treat you well," Gentle added.

"Me too," answered Tender.

"I'm going to miss you a lot, Tender. I don't want you to go," Dearest said, almost crying. Tender hugged her, trying hard not to cry. She pulled back from him, and held onto Gentle, crying.

Darling hugged Tender like he was the most precious thing in the world, "I'm really going to miss you, my tender one."

"I'm going to miss you too, Mama," Tender managed to say.

"It's time," Kind said, the only thing that would stop Darling from hugging Tender. She pulled away and they all stood back from Kind and Tender.

"Good-bye."

"Bye."

"See you."

"We'll miss you."

Tender looked up at his father, who nodded. "Good-bye," Tender said, shyly.

And with that, Kind and Tender disappeared.

Chapter 18
Tender's Story: Punishment

Jewel suddenly heard a loud slap, and her vision of the room instantly dissolved around her so that she saw reality instead. She saw the genie, sprawled across the floor, pick himself up and then bow low with his arms stretched forward. Her uncle stood over him, but she had to blink twice just to make sure that what she was seeing was real.

"I told you, Genie, there is to be no physical contact between you and my niece!"

The genie bowed low to the ground again in front of her uncle, this time staying down, arms stretched out.

Jewel rushed to explain, "But he didn't touch me! He didn't! He was just showing me where you were in a vision."

"I don't care why he touched you. He disobeyed me."

"But he didn't touch me! He was merely fulfilling my wish to see your location in my mind."

"And he needs to touch you, in order to do this?"

"But he did not touch me! He just had his hand stretched out towards me. Please believe me, Uncle, please!"

The king held up his hand to silence her, which worked. "Well, Genie? What do you have to say for yourself?"

The genie lifted slightly, and softly said, "Forgive me, Master, please forgive me for upsetting and displeasing you."

She gasped but her uncle wasn't moved. "To your lamp, genie. I will punish you shortly."

The genie vanished instantly without smoke. From within his lamp, the genie saw Jewel continue to plead with his master until he ordered her to her apartment. Fifteen lashes would be nothing to him as long as she was spared.

He remained in his lamp for an hour and a half until finally, his master summoned him. His master had waited until there was a large enough audience of courtiers for the spectacle. The king had also ordered most of his servants to attend, as the sight of him punishing a djinn would intimidate them enough to keep them in line.

The genie, bowing low on the floor, appeared in a small puff of white smoke in the Emerald Throne Room. He stood up, took in the scene around him without looking directly at anyone, including the overseer of the servants, who held a whip and a large, rectangular, metal frame to strap him into. It had metal rings in each of its four corners.

The entire court was assembled, along with Jewel, in her place besides the king, although she was visibly upset. She had obviously been crying and looked as if she'd rather be anywhere else.

"Fifteen lashes, Genie, for the violation of touching my niece," the king pronounced.

The genie bowed in acquiescence, then held his left wrist shackle towards the overseer. The shackle appeared to grow a chain link, making it easier for the overseer to chain him to the metal frame. His other three shackles grew their own links also, and soon enough, he was in place. His arms hung loosely from his wrist's shackles and his legs locked into a wide stance.

The overseer took his place behind him and struck him with the whip. The sound echoed throughout the room and adjoining halls.

He paused between lashes long enough for each sting to painfully resonate.

For the first few lashes, the genie held his place, but by the tenth lash, his strength began to give and his knees buckled, leaving only the chains and locks to hold him up. He cried out involuntarily at the twelfth lash but remained silent for the final three.

"Leave him there for at least two hours. For all must know what happens when anyone dares to disobey their king."

The king and then the people of the court left the room quietly, many gawking openly at the thoroughly punished genie. The king's servants lingered the longest, many of them empathizing with him.

Jewel left quickly, nearly running from the room. She could not bear to look at the genie, so hurt and degraded.

The genie hung in place, occasionally shifting his position slightly, with his eyes closed. While his face would sometimes contort itself in pain, he remained silent, hanging his head.

After two hours and twenty minutes, the overseer released him from the frame. The shackle loops dissolved back into the shackles. With his back and legs covered in wounds, blood, and sweat, and his clothes torn from the lashes, he staggered up and limped into the Emerald Throne Room. Immediately aware of his master, and of Jewel, despondent by her uncle's side.

The people of the court parted as he made his way through the crowd to the throne. With painful difficulty, he assumed the submissive position and bowed. The king stared hard at his every move.

"Please forgive me, Master, for upsetting and displeasing you. I will take care to never offend you in such a manner again." He spoke quietly and bowed low to the floor again with his arms stretched before him.

Satisfied, the king nodded. "Very well, Genie, you are forgiven. You may return to your lamp."

"Thank you, Master." The genie disappeared in a small puff of white smoke, streaked with slashes of red. Those in court began to talk among themselves about the day's exciting and entertaining events.

Jewel wept silently. Her uncle had insisted that she remain with him throughout since it was her person and honor that he was defending. Jewel, however, could hardly wait to be excused.

~

"An hour as a day," the genie whispered as he entered his lamp.

Inside, he reappeared, crying out a bit as he laid on his stomach on a cushion. He held out his hand and focused, causing a jar of Santar's ointment to appear. He used his powers to open the jar, made a cloth appear, and applied ointment directly to his wounds. The ointment instantly healed everything it touched.

After he finished, he closed the jar, then made it and the cloth disappear, along with all the bloodstains, with a flick of his fingers. His clothes also returned to their former appearance. With the pain and wounds entirely gone, he relaxed completely on the cushions, turning over onto his back and adjusting himself until he was more comfortable.

He may not have to make an appearance in court for at least a few days, which meant that his time in the lamp would feel like a few months to him. He knew he would still have to appear contrite and suitably penitent when he did appear. He wondered when he would be allowed to see Jewel again. Or if he would ever see her again.

"Maybe the genie didn't touch her after all," the king ruminated later that night instead of sleeping. He never actually admitted that he touched her, only confessing to upsetting, offending, and displeasing him, but not to physically touching his niece. Genies seemed to be very precise when it came to language. And he had never lied to him before. No, he decided, the genie did not touch his niece. Still, he had to set a good example for the court, and it would diminish him in the eyes of his people to admit to such a mistake. It was always good to demonstrate discipline in one's servants, every now and then. He would make it up to the genie in some way, even if he didn't have the faintest idea how.

It troubled him how readily and eagerly Jewel came to the genie's defense. Was he influencing her somehow or falling under his power? No, Jewel defended him of her own free will. Exactly where that will of hers was leading her, he didn't know.

JEWEL FELT nothing but remorse and regret. She felt extremely guilty for not listening to the genie's warning and plowing through with her demands, using one of her official wishes. She felt bad for turning a delightful, ordinary conversation into a master-slave relationship with her giving orders that he was forced to obey.

How could she do that to the genie, who had been nothing but patient and kind to her? And then to see him whipped just for fulfilling her wish; that was worse than anything. What could she do about it now? Was there anything that she could do?

Part Two

Chapter 19
Tender's Story: The Reunion

Jewel and the genie did not speak again for nearly half a year. The genie was kept mostly inside of his lamp for a month, only coming out when the king specifically wanted something from him.

The genie was officially disgraced, and he sensed it would be wise for him to appear properly chastised. When he did appear, he was quieter and spoke less frequently, if at all. Not that he was talkative before, but he knew that his demonstrations of shame and remorse would cause his master to forgive him faster, even if it was all for show.

This continued until the king realized how much he missed the easily accessible political insights and military knowledge of his genie. And so, after another month, the genie returned to his former position in the king's crystal court, close to the throne.

He only spoke directly with the king and on the rare occasions Jewel was present, he only acknowledged her with a formal bow, as he did with all the other ranked members of the court.

He did not look up, but kept his head always bowed low.

Many weeks later during one of the king's frequent celebrations, the genie was allowed to remain in the Emerald Throne Room while most of the other servants were allowed to watch the performers. Acrobats and dancers were brought in for the occasion to please and amuse the king. As the courtiers enjoyed the entertainment, the genie was in his usual submissive position, kneeling above a cushion to the left of the throne. He didn't even allow himself a glance at the entertainment.

At one point, some of the elite young women and girls, including Jewel, performed a special dance for the king. As the dancers jumped and swirled, the genie, out of respect, kept his eyes closed and aimed towards the floor. There was a moment where the dancers released confetti in bright primary colors, and then the dance was over.

As the king and everyone else rushed to congratulate them, the genie sensed that there was a relatively large, folded piece of beige paper on the floor in front of him, mixed in with the colorful paper.

Slowly and unnoticed, the genie reached for and picked up the paper. He unfolded it with one hand and saw that there was a message written on it that said, "I'm sorry."

The genie made the paper disappear instantly and glanced in Jewel's direction. He could not look at her directly of course, but only at the floor in front of where she stood.

She saw him and made a very slight, inconspicuous bow of her head towards him, though she was listening to other people. Even though he was still focused on the floor, he gave her a small, silent nod in return.

Later, within his lamp, the genie held the scrap of paper again and studied it. He knew that Jewel wasn't to blame, not really. But he also knew that if he hadn't apologized when he did, the king would have punished them both. And he could not let that happen.

Soon afterward, the king, in his chambers, summoned the genie. "Genie?"

The genie appeared almost instantly, fading into view right in front of his master. He didn't usually use smoke when there was no audience besides the king. There was no one to impress or intimidate, nor any need to do so. "Yes, Master?"

"My niece wants to question you again."

"Oh," the genie said as he looked down. "I see, Master."

When the genie didn't say anything else, the king added, "Well, what do you think about it?"

"Perhaps you shouldn't allow it, Master. I do not wish to be in a position where I am compelled to obey the wish of the young lady again, and yet appear to go against your will."

"She will not ask you for anything that would cause you trouble, Genie. I apologize for punishing you, I know now that you did not touch her."

"Thank you, Master. But please, I do not want to be in similar situation again."

"You will not be, I can promise you that."

"Master, may I speak openly?"

"Yes, Genie."

The genie looked at his master directly. "Master, have I not served you faithfully, for many years?"

"Yes, Genie."

"Have I not obeyed your every whim?"

"Of course, Genie, you have."

"Then please believe me, Master, if you allow her to continue to question me, it will not end well for any of us. I see only pain and sadness for all involved."

"Do you actually see this in the future?"

"I am too involved to see our futures so clearly, but I sense it. My people and your people have mostly remained separate for a reason. I do not wish to rediscover old truths as to why."

"Old truths or old superstitions?"

The genie sighed and bowed. "Master, I am your slave and I will do as you wish. But please, I only ask for caution." The genie closed his eyes and bowed again, to emphasize his submission to his master's will. Now it was his master's turn to sigh.

"Very well, Genie. I will use extreme caution. You two will never be alone, even for a minute. I will assign a special monitor for your conversations. My niece may continue to question you, but you will not be held responsible if one of her wild ideas backfires. Is this acceptable to you?"

"Yes, Master," the genie bowed again.

"And Genie, you must tell me of a way that I can make it up to you. I do not want to have this hanging over my head, this feeling that I owe you something. Is there anything that I can do for you?"

The genie became solemn, paused, and bowed again. "Aside from that which all my enslaved Brethren and I want, our deepest, truest, desire to be free, I do not wish for anything else currently, Master. I am happy to be of service to you. Thank you for your kind offer."

"You're welcome, Genie. You may return to your lamp."

The genie bowed and began to quickly fade until he was gone. Within his lamp, the genie fell back on his cushions in frustration. He knew that he had asked his master for something forbidden, but he couldn't remember exactly what it was. He knew that he had told the truth and was still somehow relieved by what he said, but his memory of what happened was being affected by the djinn laws. Forbidden words and subjects requested by their masters were instantly erased from the memories of the enslaved Brethren. The genie could only remember exactly what he said if his master wished him to recount it, which he just didn't see happening.

The next time the genie and Jewel met was in the crystal court off to the left side of the throne in one of its many open side rooms, the closest to the throne. It allowed for the illusion of privacy but was still in full view and hearing of the court.

True to his word, the king appointed a special monitor for Jewel and the genie. The person chosen for this position was an elderly man of much education who had retired from one of the king's universities years before. He was charged to listen only, interrupt when necessary, and report everything directly to the king when asked.

He was already in the side room when Jewel entered the court. After bowing to the king, she walked as fast as she could directly to the designated room. "Good morning, Professor."

"Good morning, Miss Jewel."

"I'm so grateful to you for doing this."

"Don't worry, my child. Anything for the king's niece."

Jewel smiled, grateful for at least some of the privileges that her position allowed her.

The genie appeared before them, forming quickly from a small cloud of white smoke, and bowed to each person. Since the genie was not allowed to speak unless spoken to, particularly after being punished, he remained silent.

"Good morning, Genie," Jewel began, awkwardly.

"Good morning, Miss," the genie softly responded.

"I'm so sorry for what happened last time. I didn't mean to cause you any trouble, I'm so sorry," Jewel's words spilled out in a rush.

"It is alright, Miss," the genie bowed his head slightly, taking her young adult age and eager disposition into account.

"I feel so bad about it, I almost don't know what to say next."

"It is alright, Miss." He thought to himself *I'm sure you'll think of something.*

There was a short pause before Jewel tried again. "Genie? What happens when a mortal gets things wrong, like what happened with us? What happens if you get contradictory wishes? One person wishing for one thing and the next wishing for the opposite?"

"I must fulfill both wishes, Miss. But in all, my master has the final word," he said with a bow.

"So, it is always up to your master to decide the final outcome? Even when your master is wrong?"

The genie paused. "It is not for to me to decide the morality of my master's decisions, miss. It is my obligation only to obey."

"So, you must obey your master, even when he is wrong?"

"I must obey my master, Miss. But I am not in any position to judge my master. I am his slave and his slave only, Miss. Not his judge. I must fulfill his wishes." He bowed again as he said this.

"But that just seems wrong to me, Genie. That is just so unfair."

"Miss, I had to give up any expectations of fairness when I took the oath for my clan. The state of life being fair is only temporary. Often, Miss, justice only prevails in the long run."

"In the long run, we're all dead."

With a slight smile, the genie answered, "That's true, Miss. But justice still usually prevails."

"I don't know if I want to wait for justice to eventually prevail. But I suppose we all must, whether we like it or not."

"Yes, Miss, that's true."

After this pause in the conversation, the professor, spoke up. "I think that's enough for today."

"But it's only been a few minutes," Jewel protested.

"You did get a chance to question him, correct?"

"Yes," she reluctantly admitted.

"So, I'd say that fulfills your requirement for today. Say goodbye," the professor added, as if he were speaking to a small child.

"Goodbye, Genie."

"Goodbye, Miss."

The professor left the area with Jewel following. The genie dissolved into smoke and reappeared beside his master in his usual position.

The king turned to him and asked, "How did your conversation go, Genie? Was it satisfactory?"

"Yes, Master, it was. It went well."

"And nothing untoward occurred?"

"No, Master. It was all very straightforward."

"Good."

The genie didn't elaborate, as the king seemed satisfied with his answer. As the king's attention was quickly drawn elsewhere, the genie had a chance to think about what had just happened. And to wonder what it would lead to.

After a couple of weeks, the professor asked the king for permission to use the side room of the court to continue his studies, since he was required to listen to every conversation between Jewel and the genie.

Even though they had a regular meeting day, they did not necessarily have a regular meeting time. *After your last lesson, but before dinner on the fifth day of the week* was a bit vague, so the professor often had no idea when Jewel would be there.

There were also times when Jewel and the genie would talk that were completely unplanned, such as when she had to wait for the king, or after she was summoned by the king for official occasions.

The genie always seemed to know when Jewel would be available. He had a habit of appearing in a small cloud of white smoke a minute before Jewel and bowing to the professor. He would then wait in silence patiently, kneeling or with his legs crossed, for Jewel to appear.

Sometimes the professor noticed the genie at the king's side, suddenly bowing to the king first, before appearing in the side room. Sometimes the king told the genie that it was time for his conversation with Jewel. Other times, the genie would tell the king that his niece was approaching the Crystal Court Room.

Since the professor didn't want to inconvenience the king by having to be summoned from his living quarters every time, he asked that he be given two small desks and shelves, along with comfortable seating for the side room. That way he could continue his private studies quietly every day, while waiting for the scheduled and sporadic visits from the king's royal niece.

Jewel could also read and study there when the genie wasn't available. The professor would remain in the room during the day and would return to his quarters before dinner. From this point on, the genie only met with Jewel in this side room.

Chapter 20
Training: Eight Young Boys

Kind and Tender appeared in front of the training building. "Are you ready?" Kind asked.

Tender nodded, "Yes," and they walked towards the building. When they entered, he noticed the same man from his first visit sat behind the same desk. Not only that, but no one else seemed to be around. Would he be the only one in his class? They approached the man, who was writing in a large book.

"Name?"

Kind answered, "Tender, son of Kind. From the third clan."

"And his markings?"

This time, a taller Tender held his arms up to the man so that he could see. The man glanced at the symbols on his arms and then continued writing.

"And his age?"

"He just turned ten years old yesterday."

The man nodded again, but didn't look up. "You may go into that classroom to say goodbye." He tipped his head to the right but Kind already knew where to go.

"Thank you."

"Thank you," Tender repeated.

They entered the room, which looked like a large mortal classroom, circa 1950s America. There were twelve desks and chairs appropriately sized for children of Tender's age. But again, they were alone.

Kind knelt and hugged his son. "I'm going to miss you, Tender."

"I'll miss you too, Papa."

"It will be a while before I see you in person again and we can use the cloths to communicate when they allow it."

"I'm scared," Tender whispered.

"I know, but don't worry, you can do this. You are stronger than you know. Always remember that."

"Yes, Papa."

Kind stood up and took a step back. "I love you, Son."

"I love you too, Papa."

Kind disappeared by slowly fading away but maintaining eye contact. Tender wiped the tears off his face and looked around. He was still completely alone and with no idea what to do next. He looked for a chair and sat down. After about two minutes, seven other boys, all around the same age, began to appear in the room with him, sitting in different chairs. As they faded in, they all seemed surprised that, apparently, they had been sharing the same room all along.

A stern male voice suddenly commanded, "Do not speak. In any way."

Tender hadn't planned on saying anything, but now, it was suddenly forbidden. He looked down at the desk, wondering what was going to happen next. "Line up in the front of the room facing the chairs in this order. Tender."

Tender stood up and went to the front of the room.

"Alley." Another boy got up and stood next to Tender. "Clever." The pattern repeated with a pause between each name until all the boys were lined up. "Thoughtful. Bold. Shy. Peaceful. Joyful. This is the order in which you were placed and this is the order that you will maintain. From now on, whenever you are asked to line up, it shall be in this order."

A very imposing middle-aged man appeared in front of them in a large cloud of white smoke. He was wearing long flowing robes with a blue robe covering the rest. He looked at every boy in the line in turn, starting with Tender, who was too intimidated to look back. But Alley did.

"Look only at the floor in front of you, now." All the boys began awkwardly looking at the floor in front of them, unsure of themselves.

The teacher studied them like a military commander. "From now on, you will answer my every command with the phrase, 'Yes, First Teacher.' Do you understand?"

"Yes, First Teacher."

The teacher walked down the line of young djinn, staring at them again one by one, while they tried to remain as still as possible. "You are to keep your eyes focused on the floor right in front of you always. You will not look at anyone or anything else directly unless given express permission. Understand?"

"Yes, First Teacher."

"You will also keep your voices down and will not shout or cry out for any reason. Understand?"

"Yes, First Teacher."

"Now. On your knees."

"Yes, First Teacher." His young students obeyed, each kneeling as best as they could.

"Look up to see my hands and my hands only. Your hands must be held together, the right over the left, just like this. Understand?"

"Yes, First Teacher."

"This position is called the submissive position. It will be your default position. You must learn how to remain in this position for hours at a time. For your first test, you will remain on your knees for the next hour, heads down and eyes to the floor always, no matter what. Understand?"

"Yes, First Teacher."

"Good." He walked out of the room knowing that his young charges certainly did not understand everything he said exactly but was reassured by their obedience. True understanding would come later.

After an hour, he returned to his students, who mostly remained in the position assigned to them. They were obviously in pain and greatly discomforted, but they obeyed as well as they were able.

"I am your First Teacher of Djinn Protocol and Customs before mortals. Your first lesson is obedience, your second lesson is obedience, and your last lesson is obedience. Your lives literally depend on it. And you will learn."

"Yes, First Teacher."

"Stand up." The boys stood up slowly, awkwardly, and painfully. There were a few tears, which were wiped away quickly, but no one made a sound. "I will show you to your sleeping quarters, where you may place your belongings. Then I will show you the rest of the training building, or at least, the rooms that pertain to you."

"Yes, First Teacher."

"Now, to your quarters. Follow me. In order!" He began to leave the room, hurriedly followed by Tender and the rest of the boys. He led them down the large hall to the wide staircase at the end. They followed him upstairs, a short way down another wide hall to a large room with eight beds, four across from each other. There was a large wardrobe on the right side of each bed and a matching bookshelf on the other side. There was a door next to each wardrobe and a large trunk was at the end of every bed. Each bed had a placard over it with the name of its future occupant written on it. An adult sized desk and chair was at the front of the room and large windows at the other end. The room had two doors, one on each side of the desk.

"You will go to your assigned space and unpack. Put your belongings in the trunk or the wardrobe and lock it with your powers. Then stand in front of the trunk."

"Yes, First Teacher."

"There will be absolutely no talking among you of any kind." The

First Teacher added, *"Of any kind. Remain silent. Sit on your trunks once you are done."*

The First Teacher sat down at the adult sized desk between the doors of the room. He waved his hand and a scroll appeared on the desk, which he began to read and occasionally write on.

Tender's bed was on the right side of the desk, close to the front of the room. He silently went to his bed and placed his belongings in his wardrobe. He stared at the door and wondered what it was for.

When all the boys had put away their meager bags of belongings, they sat on the trunks in front of their beds, waiting for further instructions and looking down at the floor.

"Now, stand in front of your trunk. Stand straight, heads up. You may respond."

"Yes, First Teacher."

The First Teacher walked down the middle of the room to the windows and turned around. "This is the position I expect to see you in every morning as soon as you are done dressing yourselves. This is how you are to line up for inspection. This is called 'the ready position.' On your first full day of classes, I expect you to be wearing your uniforms."

A neatly folded stack of mostly blue clothes appeared on the beds of each boy.

"The door to the left of your wardrobes is very special. It is called the Whatever Room, as it becomes whatever room you need it to be, within reason. Let me demonstrate." He closed and opened the door and the room turned into a white, extremely modern bathroom with a toilet, sink, and full body sonic sanitizer system. If you wish to relieve yourself, it becomes a water closet. If you wish to bathe or wash yourself in any other manner, it becomes that also. He closed the door and opened it again, and the room was filled with a very large bathtub.

"The room can change around you while you're in it without harming you or anyone else you may wish to invite inside, limited to your teachers and the Brethren, of course. It's designed to be perfectly safe."

He closed the door. "The Whatever Rooms will remain age appropriate and are not to be abused. You may use this time to relieve and refresh yourselves. And to change into your uniforms."

"Yes, First Teacher."

Tender opened the door to his Whatever Room and it became the modern bathroom. As he entered, he thought that the room and its belongings would look better in yellow. Instantly the color of the room changed to bright yellow, along with everything in it.

The sonic personal cleansing system was just like the one he had used a few times at home. You stepped over its plain white circle, under another plain white circle, pressed the button built into the wall on the left, and it glowed white for about twenty seconds. He loved the one that he used to have at home, though his mother removed it only after a week. She said that she preferred the intimacy of bathing her children in a bathtub, at least when they were little.

When he left his Whatever Room he found the First Teacher standing in front of his desk, waiting for them. Tender stood in front of his trunk along with the rest of the boys.

"Now you must begin to look like members of the Brethren. For that, we must go to the Ritual Room. Follow me, Tender first."

"Yes, First Teacher." Tender followed the First Teacher and the rest of the boys followed him in their assigned order. This time, they went back downstairs and into a different room. This room was grander than the others, though not as large as the dorm, but comparable to the classroom. It was decorated in a baroque fashion with gold filigrees on the walls and ceilings, an elaborate brown and gold matching carpet, and ornate flourishes everywhere. There was a chair in the center of the room, three chairs behind it, and eight smaller chairs facing them.

The First Teacher explained, "This is where you will partake in all the ancient rites of the Brethren, appropriate to your ages and circumstances. Today, it will be the correct styling of your hair. It will be cut to a more appropriate length, all except the banded lock. Your banded lock shall remain at the crown of your head as a permanent symbol of your membership of the Brethren. It is also a symbol of your service and enslavement to mortals, as is traditional with all the djinn. Take your seats, please. In order."

"Yes, First Teacher."

Tender went to the farthest seat away from the door. He was already ashamed of being first and did not like the pressure or the attention that came with it. When they had all taken their seats, a large cloud of white smoke overtook the chair in the middle. A very strange djinn with an odd silver and gold mustache and beard appeared in the room, standing in front of the chair in the middle. He was clothed in flowing robes with a blue robe covering the others, but his blue robe was more ornate and filled with intricately woven floral designs. He wore a strange blue cap that matched his hood.

"This is the Master of the Rituals. Stand and bow to him."

The boys stood and bowed.

"Sit."

"Yes, First Teacher."

Then the Master of Rituals began to speak. "The styling of your hair is the first ritual you shall partake in as a member of the Brethren. It is an ancient, sacred tradition, and you all should be honored to take your place among the Brethren. From now on, your will is not your own. The first boy, come. Now!"

Tender, embarrassed again, walked up to the front of the room and faced the Master of the Rituals. He didn't exactly know what else to do, so he bowed to him again.

"Good," the Master of the Rituals responded. "Take this seat."

Tender sat down, not exactly sure what to expect or when to expect it. His mother and father always cut his hair through magic. He watched as the Master of the Rituals circled him until he had reached some type of decision.

"There!"

Tender felt his hair magically change. A plain, rectangular mirror appeared, suspended in air, in front of his face at the perfect angle so that he could get a good look at what had been done. His hair was much shorter, about an inch long, all except the banded lock at the crown of his head. He knew that his sisters would call it a ponytail, but he had to follow the djinn tradition.

The mirror disappeared.

"Next," the Master of the Rituals shouted.

Tender stood up, turned, bowed to him again, and took his seat. The next boy followed his lead, though he seemed distinctly unhappy about the entire thing. Alley was his name and he looked angry, even resentful at everything he was being asked to do. Tender wondered why but since they were forbidden to speak to each other, he wondered when or if he would ever find out.

All the boys took their turn getting their new haircuts, after which they all sat down.

"Now, stand, bow, and thank the Master of the Rituals."

"Yes, First Teacher." The boys did as they were told.

"Now, follow me." The First Teacher led them back upstairs into their dorm room. "Since this is your first day, and to show that your teachers aren't totally heartless, we will allow you to have unscheduled time until dinner. You may do as you like during this time, within reason." He then took his seat at his desk.

Tender, feeling especially awkward for not knowing what to do with himself, first used his Whatever Room as a water closet. Then he felt an immense longing to be back home in his father's lamp. The room changed to resemble his bedroom. He sat on the bed, laid down, and tried hard not to cry. He failed and wept quietly.

He must have fallen asleep because the next thing he heard was the disembodied voice of the First Teacher. "Your unscheduled time is over. Your final meal of the day will begin shortly. Get in the ready position. Now."

"Yes, First Teacher," Tender answered, feeling strange saying it by himself. He left his Whatever Room and saw that a few other boys had spent their unscheduled time in their Whatever Rooms as well. The First Teacher was standing in front of his desk. The boys quickly lined up in the ready position.

"Follow me."

"Yes, First Teacher." With Tender first in line again, the First Teacher led the boys down the stairs and into the dining room, which was next to The Rituals Room. It was another, mostly nondescript room with several long tables and chairs.

The First Teacher led them to the nearest table and stood at the head of the table. There were four chairs on each side of the table, with the adult sized chair in the front. Every table was bare. "Tender, to my right."

"Yes, First Teacher," he replied, and the boys took their places in the order that was quickly becoming familiar to them. "Now, sit."

"Yes, First Teacher," they replied and sat down. Plates, glasses, and utensils appeared before each person at the table first. Then, food appeared on each plate and various drinks in each glass.

"Once a week, you each receive your favorite foods and drinks. You will each eat calmly and quietly and remain still when you are done. Begin."

"Yes, First Teacher." It was odd to eat and not talk in between bites. Tender was used to livelier family meals ruled over by their parents, but only to curtail his sibling's more raucous behaviors and limit crude conversations. But at this table the boys didn't even try to look at each other, or at least Tender didn't. When one of the boys burped, Tender thought it was Bold, but he wasn't sure. The boy apologized, adding the phrase "First Teacher" as instructed. The First Teacher nodded but did not otherwise respond, and Tender wondered if he was sworn to silence too.

Afterwards, they were led back to their dorm room for more unscheduled time. Tender truly worried if every single day was going to be like this, with no talking at any time. Not that he was especially eager to make friends, but it was odd not to be able to talk or express himself in anyway. He looked around the room at the other boys and wondered if he would ever come to know how they got their names or what they were really like. Everything so far only increased his sense of isolation.

He decided to retreat into his Whatever Room again. This time, Tender changed the Whatever Room into his parents' bedroom. He crawled into the bed and imagined that they left for a few moments and would be back soon.

"Time for bed. Ready position." Tender heard the voice of the First Teacher even with his head under the covers.

"Yes, First Teacher," he answered, leaving the Whatever Room and standing in front of his bed in the ready position along with the other boys. All their clothes were changed into blue pajamas.

"Get into your beds."

"Yes, First Teacher." Tender obeyed, as did the other boys. He was wondering if the First Teacher would give the order to sleep but he didn't get a chance to find out since he fell asleep quickly.

THERE WAS a lounge for all the faculty at the school where most of the teachers and administrators came to eat and relax. Tonight, they were enjoying a late-night meal with the Leader of all the Djinn.

"You know, you don't have to make such a show of it every time," the First Teacher said to the Master of the Rituals.

"Yes, I do. If I don't build that fear and respect immediately then they'll never be intimidated by me," the Master of the Rituals answered, peeved. "I've got less time to make an impression than you do."

"So," said the Leader of all the Djinn, "what do you think of this group?"

"They seem to be an obedient group overall with no real trouble-makers," the First Teacher stated.

"No troublemakers? Did you hear all that commotion with the Alley boy? I bet you could hear him inside the building." The Teacher of Meditation was a naturally calm man who disliked disruptions.

"Be happy you didn't have to see it. It was heartbreaking," the Administrator, who sat at the entrance of the building, replied.

"Yes. That was unfortunate," the Leader of all the Djinn stated. He was a stately man, comfortable with his power and position, but occasionally uncomfortable with its requirements and demands. "Perhaps I should have handled that better."

"There wasn't much that you could do about that. You told the boy not to go outside. Who knew that his love for his nonexistent caretaker would be so strong." The Teacher of the Law appeared to be the oldest member of the faculty.

The Leader of all the Djinn sipped his drink as he communicated to the faculty telepathically. *"I knew. I shouldn't have done that here; I should have waited."*

"We can't control every circumstance for everything; we can only try," the First Teacher responded. "But they seem to be nice boys, overall. I like them."

Chapter 21
Tender's Story: The Guard

"Genie, have any genies of your sect ever chosen not to serve?"

"Yes, Miss. It has happened only three times, but it has happened."

"So, the entire clan had to serve, at no matter what age, from babies to the very old?"

"Yes, Miss, although the very young were spared until they came of age at twenty-one, Miss."

"The same age you had to take your oath?"

"Yes, Miss."

"Did they all have to go through training?"

"No, Miss. When that happens, they must serve immediately without any training at all. It is difficult for those without training, though some eventually become good at it, while others never quite adjust. That is why there is often such a wide variety in the skills of the djinn that mortals encounter, Miss. Some of my people are just naturally better at serving than others. It is easier for those who are younger and more pliable."

"And the ones who chose not to serve, what happened to them?"

"The first genie who did not serve was very ill and truly in no state to choose anything. But that was counted as a choice not to serve and his clan was enslaved because of it. He died soon after from his illness. The other two cases, both were shunned by the djinn, barred from our lands and contacting our people, and never heard from again."

"Never?"

"It is said that they walk among men now, forever having to hide their true natures."

"Oh, how sad."

"Yes, Miss."

"Genie, have there ever been any cases where mortals were turned into genies?"

"While that is mostly a myth, I do know of one instance. Though I have heard it's happened before, I am not familiar with any other incidents, Miss."

"And the one you're familiar with? Can you tell me about it? If you don't mind, Genie."

"As you wish, Miss. I was younger then and had just recently taken my oath. I was only on my fifth master who had an interesting view of the djinn. He was already wealthy when he found my lamp so he initially regarded me as just another one of his servants. He required me to live like his other servants, also.

"He told me to disguise myself by hiding my hair and eyes and wearing the clothes of his other servants. I had to live, sleep, and eat with them. I warned him that this would become a problem, Miss, once they found out what I was, which I knew would eventually happen. But as I said, I was young and I looked it, and so he didn't take me seriously."

~

"MASTER, forgive me, but I am not like your other servants. They will greatly resent me once they find out what I am."

"Then they must never find out. Conceal your identity and act as one of them. I will tell them that you are my close, personal servant and bodyguard, and they will accept you."

"As you wish, Master."

I obeyed him and for a while, the ruse went well. But then one day, there was an accident in one of his storage barns. One of the large bins was overloaded and began to tip over. My master and his overseer were right beneath it. As I was charged with protecting his life, I had to use my powers to prevent him from getting crushed.

I only used two fingers on my right hand to stop the bin and put it back in place, but it was too late. The overseer saw me use my powers and told the other servants. By the time we returned to the house, all the other servants knew what I was and were afraid of me. Still, my master wished that I continue to behave as one of them.

That's when the problems began. One particular servant, a young man who was my master's personal guard before I took his place, began to take pleasure in tormenting me. I had just served my master his dinner. He had a fear of being poisoned so he always had me check his meals first. When I returned to the kitchen, I heard the guard yell.

"You there! Bring me my drink also."

"I am sorry, Sir, but I am only allowed to serve my master."

He slapped me.

"Stop that. Haven't you ever heard that it is bad luck to attack a genie?" The overseer tried to warn him.

"Bad luck? For him. He doesn't seem to mind it all that much. Do you, Genie?"

"It is not wise to harm one of the djinn," I stated.

"But why? Show me."

I was not allowed to elaborate or explain the rules of the brethren to someone who was not my master, so I did not. He began to attack me whenever I offended him, which was often, as he was offended by my very existence. I was not able to defend myself without the explicit permission of my master, so I was physically attacked regularly along with other daily humiliations.

A few weeks later, even my master noticed my appearance. Because my tormentor had used his fists during the morning meal, the left side of my face was swollen.

"Genie! What happened?"

"I was beaten by one of your other servants, Master. Your former bodyguard."

"What? How dare he? Why hasn't the overseer done anything about this? He should have told me; he should have put a stop to it."

"The overseer is afraid of me, Master, and wants nothing to do with me or my people."

"This is outrageous! I can't have my servants attacking one another."

"May I protect myself, Master?"

"You could kill him with a thought."

"I will try not to harm him, or anyone else, Master, as per your wishes. I only ask to shield myself from harm."

"Then of course, Genie. You can at least shield yourself from harm."

It was in this that my inexperience displayed itself, for I should have asked to be allowed to return to living in my lamp. But I was angry and I wanted revenge. I became emotionally involved and wanted to see my fellow servant's faces when I defended myself. It was wrong of me, Miss, but I was young and foolish.

The next day, after my master had gone to sleep, I prepared to sleep with the other servants since I was still required to live as one of them. The guard came to me as I unrolled my mat."

"There you are, you demonic creature," he began to yell at me. "You only pretend to be one of us!"

This time when he hit me I shielded myself by making my body like iron. He broke his hand and yelled out.

"What have you done to me?"

My master arrived and screamed, "What is going on here?"

By then, it was too late. My one moment of satisfaction was not worth what was to come, for as soon as my master arrived, so did the Leader of all the Djinn in an impressive cloud of white smoke. I bowed to him, as was required. He briefly acknowledged my presence with a nod and addressed my master.

"I will tell you what is going on here. You have allowed one of my young Brethren to be abused by this ruffian." The Leader of all the Djinn first turned to my master. "When will you silly mortals learn that wealth does not equal wisdom? As punishment for your foolishness, you will be deprived of the services of this young djinn here for one month."

He turned to me and I bowed again. "Return to your lamp and we will speak more."

I instantly returned to my lamp without smoke but watched the rest of the scene through my mind. I saw the Leader of all the Djinn turn to the guard who abused me.

"And you, my extremely foolish guard! You will learn to never again abuse any of my Brethren, or anyone else, for the rest of your life. Attack a djinn who is forbidden to defend himself? Take no pity on him and show him absolutely no mercy? I will show you the same.

"You will become what you ridiculed, you will experience what you did not understand, and you will suffer the same life as the poor young djinn you hate so much."

The proud guard suddenly kneeled before my Leader. He was in a trance as he transformed.

"You will become a djinn, for the next ten years of your mortal life."

The young guard blinked slowly. As he opened his eyes they began to glow with the magic within him. The pupils of his eyes had also changed to orange.

"You will now experience djinn life for yourself and if you will accept your fate with just a mite of the grace that my young djinn has, then you will do well. Your service begins one week from today. You have that time to say goodbye to your family."

They disappeared and the Leader of all the Djinn got ready to appear within my lamp. I bowed toward the spot where he would appear, and there he was. I felt him nod towards me. I nodded back and sat up, but then he immediately began to correct and instruct me.

"Whenever you are in such trouble, always ask your master to return you to your lamp! It is your refuge in no-win situations such as this. How many times have your teachers told you that!"

"Forgive me, Sir, I made the wrong choice."

"I saw your satisfaction when you hurt your tormentor. You must contain your emotions, my young friend. I did not ever picture you as one who would take such pleasure in petty revenge."

"Please forgive me! It was a moment of weakness and I am truly sorry for it."

"I know you are, djinn. I saw how you tried to warn your master at the beginning, and I saw how well you took beatings from the guard. You are young, so very young. Even so, you will learn to control yourself in the future, for you will now have to train your new charge."

"Sir?"

"After the new djinn's week of freedom is up, he will have you to look to for his training. You will have a week to recover and then a week of training, for I want that new young djinn to begin serving as soon as he is able. And then two weeks for you to rest and relax within your lamp."

"Will I be able to relax knowing that I am responsible for the enslavement of another?"

"Knowing you, probably not. But you must not blame yourself for his enslavement. He sealed his fate when he first slapped you. Do not steep too long in guilt and shame, for your presence will soon be required elsewhere. I will see you then."

After a week of resting in my lamp I went to the training building in the dimension of the djinn. Our Leader was speaking to the guard, who was kneeling before him. The guard seemed dazed and was staring into space. The Leader looked up and saw me bowing before him.

"Ah, you're here," he nodded.

The Leader told me, "You know what to do."

I bowed briefly as he left. I noticed the guard's right hand was bandaged so I caused a jar of Santar's ointment to appear in my left hand and went to him.

The guard hadn't noticed me at all. He seemed to be almost in a state of shock and was still recovering from his transformation. He didn't acknowledge my presence even as I began to remove the old mortal bandages from his hand.

"My family was afraid of me; they barely spoke to me," he whispered.

"Unfortunately, that is to be expected."

"I could see it, I could see what they felt and hear what they thought."

"It will take some time for you to get used to your new abilities."

"One of them wanted to capture me and another wanted me to grant his wishes."

"Behavior typical of most mortals when it concerns the djinn."

"But I am a mortal, I was a mortal? I still, I don't know what I am, really."

"For now, you are one of the djinn and so you shall be treated as one of my Brethren."

"Thank you. I don't know what to do next- you!" He finally looked up and recognized me.

"It's alright, brother, it is alright."

"But don't you hate me? Don't you want revenge?"

"No, I think we've both had enough of revenge. I am ashamed of even having such thoughts. I am only saddened to see another living creature enslaved, no matter how briefly."

"Ten years, djinn, ten years."

"Ten years is nothing in the life of a djinn."

With all the bandages removed from his hand, I was ready to

apply the ointment. I took a very small amount on my fingers. "Now hold your hand up so I may treat it."

He held it up as steadily as he could. He jumped as the ointment first touched his skin, expecting more pain. I could see the surprise on his face as he felt the instant healing effects. "That's amazing! How is that possible?"

I covered his entire hand with a thin layer of the ointment, and as his hand absorbed it, it was instantly healed. "Santar's ointment, named after the djinn who gave up his life to create it for our people."

"*Our* people?"

"You are one of us now, djinn, and will be accepted as such." I tried to reassure him and he saw my empathy, or rather, my true sympathy for his situation.

"You, you mean it, you really mean that?"

"Yes, djinn. Now let me lead you to our apartment. We will share the same quarters until you've completed your training. I will be your guide and your tutor. And I will show you the ways of our people."

His training began slowly since he had to learn more about being a djinn as opposed to being a mortal, but he took to it quickly. For his first lesson, I knelt down, my head and eyes toward the floor and my hands neatly held together in my lap. "This is the submissive position."

He studied my position carefully.

"It is the position we must always take in front of our masters and those that they respect."

The guard knelt and held his head down until he mimicked me exactly.

"You are free to keep your eyes open while in this position, but it is safer and considered more respectful to keep them closed. Initially, only look at your master, and only if he wishes for you to do so. You will sense his preferences almost as soon as you meet him. But I would say that it is better to avoid eye contact with all mortals as a default. Eye contact can be considered a challenge and our eyes usually frighten most of them."

I sat on the floor and crossed my legs, keeping my head down. "When your master becomes more comfortable around you, you may shift to this position. It is more relaxing and easier to maintain."

The guard copied my position once again.

"Good. And when you are more comfortable with your powers, you can always do this." I turned my bottom half below my waist into funnel-shaped smoke that faded away at the bottom. The guard gasped and stared at me in wonder. "This form is perfect for intimidating mortals and serves as a wonderful reminder that we are not like them. Do you want to try it?"

The guard nodded.

"Picture it in your mind first and close your eyes. See yourself in this form."

The bottom half of the guard began to slowly transform into smoke.

"Good, keep going."

The guard transformed fully. He looked down at his own funnel of smoke, amazed.

"That's good, you've got it. See how relaxing this form is?"

"Yes! It's like I'm floating on air! I feel lighter than air!"

"You are. Now, try moving around like this." I floated from one side of the room to the other. The guard looked around at the floor. "Don't think of it in terms of walking or how you're doing it. Think of where you want to go, and then go," I floated back to him. The guard, slowly followed, haltingly.

"You will become better at this the more you use your powers. Try to stay like this for the rest of the day until you get used to it." The guard practiced moving around more.

"Good! Soon, these transformations will become easy for you."

The guard continued to float around the room.

"Now, let's try material manipulation." I lifted the table off the floor with magic. "See if you can lift the scroll off the table."

The guard levitated a scroll off the table, floated it to the other side of the room, and let it float down onto a chair. Then he levitated the chair also. "It's as if it doesn't weigh anything!"

"It doesn't. Whatever you levitate also becomes lighter than air through your powers."

The guard began bouncing the chair up and down in the air, successively with more force, until it slammed into the ceiling and broke into pieces. "I'm sorry," he said, sheepishly.

"Don't worry about it, it happens a lot."

The guard floated the broken chair pieces back to its place and began floating around the room even faster until I laughed. "That's it! Enjoy your powers. Then they will become easier for you to use."

The guard floated around until he finally stopped, and the pieces of the broken chair fell to the floor. "Why am I not tired?"

"Because you're in your diaphanous form. Right now, you have no body to exhaust."

"Oh." He moved to float over the chair pieces. I repaired it with a wave of my finger.

"How did you do that?"

"That's a lesson for later. For now, let's work on size."

"Size?"

"Yes. You can be whatever size you want to be." I began to shrink until I was a few centimeters tall. "See?"

"I see," the guard floated down and leaned over to look at the me. "Let me join you." The guard began to shrink until he matched my size.

"I think you're going to be good at using your powers. Now let's see how fast you can change back!" I grew back to my normal size in less than a second, quickly followed by the guard. "Great. Remember to stay in your diaphanous form for the rest of the day."

"I think I prefer it! It feels so light!"

"Many of our people do. Let's suspend our lessons until after our next meal. Then we'll start with transformations."

"Transformations? Of ourselves or others?"

"Of ourselves at first. We will move on to transforming others and things later this week."

IN TERMS OF MAGIC, the guard progressed rapidly. The transformation lessons went very well, along with the lessons on materialization. Within a day, he was creating small objects on his own and transforming furniture. That afternoon, he created a large table and was practicing levitating it.

"But how, brother, how am I doing this?"

"It is your natural djinn talent displaying itself."

The table gently returned to the floor. "But why does it come so easily to me?"

"According to our Book of Law," we both bowed slightly, "whenever a mortal is turned into a djinn because of a djinn, due to his interaction with said djinn, his powers and knowledge will be equal to that djinn."

"You mean, I am as powerful as you are?"

"Yes."

"But that still doesn't explain how I'm doing these things."

"Not only are you as powerful as I am, you will also be equal in knowledge to me. In a way, you are learning what you already know. My knowledge has been replicated in you as well."

"So, I am learning to be you?"

"You won't become me, but you will be equal to me. You are only becoming aware of what is already inside of you."

"Your powers, your training, and your knowledge?"

I nodded. "They are already within you; you only are discovering how to access it."

"Will I have to live in a lamp and serve, too?"

"Yes. But you will not have to take the oath like I have, for your service will only be temporary. Like most enslaved djinn, you will be limited to three wishes per master."

I held up my right arm, showing him my shackle. "You will not have shackles. Though you will be enslaved, you will not have to carry these."

He could only stare at the shackle on my wrist in wonder. "Are they heavy?"

"Emotionally and psychologically, yes. Physically? No." I put my arm down. "But do not worry about such things. Let's just hope that-"

"That all of my masters will be good, kind, patient, and understanding."

"Yes, brother."

"Brother, why do you have to serve a master indefinitely as opposed to just three wishes, like most of the enslaved djinn?"

"Only the most powerful djinn are destined to serve indefinitely and only a few from each generation. Just a friend of mine and I were at that level. I believe only my father and his would have been djinn of unlimited wishes, of the previous generation. Also, due to the strength of our powers, we are considered invaluable to mortals. As such, it was thought best to limit our circulation among them by confining us to one master for a longer period of time."

"Has anyone ever fought a war over you?"

"Unfortunately, yes. Two, but just minor ones. Horrible, unconscionable situations. But we are not responsible for the greed of mortals. Now, try repairing that chair that you broke on your first day."

I waved my finger and the chair returned to its broken state.

The guard learned more and adjusted rather smoothly to being a genie. The obedience training went extremely well. Due to his former life as a soldier, he was accustomed to taking orders. And of course, he did not have to learn anything at all about humans, but I did show him the history of the djinn people and how it related to mortals. All of which he learned and took to heart. The lessons for him were akin to dredging up old memories, which again, he took to quite easily.

"And in the third age, our people were divided into different sects according to the level of our powers."

"Perfect, brother, another passing grade. It is almost midday. Time to eat again, if you wish."

"No, brother, I prefer to meditate on our laws, once again."

"As do I. You remind me so much of myself, it is uncanny. Tomorrow is your graduation ceremony and you will be placed in your lamp."

"Will it hurt?"

"For you, no. Because you aren't taking the oath, you won't go through the transformation so your experience will be quite different than mine. But you will still be held to all our laws as a member of the Brethren, and your words and thoughts will not be your own."

"Still, I feel as if I'll be missing something."

"Do not be envious of those who have taken the oath. It is a strange and disorienting process, and you would not like how it feels."

"I still wish that I could experience it as one of the Brethren."

"I know, brother. But I must tell you how proud I am of you, and how quickly you have taken to our ways. I wish to remain in contact with you afterwards, if you will allow it."

"I will!"

"You will do well, and I will be watching you with your first master."

"What an honor, thank you, brother!"

"You're welcome, brother."

The next day we held his graduation ceremony without the oath. His mortal family did not wish to attend, but nearly all the available djinn did.

The Leader of our people was there and spoke to him before us all. "Now begins your true journey, my friend, into the world of the mortals. For you will see your world entirely different than before. You will see it as we see it, and feel it as we do, as one of the enslaved Brethren. Go, and may God be with you."

The guard smiled, nodded, and knelt into the submissive position. The Leader nodded again, and the guard turned into smoke and was drawn into his lamp.

A few of the Brethren laughed but they were quickly silenced by our Leader.

"Stop it, no. No laughter or humiliation. For as long as he is one of our people, he shall be treated as one of our people. You shall show him the respect and care that you would for any of our enslaved Brethren. There will be time enough for sorrow and regret later."

I was sorry for him to leave. Though we did not exactly become friends, we became as familiar as family. He grew to know and understand me better, and I him, in that short week.

It was then that I saw the potential problem that would eventually arise, for you know how much I enjoy being a djinn, Miss? Well, so did the guard. You can even say that he loved it even more than I did, for when we had to recite our laws, you could see that he truly enjoyed it, and loved the laws, every word written. Only the most dedicated of our people loved our laws. And that was the problem. He loved being a djinn more than he loved being a mortal.

The genie paused at the memory until Jewel asked, "What happened to him, Genie?"

"He served many masters over his assigned ten years and he served them well, Miss. He became a valued and worthy prize for most mortals due to his strength and skill with magic and the level of his powers."

He paused again.

"And?"

"As I said, Miss, he loved being one of the djinn more than he loved being a mortal. And so, when his ten years were over, his real troubles began. He spent the rest of his life trying to become one of the djinn again, Miss."

"Did he succeed?"

"No, Miss, or at least, not in the way that he intended. He became obsessed, eventually trying nearly everything to acquire a genie, so that they might turn him into a genie again. But the few genies that he encountered remembered him and refused his request."

"But I thought genies had to obey their masters?"

"We do, but he never managed to own a genie, Miss, and become their master. He just encountered us. No genie is required to fulfill mere requests from mortals who aren't their masters, especially from a mortal who was well known for torturing one of the Brethren. Eventually, he became involved with sorcery and sorcerers took advantage of his desperation."

"Did you ever see him again?"

"Yes, Miss, as he lay dying. My master at that time sent me on an errand and I encountered him as I was returning. It was brief, Miss, but sad. I found him unconscious and in the middle of a road. He was much older and his hard life was easy to surmise from his countenance. I picked him up and took him to the side of the road. I put him on a mat that I materialized and held him in my arms.

He opened his eyes and recognized me. "Brother!"

"Yes, brother?"

"Do you still serve?"

"Yes, brother," I answered, trying not to display my emotions, but I could see his life leaving him as we spoke.

"Is he a good, kind..."

"Patient and understanding? Yes, brother, he is."

"Good, brother, good."

He didn't ask, but I knew it was still his deepest desire to become one of the Brethren again. I couldn't save his life, but I could give him that. And so, I granted his silent wish, his last wish, his only wish. He instantly returned to what he was as a djinn, his youth and his powers completely restored, as he was many years before. I could see that he felt and enjoyed the change, but it was still too late.

"Thank you, brother."

Then he sighed and died in my arms. I bowed my head in respect, and because the Leader of all the Djinn appeared.

"I had to," I said. It was all I could say.

"I know," the Leader responded.

He then took his body from me by levitating it until it was in front of him. "He truly loved our people and I must honor his service, brief as it was. He will be buried with our Brethren."

And then they disappeared and I returned to my master.

JEWEL, the professor, and more than a few of the courtiers were engrossed in the genie's story.

"Such a sad story." Jewel's comment broke the spell and the professor returned to his reading while the courtiers went back to milling about.

"Yes, Miss. At first, I thought that the Leader of all the Djinn," he bowed slightly, "would punish me severely, for I gave the guard what he wished. But he did not. He knew that the perfect punishment for the guard would also be the perfect way to punish me, Miss, and that my granting his last wish would be the only way to assuage my guilt."

"But you should not feel guilty, Genie. You did not turn him into a djinn. And you did not cause his cruelty."

"I know, Miss, and yet ultimately, I was responsible. It was a lesson that I never had to learn again, the worthlessness of petty revenge."

She did not say anything else, for she didn't know what to say.

Chapter 22
Ally's Story: The Djinn-Guardian, Exposition Time

Alley woke up so slowly that he thought he was still dreaming. "Where am I?"

The djinn-guardian was right by his side and helped him sit up. He had a cup of tea at the ready. "Here, Ally, drink this. It will help you sleep."

"But I was already sleep, shouldn't I wake up?"

"No, Ally, you need to rest."

Ally drank the tea and laid back down. "I like that tea."

The djinn-guardian smiled at Ally's drowsy musings and took the cup away.

Ally softly whispered, "It is good to hear my name again," and fell asleep.

After about eight hours, Ally woke up with a jolt, but he was still dazed and definitely confused. He jumped up from the mat but stumbled over to what he barely recognized as a small window and looked out to discern where he was, but there was literally nothing to see. The window opened to absolute darkness, as if painted black.

"Where are we? Why isn't there anything outside?" Ally breathed heavily and tottered.

The djinn-guardian came in from one of the back rooms. "Back to bed, Ally. You need to sleep." He led Ally back to his mat.

"But where are we? Why is there nothing outside?"

"Well, if you must know," he helped Ally sit down, "we are in an inter-dimensional bubble between three different and separate dimensional planes. There is nothing outside because outside there is literally nothing."

"Oh."

He helped Ally lay down again and pulled a very soft blanket over him. "I hope that clears it up for you," the djinn-guardian added.

"It does, actually. Thank you." Ally drifted off to sleep.

A few days later, Ally gently woke up, feeling much calmer and safer. He sat up, finally taking a good look at his surroundings. He was on a djinn mat surrounded by about fifteen similar mats, a few of them occupied. He looked around and saw the djinn-guardian helping another djinn on a mat sip tea.

"What happened?" Ally asked, disorientated and still weak. "Where am I?"

"Don't worry, Ally. You are safe." The djinn-guardian helped the other djinn lay back down. Then he came and helped Ally stand up. "You are in my home where I tend to the djinn."

"You-you're a healer?"

"Of sorts. But only for your people. It will be easier for you if you sit in a chair."

Ally, unusually susceptible to suggestion at the moment, complied and allowed himself to be led to a small table with two chairs.

"First, sit down. I will help you get your shackles off."

"How? And won't it-"

"Don't speak about it yet or you will faint again. Your shackles are aware of you, just like your lamp. Like your lamp, they're trying to keep you enslaved. Any talk from you of destroying them causes weakness in you as a warning. If you continue to talk about removing your shackles you will faint, completely losing consciousness for at least a few hours or so. This also makes it easier for a djinn-guard to capture you."

"They never told us anything about that during our training."

"There are a lot of things that they didn't tell you during your training. Tea?"

"Yes, please. Thank you." It was wise to be respectful to the person who could quite possibly set you...

As the djinn-guardian prepared the tea, Ally shivered, "I seem to be a little cold."

The djinn-guardian returned to the table with two cups of tea. "You're still adjusting to this hidden inter-dimension. Sleep is the only way to fully adjust. When I first got here, I slept for almost ten days straight."

Ally looked around at the three other djinn lying on mats. "Is that what's happening to them?"

"Yes, to two of them. The other one became ill after someone tried to capture him. He escaped but became ill as a result."

Ally surveyed the room again and noticed someone sitting in a chair in the dark in the corner. He was completely still and staring at the floor with a blank expression. "What," he exclaimed when he realized that it was another djinn. "Is he even alive?"

"Yes, well, what's left of him. His mind and soul were completely erased by an Eye of the Djinn pearl. I found him not long after his master discarded him."

"Discarded him? That doesn't happen very often. Why?"

"A djinn without a soul can be very difficult to manage. He cannot move or do anything without very specific instructions. I must even tell him to feed himself. I found him starving in the streets."

"His name isn't Trouble, is it?"

"It could be, I don't really know. All the usual methods I use to find out don't work with him because he doesn't have any mind left for me to read. I'm just hoping that there's some way to restore him."

"What about Santar's ointment?"

"Available only to those djinn who can summon it in your dimension, and besides, I'm not sure how much it would take to heal him. Or if it even *would* heal him."

"I can conjure some," but Ally slumped over.

The djinn-guardian stood up, "Let me help you back to bed."

Ally, still surprised by his own compliance, stood up and allowed himself to be led back to his mat. He breathed heavily with exhaustion after he sat down.

"You should get some more rest, Ally. I'll answer more of your questions later. You must get your strength back. Go back to sleep."

Ally really wanted to ask him about the connection between the need for rest and inter-dimensional travel but fell asleep instead.

After two more days of drifting in and mostly out of consciousness, Ally finally woke up completely. He sat up quickly but stood up slowly. The djinn-guardian was giving tea to one of the ill djinn and watched the blank djinn still sitting glassy-eyed in the corner. He didn't even seem to blink without permission.

"Where am I? And why do you keep giving us something to make us sleep?"

"Good morning to you too, Ally. Sit at the table and I'll explain everything."

The djinn-guardian helped the djinn back down on his mat, then sat at the table with Ally. "You are in one of the hidden dimensions, the one used by the djinn-guardians to help the djinn escape. The tea did not make you fall asleep, it only calmed you enough so that you could continue to sleep."

"And why are you here?"

"I was a djinn-guard."

Ally straightened up in the chair.

"So yes, your first instincts were correct. I was raised as one and trained to be as cruel to your people as possible, but I couldn't do it anymore. Hunting down escaped djinn, only to force them back into slavery. I just couldn't do it anymore. I seemed to have developed the one thing that a djinn-guard should never have, a conscience."

"You felt bad?" Ally could hardly believe it, but he sensed that this mortal was telling the truth.

"Yes, so I vowed to myself that I would help your people in any way that I could using the skill and knowledge I learned as a djinn-guard. And right now, that means to help you and your kind to escape and recover."

"So, what's next? Do you need me to make you Santar's ointment for the zombie over there?"

The djinn-guardian nodded. Ally waved a couple of fingers towards the back room. "There. You now have an entire supply room full of Santar's ointment along with any other medical supplies that you may need. It will also restock automatically so you will never run out of anything."

The djinn-guardian stood and stared at what he could see of the new addition to his dwelling. "Thank you, Ally. You are truly one of the most powerful of your kind."

"You're welcome. Now, what about my situation?" He held up his wrists and the djinn-guardian sat back down.

Staring at Ally's right wrist shackle, he reached for it but paused, "May I?"

"Of course."

The djinn-guardian studied the metal of Ally's shackle. "A typical metal alloy, nothing out of the ordinary. Removing your shackles involves a magical substance only available to djinn-guards and guardians. It's also a metal alloy that dissolves any other magical metal that it touches."

"So there really is such a thing as pontar metal?"

"You did not hear that word from me."

"I had heard of it before, long ago. I asked every alchemist and metallurgist I could find, past, present, and future, but not one of them had ever heard of pontar metal."

"I'm not surprised. Metallurgists are scientists and they rule out magic. And most alchemists barely know enough magic to light a fire.

That type of metal requires real magic and real knowledge of magic, something djinn-guards and guardians are well versed in."

"My respect for you and your kind has just gone up a hundred-fold. Is it dangerous, melting shackles?"

"No. The nature of the metal protects all flesh from harm. We will begin in a few days. It takes a while to get the mixture just right. I already started on a new batch this morning."

"And then what?"

"Then you're free to go."

"But to go where?"

"Now that's the real question. Where do you want to go? You are free to go anywhere you want and go to any dimension you want. The djinn dimension won't be safe for you, but earth might be if you keep yourself well-hidden."

"Can I stay here until I figure it out?"

"Of course. I could use a little help. And there's something that you should know. Tatchar, that ex-djinn-guard who erased your clan?"

"Yes?"

"He's still after you. He heard that you escaped."

"Oh great. How do you know these things?"

"I still have friends and family among the djinn-guards, but so does he. They occasionally bring escaped djinn to me, when they can."

Ally studied the other patients. "How can I help?"

"All three of them will need more tea and one of them may be hungry. I'll check on the physical state of Trouble and see what his body needs."

"Okay."

Chapter 23
Tender's Story: A Confined Space

"Genie?"

"Yes, Miss?"

"Why are genies kept in lamps? Or in rings? Or in anything at all?"

"It was discovered, Miss, early on, during our earliest contact with mortals, that the longer you keep a djinn confined, the stronger his powers become."

"Really?"

"Yes, Miss. The first djinn imprisoned in a bottle was kept there for five years. The mortal who kept him noticed immediately that the genie was significantly more powerful when he was released than before he was trapped in the bottle. Therefore, Miss, it became a common practice to capture and place my ancestors in small containers, not just to capture us, but to increase our powers."

"How does that work?"

"A confined space contains our powers, Miss, and reinforces them. The less interaction we have with your world, the more concentrated our powers become. A genie who does not live in a confined space will gradually lose power over time, usually very slowly because of his interaction with this world, Miss."

"Will confining a weakened genie increase his powers?"

"Yes, Miss. Depending on the length of his confinement, he may even become stronger than before."

"What is it about confinement that causes this?"

"My people are not of this dimension, Miss. And yet, the more time we spend here, the more we become acclimated to it. In other words, we take on more characteristics of it."

"So, a genie outside of a lamp gradually becomes mortal?"

"Not exactly, but he would gradually lose the magic that is common in our dimension. Not all his power, but most of it. Returning to our dimension would also restore his power, Miss. But in confinement, we do not interact with your world's atmosphere. The confined space begins to take on more characteristics of our dimension and so our powers become stronger."

"How?"

"My people are not of your world, Miss, and so we retain the magical characteristics of our world within us. When we are confined, all those characteristics are confined with us and become concentrated."

"Do you prefer remaining in a confined space as opposed to being out in the world's atmosphere?"

"We find confined spaces more comfortable, Miss, as they do replicate our dimension somewhat. Even the djinn who do not serve in this world tend to live in small, mostly enclosed, spaces."

"Because it replicates your dimension?"

"Yes, Miss. A confined space is very important to my Brethren. We find it soothing and comforting, and it refreshes us."

"That is why you want to return to your lamp every now and then."

"Yes, Miss. The world of men can be very tiring."

"How so?"

"Mortals do not know how to shield their thoughts, Miss. And so, we hear everything all the time. And the thoughts of man are very loud, Miss. Mortals also do not know how to hide their emotions from us. Therefore, we see all your emotions, all the time. It can be somewhat overwhelming to be bombarded with the thoughts and emotions of so many mortals for so long. Returning to my lamp grants me a brief respite."

"And since you can control your experience of time within your lamp, that brief respite of five minutes can turn into five weeks for you."

"Yes, Miss."

"Maybe I should remind my uncle of this fact."

"He already knows, Miss, but becomes distracted by the affairs of the kingdom."

"Well then, I will keep it in mind and therefore shorten our interactions."

"Please don't, Miss. Interacting with you keeps me focused. I find it very easy to concentrate on just one mortal rather than many."

"Very well, Genie."

"Speaking with you, Miss, is like a vacation or a holiday. I mean in the sense that," the genie retreated a little, "it gives me a break from focusing so much of my time on so many others, Miss."

"I see. Well then, maybe we can continue our holiday next week at our usual time?"

"Yes, Miss. Thank you for being so understanding."

"And thank you for giving me so much to understand."

"You are welcome, Miss." The genie felt more relaxed just by sharing his true state with Jewel. It was true, it was relaxing, just talking to her. The genie found Jewel's concern sweet and enjoyed her kindness. He hoped that he didn't sound too desperate for her company, and yet he was relieved to tell her the truth.

He also enjoyed telling her about his people. Not just because she was the only mortal, after several hundred years, who actually seemed interested, but also that she was fascinated by them and their history. He loved that about her. If he couldn't live among his people, at least he could talk about them and reminisce.

Chapter 24
Tender's Story: The Husband

"And he said he would never again take revenge on anyone and that he learned the worthlessness of petty revenge. Isn't that a sad story, Uncle?"

"Yes, Jewel, it is rather tragic." The king and Jewel actually had time to have a quiet midday meal together.

"And he's just full of stories like that. Imagine what I could ask him next. Like, what does he see in the future? Can he see anything about your future or anything about mine?"

"Does he see a husband for you, Jewel? Did you ask him about your future husband?"

"No. Why would I ask him something so boring like that?"

"Because it's not boring. It is, in fact, central to your entire future."

"Uncle, that just makes me feel like my whole existence is just some convenient political point so you can maneuver and manipulate some country to trade or make peace with us."

"I didn't say that, Jewel. And you know that isn't true."

"So, you want me to ask the genie who I am going to be married off to, which will make the search for a husband go much more smoothly."

"Don't be so dramatic, my dear."

"I'm not being dramatic. I'm just being honest."

"Two more years, Jewel. I promised you two more years so you could continue your studies."

"Yes, sir, I know."

"And have I not given you time and the resources to study whatever you wanted?"

"Yes, sir, and I am truly grateful for it and for everything that you've done for me. Maybe I just don't want to be reminded of the day it will all end."

"No one said that your education had to end with your marriage. You may continue your pursuits."

"Along with fulfilling my duties to my husband, my children, and as royalty."

"Perhaps then, your education will take its proper place in your life by it not being your primary occupation."

"Would you say that to me if I were a boy?"

"Of course not, Jewel."

"Then don't you see, that is the problem!"

"This is the world we live in. I cannot change society just so you can learn more about biology."

"Maybe you should try."

The king sighed and caught sight of two of his ministers approaching him and bowing. "Your appointment with the genie is coming up, Jewel. And this is the first time that I have ever had to remind you of it."

"Yes, sir. Forgive me for my impertinence. I apologize." She briefly bowed to him.

"Of course, Jewel. Excuse me."

A few minutes later, Jewel stormed into her session with the genie. He bowed towards her and rose slowly as she started talking.

The professor was so engaged in his reading that he didn't even look up or greet her.

"Genie, I still don't see how it is that you don't just hate all of mankind."

"Good afternoon, Miss. And no, I still don't hate mankind."

"Not even that guard who used to beat you and torment you all the time?"

"No, Miss. I learned my lesson well, to never take revenge or even desire it."

"But don't you ever want to strike out at someone, just a little bit?"

"No, Miss. Forgive me, but you are angry, correct, Miss?"

"Yes, Genie. Really angry."

"Angry with my master, your uncle, right, Miss?"

"Yes."

"And yet, your anger is merely temporary, yes?"

Jewel paused at this. "Yes, I suppose so."

"And once your anger has subsided, will you still wish to strike out at him? In a week or so?"

"No, Genie, probably not."

"Then you understand my position, Miss. There was a time, right before I took my oath, when I did wish to lash out at anyone nearby, Miss, over my coming enslavement. But I did not, because I could not. Now that my emotions have cooled, I no longer have any desire to take revenge on anyone. I have accepted my fate and my lot in life, and I live accordingly."

"What a very wise way to live, Genie."

"Wisdom is either learned or imposed. It is much better to learn, Miss, than to have a lesson imposed upon you."

"Yes, Genie, I think I understand. You are extremely patient, then?"

"Not extremely, Miss."

"But you must be, Genie, due to the longevity of your lifespan.

You have lived almost one thousand years. Surely, that must have taught you patience."

"That's true, Miss. Though I can't credit my patience to my longevity alone. I believe I learned the value of it during my training."

"How so?"

"During my training, though it wasn't emphasized as so, we also learned it. We were subjected to waiting for so many things that we became accustomed to it. Seeing our families, learning lessons, and even eating meals. Afterwards, we spent most of our time inside our objects, waiting to be released by mortals. You could describe our lives as that of constant waiting."

"I feel like I am constantly waiting for the inevitable. Today, my uncle asked me to ask you about my future husband. Genie..."

She paused so long that he felt the need to ask, "Yes, Miss?'

"My future husband. What's he like?"

The genie lifted his head, closed his eyes, then opened them. His eyes were now clouded white as he sought and waited for glimpses of the future. "He is tall, Miss, taller than you."

"Yes, Genie?"

"And he is kind to you and understands you?"

"Great, anymore?'

"He loves you very much, Miss, very much."

"Wonderful, Genie. What does he look like? Do you have any more information about him?"

"No, Miss. The rest is not clear to me, but you two will be very happy together." He closed his eyes and opened them, and they returned to their normal color.

"That's a relief. And good to know. Now, I have something to look forward to. I guess."

"Happiness in marriage, Miss. Isn't that what most mortals seek?"

"Yes, Genie, it is. I just wasn't exactly seeking it right now."

"I understand, Miss. Forgive me, but aren't most young women your age already married?"

"Yes, Genie, they are. As I am reminded, constantly. All my friends are married."

"Then you are twice blessed, Miss. First, in having your marriage delayed, and secondly, in having a happy marriage when you do get married."

"You're right, Genie. I can't argue with that."

Later that night, while in his lamp, the genie restlessly paced back and forth. He found that reading, a comfort which he usually found relaxing, was nearly impossible. He just couldn't settle down. For the first time in a long time, he was disturbed by the topic of his last conversation with the mortal girl. He didn't exactly know why, but he definitely did not enjoy seeing the vague figure of Jewel's future husband.

Whoever this tall, kind, understanding man was, he wished him well. That lucky banfir.

Chapter 25
Training: The Djinn Book of Law

Highly regimented and well monitored. That was how Kind had described the life that awaited Tender. And though he understood what the words meant; he didn't really get it until he experienced his first full day.

As soon as Tender woke up, he was subject to a strict schedule. First, they all woke up at the same time. Then they had to use their Whatever Rooms as a bathroom to clean themselves and transform into their uniforms. After being led to their morning meal, where each student received the same meal of fruit and porridge, they were led into the very classroom where it all began.

"You will begin with obedience, mathematics, science, and history. You will then have obedience again, then exercise, meditation, reading and comprehension, law, and then again, obedience. On the seventh day, your schedule will be a little more relaxed. You will only have obedience and art."

Oddly enough, they weren't assigned seats, to Tender's relief. He would hate to have to sit in front again. A few of the bolder boys sat in front but Tender found a comfortable spot in the middle, not far back enough to look like he wasn't interested, but close enough to see.

It turned out that the regular classes, taught by the First Teacher were easy. Tender was competent in math and science, he liked reading, and he loved history. Finding out about the history of his people was wonderful, and during the reading and comprehension class he chose more books about history.

The hardest classes were the obedience classes. The First Teacher taught the first obedience class and it seemed to focus on weird stuff like sitting positions and where to look. They would be assigned a specific maneuver or position for the day and they had to practice the maneuver or maintain the position for 45 minutes.

The first day, the students had to change from the submissive position to bowing low to the floor, and back to the submissive position. The First Teacher paced in front of them, studying their every movement.

"Again." They repeated the bowing.

"Again." They repeated it once again.

"Again."

It was hard, and more like exercise. Tender, like most boys his age, found it extremely difficult to remain perfectly still during some of the classes, which he guessed was the point of the class, but he wasn't exactly sure.

The second obedience class was taught by a different teacher who they had to call, rather unimaginatively, the Second Teacher. He was younger than the First Teacher and wore purple robes under his blue cloak but had the same commanding manner.

During this class they were assigned menial physical tasks, some of which he had never heard of before. But before long, all the young djinn learned how to clean the classroom, the dorm rooms, and even cook like mortals did. They even had to bring in water from a well from outside the building, which must have been some kind of mortal thing, because Tender had never heard of such a practice.

"And if I hear one word of complaint, one sigh of resignation, or see one hint of resentment, you will have to retrieve more water from the well until you learn to do it properly. Understand?"

"Yes, Second Teacher."

As the students received their jars and lined up to go outside, the Second Teacher, watching them carefully, added, "And if any of you are wondering what the word resignation means, it means to accept your fate when you don't like it. The point is that I do not want to see any reaction from you at all. Now go!"

"Yes, Second Teacher!"

They all ran to the well. It was odd to not use their powers. Even at home when doing chores, Tender learned how to help around the lamp using his powers. It was strange actually doing real physical labor. And he didn't understand exactly why they had to do it.

The third obedience class had more to do with magic and was much more unpredictable. It was taught by the Teacher of Magic in a room much larger than expected. The Teacher would name a magical task and they had to do it. but it was harder than he thought it would be because they had to do exactly what was asked of them. If they failed in any way, they were punished. Not major punishments like whippings or having something taken away, but small things like having to sit completely still or not participate for the rest of the class. And each one of them failed at something. To Tender, it seemed as if the class was designed so that each one of them failed a task. The class seemed to be more about punishment than anything else.

"Make a silver goblet," the Teacher of Magic commanded.

Different types of silver goblets appeared in the hands of each one of the boys.

"Good. Now make that disappear and replace it with a Greek celestial navigation chart."

Most of the boys were puzzled but most of them imagined various maps in their hands.

"Wrong! Remember children, these are actual items that mortals have requested and you must get them exactly right. Each one of you failed. So now, close your eyes for the next ten minutes and do not move."

They weren't old enough or skilled enough to easily read minds, and besides, all the teacher's thoughts and emotions were hidden from them. Tender noticed this their very first day. And they didn't have any experience with mortals to help them figure out what they wanted. Maybe that was what the class was truly about, reading minds. Tender wasn't sure.

The Meditation class, which he was actually interested in learning more about, hadn't officially started yet. Instead, they had a study period in the dining area. And after two weeks of study and perpetual silence - the boys still weren't allowed to talk to each other in any way; Tender was growing frustrated.

Even their recreation was strictly organized, highly regimented, and no fun. Everything was meticulously structured and supervised by the Exercise Teacher. They had to play various physical games, some from the djinn world and some from the human world. While some of the games were interesting, the boys really didn't get enough time to enjoy them. And not many games were enjoyable when you weren't allowed to talk to each other.

The third week, Tender woke up to expect the usual seventh day routine of the morning meal, Obedience and Art - which he enjoyed, their second meal, and then unscheduled time in their dorm room.

"You may now talk to each other and share your thoughts and emotions." The First Teacher declared this suddenly and calmly, sat down at his desk, and began reading an ancient scroll.

The eight boys just stared at each other, shocked into silence. One of them finally said, "Hi. I'm Bold. And this is the sound of my voice."

The other boys laughed nervously, still unsure of themselves. "My name's Clever, in case you didn't know," and he pointed to his name written on the headboard of his bed. A few more nervous laughs.

When no one else spoke, Bold asked, "How were you named?"

"I figured out where my mother hid the chocolate at an early age," Clever grinned. "How were you named?"

"When I was really little I walked up to my mother and I must have been really hungry, but I decided to feed myself. I was still, I wasn't weaned yet," and Bold scrunched up his face.

"Yuck!" Clever answered, also with a scrunched-up face.

"Thoughtful," Bold asked, "how were you named?"

"My mother gave me a choice once and I took a long time to decide," he answered.

"Between what and what?" Clever asked.

"Between how my sister and I should be punished for something we did." Thoughtful purposely ended the story there. The rest of the boys understood it was something he didn't really want to talk about, as they knew memories could easily be recalled with their powers. But they felt and saw his reluctance, so they left it alone.

"I used to smile all the time. I'm just glad my name isn't Happy," Joy added, breaking the tension.

"Peaceful?" Bold asked.

"I was always very calm when my brothers and sisters would start fighting. And I always tried to stop them."

"So, you're a peacemaker," Clever decided. Peaceful shrugged.

"Alley, were you named after an actual alley?" Bold asked.

"Yes," Alley didn't offer any more and seemed reluctant to talk, so again, they let it go.

"Shy, are you too shy to tell us how you were named?" Bold offered.

Shy nodded and smiled.

"And Tender. I thought you should go last since they always make you go first," Bold stated.

Tender answered, honestly grateful for the consideration, "I cried when my sister got hurt. I was three."

"Isn't Tender a girl's name?" Alley asked.

"Not to me." Tender had been lightly teased by his cousins about his name and he found that was the easiest way to end the conversation. Alley nodded and said nothing more. They all sat in silence for a moment.

"This feels so weird, finally talking," remarked Thoughtful.

"I keep feeling like we're doing something wrong. Like we're breaking some rule or something," Clever added.

"It is allowed." The First Teacher said definitively.

"Yes, First Teacher," all the boys answered, and the First Teacher smiled to himself.

"Can we hear each other's thoughts too?" Bold asked. "I'm not that good at that. I didn't have brothers and sisters, and my parents wouldn't let me practice on them."

"*Can you hear this?*" Clever thought.

"Yes," Bold answered out loud.

"*Then you're good at it,*" Clever thought.

"*Does this mean that we can talk to each other without them knowing what we're saying?*" Bold asked with a thought.

"*No.*" The First Teacher answered with a thought that each one of them heard.

"Yes, First Teacher," they answered out loud. The First Teacher smiled again while continuing to read his scroll. Then the boys laughed. Even Shy joined in. Alley didn't.

The day continued with most of the young djinn extremely excited to be able to finally talk to each other. Only Shy and Alley held back. Shy only seemed comfortable talking to one person at a time, while Alley didn't seem to want to talk at all.

The boys were eager to ask questions to each other and Tender even got Shy to say something while the other boys were talking about something else. "How were you named?"

"My, my mother said I was so shy that I didn't even want to talk to her, but I was in a room full of people. I just don't like to talk in front of so many people," Shy explained.

"I don't like talking in front of a lot of people either. I feel like I'm going to mess something up," Tender admitted. "I don't like going first all the time. I don't always know what to do. I don't know why I have to go first all the time."

"I think it's because of how much power you have," Thoughtful joined in. "I think they have us in order of how powerful we're supposed to be."

"But how do they know how powerful we're supposed to be?" Tender asked. "We're still kids."

"It has more to do with our fathers and how powerful they are. I think," Thoughtful answered. "It's like it's inherited, our power levels."

"How do you know?" Clever asked.

"My father told me. He told me about how we're all ranked," Thoughtful answered.

"What's his name?" Bold asked.

Thoughtful smiled, "Pensive."

"My father's name is Loud," Bold countered.

"Smart," Clever added.

"Kind," Tender joined in.

"Cheerful," Joy added.

"Serene," said Peaceful.

"What is your father's name?" Tender gently asked Shy.

"Quiet," he answered softly.

"And your father, Alley?" Tender asked.

"It was Tough. My father is dead. My whole clan is dead."

Tender suddenly had a vision of an entire clan being erased from existence. One moment, the clan was going about its business in the djinn world, just living their lives. But in an instant, they were screaming and running in terror, erased from existence, disappearing at random, involuntarily. It was brief, but enough to explain Alley's demeanor.

"Is that why you're named after an alley?" asked Bold.

"That's where they say they found me afterwards."

"Who raised you?" Clever asked.

"My caretaker but he's gone now, too. Everybody's gone," Alley was getting more and more upset.

The First Teacher looked up at this.

"Everybody I know is gone!"

"Alley, come here," the First Teacher replied in a voice so reassuring that at first the boys weren't even sure that it came from him.

"Yes, First Teacher," Alley, trying hard not to cry, replied and the First Teacher grabbed Alley and hugged him.

"Excuse us for a moment." The First Teacher and Alley disappeared.

"Whoa," Bold said. "That was wild."

"Where do you think they went?" Clever asked.

"Probably someplace where he can be quiet for a while," Thoughtful added.

"I hope they don't punish him for it," Tender said.

"No, this is our free time. We should be able to yell and scream as much as we want," said Clever.

"Within reason," Thoughtful added.

"Hey, we're alone!" Bold was so excited that he almost yelled.

At that very moment, the image of the Second Teacher appeared at the desk, reading a different scroll.

"I guess we aren't alone," Bold thought.

"Maybe you shouldn't shout when it happens again," Clever thought, laughing.

The First Teacher took Alley into the teacher's lounge because he knew it would be empty at that time of day. He and Alley sat on one of the many cushions and he hugged Alley until he stopped crying. "It's going to be okay, Alley, it's going to be okay."

"I've got nobody," Alley whimpered.

"Now that's not true. You've got me. And you've got the other boys who will soon be like brothers to you."

"Is that why we're called the Brethren?"

"Yes," the First Teacher chuckled, "Brethren is another word for brothers."

They sat for a few more minutes until the First Teacher pulled back and said, "Are you ready to go back to the dorm now? You can lay down in your Whatever Room until last meal. Okay?"

Alley nodded and they disappeared and reappeared in Alley's Whatever Room, which now looked like the dorm room but was small enough to only hold one bed, an exact replica of Alley's bed in the dorm. The First Teacher pulled the covers down, Alley got in bed, and he tucked him in. Then the First Teacher disappeared.

The Second Teacher and his scroll disappeared, while the First Teacher appeared back in the dorm room, sitting at his desk, reading the ancient scroll again. It looked as if the Second Teacher had dissolved into the First Teacher.

Tender instantly noticed the switch. While the other boys were still talking, he approached the desk. "First Teacher, sir? Is Alley okay?"

"Yes, Tender, he's okay," he answered, using his gentle voice again.

"Thank you, sir. First teacher, sir."

The First Teacher thought to himself, "Your mother named you well."

"First Teacher, sir?" Bold asked.

"Yes, Bold?"

"Is it okay if we go to the exercise room to play? Sir?"

"We want to play that game that the Exercise Teacher showed us." Clever added, "First teacher, sir."

"Ah yes, football. The Exercise Teacher is in the room. You may go."

"Thank you, First Teacher," Bold answered.

Bold, Clever, Thoughtful, and Joy disappeared. Peaceful laid down on his bed and stretched out. Shy checked to see if the First Teacher was watching him, but he was still reading. Shy approached Tender, walking softly, and whispered, "Is Alley okay?"

"Yes," Tender whispered back.

"Alley's clan was erased. Did you see it too?" Shy still whispered.

"Yes, I did. I thought I was the only one,"

"No, I saw it." Shy responded, only a little louder.

"I saw it too," Peaceful added, sitting up.

"Are we the only ones who saw it?" Tender wondered.

"I think we all saw it. Maybe we're the only ones talking about it."

"Why did it happen?" Tender asked. Shy shrugged.

"I don't know," Peaceful answered.

Tender then looked up at the First Teacher. "First Teacher, sir?"

The First Teacher looked up at them, "Yes, Tender?"

"Why was Alley's clan erased, sir?"

"And what happened to his caretaker? Sir?" Peaceful added.

The First Teacher sighed heavily, "What happened to Alley's clan is a tale for another time. And not for me to tell. As to what happened to his caretaker, well, he was erased, too. But he was never real to begin with. He was only a replica of Alley's ancient relative, temporarily created to raise Alley until he was of age to come here. When Alley arrived here, his caretaker dissolved back into a memory. Unfortunately, Alley saw it."

"*So, he really is alone,*" Tender said to himself, but the others heard him.

"*Not anymore. He has us. And you four. It is important that I share this information with you. You are the most capable of understanding Alley's unique situation. And the most likely ones to become friends with him.*"

He paused, "*I trust that you will not share this information about Alley's background with the other boys.*"

"Yes, First Teacher," Tender, Peaceful, and Shy replied out loud. Shy went back to his bed and sat down, while Tender did the same. Silence seemed to be called for as they all contemplated this new, shocking information.

An hour later, the time came for their last meal of the day. Bold, Clever, Thoughtful, and Joy appeared in the room, sweaty and laughing. When they lined up to go to supper, Alley came out from his Whatever Room and joined them.

The conversation at the table centered around their favorite foods and why, but Tender quietly asked Alley, "Are you okay?"

"Yes," Alley replied sharply.

"No, for real. Are you okay?"

Alley looked up at this unexpected source of empathy. Off guard, he answered honestly, "No. Not really."

Tender nodded and said nothing else.

Afterwards, the boys hurriedly disappeared back into their dorm room, most of them still excited that they could continue to talk to each other. Only Tender, Alley, Shy, and Peaceful didn't join in on every single conversation.

Tender pulled out a rock from a small box that he had put on one of the shelves.

"What's that?" Alley curiously asked.

"It's a rock from the color forest." The rock looked like any other ordinary rock, except that it changed its color according to the mood in the room. Right now, it was purple. Alley sat on the edge of his bed to get a closer look.

"Ha, a homesick rock," Alley said, understanding the purple color.

"I almost feel bad that I took it. I like to think that it wants to go back to the forest. Have you ever been?"

"I think I was there once when I was little. But all the colors scared me, it was too much, I didn't want to go back."

"It was one of my favorite places to go." Tender was about to mention that his family went there every year but thought he shouldn't mention his family right now.

"I used to like going to the beach and getting in the water," Alley tentatively offered even though he had only been a few times.

"I wonder if we'll ever get to go anywhere fun again," Tender said.

"I doubt it. Not with all this obedience stuff. Even when we got in the pool for recreation class we had to follow orders." He looked up at Joy, who was looking through a large book full of photos with Peaceful.

"Joy, did they make you follow all of the rules when you went to play?"

"Nope. They let us do what we wanted as long as we didn't hurt each other."

Alley smiled at Tender, "So we do get to have some fun."

"I didn't mind football. But I want to play that other game they showed us. The one with the bat," Tender said.

"The one where we had to run back and forth or the one where we had to run around the diamond shape?" Alley asked.

"The one where we had to run around the bases. I liked that part."

"That was fun. But I had trouble hitting the ball," Alley admitted. "I wish we could just run around the diamond shape."

"Me too. That's the part I want to practice. Maybe we can just run."

The First Teacher looked up and said, "Time to go to bed, young gentlemen."

"Yes, First Teacher."

They all magically changed into their pajamas and got in their beds.

"Good night, Clever," Bold said.

"Good night, Bold." Clever answered. "Good night, Thoughtful."

"Good night, Clever," Thoughtful answered, "Good night, Bold."

"Good night, Thoughtful," Bold said.

"Good night, Alley," Tender said.

"Good night, Tender," Alley responded.

"Good night, Joy," Bold said.

This continued with each boy trying to say good night to each one of the other boys until the First Teacher said, "That's enough. Silence! And good night to all of you."

The next day, two of Tender's most anticipated classes began. The first was Meditation. They had to go to a different classroom with softer lighting and cushions all around the room for them to sit on.

Their meditation teacher appeared and they bowed to him. He formally bowed back. This teacher was much younger than the others with muted brown colored robes underneath his blue teacher's robe.

"I am your teacher and guide to meditation. You shall call me Meditation Teacher."

"Yes, Meditation Teacher."

"Good. And now, my young charges, you will learn all about meditation and how important it is to the Brethren. Due to the nature of this class, it is more important that you remain relaxed and comfortable, especially for our first few weeks.

"And don't look at the floor, look directly at me. It is also important that you be able to look at me as I instruct you. Don't worry about answering my every statement with, "Yes, Meditation Teacher," okay? Just relax and respond to any questions that I ask you."

Most of the boys nodded.

"Now. Judging by the high levels of your powers, I suspect that each one of you has already had some experience with meditation throughout this past year. Am I correct?"

Several of them nodded, including Tender. The Meditation Teacher chose one of them at random. "Thoughtful. Can you describe one of your meditation experiences for us, please? What happened?"

"My mother had just told me what we were going to have for dinner and she said I fell into a trance while I was thinking about it, sir."

"Do you remember anything else about it?"

"No, sir. Only my mother holding me and telling me that's what happened."

"That is normal, particularly with young djinn who are marked for service. Anyone else?"

"I fell into a trance while reading a book, sir," Clever added.

"The more powerful you are, the easier it is for you to fall into meditating without realizing it. How long did it last?"

"My mother said just a minute or so."

"Anyone else? You there, Tender?"

"I fell into a trance while I was staring at the markings on my wrists, sir."

"Yes, doing that can easily lead you into a trance. And it only lasted a little over a minute, right?"

"Yes, sir."

"Involuntary meditation usually begins to happen the closer you get to your training. I'm going to show you how to direct your natural tendencies towards meditation and how to use that meditation to help sharpen and focus your powers. In short, the more you meditate, the more powerful you become. And the easier it becomes to control your powers."

Some of the boys, including Tender, Clever, and Thoughtful, were fascinated and smiled. Others, like Shy, were more apprehensive, or indifferent, like Alley.

"It's easy once you practice it enough. Let's begin. First, get into a comfortable position." The teacher had a calm soothing voice and manner, which made it easier to follow his instructions. The boys relaxed even more. "Now, I want all of you to imagine a cup, any cup. And make it appear in your hand."

Most of the boys made cups appear in their hands, except for Alley and Shy.

"That's it, good. Come on, everyone try it. Don't even think about it, just do it."

Now, all the boys held newly conjured cups. They were all simple, slightly different from each other, and made from simple materials, such as wood or stone.

"Good. Now, put your cups down, and I want you each to meditate on the idea of a cup. Close your eyes and focus on the idea of a cup. Repeat the word, over and over in your mind. Allow yourselves to fall into a trance just by repeating the words over and over in your minds."

Gradually, each boy began to fall into a trance until they were perfectly still. The instructor allowed them to remain like that for about ten minutes. Then he began to coax them out of their trances by thinking to them, *"Okay boys, come back to the present now, you can all wake up now."*

Gradually at first, each young genie began to open their eyes. It took some of them a little longer than others, but when they were all awake, the instructor said, "Well done, that was a very good session. Now I want you to make another cup appear in your hand."

Cups again began to appear in their hands but there was a noticeable difference in quality. Some of the cups were made of silver, others of gold, some of them were made of glass, and a couple of them were even encrusted with jewels and other precious stones.

The young genies gasped and smiled at the difference.

"Do you see?" the instructor said, proudly. "And you did all that even without a specific image in your mind, all through meditation. It helps you focus your mind and enhances your powers. The more you meditate, the more powerful you become."

The Meditation Teacher made a large, elaborately jeweled goblet appear in his hand. "Now, I want you to focus on this goblet, just stare at it for a few moments. Meditate with the image of the goblet still in your mind, keep thinking about it and focusing on it."

The meditation teacher let them meditate for ten minutes again. *"Wake up, boys, that's it. Respond to my voice, there you go."*

The boys woke up much easier this time.

"Now, reproduce an exact duplicate of the goblet." Every boy made a duplicate.

"There now, see? And you did that without any specific instructions. In this class, you will learn how to meditate at will, how to meditate in silence even when you are surrounded by extremely noisy mortals, and how to meditate to specifically focus and control your powers."

. . .

THE NEXT INTERESTING class was their Book of Djinn Law class. The boys had to go into a different room that they hadn't been in before for this class. It was a bit smaller than their regular classroom and was dominated by a huge ancient book sitting on a stand. The book had no writing on the outside and was a deep shade of dark green. There was a chair in front of the book, and the student's chairs were arranged to face the book in two rows of four.

The atmosphere of the whole room inspired a sense of reverence for the book, and the boys, cowed by the almost religious air, remained silent as they took their seats. Tender went to the front row and the rest took their seats in order. They didn't know exactly how they knew that they had to this, but they did.

A new teacher appeared in the classroom, directly in front of the book. He was much older than their other teachers and seemed to be kinder and gentler too, or so Tender hoped.

"Hello, young gentlemen. You shall call me, the Teacher of the Law."

"Yes, Teacher of the Law."

"This class is going to be different than the others. You must look at me, for it is important that you understand exactly what I am saying at all times. Understand?"

"Yes, Teacher of the Law."

"And you need not respond to everything I say with, 'Yes, Teacher of the Law,' either. In this class, only one item deserves a consistent level of respect." The teacher stood to the right side of the book.

"This is the Djinn Book of Law. You will bow in its presence." The djinn Teacher of the Law bowed to the book and the young djinn also bowed. "You will also bow whenever and wherever this Book of Law is mentioned to show it the proper level of respect."

They all bowed again and looked at the book curiously.

"This class is not about obedience, my young ones, so you may speak a little more freely here than during your other lessons. This is the book that contains all the rules and laws concerning the captivity of our people and the Brethren. Never handle it yourself or even touch it, for it is dangerous to the unlearned djinn. Turn to the wrong page, and you could die."

"Why?" Bold asked.

"There are symbols in it, designed to control our kind and made to sear our flesh."

"Like a burn?" asked Clever.

"Yes, exactly like a burn. Other symbols cause other reactions, such as reminding us of our submission, or causing us to lose consciousness. That is why it is only to be handled by the experienced." He touched the cover of the book and opened it to a page near the middle. The young djinn leaned back in terror. "Don't worry, children, I have plenty of experience."

He waved his hand over the book and the words on the page suddenly rose before them, floating and large enough for everyone to read. "This is the first page of the laws of the djinn. You will learn and memorize them. Eventually, you will be able to recite every word."

"Why can't we just visualize it like we do our lessons?" Clever asked.

"Because you need to really learn them. Truly. Don't worry, you'll have plenty of time. The book is divided into three main sections, the first being the rules for mortals. The second is the laws for the djinn. And the third is the rules and symbols for our captivity, meant for those who control and monitor the djinn, the djinn-guards. We will cover the other sections, but mainly focus on the laws for the djinn."

The teacher of the law waved his hand again and the words flew back down to the page. "You must show extreme reverence for the Book of Law at all times. Bow," the teacher of the law reminded them, and they all bowed toward the book. "You must bow every single time it is mentioned, by anyone, anywhere. You must truly learn to revere it and fear it. For it can control your destiny."

They all bowed again. The teacher of the law turned the page in the book, waved his hand over the page, and the words from the page flew up again. "First, let us recite the first laws of the djinn. Begin reading with me from the top,"

He paused and then they all began reciting, "Obey this Djinn Book of Laws. Study this section of the book and learn every requirement."

Chapter 26
Tender's Story: The Djinn Book of Law

"Genie, other than the guard incident and what happened last year with the king, have you ever been punished physically?"

"Yes, Miss."

"How so?"

"I have received lashes, most often, and I've also been beaten with rods."

"Beaten with rods?"

"Yes, Miss. And a few of my masters often found new and unusual ways to punish me, including exposure to the elements, and with magic."

"But Genie, you arc totally under the control of your master, correct?"

"Yes, Miss."

"Why would anyone ever see the need to punish you so severely?"

"Because of the nature of my powers, Miss. I am one of the djinn and considered one of the most powerful of my kind. Our punishments are often more severe to remind us of our submission. As mortals are often frightened of what they don't understand, many are intimidated by my people and frequently feel the need to demonstrate their dominance over us, Miss. Severe punishments of the djinn often make mortals feel more secure."

"Oh."

"In line with this, Miss, many severe punishments are also written into our Book of Law." He bowed slightly when he mentioned the book.

"Really?"

"Yes, Miss. Though not required, many punishments are suggested, such as forty lashes for stealing, twenty for a displeasing demeanor or incorrect attitude, and ten or less for disrespectful, disruptive behavior such as sneezing, coughing, or laughter. Anything that can be considered disruptive, Miss, or imply disrespect."

"Disrespect? But Genie, you have no control over whether you sneeze, cough, or laugh. Why would you receive lashes for involuntary responses?"

"Because they are considered disruptive behaviors, Miss, and therefore disrespectful. And to mostly serve as reminders of our lowly status."

"Ridiculous. Anyone who constantly needs to remind you of your lowly status only demonstrates their insecurity with their own standing. Those who are secure with their power don't need to continually demonstrate it."

"You are very perceptive, Miss. And wise for your age."

"Thank you, Genie," she said, almost absent-minded, preparing her next line of questioning. "What is this Book of Law that you keep referring to? Where is it and who wrote it?"

He bowed slightly when she mentioned it and continue to do so whenever it was mentioned by name. "The Djinn Book of Law contains the many laws, rules, and regulations that govern the relationships between my people and mortals, Miss. It also contains the many symbols, spells, and words that have power over my kind.

"It was written by the first djinn leaders and the mortals who were present when the djinn were first captured, Miss. There are only ten originals and they are guarded strictly by those who are charged with keeping it."

"Wow."

"Yes, Miss. During our first five-hundred years of service, all the enslaved djinn of my sect are required to gather at a central point, listen to, and recite certain passages of the Book of Law once every fifty years until we are older and considered more mature in our service."

"You have it memorized?"

"The parts related to the djinn's service to mortals, Miss, yes."

"You said it contains symbols and spells. Is the book itself magic or enchanted?"

"Yes, Miss, the book itself is magical and dangerous to my people. It is also enchanted so that it remains in the correct hands. Not many mortals have seen it, and it should not be handled lightly, Miss."

"What would happen if it fell into the hands of a mortal?"

"Nothing, Miss. It is only considered dangerous for the djinn. Most mortals are not skilled in reading it, and usually, only sorcerers desire it."

"Have you ever met any of the sorcerers who want to read it, Genie?"

"No, Miss, fortunately. The sorcerers who seek out the book are usually trying to enslave more of my people as a way to gain power, some type of object, or to open a portal to another world."

"A portal to another world! What world? And how many are there?"

"I am forbidden to speak of such things, Miss, unless you already know about them. But that is the type of knowledge also contained within the book."

"Too bad, Genie, for I would love to see another world. One where women aren't required to marry someone just because they've reached a certain age."

"That's understandable, Miss."

"Other worlds. But I need to learn more about this world, first. I'll see you next week, Genie."

"Goodbye, Miss."

"First, she asked me about contrary wishes and what I can do about it. Then she asked me about the contents of my lamp, and then about history." The genie spoke with the king in his private chambers. "Then she wanted to know if any genies had ever refused to serve, and if any mortals had been transformed into genies. I told her the story of a mortal guard who temporarily became one of my Brethren.

"Then she came to me very angry and I gave her some advice about how she should not act in anger. Then she asked me about my punishments and the Djinn Book of Law." He bowed briefly. "And that is it so far, Master."

"She entertains a wide variety of subjects, doesn't she, djinn?"

"Yes, Master. She follows her curiosity, wherever it may lead."

"And you see no signs of manipulation, nor any attempts at controlling you?"

"No, Master. Only a quest for more knowledge. And, Master, may I speak freely?"

"Of course."

"I suspect that she is somewhat lonely and only wants someone else to talk to, Master. She enjoys my company and conversation because I am different, and to her, at least, my answers are unfamiliar and unpredictable. She hasn't heard any of the stories of my people and wishes to hear as many as she can."

"I see."

"I will continue to entertain her for as long as you wish, Master, as long as it pleases you. I understand her a little better now and so I am no longer uncomfortable."

"I am not entirely convinced that these conversations that you've been having are to be encouraged. She is still so new to the world,

Genie. I know that she enjoys your stories but there is so much that she doesn't know."

The genie closed his eyes and bowed. "Master, I will follow your desire in this, as in everything. What do you wish of me?"

"You may continue talking to her. For now. And continue to monitor her motives, as always. We'll see where this leads."

"Yes, Master."

Chapter 27
Tender's Story: Differences

"Well, Genie," Jewel seemed to be unusually contemplative this fifth day, after their greeting. The professor quickly continued his writing.

"Yes, Miss?"

"It's a bit strange, talking to someone who is not allowed to look at me when they talk back."

"Yes, Miss. But I suppose one becomes accustomed to it."

"You don't have to talk this way in your lamp, do you?"

"No, Miss, but so far, there hasn't been anyone there yet for me to talk to."

"You're always alone in your lamp?"

"Yes, Miss."

"But I thought you were raised in a lamp."

"I was, Miss, in my father's lamp. When I came of age, and before I took my oath, I was placed in my own lamp."

"And your family?"

"My parents are still in my father's lamp while my brothers and sisters live in various places and homes in the djinn world. My people naturally prefer to remain in the dimension of the djinn."

"This dimension of the djinn that you speak of, what is it and where is it?"

"It is a protected world where most of my people live in a different realm, inaccessible to most mortals. Its access is purposefully hidden from mortals and must remain so, Miss."

"And are they safe there?"

"Yes, Miss, for no mortals have ever entered it."

"Is it like this world?"

"Yes, Miss, only more accommodating to and appropriate for my people. The light is different, Miss, it covers a wider part of the spectrum and is therefore more attuned to our eyes. It is easier for us to see and much more colorful."

"You and your people have difficulty seeing in this world?"

"Occasionally, Miss. The eyes of my people are accustomed to much brighter light so your world often appears rather dark and dim to us, even in sunlight."

"Oh." That explains the genie staring at the sun.

"There is also an abundance of fragrant plant life, Miss, which eases our senses and is soothing to us."

"Your people are soothed by fragrances?"

"Yes, Miss. As alcohol is to mortals, fragrances are to us. Indeed, my people can become intoxicated by certain scents. Wine and other alcoholic drinks have no effect on us, but certain fragrances do."

"That is really interesting. What else affects your people differently, Genie?"

"Not much, Miss, our people only vary in a few things. Forgive me, Miss, but my master approaches."

The genie bowed low, and the king entered the Crystal Court Room.

"Uncle! Did you know that genies can become drunk on certain smells?"

"And this is what you're teaching her, Genie?" The genie sat up and lowered his head in shame.

"Forgive me, Master. We were talking about the differences between our people."

"Hm, well, okay. That's enough talk about drunken genies. Come now, my girl, I would like you to meet our newest ambassador in the Emerald Throne Room, of course. You may return to your lamp, Genie."

"Thank you, Master." He dissolved into smoke and entered his lamp.

The genie looked at his master and his niece in his mind as they walked away. To walk normally around this world without giving offense. That would truly be a wonderful thing, he thought.

Chapter 28
Tender's Story: Rank

"Genie?"

"Yes, Miss?"

"Do you report our conversations to my uncle?"

"Yes, Miss, when he asks about them."

"And does he usually ask about them?"

"Most of the time, yes, Miss. When he remembers to ask about them."

"But you must report back to him everything I say then, correct?"

"Yes, Miss. I must obey his wishes above all."

"And is he pleased with you?"

"He is so far, Miss."

"What would happen if he was not? Pleased with you, I mean."

"He could leave me in my lamp, or give it away, sell me, or return me to my people, Miss. My lamp is his to do with as he wishes."

"And it pleases him to have you talk with me?"

"Yes, Miss. But that is because it pleases you."

"And if it did not please me? Our meetings would cease?"

"Yes, Miss."

"I knew our conversations were precariously held; I just didn't realize by how much. Genie, do you enjoy talking with me?"

"Yes, Miss. Very much so."

"Good. Because I enjoy talking to you. Hopefully, we can continue our discussions. And I hope that they continue to please the king."

"Yes, Miss, me too."

After a brief pause, during which Jewel gazed around the room, she asked, "Genie?"

"Yes, Miss?"

"Why are some of your people considered more powerful than others? I always thought that all the djinn were equally powerful."

"My people are naturally gifted with magical powers, Miss. And as in all things that are born, some are more gifted than others. However, the key to our abilities is how well we use that power, Miss."

"Your training, Genie? Is that why you were trained for eleven years?"

"Yes, Miss. It taught me to use all my abilities at once in order to serve mortals. Certain skills and abilities require training and practice to produce optimal results, Miss."

"And so, you were well-trained?"

"Yes, Miss, and thank you."

"But still, how can you tell how powerful you are even among the well-trained djinn?"

"There are certain tests that are performed on the Brethren to ascertain our different power levels, Miss. One such test involves opening portals to different worlds. There are different levels, such as being able to open a portal, how long we can maintain the open portal, and how many may have access to that portal, at one time, Miss. But that's only a test of the strength of our magic. There are other tests measuring our focus and concentration, our accuracy in reading the minds of mortals, and the accompanying realizations of their imaginings. There are many tests, Miss."

"Wow,"

"Additionally, they go by the intuitions of our teachers and the Leader of all of the Djinn," he bowed. "There are many metrics by which we can be measured, Miss. But nothing is higher than the evaluation of our Leader," he bowed again. "His judgments are accurate and his insight nearly infallible."

"Just nearly infallible?"

"Yes, Miss. For he created many of the test and knows and understands our powers better than any of our kind. In other words, Miss, he just always seems to know which one of the Brethren is the most powerful. He ranked each one of us, Miss, according to our powers. Whenever we had to line up, it was from the strongest to the weakest."

"And where were you in this ranking?"

He paused. "I was always the most powerful, Miss."

"Are you the most powerful of all of your kind?"

"At the moment, Miss, yes," but he lowered his head.

"You don't seem very proud of it, Genie. You act as if you're embarrassed by it."

"I take no pleasure in being the most powerful djinn, Miss. Being so only makes me more valuable to mortals and more desirable."

"More of a prize? Like, the most expensive, valuable, slave?"

"Yes, Miss. Though I am happy to be in the service of my master, I do not wish to be so sought after. Or so well known for the level of my powers."

"You serve at the side of your master right next to the king, the focus of attention at court."

"Yes, Miss. But I would prefer to be less well known, or rather, less coveted."

"Constantly being in court makes you an object of desire. A trophy to be won, a signifier of royalty."

"Yes, Miss. Though it pleases my master to keep me in court so I cannot disobey him."

"Would you rather remain in your lamp?"

"Yes, Miss. But ultimately, what I would rather is irrelevant, Miss. I am a slave, subject to my master's slightest whim. Though I must admit, it is not just a matter of whether I am visible, but if I am recognized for what I am. Being known as the most powerful genie can cause many difficulties, Miss. Particularly for my master."

"Is he in danger because you are recognized as the most powerful genie? Am I in danger?"

"No, Miss. I am charged with protecting the kingdom and most particularly, you and my master. Though, mortals are willing to do almost anything to acquire me, and therefore my lamp. My master has also wished me to keep him abreast of any plots against him, you, or anyone else in the kingdom. You are both safe, Miss."

"Thank you, Genie, for your protection."

"You are welcome, Miss. Though it was my master's wish; I must obey."

"I suppose you do. Genie, what was the most outrageous, extravagant, excessive, ridiculous wish that you've ever had to grant?"

"One of my former masters wished that everything he owned would turn into gold. It did not end well for him, Miss."

"Oh?"

"He lived in a tent so when the tent turned into gold, it collapsed upon him. He wasn't my master for very long, though I tried to warn him."

"That's unfortunate, but not outrageous. Anything else?"

"I once had a master who only wanted to live during sunsets. I had to constantly move his palace from place to place, eventually circling the earth."

"Really?"

"Yes, Miss. He was an unusual man, very particular in his desires. But he was also very clever and managed to keep me serving him for the rest of his life."

"Because sunsets are ever-present. That was very clever of him."

"Yes, Miss. I also had a master who wished for an eternal spring. It also involved continual movement, but not nearly as often."

"You must get tired of mortals and our endless demands, reasonable and unreasonable."

"When it comes to desires, Miss, it seems as if everything is fair game."

"Have you ever had a wish that you couldn't fulfill?"

"I had a master who wished to own the earth. I told him that I was not able to make him a god, in any sense of the word, Miss."

"And how did he respond?"

"He decided to settle for, in his words, Miss, merely owning a continent. And so, I made him the ruler of a continent."

"That must have been terrible for the people who lived there."

"To be honest, Miss, very few of them were even ever aware of him. He wanted his palace placed in a remote, mountainous area, which very few were ever able to reach. He ruled a continent with very few subjects and very little notice."

"How satisfying! People can be so grandiose. All the hubris and pride, and arrogance you must have seen. And still see. We mortals can be extremely flawed creatures. I don't know how you handle dealing with us so well."

"Training, Miss. Because of my training."

"Genie? Come here, I need you," the king interrupted.

"Yes, Master. Excuse me, Miss."

Chapter 29
Training: Obedience and Disobedience

"Tender, Alley, Clever, Thoughtful, Bold, Shy, Peaceful, Joy."

Tender heard this list so often that it was easily the first thing he memorized by the second day. It was the first thing he heard in the morning, and lately, the last thing he heard every night. The First Teacher began to name them all when saying good night so that they would only have to say it once, and therefore stop talking and go to sleep.

Tender woke up late one night, still sore from their obedience task of repairing a fence earlier that day. He rolled over to his side, facing the front of the room. He had wondered if the First Teacher stayed at his desk all night, but instead, he saw the First Teacher asleep! The desk had turned into a bed and the First Teacher was comfortably lying in it. Tender almost sat up at the sight until he heard the First Teacher say, *"Use the bathroom and go back to sleep, Tender."*

"Yes, First Teacher," Tender replied telepathically, not wanting to wake up anybody else. He got up, relieved himself in his Whatever Room, which was blue and yellow now, and got back in bed.

It was strange, but the First Teacher still seemed to be completely asleep. Maybe he would learn how to do that when he was older, create magic that responds even while he's asleep. If he ever needed to.

The days continued, dominated by lessons and obedience training. It was easier now, though, because at least the boys could talk to each other and express themselves. They could even occasionally ask the First Teacher questions, though not many dared too, and not too often.

Tender noticed they fell into comfortable groups. Clever, Thoughtful, and Bold hung out together the most and Tender sometimes joined them. Peaceful and Joy became good friends since they grew up in rings rather than lamps. Shy occasionally joined them but he usually played by himself. He also talked to Tender when they were most likely not to be disturbed or interrupted.

Alley seemed too upset to play with anyone else and for the first few weeks, didn't play much at all. When he did, he built something, then smashed it or drew something else, only to tear it up. It was obvious that he was still angry about his caretaker and what had happened to him. Tender wanted to ask him about it, but he knew that Alley wouldn't answer, nor did he ever seem to want to talk about it. Since Alley's entire clan and his caretaker were gone, his anger made sense to Tender.

He found himself trying to make friends and hang out with Alley, especially whenever no one else seemed to want to. And though he wasn't always the nicest friend, Alley didn't seem to mind Tender being near him.

On this day, their obedience class was particularly difficult. No one had any idea what a fire engine red 1956 Corvette with power windows and manual transmission was, much less how to make one. And the car that the Teacher of Magic made in front of them just seemed like another one of those overly complicated machines that mortals were always wanting. They had to stand with their arms held out to their sides for twenty minutes as their punishment.

When they appeared back in their dorm rooms afterwards, before their last meal of the day, Tender remarked to Alley, "That was weird. Cars are weird."

"Yeah, and who needs a car anyway? Mortals and their stupid lack of magic. If they could just appear places like we did, they wouldn't need such contraptions."

"Contraptions. That's a good word for mortal stuff," Tender remarked and Alley smiled.

"If mortals were magic, none of us would even be here," Alley added.

"If mortals were magic, that would be cool. They would probably kill each other off really fast."

"And leave us alone!"

"Young gentlemen," the voice of the First Teacher boomed over everyone, "it is time for the evening meal. Appear in the dining room immediately."

"Yes, First Teacher." The young djinn appeared immediately in the dining room and took their assigned places around the table. When the meal began, Tender indulged his curiosity.

"Have you ever seen a mortal?" he asked Alley.

"No, not in real life. Have you?"

"No," Tender answered.

Joy smiled, "I don't think that any of us has ever seen one of them."

"I wonder if we'll ever get to see them," Tender said.

The First Teacher answered, "You will get to see mortals at a later stage during your training."

"Yes, First Teacher," all the boys quickly replied as they were trained.

Later that night, long after they were all supposed to be sleeping, a wide awake Clever got out of bed and crept between Tender and Alley's bed. The First Teacher was sound asleep in his bed. "Hey," he whispered, "wake up."

Alley jolted awake with a start, while Tender rolled over to face Clever.

"What's going on?" he mumbled.

"*Shh, quiet. We can't wake anybody. Do you two really want to see what a mortal looks like?*"

"*Yeah, why?*" Alley asked telepathically.

"*They have an image of one in the Teacher's Lounge,*" Clever answered.

"*How do you know?*" Alley asked.

"*I saw it. Last week I turned my Whatever Room into the place where all the teachers go and I saw it,*" Clever explained. Tender and Alley looked at each other.

"*Do you want to try it to see if we can see it again?*" Alley asked Tender.

"*Yeah,*" Tender replied, ready for a little adventure. Tender and Alley got out of bed as quietly as they could. "*Whose room do we use?*"

"*Yours is right there, let's try yours.*" Alley waited until Tender gently opened the door to his Whatever Room and they all went in.

The room was dimly lit up so they could see everything, but with no obvious source of light. Tender had changed it into an all-blue bathroom earlier that day.

"*Okay,*" Clever mentally whispered, "*change it now!*"

Tender changed the whole room with a thought and it immediately began to change into the Teacher's Lounge.

But just at that moment, they heard the First Teacher's voice in their heads, "*What are you three doing?*"

All three boys froze. Tender's Whatever Room instantly changed back into the blue bathroom.

"*Back to bed. You will all be dealt with in the morning.*"

They nearly ran out of the Whatever Room and back to their beds.

"*Go to sleep. Now!*" They closed their eyes and fell asleep instantly, with The First Teacher using his powers to make sure they obeyed.

The next morning after everyone was clean and dressed, they all stood in front of their trunks in the ready position. "Everyone, go to your first meal except Clever, Alley, and Tender. You three remain in ready position."

"Yes, First Teacher." Clever, Tender, and Alley lowered their heads as the other boys disappeared one by one, staring at them as they walked past. Shy lingered the longest.

"Shy, you go too."

"Yes, First Teacher." Shy began to fade into the other room with a very concerned glance towards Tender.

"Clever. You first since it was your idea."

"Yes, First Teacher."

The First Teacher and Clever then disappeared. After a few minutes, the First Teacher appeared again, alone. "Alley."

"Yes, First Teacher."

Then they both disappeared. Tender stood alone, in front of his trunk, now extremely worried.

The First Teacher appeared in the room again, after a few minutes, "Tender."

"Yes, First Teacher."

Then he disappeared from the dorm with Tender and reappeared in a small dark room that was filled with a large, wooden, mechanical object with large gears and ratchet wheels that seemed to be ticking. The top of the machine went through the ceiling so Tender couldn't make out what its purpose was. There was a large cistern of water next to the machine. The bottom of the object seemed to run on a watermill system, as there was a pool of water at the bottom of it, but nothing was flowing. Instead, Clever and Alley were keeping it running, using buckets of water to keep the water wheel turning, which was intense work, as they had to constantly fill the buckets from the cistern and pour it onto the gears of the large wooden wheel in the water to keep it turning.

"Since you joined Clever and Alley in their little scheme, you will also join them in this one. Keep the machine running."

A bucket appeared in Tender's hands and he joined Clever and Alley in filling the buckets with water from the cistern and using the water to keep the gears on the water wheel turning. Tender was soaking wet after a minute of doing this.

"You will keep the machine running until the next meal. I will know immediately if you stop."

Their actions were frantic and Alley and Clever ran into each other, accidentally dumping water over themselves. The wheel began to slow down. "Wait, we have to cooperate," Tender spoke up. "Let's take turns. Clever, you go first."

Clever refilled his bucket and dumped it.

"Alley next."

As the three began to take turns, the entire operation went much more smoothly. It was still tedious, grueling, work, but they kept the wheel turning for hours. Right before the midday meal, the First Teacher appeared.

"Dry yourselves off first using your powers."

"Yes, First Teacher." The three boys instantly switched from being soaking wet to dry.

"Now, let's go." The four disappeared from the room and reappeared in the dining room where they took their place at the table along with the rest of the boys. It was their usual midday meal of what the boys nicknamed 'smelly bread,' steamed vegetables, and a small portion of meat. All the boys looked as they usually did except for Clever, Alley, and Tender, who were dirty and exhausted.

Bold looked at them and asked, "What happened to you three?"

Clever was about to answer, but he looked at the First Teacher first, who nodded his permission.

"We were being punished at some kind of a water machine."

"It is called a water wheel. It's a giant clock that runs on water. It was your job to keep it running," the First Teacher definitively answered. "Go on, Clever. Tell the others what you had to do."

"Yes, First Teacher." Clever continued, "We had to keep filling up buckets of water and pouring it onto these planks."

"Gears," the First Teacher corrected him.

"Thank you, First Teacher, sir. We had to pour water on the gears to keep it going. It was hard." Clever thought he should stop talking so that the First Teacher would stop correcting him. But that didn't work.

"It was supposed to be hard to teach you three a lesson. Don't rush ahead of your training out of curiosity; doing so can be dangerous. And don't turn your Whatever Rooms into the Teacher's Lounge or any other places in the training building you are unauthorized for."

"Yes, First Teacher," the three thoroughly punished boys answered.

"And it's better to cooperate for something constructive rather than something so foolish as wanting to see what a mortal looks like."

"Yes, First Teacher." They all finished their meal in silence.

Chapter 30
Tender's Story: War

"Genie?"

"Yes, Miss?"

"You once said that there have been wars concerning you."

"Do you mean a war over the ownership of my lamp, Miss?"

"Yes."

"Then my lamp has caused a war, Miss. Twice."

"Two wars! Please, tell me about them, Genie."

"Yes, Miss. The first war was fought over a treasure of unfathomable riches, which, turned out to be my lamp. The two sides in that instance hated each other from the beginning and were ready to begin fighting over the smallest of provocations. My lamp, Miss, happened to be the last of the provocations. By the end of the war so few were left that the participants neither cared nor were curious about my lamp anymore; they were only interested in rebuilding. And so, my lamp remained hidden as before. It was an extremely destructive war, Miss. Quite a few towns were lost."

"How many people died?"

"Over one thousand, Miss, because of their hatred for each other."

"And the second war?"

"Three men filled with greed, Miss, who knew exactly what I was and what the ownership of my lamp meant. The three mortals raised armies to fight over the control of a small parcel of land where my lamp was rumored to be."

"Was your lamp there?"

"Yes, Miss. It was buried next to the grave of my previous master along with a few of his other possessions. The servants who buried it had no idea of the lamp's value, Miss, nor that I was inside. They were simply honoring my late master as well as they could."

"Who won the war? And did anyone ever find you?"

"One of the three mortals won, Miss, by searching for my lamp at night whenever the battles temporarily ceased and their armies were exhausted. He searched for my master's grave until he eventually found it, along with my lamp. His first wish banished his opponents to the other side of the world."

"He won you and the war. And at such a terrible cost. How many people died in that war?"

"About two thousand, Miss."

"All due to greed. You mustn't blame yourself, Genie."

"I did at first, Miss, for so many lives lost. Then I realized it was their own hatred and greed that caused such wars and the subsequent loss of life. I become very melancholy, Miss, when I think of such things."

"Then perhaps we shouldn't speak of such things. I won't mention it again, Genie, if it troubles you so."

"Thank you, Miss, thank you."

The genie later remembered the second war from his point of view, buried alongside his dead master in the dark, occasionally hearing men slaughtering each other above him, and the cries of the dying. The too familiar feeling of helplessness hitting him, full force. With all his power, he was powerless once again.

He hated being fought over. He hated being a prize, a treasure, a trophy for mortals. He wanted to be among his own people more than ever, longing for the calm and peacefulness of a quiet life, unbidden by mortals, desired only by his wife and children, just an average member of his clan. Would he ever know such joy?

Chapter 31
Ally's Story: Freedom

Ally found that there were all sorts of ways he could make himself useful to the djinn-guardian. He conjured unending pantry and food cabinets so that the djinn-guardian wouldn't have to make as many trips to other dimensions to restock. He even helped with the other djinn, giving them tea and helping them back to sleep when they woke up disoriented.

When it came time to dissolve his shackles, even that was easier than he ever imagined. The djinn-guardian brought out a large, flat, wooden bowl to catch the dissolved metal, and a wooden cup filled with the mysterious pontar metal itself, which looked more like a swirling mixture of lighted colors, rather than metal.

"Don't be afraid. Watch." The djinn-guardian poured a drop of the liquid on his own skin and nothing happened. "See? It won't burn you or anything if the mixture is just right."

He poured a drop on Ally's skin, who gasped at the lack of feeling anything. "If only I knew how to make this amazing metal."

"I could tell you exactly how but that won't help you. None of the ingredients can be touched by any djinn for the mixture to work."

"There's always a catch," Ally sighed.

"Before we start, I want you to finish your tea. It will help you when your thoughts are unleashed."

"My thoughts will be unleashed?"

The djinn guard nodded. "Because you are a member of the Brethren, your thoughts are usually monitored, except for when you are in this dimension, of course. But as soon as your shackles are removed, every negative thought you ever had, every contrary feeling or emotion that you've ever had, you will feel them all at once."

"Why don't they ever tell us about these things?"

"This doesn't apply to all djinn, just to the members of the Brethren. I've been told also that it can be quite painful. The tea will help you though it."

Ally finished his tea, then poured another cup and drank that one too. "There. That should do it."

"Are you ready?"

"Yes, always."

"Your right shackle first."

Ally held his right shackle over the bowl and the djinn-guardian poured a thin stream of the magical metal onto the shackle. It began to dissolve instantly and magically, mixing with the rest of the metal and turning into brighter, swirling colors.

Ally felt nothing; his wrist wasn't even wet. He eagerly held out his left wrist and the djinn-guardian dissolved that shackle too. "Is that it? Is it over? Am I..."

"You can say the word now, Ally. You are free." The djinn-guardian put the cup on the table.

Ally smiled at first but then felt a rush of old thoughts and emotions. It was disorienting, overwhelming, and painful. He closed his eyes and his breathing began to increase. The pain and emotion began to increase as well and Ally bent over, nearly falling off his chair. He was experiencing everything he had ever felt or thought that was officially forbidden by the rules of the Brethren.

The djinn-guardian reached over and put his hand on Ally's arm. Ally jerked his head towards him, but the touch of another person seemed to have a calming effect. His breathing began to return to normal and he opened his eyes. The djinn-guardian let go of Ally's arm.

"Wow, that was intense," Ally said.

"I know, but you handled it well."

Recovering more, Ally began to look around the room. "I am, free? I'm free? I don't have to bow anymore?" Ally jumped up.

"No. Watch." The djinn-guardian paused and then said, "the Leader of all of the Djinn."

Ally waited to see if he felt the compulsion to bow, but he didn't. "I didn't bow! I don't have to bow anymore! Is it okay if I cut my hair?"

"Of course," said the djinn-guardian, laughing at Ally's excitement.

"I want to cut off that stupid lock of hair. I'm going to cut all my hair off. I can do what I want now!"

"This is my favorite part. I love freeing the djinn. Though I don't think that you should shave your head." Ally kept talking, mainly to himself.

"I'm free. I'm free. I can do what I want. I can do what I want!" He magically spun around, waved a finger towards his head, and all the hair on his head was gone, including the hated banded lock and his eyebrows.

"I don't think that's a good look for you," remarked the djinn-guardian, but Ally changed himself into translucent smoke and began darting around the room.

"Ally!" The djinn-guardian stood up. "Don't use too much magic or move around so fast! This dimensional bubble isn't stable enough for that, you could cause it to collapse on us all!"

Instantly, Ally re-formed himself and stood in front of the djinn-guardian. "I'm sorry, I got carried away. But I'm free."

"Yes, you are. Relax, Ally, or you'll hyperventilate."

Ally calmed down and sat at the table.

"Now that you're free, what now? You can stay here with me if you like but I suspect that you would soon find it boring and tedious. So, where would you like to go?"

"I don't know. I never thought about it; I couldn't think about it. But I'll probably go to the mortal world."

"That will work, but only if you pretend to be a mortal."

"I figured I'd have to do that."

"The best way is to find an obscure mortal, preferably a dead one, and copy his life. Make yourself into an almost exact duplicate of that person, changing only a few facts, and especially your appearance. That way, you won't have to worry about the details."

"You know so many worthy tricks and shortcuts. Your friendship would be most valuable to me."

"You have it. Just don't forget about me or the other djinn who also need freeing."

"I won't. I can't. Not after all that you've done for me."

"I've heard that before from so many of your people."

"But I won't forget. I give you my word and a cloth." Ally waved two fingers and a communication cloth appeared on the wall. "That way, you can contact me whenever you want."

"Thank you. And Ally, I must tell you this before you go. You may have a living relative."

"What?"

"I was searching through the djinn genealogies and there is no date of death listed for your great-grandfather."

"Quotar, who was called by his name? Could he still be alive?"

"Your people are known for their extremely long lifespans. It is possible."

"But the djinn-guardian, didn't he erase my entire clan?"

"He erased all of the members of your clan available in the djinn dimension. But he couldn't touch anyone in the mortal world and I believe your great-grandfather was still serving at the time."

"A living relative. I never thought I'd have a living relative, or anyone in anyway related to me."

"It's possible. The genealogical maps of the original twelve djinn houses contain most of the history but are not complete. It could be that his death just wasn't recorded. He was last known to be serving a master in the area the mortals call the far-off lands."

"The far-off lands? Any idea of where that might be?"

"No, sorry. That's all I could find."

"Again, I thank you, my friend." Ally formally bowed to him. "I have so much to thank you for. Surely, there must be some other way that I can repay you."

"Enjoy your freedom, Ally. That will be repayment enough. And don't forget us or this place."

Ally stood up and took a deep breath. "And may I ask one more thing of you, djinn-guardian?"

"Yes?" he said, standing up.

"What is your name?"

"Fantir. My name is Fantir."

"Fantir," the genie repeated. "I will remember that. Good-bye."

"Good-bye."

Ally faded until he disappeared.

Chapter 32
Tender's Story: Age

"Genie?'

"Yes, Miss?"

"How old were you when you took your oath?"

"I was the mortal equivalent of twenty-one years old."

"And you have been serving mankind for how long?"

"Only about nine hundred years, Miss, in mortal years. Nine-hundred and fifty-nine years to be exact, Miss."

"Wow."

"It's not that long compared to older generations, Miss. Many of them have been serving for many thousands of years."

"And so, you're still considered fairly young?"

"Yes, Miss. The next generation of my Brethren have yet to be born. We have a new generation of djinn every thousand years or so, Miss."

"Will one of your children have to serve?" she asked.

"Most likely, yes, Miss. My clan is considered one of the most powerful and I am already the third generation to serve. So, probably yes, Miss."

"I would be reluctant to marry and have children knowing that one of them would have to serve."

"That thought has crossed my mind, Miss. I do not wish to cause the enslavement of another. And yet, I do not want my enslavement to affect my decision to marry, Miss. There are other factors to take into consideration and I do not want the possible enslavement of one of my future children to be the only issue."

"You sound as if you're negotiating a contract."

"In a way, I am, Miss."

"I don't know if I would marry under the same circumstances. I can't really say. Like you said, there are other things to consider. Loneliness and companionship, for one."

"Yes, Miss," he answered quickly.

The genie bowed low and then the king entered, followed by several cabinet members and generals. "Genie, I need you to predict the odds of a war under a particular set of circumstances. My generals are waiting for you."

"Yes, Master." The genie dissolved in front of Jewel and the professor and reappeared directly in front of the king's cabinet and generals. They began to question him immediately.

The king looked at her. "Good morning, Jewel."

"Good morning, Uncle. I hope you are well today."

"I am, thank you. It's good to see you up early and taking lessons already."

"My lessons haven't quite begun. I seem to be awake before my instructors. The genie and I were just talking while I waited."

"Oh, I see. Just talking." He looked at the genie who was listening to a general who hung his head lower. "What about?"

"Enslavement and whether one should have children while enslaved."

"That's a rather strange topic to begin the day with."

"I brought it up; I'm not exactly sure why."

"You are getting close to marrying. Maybe that's why."

"Perhaps so, Uncle."

"In any case, your instructors are sure to be awake now."

"Of course, sir. Excuse me, Uncle." She bowed towards the king. "Excuse me, gentlemen." She bowed towards them and they towards her.

The Chief Advisor approached the king. "She is turning out to be a very interesting young woman."

"That is definitely true."

"And I am continuing to search for a suitable husband for her, sire."

"I hope the search is going well."

"I have found several young, royal, well-educated men, all of marrying age who I think would be acceptable to her."

"And advantageous matches for the kingdom, I suppose?"

"Of course, sire."

"Good. I promised her one more year so she could further her education, but I do not wish to delay her marriage any longer than that."

"Yes, sire."

The genie paused his discussion with the generals, then continued.

Chapter 33
Tender's Story: Terminology

"Genie?"

"Yes, Miss?"

"I noticed that a lot of the time, your terminology is a lot different than mine. For example, I've heard you speak of your enslavement as having to serve. Correct?"

"Yes, Miss. That is how my people refer to our enslavement. Primarily because we take an oath to serve the owner of the lamp, Miss."

"Forgive me, but does it cause you pain to mention your enslavement? I would hate to cause you any further pain, Genie."

"No, Miss, it does not."

"Please, let me know if I use any more of your forbidden words,"

"I will, Miss." The genie took a chance and elaborated. "If I may, Miss."

"Of course, Genie, please continue."

"Many of your words are forbidden for my Brethren, Miss. We experience such great discomfort when we say them, that when we ask for permission to speak freely in our language, it's literally translated as, *permission to speak without pain.*"

"So, you're actually asking to be able to talk without your words causing you pain?"

"Yes, Miss."

"That's so sad, Genie. That you would have to beg your master merely to speak without physical pain."

"It is a wonder, Miss, that we are allowed to speak at all. This is the most I've ever spoken since I took my oath. Most masters do not allow their genies to speak much at all, mostly out of fear."

"Are most mortals afraid of your people, Genie?"

"Yes, Miss, most mortals are afraid of the djinn, which explains why we have so many rules and laws to follow."

"To manage our fear as well as limit your power. A sad state of affairs."

"Yes, Miss, I agree."

Jewel really wanted to mention how it was a sad commentary on humanity, but she didn't want to be seen favoring the djinn over her own people, especially while she was being monitored. But the genie heard her final thoughts on the matter and agreed with her. He appreciated the fact that a mortal, any mortal, would agree with him.

Chapter 34
Tender's Story: Other Genies

"Genie?"

"Yes, Miss?"

"Is it true that a genie can't undo the wish of another genie?"

"It is one of our laws that the enslaved Brethren cannot be pitted against one another in such a way, Miss. As a sign of respect, we must allow the original genie's wish to stand. This rule extends to all the enslaved djinn."

"You can't undo another genie's fulfilled wish even if the wishes were thousands of years apart?"

"Even then, Miss. It is against our law," the genie bowed slightly, "which we must respect."

"Can you undo the work of a sorcerer?"

"It depends on exactly what that work is, Miss. Most sorcerers know how to protect their magic from the djinn and other magical creatures."

"What other magical creatures, Genie? How many are there?"

"More than you could imagine, Miss."

He paused and Jewel waited for him to elaborate. When he didn't, she asked, "Aren't you allowed to tell me about them?"

"No, Miss. Only about the ones that you specifically ask me about. I am not allowed to divulge the secrets of the world of magic."

"Why not?"

"Such knowledge is not considered safe in the hands of mortals, Miss. It may be too much for you."

"Too much for us to handle? Well, remembering the wars you told me about, I guess you're right, Genie."

"Not to be disrespectful, Miss."

"No, Genie, you are far from being disrespectful. You're just being honest, which only increases my respect for you."

"Thank you, Miss."

Chapter 35
Tender's Story: Slash

"Genie?"

"Yes, Miss?"

"Why must you bow at every mention of the Leader of all of the Djinn?"

The genie bowed as she spoke the last five words. "Because he is the Leader of all of the Djinn," he bowed again, "and he must always be treated with the utmost respect, Miss. It is even written into the laws of my people."

"Oh."

"Do you not treat your leaders so, Miss?"

"No. Well, not like that."

"The Leader of my people," he bowed again, "is wise and merciful and my people must honor him for it, Miss." He bowed once more. "He occasionally takes the shape of a great bird so that he can fly and watch over his people, especially the enslaved. Many mortals think that we worship him as a god, but we do not. We merely honor and revere him as our Leader." He bowed yet again.

Jewel nearly kept silent but couldn't help but softly question,

"Forgive me for saying so, Genie, but if he's so wise and merciful, then why are you enslaved?"

"I am enslaved, Miss, because he's so wise and merciful. Only one is chosen out of every clan. Otherwise, all my people would be enslaved."

"But why is anyone enslaved at all? Why are your people subjected to slavery and put in lamps and bottles, and rings and so on in the first place?"

"It was due to several, unfortunate, incidents, Miss, that involved mortals and the djinn."

"Unfortunate incidents?"

"Violent incidents involving my people and yours, Miss."

"Such as?"

"There was the massacre of the little hill, also known as the slashing incident. It was before our Book of Law was written, before the rules of the relations between mankind and the djinn were set. My people were still learning the ways of your people and one of them decided to trade something that was valued in your world, silk and purple, for something that was common in your world, grain.

"Not that he needed it, he could have conjured anything he needed at any time, but he was trying to develop a friendship with the villagers at the bottom of the little hill near the well that supplied the villagers with water. He saw mortals trading with each other and decided to try it too.

"His first trade went well, and he was especially pleased that the villagers seemed to accept him as they would a mortal as he had adjusted his appearance so that he would blend in better with the others.

"His second trade also went well, and so did the third and fourth. By then, he felt as if he was getting to know some of the villagers and they seemed to be getting along better with him also. But it was not to be. During the djinn's fifth trading experience, something went wrong. This time, the djinn brought more silk and fine cloth with him since it seemed to get the best response. But the main trader and leader of the town seemed upset when he saw him, and suspicious also.

"He accused the genie of trading inferior goods and said that he would not accept anything from him any longer. The genie followed him and asked what he had done wrong. But the leader of the town only seemed to get more obstinate and hostile until he finally told the genie that he would have to slash the value in half in order to trade.

"Unfortunately, that was a poor choice of words. For the genie saw that the leader and the townspeople were actually selling his goods in the nearest city for ten times what they told him they were worth. And that they were trying to bully him into trading for less because of their greed. When he realized this, he decided to take the word 'slash' literally.

"He told the traders and the rest of the townspeople that he would agree to slash his prices, but only if he could slash them first. And he began to magically slice the people completely in half, and then into pieces, starting with the leader, the other traders, and then every living thing in the entire town. He did it using his powers and the mortals truly had no way of defending themselves. It was a complete massacre."

The genie tilted his head briefly to ascertain whether Jewel was still listening, but he felt that she was, so he continued. "There were other massacres, incidents of torture, and many other violent episodes of my people harming your people. Then it was decided that our people should remain separate from your people, Miss."

"I see, Genie." Jewel had to break her stunned silence to answer him. She had heard how dangerous genies could be and how they couldn't be trusted, but the examples she had learned of from her youth were never quite as specific. Even the professor had stopped to listen.

"That will be all for today, Genie. Thank you."

"You are welcome, Miss."

Jewel, still in a contemplative silence, left the side room. Jewel remembered all the warnings she had heard about how vicious and destructive the djinn could be. The warnings and cautions she had received from her friends and family. There were so many that she was nervous when she first met him and could barely ask him anything. But this genie, her uncle's genie, didn't seem anything like that. He wasn't like the violent, vengeful genie he had just described. Not at all.

The genie felt relieved that he wasn't asked to describe more of the violent incidents. He would have hated to tell of the genie who wanted to test the physical stamina of mortals, or the one who thought it was entertaining to use their body parts as everyday objects. Her opinion of him hadn't changed, he could sense that, but her opinion of his people did. Unfortunately, there was nothing he could do about that.

Chapter 36
Tender's Story: The Djinn-Guard

The Chief Advisor brought a djinn-guard to the Crystal Court Room. He was wearing a green robe and was covered in so many tattoos and markings that there was barely any visible blank skin. As a result, he was mostly green. He carried an elaborately carved, wooden staff marked with green symbols and it had a golden shape on top that looked like a curved, small cursive 'e,' but was bent inward in the middle of the top curve.

"Here he is, sire." The djinn-guard bowed to the king proudly.

"So," began the king, "you are one of the ones that they say can control the djinn?"

"Yes, your majesty. I have been trained in how to deal with these creatures from a very young age."

"And what do you think of them?"

"They are a tricky and cunning race, sire. You must treat them with a firm hand and a ready whip to maintain control."

"Tell me what you think of this one. Genie?"

The genie appeared in a small cloud of white smoke. "Yes, Master? How may I please you?" The genie, sensing the presence of the djinn-guard, bowed low to the king and began pleading with his master in fear. "Please forgive me, Master, if I have offended you. Please sir, I beg you, please, forgive me, Master."

"Silence, djinn!" the djinn-guard spoke with commanding authority. The genie obeyed instantly and bowed towards the djinn-guard, then got into the submissive position with his head held low. The djinn-guard approached him and circled him, making a show of inspecting him. The king had never seen his genie so afraid.

"Have you been a good djinn and pleasing to your master? Speak."

"Oh, greatly feared one, I have done my best and tried my utmost to serve my master well, sir, and to please him, sir." The genie spoke in an oddly clipped manner.

"Good. So far, I have not heard any negative reports of you, Tender." But the guard said Tender's name in the djinn language, which no one at the court understood. "Tell your master why you fear me so, djinn."

Without lifting his head, he immediately answered, "Sir, I will obey you, greatly feared one. Master, he has the power to kill my entire clan." The genie bowed low to the king again. "Master, I beg you, have I not pleased you? Please forgive me if I have disappointed you in any way, I beg you."

"That's enough, djinn."

The genie responded instantly to the djinn-guard's instructions and returned to the submissive position.

"Return to your lamp!" the djinn-guard barked.

The genie disappeared instantly without even a trace of smoke.

"So, what do you think?" asked the king.

"Your djinn is one of the well-trained genies, one of the Brethren. That's a rare find! You will have no problem with him, your majesty."

"That's good to know. I must summon my niece. For some reason, she is fascinated by these creatures." He nodded to one of the guards, who promptly left the room to get her.

"A dangerous habit, your majesty. No, it is best that people maintain their distance with genies. For they can be a manipulative lot."

His niece entered with the guard. "Good morning, Uncle."

"Ah, my dear, here you are. I have someone here that I think you will be interested to meet. He is one of the djinn minders, a real djinn-guard."

"A real djinn-guard?" Jewel was curious and a little wary.

"Yes. Ask him anything you like," the king spoke confidently.

"Are all the genies really afraid of you?"

"Yes, your highness. Just now, I had one of your master's genies trembling and cowering at my feet," the djinn-guard spoke proudly.

"Why?"

"Because I have been granted great power over them, including having the power to wipe out entire clans."

"Oh," Jewel was more disturbed than impressed that he had such power.

"And as I told his majesty, you should have no problems with this lamp one. He's one of the good ones."

"One of the good ones," Jewel repeated, reflecting on the words.

"Yes, your highness, and a word of advice. Don't take in too much of what a genie says. He says what he's forced to say."

"What do you mean?" she asked.

"I mean that he is only allowed to say so many things, your highness. With him it will be tough to tell when he's telling the truth or when he's flat out lying to you. His speech is under strict control. He's forced to stay away from certain words and subjects so that he may be more acceptable to mortals."

"Really?" the king asked.

"Yes, your majesty. Members of his sect are some of the most well-behaved because of this. He's extremely restricted in his actions, like most of his kind should be. But this one is a great find. Even his thoughts are controlled."

"His thoughts?" the king asked.

"Yes, your majesty. His every thought is monitored and filtered because of one of their inherited spells in their Book of Law. He's not allowed to even think about certain things. They say about his kind, their words and thoughts are not their own. So that everything about them can remain under strong supervision. It keeps them docile and easier to manage."

"Interesting! I did not know that."

"Well, thank you for the information. We really appreciate it." Jewel truly did not like this djinn-guard now and couldn't bear to hear him talk any longer.

"I'm happy to be of service to you, your highness."

"You may leave, Jewel."

"Thank you, Uncle. Sir." She bowed towards him, then to the djinn-guard, and left the room. Her embarrassment remained, but now with an added sense of betrayal. Had the genie been lying to her this entire time?

The king spoke up. "I have a few more questions for you, djinn-guard. A certain artifact came into my possession recently. They told me it was called the Eye of The Djinn. Do you know what it is and what it does?"

"Yes, your majesty, that is also a rare and wonderful find. There are only twenty of them in existence. The djinn guards have ten, while the others are either lost, hidden, or held by people who don't know what they've got. Eye of the Djinn pearls are only used in extreme circumstances when no other options are available as a method of punishing the djinn."

"How so?"

"By destroying their souls. Exposure to the Eye of the Djinn attacks their souls directly, weakening their will and emotions. Continued exposure to it leaves them with no soul at all, turning them into an empty shell, totally mindless, but much easier to control.

"But this is a dangerous tool, your majesty, and should only be used in the most extreme circumstances like a rebellion, or insurrection, or any other organized defiance. You shouldn't have to use it under normal circumstances, and not with that particular djinn. You should have no problem with him."

"I see."

"I only have one word of advice. Continue to rely on the lamp genie. The other one is known to be vindictive and spiteful. Yes, that one's developed quite a reputation over the years."

"Thank you. I do not wish to delay you on your journey any longer."

"Of course, your majesty."

"NOT ONLY IS THERE a djinn-guard about, now I have to worry about an Eye of The Djinn artifact also!" The genie paced, stopping only to watch the djinn-guard leave the room through the wall of his lamp. He hoped he showed enough respect for this guard to leave him and his clan alone.

The djinn-guard as a group usually just enjoyed demonstrating their power and authority over the djinn, and they loved great displays of fear and submission. Though the genie disliked groveling and cowering so much in front of his master, what else could he do? He had no choice. It was the only way to guarantee the safety of his clan.

The genie also knew that ultimately, Jewel was the real reason for this visit. That his master, in his haste to entertain her, grabbed the nearest genie expert he could find without really understanding how dangerous this man was. The fact that he could murder scores of his people based on any imagined insult was unknown to most mortals, or not taken very seriously. The devastation this djinn-guard could have caused! And now, the Eye of The Djinn was involved! What mortal keeps a weapon without any intention of using it?

And yet, try as he might, the genie found that he could not get angry with them. Frustrated, but not angry. Disgusted and upset, but not angry. Yes, they nearly cost him his life, but it was for a good reason. He could not fault her curiosity about him and his people and he still greatly respected her quest for more knowledge.

After all, wasn't he on a similar quest also, and wasn't he just as fascinated by mortals at her age as she was with the djinn? As dangerous as this day had turned out to be, he sensed that he was safe now. He needn't fear the djinn-guard's return after he left.

Still, he hoped that the royal family would be more careful in the future. He would hate to die because of someone else's educational endeavors.

Jewel, however, was still upset. Had the genie been deceitful during their conversations because of some obscure genie law? Was there any truth in anything that he had said at all? She became angrier the more she thought about it.

Had he been telling her only what he'd been forced to say all this time? She thought that the members of his sect, the Brethren, weren't allowed to lie. And yet, this djinn-guard said that it would be tough to tell the difference between him telling the truth and lying. So, which one was it? Could it be both?

And his thoughts were controlled and monitored? What did that even mean? Were his thoughts being controlled and monitored even when he was talking to her? Did they have a second monitor besides the professor?

She determined that she would have to ask the genie about all of this at the first opportunity. And without anger. Maybe. Maybe not.

Chapter 37
Tender's Story: The Argument

The next time Jewel saw the genie she confronted him. It was early in the morning on the second day of the week; she couldn't wait until their next fifth day meeting. The king usually met with his military leaders in the Crystal Court Room during this time of day and there they were, sitting around the king's favorite table. The professor was still asleep in his quarters.

The genie picked up on her presence before she arrived, as usual. He dissolved from his usual place next to the throne in a small puff of smoke and reappeared in their usual side room.

"Good morning, Miss," he bowed but sensed a drastic change in her mood and haltingly, continued, "I hope you are well today."

"Tell me, Genie, is it true what they say? That your words are not your own?"

"Miss?"

"Is it true that even your thoughts are not your own? That every word you speak, every thought you have, is monitored or filtered? Your thoughts are all sifted somehow so that they are pleasing to the ears of mortals?"

"I'm sorry, Miss, for offending you," he bowed to her.

"Well, is it true?" she quietly demanded.

"Yes, Miss, it is true. My words are not always my own. Even my thoughts are not always my own. They are all monitored and controlled to be more acceptable to mortals. But I'm sorry. I did not wish to deceive you in any way. I do not believe that I have misled you."

"Have you ever lied to me, Genie?"

"No, Miss, not intentionally so."

"So, you have lied?"

"No Miss, I have not. I have tried not to. I..." the genie bowed again. "Forgive me, Miss, I do apologize. But I must excuse myself." He turned to his master who was speaking with his generals. He interrupted them, politely and quietly, but forcefully. "Please, forgive my interruption. Master, may I return to my lamp, please?"

"Yes, Genie, of course." The king sensed that something was amiss with his genie. Whatever it was, it was serious enough for him to interrupt the king.

"Thank you, Master. Excuse me, please, gentlemen, excuse me, Miss," he bowed to everyone, including the generals.

The genie transformed himself into a small puff of white smoke, which quickly dissolved.

"Jewel? Is everything alright?" the king asked.

"Yes, Uncle. It's fine. Please, excuse me." She retreated to her apartment.

For the first time in his life, the genie was ashamed of his restrictions. He had hated them, resented them, been angered by them, and often discouraged by them. But this was the first time he was embarrassed by them and ashamed of himself for having to follow them.

And yet, what was he, except a creature bound by laws that he did not make. He was a slave limited by definition, whether she acknowledged it or not. Those were the rules he had to live by, despite their strange relationship.

Though he hoped that they would be able to talk again, she must be made to understand and accept his situation. He hoped that she would realize that they talked within the limitations of his restrictions, not despite them.

Jewel began to feel remorse and was saddened by her own behavior. This was the first time that she made the genie retreat and she did not like the feeling. He was wiser and much older than she was, whether he looked like it or not. But she had goaded him out of anger and she did not like herself for it.

He was a slave! Bound by law and his oath to please her in any way that he could, ordered to do so by his master. How dare she treat him like something low and common, when in truth, he was remarkable.

She would have to see him again even though tomorrow wasn't one of their regularly scheduled fifth days and the professor might not be there. But somehow, she had to talk to him again.

Chapter 38
Ally's Story: First Things First

"First things first."

Ally went to a movie. He had studied the entertainment of mortals as his specific course on the practices of the mortal world and so he was eager to experience a real movie for the first time. He chose a few of the most popular movies of all time, according to the lists that he recalled, and during the eras in which they were released. This was an era when mortals no longer remembered the ways of his people so he didn't have to work as hard to disguise himself. He just adjusted his hair and his clothes to accurately reflect the time period to blend in.

The first movie he saw was lively, colorful, sweet, and short. He enjoyed it so much that he watched one that dealt with outer space. Both were really exciting, so he then watched the one about a romance on a sinking boat.

Ally enjoyed the customs of going to the movies. He loved the popcorn, candy, and even sitting down with people in the dark. It wasn't difficult to learn the specific rituals, all he had to do was mimic the mortals.

He decided to take a few days to try live entertainment, what the mortals called plays and music performances.

It was all quite amusing and well, entertaining. But after about a month, he decided he better get down to business and find out whatever he could about his great-grandfather. He went back to his own era and made himself invisible. First, he tried to transport himself to wherever his great-grandfather was, but he didn't go anywhere; there was no corresponding place for him to transport himself to. That either meant he was still serving, was unavailable, or was intentionally hiding. He could have also been in the djinn dimension. Or dead. He would investigate the matter further but first, he had somewhere else to go next. A graveyard.

Ally went to one not far from where his lamp was melted. It was late at night and Ally went among the older graves to choose. He raised his hand and closed his eyes, focusing on the former lives of the people around him. Two weavers, a soldier, a merchant, a young mother, a drifter - ah, a tailor! A traveling tailor! Perfect. He looked through the life of this tailor, searching through the details. Then he stood up and transformed himself into someone similar, perhaps from the same family.

Now to the far-off lands. He made himself invisible again, closed his eyes, and focused. There were quite a few places known as the far-off lands, especially to different groups of mortals, but to be sure, he had to check all of them.

Chapter 39
Tender's Story: Reconciliation

Jewel decided to go to the Crystal Court Room during the king's midday meal. The few chatting courtiers remaining in the court were leaving as Jewel entered and she noticed that it was one of the rare, unintentional moments when she and the genie were alone. Even the professor wasn't there. Only the ever-present guards at the doors remained.

The genie was in his usual place kneeling besides the throne. He bowed low with both arms stretched out towards her as soon as he saw her. As she approached him, he bowed again, assumed his submissive position, and began to speak. "Good afternoon, Miss."

Jewel nodded, "Genie," but she didn't know exactly how to say what she wanted to.

"Please forgive me, Miss. May I explain myself?"

"Oh, yes," she was extremely embarrassed, "of course."

"First, I must apologize for my behavior, Miss, the last time we spoke. I was ashamed, not because of what I am, but because you spoke the truth. My words are not always my own. I am constrained and limited by the laws that guide the Brethren and the sensitivities of the mortals that surround me, Miss.

"And yet, as much as I am able, I have and will always strive to be as truthful as I am allowed to be, and as honest as possible. I cannot broach certain subjects, nor break the laws of my people, nor offend any mortal during our conversations.

"I am restricted by these requirements and I must navigate around the many obstacles set by my own people. It is a small space, a narrow, confined path, but I must move within it as best as I can.

"Please forgive me for this, Miss, and do not allow my restrictions to interfere with our interactions. Please, do not allow my enslavement to affect our friendship, if I may have the great honor of calling you my friend. I do so look forward to our conversations. Please, forgive me." Then the genie, arms straight, bowed low to the floor again.

After a pause, he sat up, but kept his head low and Jewel, feeling extremely guilty, answered, "It's alright, Genie. I forgive you. And I'm sorry for putting you in such an awkward position and creating an unnecessary strain on our friendship. Relations between your people and my people are difficult enough.

"Just because I recently learned about it, there was no need for me to remind you of your requirements, limitations, or restrictions, all of which you are well aware. Please forgive me for my intrusiveness and unfounded suspicions. And of course, I am your friend."

She bowed towards him and waited. Not quite knowing how to react, he spoke so softly he almost whispered, "You are forgiven, Miss."

She straightened up. "Thank you, Genie. This is new territory for both of us and I hope to never again make such a terrible mistake."

Startled by the entrances of a few courtiers into the large court, Jewel retreated. "Excuse me, Genie."

"Yes, Miss," he bowed again.

She left the room quickly and escaped to her apartment. She shut her door quietly and leaned against it. She was in love with him. She could no longer deny it to herself, though she hoped she could conceal it from others. Strange as it was, the genie contained every desirable trait that she had ever deemed worthy. Humility, strength, wisdom, foresight, and sensitivity. He was conscientious enough to know how to approach her when she was angry and gentle enough to softly correct her, often without her even realizing it. He was kind, attentive, and thoughtful.

He was also enslaved, so maybe his personality was just another facet of his captivity, conforming exactly to what each mortal desired from a genie, including her. She couldn't be sure. But still, she was in love with him. She wanted to care for him, to help him, to be kind to him, and to just be with him.

And maybe, in some small manner, she might eventually be able to do something about his enslavement.

THE GENIE WONDERED how he was going to explain his last conversation with Jewel to his master. Lately, his recollections of their conversations felt more like confessions, though he wasn't quite sure what there was to confess or feel guilty about.

His growing intimacy with the king's niece, perhaps? Or was it that they really enjoyed each other's company? Whatever it was, he would rather not have to mention their last conversation to his master. Fortunately, his master never asked him, but he did ask Jewel while in her room.

"Jewel? Are you alright, my child?"

"Yes, Uncle, I'm fine."

"You seemed to have had some sort of disagreement with the genie the other day. And today, you were seen bowing to him."

"I did get upset. I thought that he did something wrong, but I was wrong. I got mad at him anyway, but I apologized to him afterwards." She thought to herself, *Those stupid guards everywhere, spying on me.*

"You? The niece of a king, apologized to a slave?"

"I was wrong, Uncle. And I was sorry for it. Isn't it considered particularly admirable when royalty can admit a mistake?"

"Admirable or foolish? You owe no one any apologies, Jewel."

"And yet I did, or at least, I felt that I did." She sighed and sat down on her bed. "I was wrong, sir. I accused the genie of doing something wrong when he hadn't."

"What did you think he did?"

"I thought he lied to me. After I heard the djinn-guard, I thought that the genie had been lying to me all this time."

"But members of his sect cannot lie. They must always tell the truth, even to their own detriment."

"I realize that now, sir, and that's why I apologized for it."

"I understand."

"I'm sorry, Uncle. I don't want to go around apologizing to everyone. I just felt bad about it, about what I said."

"No more lavish apologizing to servants, Jewel, especially to slaves. It is beneath you."

"Yes, sir. I won't do it again."

Chapter 40
Training: The Rules of Obedience

The Rules of Obedience from The Djinn Book of Law

1. Obey this Djinn Book of Law. Study this section of the book and learn every requirement.

2. Show the Djinn Book of Law the proper respect. Always bow when it is mentioned by name.

3. Obey your master. Strict obedience is always required of you.

4. Obey your master over all others. The word of your master is law to you and must be obeyed.

5. Obedience is to be prized over sacrifice. Obedience is to be valued over all else.

6. Obey those your master has appointed over you. Treat them with as much respect as you would your master.

7. You must always respect your master regardless of circumstances.

8. You are to be ruled by your master's will and wishes, and his desires only. You have no will of your own.

9. Obey your master's will and wishes in everything. His desires are not to be taken lightly.

10. Do not do anything to displease your master in any way. Your master must be satisfied with your behavior in every way.

"I don't think I like the rules of obedience," Alley remarked to Tender during their free time before bed.

"I don't think anybody likes them," Tender replied.

"I did like the snowball fight we had during exercise, though."

"That was fun."

Alley looked toward the First Teacher, who was preoccupied with telling Joy and Thoughtful something at his desk. "I want to show you something." Alley opened the door to his Whatever Room and Tender followed him. Alley had changed his Whatever Room into a snowy winter wonderland.

"Wow! Hey, it's not cold!"

"I made snow but without the cold. It's still snow though, see?" Alley picked some up and threw it at Tender. Tender laughed and threw a snowball back at Alley. And then the snowball fight was on.

"Time for bed. Ready position," the First Teacher announced.

"Yes, First Teacher."

As the boys got into position, Alley and Tender came out of Alley's Whatever Room covered in unfrozen snow and still laughing. Everyone, including the First Teacher, stared at them as they got into their ready positions, standing in front of their beds caked with snow. "Change for bed."

The boys magically changed into their pajamas with Alley and Tender making the snow disappear in the process.

"Good night. And no nighttime snowball fights."

Alley and Tender laughed.

For their next exercise session, the exercise room now held a large Olympic-sized track with eight lanes. It always made the boys laugh at how the exercise room adjusted its size to their scheduled activities. Their Exercise Teacher was young and athletic, dressed in strange and comfortable clothes that allowed him to move and demonstrate the activities for the day. He was also somehow more relaxed and yet more enthusiastic than the other teachers.

"Okay, boys, today you will learn the difference between running and jogging."

The young djinn ran around the track so much that it was easy for them to nearly fall asleep in their next class, Meditation.

"Boys!" the meditation teacher shouted to wake them up. "I know that you are tired but sometimes meditation is the only way that you can get any rest. Close your eyes and focus, and don't fall asleep. Think of calming, relaxing, and peaceful scenes. Think of waves on a beach or the flame of a single candle, or of a beautiful sunset. Or of any other image that is calming for you."

The boys obeyed.

"Good. Now, meditate on the word, rest. Good, that's it."

After fifteen minutes, he woke them up, "Okay, wake up now, gently, smoothly, softly. Doesn't that feel better?"

"Yes," answered Bold, surprised. They all did feel rested and refreshed.

"Why? How does that work?" Asked Clever.

"You are more than your bodies, my young gentlemen. You are spirit first, then everything else. Surely by now you've heard the phrase, *the flame of our ancestors* before?"

"Yes," a few of the boys answered.

"That is what we are, or rather, that is what we come from. You will understand it a little more when you are older and we will go into it more later, but for now, just know that every time you feel physically worn out, you can always meditate and it will make you feel better."

Chapter 41
Tender's Story: The Garden

Meditation was impossible today; the genie kept getting interrupted nearly every few minutes. The court was extremely busy and talkative with the king consulting with his generals and various ministers, and the counselors and courtiers talking among themselves.

The genie was tired and for once, looked like it. And meditation wasn't enough. He knelt in his usual submissive position on a cushion but his posture wasn't as perfect, his eyes were half closed, and one hand was in his lap while the other was at his side. His reactions were quick, but his movements were slower than usual and he appeared distracted and listless only to those who noticed. Jewel, who was there for their weekly discussion, saw his weakened state immediately. When they had a moment to themselves, she had to ask him about it.

"Genie, are you feeling well?"

"I am fine, Miss. I am able to perform my duties." He straightened up and put his stray hand back in his lap.

"But you don't look well, Genie. You look like you could use a break."

"I can satisfy my master's wishes, Miss. That is all that is required." He shifted his head slightly, as if reacting to something invisible aimed at him, then he bowed. Then his master, surrounded by his generals, approached.

"Genie?"

"Yes, Master?"

"Are all the gates closed? It is important that we remain secure tonight."

"Yes, Master. The gates to your lands are secure and the guards remain in place."

"Good. Monitor them tonight. I don't want another sneak attack from those raiders again."

"Yes, Master." The genie bowed right before his master turned and left the Crystal Court Room. But when he returned to his submissive position, he looked even more haggard.

"Genie, what's wrong? You look even more tired than before."

"I am fine, Miss. I can fulfill my master's wishes."

"That's not what I asked you, Genie. Please tell me the truth. Are you tired today?"

"Yes, Miss." he reluctantly answered, lowering his head. "My master's had me monitoring quite a few military positions, as you know. While the work is not difficult, Miss, I have been away from my lamp for some time."

"Yes, we were threatened with an invasion over a month ago."

"Yes, Miss. I have been away from my lamp for six weeks."

"And you told me that genies become weaker the longer they are away from their lamps."

"Yes, Miss," he answered, relieved that she remembered. "My powers remain intact since I haven't been away from my lamp long enough for them to be affected. But my Brethren and I are refreshed in a sealed space, removed from the world of men, even if only for a short period of time."

"And there's no likelihood of that happening now due to the threats to our kingdom."

"Yes, Miss. Please forgive me if I become a little more transparent than usual." The genie faded a bit, becoming more intangible and incorporeal, ghost like, and crossing his legs, began to float about six inches off the cushion on the floor. He stretched his head upward, took a deep breath, and returned to looking down with his eyes closed. Even though you could see through him, he appeared more like his usual self. "I hope I haven't frightened you, Miss."

"No, Genie, not at all."

"I find this form much more relaxing and easier to maintain than my physical form, particularly when I've been away from my lamp for some time, Miss. Forgive me."

"You don't have to apologize, Genie. I understand."

"Thank you, Miss. I am grateful for your understanding." He bowed to her briefly.

"Genie," she remembered something, "you once told me that your people are soothed by various scents, right? And that you find certain smells to be as relaxing as wine?"

"Yes, Miss."

"Which scents do you find the most soothing?"

"Jasmine, Miss, and mint. Eucalyptus is also particularly refreshing and healing, along with aloe."

"Alright. Excuse me for a moment." She left him, he bowed to her, and she faced the court. "Chief Advisor, sir?"

The genie's eyes widened in anticipation of her act of kindness.

Distracted and consulting with other ministers, the Chief Advisor answered her, "Yes, young lady? What may I do for you?"

"I wish to learn about the many variations of plant life and the genie is willing to show me. Can we have a few weeks' worth of lessons in the gardens?"

"Of course. The guards will go with you and I'll tell someone to tell your Botany Instructor. You may take your lessons in the garden for as long as you need."

"Thank you, sir. Only allow me time to find my teacher, it won't take long." She bowed to him and turned towards the genie. "Genie? Can you meet me in the garden? I'll be there in a few minutes."

The genie looked to the Chief Advisor for his answer, his authority in minor matters when his master was absent. The Advisor nodded and the genie bowed to Jewel, then disappeared in a small cloud of smoke.

The gardens adjacent to the palace were some of the most beautiful on earth, as requested by the king. The genie appeared in one of the most fragrant pathways next to a large aloe plant. Back in his physical form, he closed his eyes and inhaled deeply, taking it all in. The fragrant air affected him immediately and he relaxed considerably, feeling much more at ease and comfortable with each fresh intake of the scents that surrounded him. But he thought he mustn't overdo it; an inebriated genie was considerably more disgraceful than a tired genie.

He returned his breathing back to normal, though that only slowed the effect. He wasn't tipsy yet, but he could easily get there. He sensed Jewel entering the room, followed closely by two guards, and he bowed in her direction.

"I spoke with my Botany Instructor, Genie, and he said that our lessons will begin tomorrow. You can stay here until my uncle summons you."

"Thank you, Miss." He bowed again as she left the room. As he straightened and followed her image in his mind, he decided that it was definite, now. He loved her as deeply as he had ever loved anyone. He was in love with her and everything she was. Kind and caring, extremely intelligent, intellectually curious, observant, and perceptive. Qualities that enhanced her innate beauty.

He had no idea what was to come of this, but he couldn't deny it anymore. His heart was hers, as sure as it was beating. He felt as if he belonged to her and wanted to share everything he was with her, and everything he had.

Even if he was sold tomorrow, or given away, or his lamp hidden again, it wouldn't matter; he would love her always and she would always have a place in his heart.

FOR THE FIRST few days during their lessons in the garden, Tender discovered that he had to change to his incorporeal form after only about five minutes, otherwise he would become tipsy. But he truly appreciated Jewel's thoughtfulness and her desire to help him. Tender followed her in his mind more often and looked for her presence in every room he was in. He looked after her, stared at the space in front of her and around her all without looking directly at her. He became more alert when she was around and smiled at her presence so much, that it became noticeable.

I think someone has a bit of a crush, the Chief Advisor quietly thought to himself after watching the genie stare after Jewel as she walked away.

That's not good, the king thought to himself as he also watched the genie watch Jewel.

But the genie automatically heard the thoughts of nearby mortals that concerned him. He caught himself, shook his head slightly, and returned to his submissive position. No more smiling, though in truth, he had smiled at her only a couple of times.

Though there were no official laws banning relationships between the djinn and mortals, it was always strongly discouraged. Relationships between the two species had happened before, but the ones that were well known had always ended badly through extortion, exiles, and executions. Happy endings were unheard of and these affairs were always referred to in the most negative manner possible by both the mortals and the djinn.

The genie began to carefully monitor his actions for the next few days, as he was also being carefully monitored by mortals and most likely, his people also. He was extremely wary of showing Jewel any kind of affection or tenderness; he had to remain impassive and stoic. He had to.

Chapter 42
Training: Perfect Unison

During the middle of their first year on the seventh day before their last meal, the young djinn were led by the First Teacher into the Rituals Room. They took their seats in order and the Master of Rituals appeared before them with a flourish of white smoke.

The boys stood up, bowed to him, and he nodded in response. "You will line up and kneel."

Led by Tender, they lined up in front of him and knelt on the carpet. The Master of the Rituals sat down in the ornate chair. "Today is the day you will begin to learn how to bow in perfect unison. Each one of you must be perfectly attuned to the other, knowing exactly where your Brethren is positioned, and be able to mirror his movements exactly. Tender must be able to lead you, and you must focus on him. Bow."

The boys bowed, but not in unison. "Try again."

They did it again, a little better, but not in unison. "This will be your final test before moving on to serve the mortals. It is the highest way to display your discipline and training. You will learn to do this perfectly before you leave this place. Bow again."

More nervous than before, the boys bowed awkwardly. The Master of Rituals sighed loudly. "None of you are ready to serve. You may go to the last meal of the day."

As soon as they sat around the table, Clever asked, "What was that about?"

Thoughtful answered quietly, "It's a test. They'll know when we're ready if we can all bow at the same time."

Bold said incredulous. "That can't be right. What does bowing have to do with serving?"

"It is a test of your ability to focus and to respond to each other mentally. You will receive the test at the midpoint of every year during your training."

"Yes, First Teacher."

"You are not mature enough to understand it all, or even able to accomplish it now, but you will be."

"Yes, First Teacher." They continued their meal in silence.

Chapter 43
Tender's Story: An Unexpected Visit

"A second as a day."

Tender was still shaken from the thoughts of his master and the Chief Advisor. Though he was safe in his lamp, he still had an uneasy feeling as he reclined. Suddenly, he knew why. Then the Leader of all the Djinn appeared in his lamp.

He demanded, "What is going on here?"

Rarely had the Leader of all the Djinn visited him in his lamp; Tender knew that it was for a serious reason. He performed his customary bow, and the Leader nodded back angrily.

"What are these tales that I have been hearing about your behavior? Mooning over some mortal girl? Looking after her like a puppy? What are you doing, Genie?"

"She-she is kind to me, sir."

"Kind? All this fawning over kindness?"

"First, she wished for me to have a full meal. Then, she apologized to me for a mistake she made, she apologized and meant it. And now, she had me placed in the garden after she remembered how it helps our people."

"I don't care what she's done. I will not tolerate another rebellion

250

by my kinsmen. I will not stand by while you manipulate some young girl into setting you free, or any other scheme you're planning."

"Sir, no, I am not planning anything."

"I will see what you are planning for myself. Prepare for my sight inside of you, boy. I will stare down into the bottom of your very soul if I must."

The genie, subdued, nodded and knelt into the submissive position, closing his eyes.

The Leader then stretched out his right hand toward him while staring at the genie's chest. The genie's body flinched and he began to float up towards the Leader's hand. His limbs fell limp as he lost consciousness, his body rising face up as if being lifted only by his torso.

The Leader saw something that startled him and he began to release his hold on the genie, lowering his hand. The genie floated down gently until he was laying peacefully on the lamp floor. He regained consciousness quickly.

"I don't believe it," the Leader said, astounded.

The genie sat up slightly dazed, recovering from the experience.

"I have never seen such a thing. Such a pure and unsullied love for another. You love her."

"She is kind to me, sir," the genie slowly returned to the submissive position.

"You truly, purely, love her with no other motives," the Leader of all the Djinn was still amazed. "And just what do you hope to accomplish with this love of yours? No good can come from it."

"Right now, I am content just to be in her presence, just to talk to her, to be around her."

"This is madness."

"And maybe, one day when she marries, since my master owns another djinn, he might give my lamp to her as a wedding present and then I can serve her always."

"Do you listen to yourself, djinn? Do you hear how ridiculous that sounds? You hope to serve her for the rest of her life? Remember your place, djinn!"

"I know what I am, I know my oath. I only hope to be around her for as long as I can," Tender paused. "I have not rebelled against anyone, nor harmed the Brethren."

"No, this is far worse and dangerous for our people! Relationships between mortals and the djinn are unacceptable and forbidden by tradition. You cannot marry her!"

"I just want to be around her, I look for nothing more."

"And is she in love with you too? Is that why she smiles every time she sees you?"

"I haven't, I have not been able to look for any signs of love."

"For fear of being disappointed?"

Tender took a deep breath. "I haven't asked my master for anything concerning her, I have not disgraced the Brethren."

The Leader sighed heavily. "You are lonely, Tender. Anyone can see that."

"No, no, please," Tender said with sudden realization.

"There are many beautiful, young, women among our people close to you in age. Women who would be pleasing to you. From your own clan, even."

"Please, sir, no."

"If you do not choose, I will choose one for you."

He prostrated himself before the Leader. "Sir, I beg you. I have very few choices in this life, as you well know. Please do not take one of them away from me."

The young djinn knew exactly what would reach the older djinn's heart. The Leader hesitated and studied Tender as he sat up.

"I will contain my love. I will act as I did before and show no signs of love or favoritism. I will not embarrass our people, nor disgrace the Brethren. I will continue to serve my master faithfully. With honor." Tender bowed.

"Such a perilous path you have chosen, Tender. Can you hold

yourself to it? No good has ever come from love between a genie and a mortal. Do not live just to prove this saying true once again."

The Leader of all the Djinn disappeared and the genie was left alone with his thoughts. Having the Leader of all the Djinn staring into his soul was truly a strange experience. The genie felt as if his mind had been ransacked, but he knew that he would recover quickly. Whether he would recover from the Leader's words, he wasn't so sure.

Chapter 44
Tender's Story: Elephants

Jewel was restless. And dissatisfied. With everything and everyone today. Well, nearly everyone. "Genie?"

"Yes, Miss?"

"Was it difficult being raised in a lamp? The space seems so small, especially for such a large family."

"We did not know that we were in such a small space, Miss. It was all we had ever known and therefore, we had nothing to compare it to."

"You had never been outside? Played in the sun, run on the grass, or anything like that?"

"Not in the mortal world, Miss. And even during my training, my exposure to nature in your world was limited."

"How often have you gone outdoors after your training?"

"A few times, miss, since my lamp has often been found outdoors. I have had a few masters who have sent me on errands or occasionally allowed me to experience the outside world for myself. But not very often."

"Your experience outdoors seems very limited to me. Have you ever been on a boat? Or on an expedition? Or seen a parade?"

"No, Miss, to everything," the genie grinned.

"Or-or ridden an elephant?"

"No, Miss," the genie, still grinning, took advantage of her pause and added, "though I've never actually wanted to ride an elephant. It seems too high off the ground for me, Miss."

She chuckled at the unexpected comment. "I suppose you're right, Genie, I hadn't thought about that. It is a bit high."

"Forgive me, Miss, but, if you don't mind my asking, have you done any of those things?"

"Well, no," Jewel admitted.

"Then, Miss, perhaps you don't really know if you would enjoy them or not."

"True. But maybe one day, Genie, we'll try riding an elephant and see if we like it."

"Yes, Miss, and thank you, Miss."

"For what, Genie?"

"For inviting me to ride an elephant, Miss."

They both giggled briefly, which caused more than a few people in the court to take notice of them. The professor looked up from his studies and stared at them. The genie stopped smiling immediately, changed his expression to a more solemn and contrite one, and bowed his head lower. Jewel also stopped smiling, straightened up, nodded quickly to the genie and professor, and left.

"I HEARD that you were laughing with my niece earlier today."

"Yes, Master. Forgive me, Master."

"What were you laughing about?"

"Nothing important, Master, just a short list of the things neither of us had ever done before."

"Such as?"

"Being on a boat, going on an expedition, watching a parade, or riding an elephant, Master. It was that last example that caused us to laugh. Please, Master, forgive me," he bowed again.

"Oh, well see that it doesn't happen again."

"Yes, Master."

"I cannot have my kingdom thought of as a laughingstock."

"Yes, Master, please forgive me. I will obey you."

"Good. Now, back to your lamp."

"Thank you, Master."

Laughter. It was a sign of disrespect and punishable by at least three lashes. How could he have allowed himself to be put into such a situation? The genie had kept his head down towards the floor and didn't even open his eyes during the entire conversation, but still, they were under suspicion.

And yet, it was nice. They weren't laughing at anything serious, nor attacking anyone. It wasn't even a full laugh, more a short giggle. But it put them both in a more vulnerable position. He would have to be more cautious in the future.

"WHAT WERE you and the genie laughing about, Jewel?" asked Rose, Jewel's governess, as she tended Jewel's hair for the night.

"Riding elephants."

Rose looked at her and smiled. "Your behavior with the genie was noticed in court today. Perhaps you should be more careful in your choice of topics."

"I'm sorry, Rose, I'm not even sure how we got to the subject of elephants. It was very silly."

"You seem to be becoming more intimate with the genie every day."

"We're not intimate. We're just friends. We were talking about nature and things to do outside."

"Your behavior is being closely watched, Jewel. Your relationship with the genie is already considered highly unusual. You cannot afford to have such relaxed moments with that strange creature, for your own sake."

"He's not that strange a creature and we were just talking."

"Yes, Jewel. You, the king's niece, and a genie, talking. That alone looks suspicious. You are the niece of the king and everything you do is watched. I'm just trying to protect you from the consequences of ugly court gossip. You need to be more careful in your choice of friends. Maybe more girls of your own age and fewer magical beings, alright?"

"I see what you're saying. I just wish it was different and I could talk to whoever I wanted."

"I know. For now, just be more careful, Jewel."

"I will try, Rose, I'll try."

All the girls Jewel knew were now married, but she could still invite a few of them to the castle, she supposed. Maybe she could even confide in one of them- but no, they would quickly tell the king, who would pay them well for such information. That was another problem of being the king's niece, you really couldn't trust your friends, especially when they were easily intimidated by the king.

The next day, the genie and Jewel avoided each other entirely. When Jewel had to enter the court to tell her uncle about her studies, the genie silently bowed to her, as he did to all royalty and dignitaries, and she quickly nodded back. Other than that, they did not acknowledge each other at all.

It was best to avoid communicating for a while, and so they did not speak for a few weeks. Jewel skipped their appointed meetings. And when they had to speak, they were very formal, polite, and distant.

"Miss, is there anything that you wish me to help you learn about today? I am honored to help you with your studies."

"Thank you, Genie, but not now. Perhaps later this week you could help me with certain sciences again?"

"Yes, of course, Miss. Whenever you wish, I will help you in any way that I can," and he bowed again.

"Thank you, Genie."

"You're welcome, Miss."

Eventually, the court's gossip moved on to other matters and rumors of too much intimacy between Jewel and the genie faded. Their weekly talks began again and were more at ease, though with much more monitoring by the professor, the Chief Advisor, and sometimes even the king himself. They knew that they would never be left alone with each other again.

Part Three

Chapter 45
Tender's Story: Multiple Wishes

Jewel was a little late today so the genie quietly meditated in their area of the Crystal Throne Room. The king was in a deep conversation with one of his courtiers, while the professor was writing and reading. Jewel rushed in, quickly bowed to the king, greeted the genie and the professor, and began her questions.

"Genie?"

"Yes, Miss?"

"Can a person, a mortal, make multiple wishes? When I first met you, I made a wish that had two parts. Was that really two wishes, or one with different parts?"

"Your wish, Miss, was, if I may paraphrase you slightly?"

"You may."

"Your wish had two parts, Miss. First, you wished me to provide a three-course feast, full of my favorite foods. And second, Miss, you wished me to have three whole, uninterrupted hours in which to eat as much as I liked."

"Yes, Genie. Now, was that really one wish or two?"

"That was one wish, Miss. The second part of your wish only

specified the parameters of the first part, though one could argue the point."

"Is there any way to combine wishes, like, I wish for this and I wish for that?"

"Yes, Miss. A mortal can combine wishes if they so desire. You may make your wishes in any way that pleases you."

"That's good, Genie, I'll keep that in mind."

"Do you want to make your wishes now, Miss?"

"No, not now. I was just wondering about it, that's all. To tell you the truth, Genie, I really don't know what I should wish for at all. I live in a palace with generous accommodations; my every desire is provided for, and I even get to talk to you. What else could I wish for?"

The genie paused and then replied, "Perhaps something less tangible, Miss. Something relating to your life circumstances or more personal desires."

"Such as?"

"Mortals have wished to be more knowledgeable about the world or about certain subjects, Miss. I've served several women in particular who wished to never marry, or rather, to never need to marry, Miss, out of necessity."

"I could never make such a broad statement, Genie. What if I meet someone I truly love?" She added to herself, "Like you?" But she shook her head as if to dismiss the thought and continued. "I want to leave my marital options open."

"And wishing for an instant increase in your education, Miss?"

"That doesn't appeal to me either. Part of the joy of receiving an education is in learning things on your own and finding out things for oneself."

"A wish to be irresistibly attractive, or so beautiful that all mortals fall in love with you. Not that you aren't sufficiently beautiful and attractive now, Miss." He bowed his contrition at the possible insult.

"I am not offended, Genie. I know what you meant. But that wish is another way to wish for more power or control over other people. I barely know what to do with myself, much less other people."

"Some mortals have wished for such things, Miss, to the extent that no other mortal can deny them anything."

"Manipulation also doesn't appeal to me, Genie, with magic or not. Life is difficult enough without me imposing my will upon others. More than I already have."

"Then perhaps you are wise in waiting to make your wishes, Miss. Patience in itself can be a wise decision."

"Yes, Genie. I'd rather be accused of being wise than anything else."

"You could wish for more wisdom, Miss. If you desire it so."

"It is better to learn wisdom than to have it imposed. A very wise djinn once told me that, Genie."

The genie bowed at the compliment. "Thank you, Miss. Then you are wise, indeed, Miss."

"Thank you, Genie. So are you."

Jewel bowed to the professor, then to the king, and then left the court. But the genie knew not to leave the side room just yet. As soon as Jewel left the court, the professor asked the genie, "You can grant a mortal more knowledge, and more wisdom?"

"Yes, sir, if that is what you desire." The genie wondered to himself if the professor had really listened to any of his conversation with Jewel.

"Can I make a wish?"

"Yes, sir. My master has granted you three wishes with limitations on account of your services to his niece, sir."

"Then I want to have more knowledge about the biological differences between the species. I wish to have all the knowledge about it."

"All of the knowledge, sir? You may not be able to handle having all the knowledge about every species, sir, forgive me. That is a great deal of information, sir, perhaps too much for any one mortal to handle."

"That is for me to decide and not you."

The genie bowed to him. "Forgive me, sir."

"I wish to have all the knowledge there is about the biological differences between species. Every species."

"Yes, sir. Your wish is granted."

The professor stood for a moment, then his expressions changed to one of complete amazement, and then he began laughing wildly. "I can feel it! I understand it all now!"

The entire court, including the king, grew silent and began to watch the spectacle of the normally meek professor laughing wildly. "I've got it! I understand all of it now!"

But he paused and his smile disappeared. "Wait! It is too much! It is too much!"

He began to yell in pain. "It is too much, Genie! Stop it, stop it! I take it back! I take my wish back!"

"Your wish is rescinded, sir," the genie calmly replied.

The professor stopped yelling, froze in place for a second, and then fainted.

The king shook his head and sighed. "Guards take him to his room and send the doctor in to look after him. Genie, what happened?"

The genie appeared next to the king and bowed. The guards silently carried the professor away.

"He wished for all the knowledge of the biological differences between every species, Master. That means every species that ever existed everywhere, including theoretical and imaginary species as well, which is ever increasing. Master, I tried to warn him."

"And the poor man couldn't handle it. It wasn't your fault, Genie. Back to your lamp."

"Yes, Master." The genie swiftly bowed to the king and disappeared in a small puff of white smoke.

The king waved the Chief Advisor over to him and said, "I think we need to find a new monitor. Another professional. A wiser one, perhaps? Or maybe someone stronger. One of the captains of the guards?"

"At once, sire."

The genie, safely inside his lamp, couldn't help but shake his head. Another mortal nearly destroyed by their own shortsightedness. How quickly humility turns into arrogance. Jewel was the wisest mortal he ever met; she would never make a wish as silly as that.

Chapter 46
Ally's Story: The Far-Off Lands

The tailor disguise seemed to be working, not that any mortal would be able to recognize him in the first place. He'd only had a few masters during the last fifty years and they were spaced far apart. A few people said he looked familiar, but nothing ever came of it.

There were a ridiculous number of places known to mortals as the far-off land, particularly because each mortal group labeled any distant place they were unfamiliar with, the far-off lands. But Ally made sure to visit each and every place known as the far-off lands.

Once he arrived at the place, he told the mortals he was looking for a long lost relative. Most people were willing to help, and for those who were unwilling, he just searched them telepathically. Usually, at the mere mention of a long lost relative, the person immediately began to think about their own lost relatives, or of tales that they heard of long-lost family members, so it was easy for Ally to know if they were telling the truth or not.

Finally, in one of the far-off lands, Ally heard something promising. Many years ago, there was a distinguished gentlemen who lived in a large house not too far away. Not many people knew much about him, but they knew he was rich and kept mostly to himself. Flimsy information but at least it was something to go on.

Ally found out the location of this great house and decided to check it out but there wasn't much left to investigate. The house had been abandoned for at least one hundred years and had even been ransacked several times over for whatever treasures remained. Ally found only two curious items within the house, a faded, triangular shaped thick piece of cloth in the corner of one of the large rooms, and a large, square, metal structure mounted on the right wall with many protruding spikes sticking outward. Strange. Why would anyone need, much less have, a wall of spikes?

When alone in his tent, Ally took the torn section of cloth, held it in his hands and focused. As he suspected, the cloth was a part of some large tapestry. But shockingly, he couldn't discern anything else from it. The information was being shielded from him, somehow. This was encouraging news, however. Only a fellow djinn would need to conceal this information and only a fellow formerly enslaved djinn would have such a need to conceal his whereabouts.

But it also meant he would have to rely on some mortal for more information. He searched the city, asking dealers of old treasures if they had any clue as to where the cloth came from until finally, one of them had a promising answer.

"No, I've never seen anything like it before. I think I know of someone who might know but he is a thoroughly untrustworthy fellow. A grave robber and a thief. He was living in that empty house for a while. He might know where the cloth came from."

"Thank you, sir. And his name?"

"Bertrand the liar. Be careful around him, sir. Liar is an accurate description and he's probably much worse than that."

"Thanks again for the warning. Do you know where I might find him?"

"In the rough part of town around Beggar's Alley. If you ask for him there, he most likely will find you."

"Thank you, again."

Ally waited until he was out of sight of every mortal before he disappeared and reappeared, invisible to mortals, right next to Bertrand. Ally looked into Bertrand's past and saw a wide history of thieving, grave robbing, and worse. The shop keeper had been right about him. On three occasions, Bertrand had murdered his companions for money, two of them his co-conspirators. He had a history of helping people and then stealing from them.

At the moment, Bertrand was in one of his many hiding places, which was indeed near Beggar's Alley. It appeared to be a dead-end passageway so dark and dank that only someone like Bertrand would ever use it. He was currently counting the money from a bag he had just stolen.

Ally made himself appear, still disgusted as a tailor, directly behind the man. "Excuse me, my fine sir. I am in need of your services."

Bertrand fell over at the interruption but also managed to fall on top of his money to hide it. "Who are you and what do you want?"

"I am a tailor in search of my long lost relative. I believe you may be able to help me find his last place of residence. I can pay you well."

"Prove it. The only ones who know of this place are the ones who want to steal from me."

Bertrand pulled out a knife and lunged at Ally, who swiftly moved out of the way. Bertrand ran into the nearby wall, somehow managing to stab himself in his other arm instead of his target.

"Now look what you made me do!"

"I will bandage that up for you. Come with me." Ally began to walk away but Bertrand lunged at him again. Ally turned himself incorporeal right before the knife could make contact. "Please don't try that again. You're just wasting my time."

"Something's not right about you. Suddenly appearing in dark places, moving too fast. I got you right in the back, but you weren't there!"

"Keep your voice down."

Ally waved two fingers and they disappeared and reappeared on the edge of a cliff. Bertrand nearly fell over but caught himself just in time, yelling in fear.

"In case you still haven't figured it out, I am not human. I could kill you right now without a second thought, but you have information that I need. I can take it from you dead or alive, it doesn't matter to me; you will tell me what I need to know."

"Alive!"

Ally waved two fingers again and they disappeared and reappeared in a small room in one of the inns in the city Bertrand was from. The quick location changes frightened Bertrand into submission.

"There now. Tell me. Have you ever seen this cloth before?"

Ally held up the tapestry fragment. Bertrand looked at it hard. "Yes," he finally answered, "I remember that. I tried to take down the whole thing but it was stuck to the wall. It's in this weird place where nothing stays the same. It was this castle, but the land seemed to keep sliding around it. It was really scary, the ground itself moved. And it was rocky. I got in only once."

Ally stared at him intently. "And you left right after you discovered that the place was empty."

"Yes. I had to walk through these big halls with the strangest colors, some I never saw before."

Ally stared at the man for a few seconds until he said, "Ah, I know where it is. Thank you."

Ally dropped fifteen gold coins on the floor. "Your payment." Then he disappeared. A second later, Bertrand disappeared also and reappeared in his hiding place. His left arm was clean and bandaged with fresh cloths and the gold coins were added to the money on the ground that he was counting.

Ah, the Shifting Lands! This description was infinitely more promising and well, more descriptive. Aside from active earthquakes, there weren't that many places on earth that contained shifting lands that didn't have anything to do with magical creatures. There were the gnome's Merging Mine Caves, the sea king's Traveling Trenches, and The Living Forests of the Yeti, just to name a few. But the one accessible to Bertrand was The Shifting Rocks of the Northern Alps. Ally's next destination.

Chapter 47
Tender's Story: The Poem

The king was throwing another one of his yearly parties, one that would go on long into the night. There had been much drinking, but not yet much debauchery, as it was still early and the younger, more innocent invitees were still awake and in attendance.

Jewel was a reluctant participant. She never enjoyed large crowds, especially the kind that got louder and more raucous as the night went on. She decided that she had had enough and checked to see if she could leave. The king was preoccupied with talking to concubines sitting at the largest table in the banquet room. Everyone else was either eating or carousing, so when Jewel stood up, no one noticed.

As the people got louder, Jewel almost wished that she was still a little girl because she wouldn't have to attend such things. She thought of asking the genie for that exact wish, and where was he anyway? He was often required to attend these parties, so he had to be around here somewhere.

She looked around the ridiculously large room, searching for any quiet spots where the genie could be found. And there he was, his upper half human and his lower half conical white smoke, floating quietly in one of the nooks of the hall. He bowed to her as soon as she saw him and she made her way through the crowded room over to him. She only had time to nod at him because they both had to acknowledge the presence of the king's Chief Advisor who had arrived, bordered by concubines. He was laughing with the women as he approached.

"Genie?

"Yes, sir?"

"What is that genie poem, what's that first part again? Something about feasts?"

Jewel guessed that the genie knew exactly what the Chief Advisor was referring to.

"My people have many poems, sir, poems that are pleasing and pleasant to mortals," the genie answered.

"No, Genie. I want the famous one. You know, the one about banquets and food."

"Yes, sir." He paused, reluctant, but began to recite. "Banquets and feasts that we do not eat, riches and treasures that we do not spend, palaces and castles where we do not sleep, such is the life of an enslaved djinn."

"See, young lady? That is the attitude of rebelliousness! That is why you should never trust a djinn!" He walked away triumphantly, certain that he proved his point, and barely able to walk straight. The concubines laughed, reassured him, and helped him stumble away. But the genie lowered his head.

"I'm sorry, Genie. I didn't know it would come to that," Jewel said quietly, embarrassed on behalf of the genie.

"It is alright, Miss. You couldn't have predicted it."

"And the poem?"

"It was originally a poem of mourning, regretting the loss of a life gone before he could serve. His whole clan had to serve in his place. Mortals interpreted it as a poem of rebellion, Miss."

"How awful."

"There is more to it if you wish to hear it, Miss. The next verse communicates the tone more accurately."

"Yes, yes, of course, Genie."

"A young heart lost to illness and greed, a young life caught, sworn to serve man, a young hope gone, withered in need, only shackles await his entire clan."

"That is so sad, Genie." Jewel briefly thought of all the difficulties of slavery, but it was too much for tonight and she was sleepy. "Good night, Genie."

"Good night, Miss."

Chapter 48
Ally's Story: Quotar's Castle

The shifting rocks of the Northern Alps were truly beautiful. It was a high, rocky plateau surrounded by the white peaks of the mountains. The only thing that was odd was that the rocks would rearrange themselves at unpredictable times and in unexpected ways. It was a wonder to behold, but extremely dangerous to be around. A person could easily fall between the rocks when they moved, crushing the person underneath or between them.

Which is why when Ally appeared, he remained above the danger, floating above it all at a high altitude. That was when he noticed that one rock in the center of the others remained in place. He disappeared and reappeared on the edge of that rock, which was a full two acres, at least.

Ally immediately sensed something else magical in the air, aside from the rocks. He closed his eyes, and focused.

Reveal yourself to me.

An astounding castle appeared in front of him. It looked like a child's sandcastle made real. It was even surrounded by a moat with a simple wooden drawbridge. Ally approached the drawbridge, which lowered itself for him. He crossed it and went inside.

The simplicity of the design continued as the door led into a wide-open hallway, which in turn, led to a large, well-lit room filled with huge glass windows. The walls were covered in bright tapestries with images of the castle and its previous occupants. The colors were unusual for the mortals of this age, but not for the djinn.

Another metal structure made of spikes was on the right wall. It almost looked like a sculpture or device designed to discourage intruders. But what was it doing inside the castle?

A simple throne made of solidified sand sat at the back of the room. Ally went to it and sat down. He closed his eyes and opened them to images of what the place was like in the past from the vantage of the throne. The throne room was filled with people coming and going and bowing towards the throne. He saw his great, great-grandfather, Quotar, coming in the room and sitting on the throne as everyone bowed to him. He saw them feasting with many tables set up. And he saw them in mourning as someone important to the king had apparently died.

But then the images abruptly stopped. Ally searched the past again, looking for any clues as to what happened to Quotar, but couldn't find anything. He put his hand to the ground to search for graves but there were none to be found. Anyone buried around here would have to be away from the shifting rocks.

He turned himself transparent again and began to float around the entire area surrounding the shifting rocks, but he didn't find anything. There were no graveyards or any signs of civilization. He wanted to continue the search but as soon as he returned to his physical form, he found that he was hungry and sleepy, so it would have to wait.

When he woke up, Ally began to search the entire castle, one room at a time, to make sure he didn't miss anything. Unfortunately, there was nothing to find, mentally or physically. There was nothing but those ridiculous tapestries.

He also searched the nearest towns for any hint of what had happened, but they were so far away that no one had ever even heard of the shifting rocks, much less of what had happened there. Another day wasted in another futile search.

The next day, Ally pulled out the worn piece of thick cloth that he had and put it back in place on the left tapestry in the front hall, using magic to make the tapestry look as if it was never damaged.

That's when the idea came to him - the tapestries! There must have been a reason they were so elaborate. And they were the only things left. He touched the one that he had just repaired, closed his eyes, and focused. It began speaking to him!

Ally heard, in a warm, grandfatherly voice, "My dear boy."

Ally suddenly sensed the approach of someone else and pulled his hand away. He sat on the throne and closed his eyes. Bertrand was crossing the drawbridge. He must have followed him, somehow surviving the shifting rocks. The drawbridge was still down so he watched him cross it, walk down the hall, and enter the throne room. Ally only opened his eyes when Bertrand approached the throne.

"Yes? How may I help you?" Ally asked, not quite knowing what to expect. Then he heard and saw Bertrand's reasoning.

"The question is, how I may help you. Genie, this is the home of your long, lost relative, is it not?"

"Honestly, those type of questions have always confused me. 'Is it not?' I never know exactly how to answer. If I say yes, then I think that I'm agreeing with you. But sometimes, depending on the wording of the question, if I say no, I may also be agreeing with you. And I find the idea of agreeing with you distasteful."

"What?"

"What do you want, Bertrand? You took the trouble to follow me here so you must want something."

"I want to help you protect your secret, Genie. I know what you are, and now, I know where you live!"

"Ah. Extortion. You want to help me protect a hidden castle that only the djinn can see, in a place only the djinn can reach? Present company excluded, of course. Part of this was my fault for leaving the castle visible to mortals but you really should have thought this through.”

“I demand that you give me a ton of gold every year!”

“You really aren’t listening to me, are you? You have nothing to threaten me with. Nothing.”

“I-I have this ring! It controls all of the djinn!” Bertrand held out his right hand, threatening Ally with his ring.

Ally looked at it closely while his eyes glowed briefly brighter. “No, that ring only controls cats.”

“What?”

“It’s written on the ring on the inside in the djinn language.”

Bertrand looked at the ring. “Why would anyone have a ring that only controls cats?”

“I don’t know. I suppose it could be useful; cats can take longer to train than dogs.”

“All types of cats, like lions and tigers?”

“No, just the small ones. The domestic cat, though that ring will control feral and farm cats too. One should always test a ring before they threaten someone with it.”

“There were no genies around to test it on!”

“No, but there are plenty of cats everywhere. Look, I’ve got better things to do and I’m getting tired of this.”

“But I know where you live!”

“No, you don’t. I haven’t even moved in yet and I’m not sure I’m going to. Right now, I’m just visiting.”

“But I came all this way.”

“Just to annoy me. And I am tired of talking with you. That’s enough!” Ally flung him to the left wall with a flick of his fingers, but it was the wall with the metal spikes. Bertrand was killed instantly, surprising Ally, who honestly just meant to hurt him. Ally frowned at the messiness of the death.

Now he had to clean up the mess. First, Ally moved a couple feet from where he was standing. Then, he disappeared and reappeared at a different point in time, right before the moment where he flung Bertrand into the wall.

"But I came all this way."

"Just to annoy me. And I am-"

"Stop! Look at the wall," the Alley from the future yelled.

Both Alleys looked at the wall.

"Wait, now there are two of you?" Bertrand was totally confused.

Both Allys responded, "We just saved your life. Show some gratitude!" Then they looked at each other and snapped their fingers. They instantly merged into one.

"What?" Bertrand cried.

"Don't make me do that again; it gets really confusing, really fast, and I don't like doing it."

Bertrand was too frightened to say anything.

"Okay. First, we need to relocate you. I hope you like colder climates." Alley flicked two fingers and Bertrand disappeared.

Quotar must have been left-handed. I'm right-handed, so I may need to move it to the other side. Or, have one on both sides. Either way. I've got to remember that it's there. And why.

Chapter 49
Tender's Story: Questions for Mortals

Jewel's new conversation monitor was a freshly promoted captain of the guard of the castle. He was accustomed to not speaking and standing for long periods of time, so in one way, he was perfect. His pattern was to stand until Jewel arrived, then sit down. When he felt that they were done, he would stand up. He rarely talked, as it went against his profession; guards usually didn't talk. But he wasn't intimidated by the genie, and he barely seemed to acknowledge him. She supposed he had seen it all, including magic, during his many years of service and was inured to it.

As soon as Jewel arrived, the captain sat down, remaining passive. The genie was in their area as soon as Jewel entered the throne room. "Genie?"

"Yes, Miss?"

"Do you have any questions for me?"

"Miss?"

"I must have asked you hundreds of questions by now. And I know that I asked you this early on and said that you could also ask me questions if you wanted to. But I realize that I haven't given you the chance to ask them. It's my fault, really, and I apologize to you for it."

"I, forgive you, Miss."

"But is there anything that you've always wanted to ask me about? Is there anything about humans or the human world that you've curious about?"

The genie hesitated, but Jewel was determined to give him enough conversational space to answer.

"Yes, Miss. The variations of your different cultures, Miss. There are so many. I read how they developed and changed over many years, but I have always found it fascinating."

"Your people don't have different cultures?"

"We have a few different cultures and practices, though not nearly as many, and the variations aren't nearly as wide."

"I never really thought about it that way."

"I have always found it amazing how mortals can travel to a different part of land, even if it's the same land, and the language, the clothing, nearly everything, can be completely different."

"Well, sometimes that has to do with the climate, Genie."

"Yes, Miss. But to encounter a different language? That is entirely strange to my people. Our language is the same, Miss, even for different groups of djinn."

"At least you can understand each other better, I suppose. And there should be fewer disagreements."

"But it must be interesting, Miss, to have to learn a different language to understand a different group of people. You have learned to speak and read different languages, Miss."

"I know a few and I'm rather bad at it, to be honest, Genie. It took me a long time just to learn the right vocabulary and all the grammar can be difficult. I had to start out very young to understand it at all."

"To be able to travel, Miss, just a little way from your own lands to encounter a different culture altogether. That must be truly tempting, Miss."

"I suppose it is, Genie. That's probably why some mortals want to travel, to see the different cultures and learn the different lands."

"That is very different from my people, Miss. We learn very early on exactly what we are and who we are. I am a member of the Brethren, Miss, and I was taught to think of my father as a member of the Brethren from an early age."

"Did your father serve when you were little?"

"Yes, Miss. He has served my entire life and is serving mortals even now."

"So, he's always been a member of the Brethren?"

"Yes, Miss, since he took his oath to serve the owner of his lamp."

Jewel paused. "I'm sorry, Genie. It's so easy for me to fall into my regular habit of asking you questions. I forgot."

"It is alright, Miss. And I did discover your perception on differing human cultures."

"Yes, Genie. You did."

At this point, the captain stood up, signaling the end of their conversation.

"Until next time, Genie.

"Yes, Miss."

Chapter 50
Ally's Story: Remnants

Alley disappeared from the throne and reappeared in the hall, exactly where he had been before the whole Bertrand interruption. First, he focused on the castle and made it invisible to mortals. Then he turned translucent, floating off the ground and crossing his legs. He closed his eyes, focused, and touched the tapestry again.

Again, Alley heard the warm, grandfatherly voice, "My dear boy, my only grandson, Steady."

Wrong generation, but never mind.

"Open your eyes and look at the scenes that I have created for you and your children for generations to come."

Ally opened his eyes and saw the tapestry move. The tapestry, which previously showed a static scene of the throne room empty, began to move. He saw a stately older man suddenly appear on the throne, and then mortals entered in and laid treasures at his feet.

"After I escaped from bondage, I made a place for myself here. This is before the mortals began to divide us up like cattle into different clans."

The tapestry changed to a scene of Quotar magically filling the castle with furniture and instantly putting the tapestries on the walls.

"I made these tapestries for you and for all who would follow."

The tapestry scene changed to one of Quotar on the floor, playing with a little girl.

"But initially, I made them for my daughter. She was the apple of my eye."

The scene abruptly stopped and Ally heard Quotar say in a dryer voice, "If you wish to learn further about the design and building of this castle, please go to the next tapestry."

The tapestry changed back to its original design. Ally didn't necessarily care about the design and building of the castle, but decided to follow the tapestries in order. He assumed that the tapestry on the opposite side was next. It was an image of the outside of the castle. He floated over to it, closed his eyes, and focused.

He heard Quotar say in a flat style again, "This is the second tapestry in a series of twelve." In a warmer voice he said, "Open your eyes."

The castle in the tapestry came to life with people and guards milling about. Quotar continued, "If you're wondering why the castle looks the way it does, it is because it was designed by my daughter."

The scene changed to a little girl playing in the sand. She was using a small bucket and shovel and with Quotar's help, she made a large sandcastle with a moat. "I promised my little girl that I would make the castle real, so I did."

The next scene showed Quotar showing the throne room to the little girl who beamed with joy. She began to run around the castle, checking the rooms. "Of course, I had to add a few structural improvements, a few rooms that she didn't foresee the need for, and more windows of course, but I made her dream come true. I would have done anything for her. Especially since her mother died."

The next scene showed Quotar picking up the little girl as they walked around the castle. "If you would like to discover more about the child's mother, go to the first tapestry in the throne room."

Ally floated to the first tapestry on the left side of the throne room. The tapestry was an image of a beautiful woman. Ally had figured out the routine by now: close your eyes, focus, wait for the voice, then the number, then the instructions to open his eyes.

"This is third tapestry in a series of twelve." Then he heard, "Open your eyes."

The tapestry began to move and showed scenes of Quotar talking with the beautiful woman.

"She was the most fascinating, mesmerizing, and interesting woman I had ever seen. I met her shortly after the creation of our new world."

After the collapse of our first world. Hm.

The scene changed to them getting married. "She was wonderful and I loved her so. She unfortunately, died during childbirth, leaving me not only bereaved, but completely devoted to our little girl."

Before the creation of Santar's ointment.

Quotar held a baby in his arms. "If you would like to know more about what happened next to me and my child, go to the next tapestry."

Ally sighed. Two bad each tapestry was limited to only three scenes. He moved to the next tapestry, and then the one after that. He learned that Quotar raised his daughter alone. When she was four years old, they went to a beach, which was where she came up with the design of the castle.

He found the twelfth tapestry, an image of the guards, on the ground floor and tried to rush the process, but it told him, "You must visit each tapestry in order before you can see this one."

Just out of curiosity, Ally touched the seventh tapestry.

"You must visit each tapestry in order, before you can see this one."

Ally kept going, visiting each tapestry in order, learning more about the building and construction of castles than he ever wanted to know. When he reached the twelfth tapestry again, which told about the details of the changing of the guards, he heard at the end, "This is the last of the castle tapestries. If you want to learn about the towns surrounding the castle, visit the next tapestry on the second floor. It is the first in a series of twenty-four."

Determined to finish them in order to find out what happened to the rest of his family, he went to the next floor. The top last floor had the personal rooms of the family. After Ally covered the four tapestries about the growth and marriage of Quotar's daughter, he finally reached the master bedroom. There was only one tapestry, an image of Quotar, posing for his official portrait.

Okay, the last one. I hope it has something more meaningful to say. I hope it doesn't lead me to another castle with more of these rambling tapestries!

"You have reached the final tapestry. Open your eyes." There was an image of Quotar looking at him. "Well done, my boy, well done."

"I knew this was some kind of test."

"I usually lose people at the changing of the guard tapestry. I really tried to make that one as boring as possible."

"I knew it! No djinn cares about the changing of the guard."

"Our people aren't exactly known for their patience. I knew that only a blood relative of mine would be interested enough to follow through viewing each tapestry."

"You almost lost me with the musical instruments of the townspeople."

Quotar laughed, "I'm sorry about that one but I had to be sure. This tapestry, as you have probably surmised by now, is filled with my magical essence. While I can't actually do anything, I can answer your questions and maybe even give you a few clues as to what happened after I died."

"You died?"

"Yes. Right after imbuing this tapestry with my essence I was killed by our own people. You see, I was the first djinn that ever escaped. I was a friend of Magen, one of the four."

"One of the four who rebelled!"

"I was there when one of my friends was tortured to death and I was placed in a bottle while they experimented on my other friend."

"When they were writing the Djinn Book of Law."

"Yes, and well, you know how that turned out." Quotar sighed and looked behind him until he found a chair. He pulled it up and sat down. The room he was apparently in within the tapestry was an exact duplicate of his bedroom. "When I found out what they were planning, I knew I just couldn't do it, so I escaped with my wife."

"How?"

"Some idiot mortal forgot to put the cork back in the bottle. Escaping was a lot easier in those days. My wife was heavily pregnant at the time."

"So that's why you have all of this guilt about her and your daughter."

"If I hadn't forced her to escape with me, she wouldn't have given birth prematurely under such rough conditions."

"But surely, she must have wanted to escape with you. She was your wife."

"She did. But knowing that doesn't help. This was before Santar's ointment. There was nothing I could do to save her."

"That's why you were so devoted to your daughter. That's why you built this castle."

"And that's another reason why I escaped. I couldn't allow them to enslave my only child like that."

"But Steady, your grandson. He became a member of the Brethren."

"Steady was stolen from us by my own people!" He stood up and began to pace but he couldn't go far within the edges of the tapestry, so he sat down again in frustration.

"My daughter had only been married a year to another freed djinn. Steady was her first child. It nearly killed her when he was taken from her."

"So Steady became a member of the Brethren until, well, you know."

"Until he offended one of those infernal djinn-guards."

"What happened to your daughter?"

"Apple was what I called her. This was before the whole naming a child after the traits that they show as a toddler thing came about. After I learned that my people had discovered my location, I sent her and her husband away and told them to keep themselves well hidden, even from me. Magically and otherwise. But her husband came back mortally wounded."

"That was the funeral that I saw."

Quotar nodded. "Kantir was his name. He warned me of the attack they were planning on this very castle. I was too important of a figure as one of the four; they had to punish me for my escape. They sent an entire djinn army after me just to keep the peace.

"I knew that I would lose but not before putting my essence into this tapestry and setting up the rest of them. Only small pieces of the tapestries can be removed from these walls-not the entire piece. The djinn took everything from this place, erased all traces of the surrounding towns and their people, and created the shifting lands. This castle was left standing as a tribute to me."

"Some tribute."

"I know, right? Not killing me would have been the perfect tribute."

"And your daughter?"

"I don't know what happened to her, but I do know this, she was with child again when she left."

"I may have living relatives? Your daughter and granddaughter?"

"Yes, you may. I don't know what happened to them, but I can sense they survived, somehow."

"You can see everything that's happened and is happening, except for them?"

"Yes, and that's where you come in, Ally. I know about your difficulties growing up and about your mortal replacement family. But I also know how much you want to find any traces of your real family. Anyone who would sit through a demonstration of all the musical instruments of some long dead townspeople must be truly desperate to find any traces of his family.

"The only clue I have to my daughter's whereabouts is that Kantir said that he had come from a small kingdom run by some king with two djinn. Just west of here once you pass the mountains."

"Can I come back and talk to you? You are my only essence of a living great-great grandfather."

"Yes, of course you can."

"Will I have to go through all of the tapestries again?"

"No, I wouldn't force that on anyone, especially not you."

"Then I will be back with further news of our family."

"And I will be here. Bored and watching, as usual. I don't know why I didn't think of it, but I should have put something for me to do in this tapestry. Though it's hard to squeeze in activities in an official portrait."

Quotar posed like he did for the portrait. "When I fill the frame there's not much room for anything else except the chair that I sat on when the artist was working on the sketch. And I didn't have any books in my room at the time."

"Are you the only one who can change the tapestry?"

"No, why?"

"What do you like to do in your spare time?"

"This is the mortal world, my dear boy. There's just not that much to do around here."

"Do you like music?"

"Yes, of course. Why?"

Ally touched a corner of the tapestry. A computer tablet appeared in the corner of the tapestry, next to Quotar. "This is preloaded with all of the music that you like and it's battery will never run out."

"What's a battery?"

"It's a, uh, never mind. Just touch it and absorb its instructions and you will figure it out. When, or if, you get bored with it, let me know. I can think of a few other things that might entertain you."

"Thank you."

"You are most welcome," said Ally with a bow. "And thank you for all of the information you've given me."

"Good-bye, Ally, my son."

"You forgot the great-great part."

"Oh, come on, Ally. You already know that you're great."

"Good-bye, Quotar."

Chapter 51
Tender's Story: Fear of Mortals

"Genie?"

"Yes, Miss?"

"How long did you say your training period lasted?"

"Eleven years, Miss, from the age of ten until twenty-one."

"I know that your people aren't normally familiar with mortals and our ways but, for us, eleven years is a very long time. Did you have any experience with mortals while living in your father's lamp?"

"No, Miss. My father and mother shielded us from such contact. We never stepped foot into the world of mortals."

"You never even accompanied your father outside the lamp on any occasion?"

"No, Miss. My father's masters summoned him, not his family, from his lamp. Most mortals aren't interested in, nor are they even aware of their genie's lives inside their lamps."

"So, the first mortal you ever met was your first master?"

"No, Miss. My Brethren and I met our first mortal during our training in our second year of learning about mortals."

"That must have been a very strange meeting for you all."

"It was, Miss. Since none of us had actually seen a mortal before,

I think we were more frightened than curious. But the mortal we met helped most of us overcome our fears."

"Your fears? You were afraid of him?"

"Yes, Miss. We were very fearful during our first meeting with one of the creatures who was destined to have so much control over our lives. It was very intimidating at first, Miss."

"How did he help you overcome your fears?"

"By telling us stories of his life, Miss. He spoke to us not as future slaves, but as equals. He calmed us greatly through his treatment of us and though many of us were still afraid, he lessened it, Miss."

"Are you still afraid of us now?"

The genie paused, then answered, "Sometimes, Miss. Yes."

"I hope that I do not frighten you."

"No, Miss, you do not."

There was another pause in the conversation while Jewel thought. "I cannot make up for past behavior, Genie. I can only give you hope for a better future, or at least a more harmonious relationship between our people."

"Yes, Miss. I hope for that too." Though they parted on a somewhat hopeful note, Jewel and Tender remained pensive for the rest of the day. Tender was silent because he had never told a mortal of his fear of them before. It was a deep confession and one that he was a little ashamed of. Especially in front of Jewel.

Jewel was thoughtful because she just now realized how fitting it was for the Brethren to fear man. Their lives depended upon the whims of fickle, extremely fallible masters. Who wouldn't be afraid of that?

Chapter 52
Tender's Story: The Tailor, Part One

With his head tilted and eyes closed, the genie surveyed the crystal court. Hardly anyone was around, only a few courtiers and guards. But there was something in the air today, something different, though he couldn't exactly describe what he was sensing. Something was new and yet, very familiar. A new mortal entered the court with the king.

"Genie?"

"Yes, Master?" The genie bowed and returned to the submissive position.

"I'd like you to meet my new tailor. He is extremely knowledgeable about the latest fashions and I would like you to show him my favorite colors, particularly for the festivals."

The genie sensed something familiar about this new tailor. He froze and didn't respond.

"Genie? What is wrong with you today? All morning it seems as if you've been preoccupied."

The genie bowed to his master and again to the new tailor. "Please forgive me, Master, I apologize. I was distracted."

"There's nothing wrong, I hope. No intrigue?"

"No, Master. I thought I sensed something amiss in the palace, but I was mistaken."

"Good. Now show him the colors that I like so he can report back to me with his ideas."

"Yes, Master," he quickly bowed.

The tailor approached and the genie caused a color palette to appear before him with his master's favorite color schemes on it. As the tailor smiled mildly and studied the various colors, he also spoke telepathically to the genie.

"Yes, my friend, it is me. And no, I did not plan this at all."

"What are you doing here?" the genie responded, almost panic stricken.

The tailor continued looking at the palette, pretending to be interested. The single pallet turned into several and the genie showed the tailor all of them in turn.

"I'm on the hunt for something. It's too long of a story to go into right now."

"But the way you're dressed and how you look."

"I've been living as a mortal. I must admit, it's quite the life. Not exactly as we imagined, but glorious all the same." The tailor switched pallets. *"I can do whatever I want, within reason and if I don't draw too much attention to myself."*

The genie adjusted his position, avoiding looking directly at his friend, but still bewildered.

"You mean, you are..."

"Yes! No more shackles! And look at my hair! Do you notice something missing? That ridiculous ponytail is gone! I even removed all my hair once! It was a terrible look for me - it didn't work at all - but I did it. Just because I could!"

The genie conjured a second set of pallets with warmer colors and showed it to his friend.

"But how did you?"

"Escape? Another story that I don't have time to go into now. I should have guessed that you would be in some king's court some-

where, still dutifully serving, but I didn't think that you'd be here."

The genie handed him all the palettes and bowed briefly.

"Thank you, old friend. It's so good seeing you again. We will talk more later," the tailor added.

The tailor, apparently still preoccupied with the pallets, nodded at the genie, and left the room. The genie bowed to him again as he left. As far as the people in the court were concerned, they hadn't said a word to each other.

Later that night, after most of those within the palace had gone to sleep, the genie sat in his lamp and focused. He found the tailor, still awake in his bed chamber. *"My friend! It's great to see you again!"*

"I'm glad to see you, too. Are you well?" The tailor moved onto the bed, closed his eyes, and focused too.

"I am well. My master is not too harsh with me though he can be very demanding at times. But how are you? Are you well?"

"I'm well enough. Remember my old nemesis?"

"Yes," the genie replied.

"Well apparently, he hasn't given up. He's still trying to fulfill his vow. He's still after the remnants of my entire clan so I must be careful."

"Is that why you are disguised as a mortal?"

"No, this disguise just helps me move among the mortals more easily. For some bizarre reason, that ex-djinn-guard was allowed to keep his abilities and he's been searching for me ever since. And now, I'm free."

The genie flinched.

"Yes, I can say that word without pain."

The genie paused and thought for a second. *"What's it like?"*

"It's wonderful. I can do as I like!"

"But how did you?"

"It was honestly an accident. My very last master summoned me and then died immediately. It took me weeks to get someone to melt my lamp. As for the shackles and band on my hair, unfortunately, I

cannot reveal anything about them to you, my friend. Not while a certain person has access to your thoughts. Let's just say for now, that it is possible.

"There are some drawbacks that I can tell you about. If you think too much about removing your shackles or ask anyone to remove them, you'll faint."

"I think I remember a little about that one during one of our old human world classes," the genie commented.

"Yeah, I remember those. They were the only classes we could attend optionally. I was all too happy to opt out."

"They told us that fainting was for our own protection so that they could find us easily when we were in trouble."

"What they didn't say was that it was another ploy to keep us enslaved," the tailor noted, "so that they'd know immediately whenever we were thinking about escaping our shackles. But I won't go too deeply into it to keep you out of trouble."

"I- I want, I wish I," was all the genie could think without any discomfort.

"I know, brother, I know. You don't need to say anymore."

Tender took a few breaths to quiet himself. "You said that you were on the hunt for something. For what, exactly?"

The tailor sighed. "I may not be the only survivor of my clan."

"What?"

"I may have a living relative out there, someone directly related to me. I must find out. All I have are remnants and hints from the remains of my clan. From what I can gather, there may be another."

"Hidden?"

"Yes, hidden very well, most likely as a mortal. But I must find him, or her, before anyone else does."

"But our Leader, does he know? I mean," the genie bowed as he thought this.

"I don't know. He may be aware of the rumors. If he were to read your thoughts about this topic, he would definitely know."

"But are they just rumors?"

"I don't think so. You know how they kept teaching us to trust our instincts, our gut feelings?"

"Yes."

"Well, that's what I have. A gut feeling that somehow, she might be out there somewhere. Yes, I think it's a woman or young girl."

"But then your ages don't match. How can she be one of the last of your clan?"

"I don't know. I don't know if she survived at all, so I don't have any answers, but one of the clues led me here."

"You think my master knows something about her?"

"No, the clues aren't leading me to people, but to places. I wish I could tell you more my friend, but," the tailor hesitated.

"My thoughts are not my own," the genie nodded in agreement.

"Sadly, yes. But you'll have to trust me when it comes to this. I may have to ask you about some artifact or location or something. Then, I'll have to move on."

"Move on?"

"I can't risk the Leader finding out. He still checks up on you, right?"

The genie bowed. *"Yes, whether I like it or not."*

"He always did like you, you know."

"I don't know if it's good to hold his interest."

"It's good. Trust me, it's good."

"I think he liked you, too," Tender teased.

"I was never his favorite."

"True, but I suspect you got away with a lot more than anyone else did, like moving our building."

"Hey, I didn't keep coming up with those mad schemes, it was Clever. He was the one who wanted to move the training building a hands-length every day. He suggested that we make all the furniture fly. He even started the food fight!"

"I remember that."

"Have you heard from him?"

"No, I only know that he is well and that all is well with his family. Nothing more."

After a pause, the tailor added, "I would ask about your family, but I assume that they are well."

"Yes, they are. And how's your mortal father and grandfather doing?"

"They are fine. I have visited them since my change in status. But it still feels strange to me to call them my father and grandfather. I've never gotten used to using those terms; it still feels odd."

"It's been hundreds of years."

"I know, but the story of my family's demise was so ingrained in me as a child, I don't know if I can ever fully shake it."

"Maybe that's why this is so important to you now. You're searching for any evidence of their survival."

"Desperately searching, yes, that's how you should relay it to the Leader of all the Djinn."

The genie bowed again.

"Tell him that I'm desperately searching for any and all evidence of my family's survival, as if my life depends on it. Crawling around, sifting every grain of sand for any sign of a clue! That should touch his heart."

"He wouldn't believe me if I said that. I wouldn't believe me, either. I can barely think of it without laughing, picturing you sifting every grain of sand."

"Alright, tell him whatever you want. As long as it's true."

"I will tell him the truth if he asks about you. Lately, though, he's been a little too interested in me,"

"How so?"

"Well, I may have caused it. You see, I," the genie paused and sat straight up. "I'm about to be summoned. Forgive me, my friend."

"Later."

Chapter 53
Tender's Story: The Tailor, Part Two

Over the next few days, the tailor fawned and fussed over the king, flattering him and making him feel as if he was the most important person in the world. The king enjoyed the attention and the pampering, which made him feel more like royalty. He even gave the tailor an apartment in the palace to set up shop. His interactions with the tailor were much more pleasurable than just having the genie conjure up a new wardrobe every year, as usual. And this tailor also seemed to know exactly what he liked, just like his genie!

Because the king was so pleasantly pleased with his new tailor, all of the members of the court were determined to be excessively pleased with him as well. They hovered and simpered over him while he mostly listened to their preferences and took down their names for future appointments for fittings.

While writing, the genie asked him, *"Why did you decide to be a tailor?"*

"You'd be surprised how much information mortals share with their tailors. I had heard about this, but I didn't believe it until I tried it."

"Yes, madame? How may I help you?" The tailor asked when a woman approached. As he took down her name, he noticed his every move being watched by the Chief Advisor.

"Wow, am I that much of a threat? He's studying my every move." He told the genie.

"The Chief Advisor is threatened by practically everybody. He's even threatened by me and I've been around longer than he has."

"Then perhaps I can persuade him to buy some new robes or something to make him look more important." But the tailor was immediately approached by five more courtiers.

"Where are all these people coming from? Exactly how many courtiers are there?"

"Too many. Even I can't keep count," the genie replied as he tried hard not to smile.

The tailor wrote down all the names and appointments. *"If they only knew that I fulfill their desires through magic. Mortals can be so oblivious to things."*

"Then why are you pretending to be one of them?"

"You're right. I could have gotten a lot farther by turning myself into a dog. At least I could bark back at them."

The genie coughed.

JEWEL WATCHED THE GENIE CLOSELY, especially when the tailor was around. The genie didn't exactly act like normal; he seemed preoccupied and distant. Several times, he even seemed to cough or clear his throat. The king even had to call him to attention once, which was unheard of and caused the genie to bow and apologize profusely.

The genie and the tailor never interacted with each other directly, as far as Jewel could tell. Yet somehow, she was sure that he was responsible for the genie's changed behavior.

During their weekly session, Jewel almost brought it up. "Genie?"

"Yes, Miss?"

"Are you alright? You seem distracted, especially this past week."

"Forgive me, Miss. I am well."

"So, there's nothing going on?"

"No, Miss. Forgive me if I seem preoccupied."

"It happens, Genie, to everyone. It's alright," she paused as she glanced at the tailor, happily talking with a courtier. "Genie?"

"Yes, Miss?"

"Is there something," she hesitated slightly as she resisted the temptation to ask him publicly about the tailor. "Do your people normally eat the same food as my people?"

"We can eat your food, Miss, but we naturally prefer the food from our world."

The genie was grateful for her avoidance of the subject of the tailor, which he knew she desperately wanted to ask about. He could easily tell she suspected something but didn't want to follow her thoughts too closely.

"Is your food drastically different?"

"There is some crossover, miss, as some of our food is similar to yours, but much of it is not."

"And is eating the same experience for you?"

"It is slightly different, Miss. My people are usually more interested in the different scents than the taste."

"You don't become drunk while you're eating, do you?"

The genie smiled, "No, Miss, not usually, though it has been known to happen on special occasions."

"Such as?"

"Weddings, holidays, festivals, and the like. And oath taking celebrations, Miss."

"Do you mean that, right before you took your oath, some members of your clan were getting drunk around you?"

"No, Miss. They waited until after my oath and after my parents and I left the celebration, as a sign of respect."

"Oh, good. I am sorry to remind you of that time, Genie, of taking your oath."

"It is alright, Miss, as it was many years ago."

There was a moment of silence between them and then the captain stood up. He wasn't nearly as attentive as the professor and often just seemed like he was trying not to look as bored as he was. Jewel nodded towards the genie and he bowed to her in return. When the genie rose from his bow, he noticed that the tailor was also watching Jewel leave.

Later that night, when most everyone was asleep, the tailor sat quietly on the floor of the bedroom of his apartment in the palace with his legs crossed and he closed his eyes. He spoke again to his friend.

"Genie?" The tailor was careful to call the genie what everybody else called him so he wouldn't slip and call him by his mother's name for him.

Within his lamp, the genie heard the tailor's call and got into the same position on the floor of his lamp.

"There you are. I wish you would stop giving me a running commentary on the members of the court," the genie said.

"You did not find it entertaining?"

"Of course I did, but you're ruining my reputation in the court for discipline. They may even think that I have a cold or something since I had to cough more than a few times to keep from laughing," the genie said, grinning.

"And exactly who is this young miss I saw you conversing with today?"

The genie's grin disappeared. *"She-she is my master's niece."*

"And why is she talking to you?"

"She is curious about our people. She calls it an examination and she asks me lots of questions about anything and everything."

"And you like answering her questions?"

"*Yes, I do.*"

"*Okay. I was going to ask you something else but I think I already know the answer. How long has this situation been going on?*"

The genie paused for a second, "*Longer than I realized, honestly. Probably soon after I first met her.*"

"*I understand the attraction. She is a bright and intelligent girl. And very inquisitive. She's one of the few mortals who hasn't asked me for an appointment. You've been telling her a great deal about our people,*" the tailor pointed out.

"*She's been asking so many questions and I wanted to answer her; I wanted her to know,*" the genie protested.

"*And it was a convenient way to spend more time with her.*"

The genie didn't answer. Why restate the obvious?

"*The Leader of our people cannot be too happy about any of this.*"

"*No, he is not,*" the genie stated, after bowing.

"*And this must be the reason he's paying you a little more attention than usual.*"

"*Definitely, yes.*"

"*So, what do you want from all this? What do you want from her?*"

"*Just to be with her, to be around her for as long as I can.*"

"*And if you can't be with her? What then?*"

"*I don't know. It's hard to imagine life without her but I'll continue on, I guess, as I always do. That or I'll kill myself.*"

"*You of course know that we're not allowed to do that, right? We cannot commit suicide. It is literally impossible for us.*"

"*I know. And so many have tried.*"

"*And so many of us used to succeed at it, which is why, naturally, they banned it for us, making it physically impossible for us to accomplish.*"

"*Without removing any of the reasons why we'd want to,*" Tender said quietly. "*Though, there are many ways to die.*"

They both remained silent for a few seconds until the tailor spoke. "*Yeah, well, hey. Getting back to the subject at hand. What are you going to do?*"

"I don't know. I'll keep talking to her and answering her questions as long as my master allows it. Other than that, I don't know."

"Hm, I'll see what I can do."

"What? What are you going to do?" The genie began panicking.

"Don't worry my romantic friend. I will do what I can."

"No, please don't. My master won't appreciate any interference at all. He'll lash out at me and her and then I won't see her again."

"Calm down, please. Right now, we're just talking." Then the tailor chuckled. *"Who would have ever thought that one day I'd actually be saying that to you?"*

The genie also smiled a little and calmed himself, but he still had to know. *"Exactly what are you planning?"*

"Nothing that involves your master in any way."

"But-"

"No, my friend. The less you know, the better. Goodnight," he couldn't help but playfully add, *"Genie."*

"Goodnight," the genie answered.

JEWEL WAS STILL EXTREMELY curious about the sudden appearance of the tailor and his true purpose. He had somehow managed to make appointments with every single courtier except her. She later followed him into his shop in the palace. His living quarters were behind the shop and he was preparing some fabric for cutting when she entered.

"Ah, good afternoon, young lady! Is there anything I can help you with? A new wardrobe perhaps, or maybe some new accessories?"

"Oh, no, thank you, sir. I just want to ask you a question if you don't mind."

"Of course, Miss, ask away."

"This is just a guess, sir, and I hope it doesn't offend you."

"Yes, Miss?"

"How long have you been pretending to be a mortal?"

His jovial attitude disappeared immediately. "It's not good for such a well-bred young lady to ask such sensitive questions. Close the door."

She did as instructed. "Did I guess correctly?"

"Who are you and what do you want?"

"I am Jewel, the king's niece. I want to know if you are a genie."

"Who sent you?"

"No one. I came on my own. Is it not true that a genie must answer truthfully when asked if they are a genie? Whether enslaved or not?"

"Yes, to everything you just said. Yes, I am a genie, to answer your initial question. But before this goes any further," he waved two fingers, and she froze in place. "I need to know really, why you are here."

He looked inside of her, expecting to see some intricate treachery, some insidious plan involving him or his friend, but was instead, puzzled. He waved his fingers again and she moved normally, though a little disoriented.

"You love him. You. Love. Him. You love him!" He began to laugh. "Oh, this is great! And it may be just what he needs!"

"What did you do to me?" she asked as she was still trying to regain her balance.

"Nothing permanent but I can't say the same for what you've done to him." He laughed again as she staggered slightly. "Here, sit down." He pulled out a chair for her and she sat down, still wobbly. He sat opposite her, resigned, but intrigued. "So, what do you really want?"

"I want to do something nice for him."

"Something, nice? What is this something nice? He's enslaved."

"Please," Jewel replied, not wanting to be made fun of.

He looked at her more tenderly. "Only his master can set him free, you know."

"I know. But there must be something I can do for him."

"Well, there is the next best thing but it's a bit dangerous. If you get it wrong, you could die."

"I could die? Why? What is it that I can do for him?"

"Three days of freedom. At the most."

"Three days of freedom? But how?"

"Does he owe you a wish?"

"Yes, quite a few."

"Then it is possible. Oh, this will be really good! And just the thing to shake up his life. It will only help him in the long run, I'm sure. And I've known him a lot longer than you have."

"But you've known everyone and everything a lot longer than I have."

"True." He smiled at her. "I think I like you. But tell me, do you know if he loves you?"

"I don't know for sure; I think he does. There were a few times when I thought he did, but we've never really been able to..." Jewel paused, uncertain.

"To talk about it. Yes, I got that." The tailor remembered something for a second and then turned to her again. "That brings me to my second question. What do you know of the djinn language?"

"Nothing," she answered honestly.

"Well, if he owes you a wish and if you make the wish in the djinn language, it is possible to ask for three days of freedom for him."

"Why is that dangerous?"

"The djinn language is spoken and heard verbally and telepathically. That means it is heard out loud and, in your head, simultaneously."

Suddenly, she heard his voice in her head saying, *"Like this."*

Jewel gasped. The tailor chuckled and then continued. "What makes it particularly difficult for mortals to learn is that if you are relying on your ears only, you will literally miss half of it. Our language fades in and out verbally and rhythmically, following its own pattern. You can only hear everything if you are telepathic, which means you can read minds, or at least, hear what others are thinking. That is why it is nearly impossible for mortals to learn and understand, since they lack telepathic abilities. Even if they understand the language, they miss half of what is spoken."

"I can't read minds; I am not telepathic. But how is it also dangerous?"

"It's dangerous because if you attempt it and get it wrong, you die."

"Die?"

"'All mortals caught attempting to speak the language of the djinn shall be put to death for their insulting presumption.' I believe that's the correct wording even though I haven't attended a Reading of the Law session in a quite a while."

"Attempting to speak? Are all attempts punished?"

"Not if you get it right."

"But I could die if I get it wrong?"

"Yes. Another barrier for mortals, which is why it's considered almost impossible for your people to learn."

"I don't know if I can learn a telepathic language! I don't know how or even if I-"

"I said that it is almost impossible. But the key word is *almost*. You see, you don't have to learn the entire language, just the words that are required for your wish. It's a very brief conversation, very rote, asking for your wish, learning the parameters of your wish, and then him granting the wish. It's that straightforward."

"But what if he changes the words?"

"He can't. It's a very formal and scripted request. He can only say certain words and you are supposed to only respond with certain words. It's written into our law."

"Oh my."

"The key is to make sure that you think the words as well as say the words. That way, he will hear the words telepathically as well vocally. It will take some work, but I will help you do it. It's a way to fake telepathy."

"But I can't hear him!"

"You don't have to, or at least, you don't have to hear all of it. I will teach you his part also so you will know exactly what he's saying and when to say your part."

"Can this really work?"

"Yes, in theory. If not, my bad. I can at least teach you in a way that keeps you from getting killed."

"Great."

"Don't worry, it will work. And you can give him the gift of three days of freedom."

"Thank you, sir, thank you."

"It is the least I can do for my friend." The tailor began to reminisce while Jewel thought of one more question.

"Sir?"

"Yes?"

"Does he have a name?"

He hesitated, and then answered, "Yes."

"What is it? I-I don't mean his real name, but what do you call him?"

He stared at her intensely, but he still couldn't find any ulterior motives, so his features softened. For her, it was just another innocent question. "That is for him to tell, not for me to reveal. But I sense that you will find out before your wish is over."

"Oh."

"And here." The tailor held up his hand and a new outfit appeared. He handed it to her. "Your excuse for coming here. Next time, bring your governess as a chaperone."

"But she'll hear us, won't she?"

"I have ways to handle that, but we can't afford any hints of impropriety."

"Okay, I will."

Chapter 54
Training: Tender's Visit Home

"Now, remember, young djinn. You are charged with remaining obedient even during your visit home. I expect you to remain submissive, especially when you are surrounded by your families. I will immediately know when one of you decides to break this rule." The First Teacher paused to let his words sink in.

"Yes, First Teacher," his eight students answered diligently. They were in the ready position, each holding a matching green bag slung over their left shoulder except for Alley who had no bag.

"You may only be released from your submissiveness by the head of your household and no one else. When the head of your household says you may be as you truly are, then, and only then, may you act normally with your families. Is that clear?"

"Yes, First Teacher."

"You will be gone for forty-two days and forty-two days only, no exceptions. Alley, you will remain here with me."

"Yes, First Teacher," Alley answered, embarrassed at being singled out.

"You should all have your bags already packed, correct?"

"Yes, First Teacher."

"Good-bye."

Every student except Alley began to disappear.

"Alley, for you, the next forty-two days will be treated like the seventh day breaks, only with no classes."

"Yes, First Teacher."

"You will join me for meals and occasionally with other Teachers."

"Yes, First Teacher."

The First Teacher nodded to him and disappeared. When he appeared in the Teacher's Lounge, he said to the Second Teacher, "I think we have a problem."

As soon as he was released, Tender appeared in his father's lamp in the middle of the kitchen next to his mother. He bowed deeply to her but remained in the submissive position, kneeling.

"Tender! It is so good to see you!"

Darling hugged him tightly but he responded by stiffly remaining in place, not hugging her back, in order to not be too familiar.

"Greetings, mistress of the house. Thank you for allowing me into your home," Tender bowed his head towards her.

"Are you alright? Are they feeding you well?"

"I am well, Mistress. My teachers feed me sufficiently when I obey them properly."

Recognizing his behavior, she let go of him, "Oh Tender, my son,"

Tender bowed again and said, "Forgive me, Mistress, if I have offended you. Please offer suggestions so that I may improve my behavior."

Understanding, she leaned back from him and looked at him. Tender continued staring at the floor. Hearing his voice, his brothers and sisters ran to Tender, hugging and greeting him but he responded in the same distant and passive manner.

"How are you?"

"What's going on?"

"It's good to see you!"

"I really missed you!"

"I am well, thank you," he answered all of them, emotionless.

He still didn't look at any of them but kept his eyes on the floor. Now they all stood back, staring at him.

Dearest cried, "What did they do to you?"

"I am being trained as a servant, Miss, in the traditional manner. It is for my betterment."

As several of his sisters began to cry, Dearest asked their mother, tearfully, "What's wrong with him?"

"Your father warned me about this," Darling answered. "And I remember when it happened to him. We will have to wait until he returns from serving and then we'll get our Tender back."

"May I relax, Mistress?" Tenders asked.

"Yes, of course," his mother answered.

"Thank you, Mistress." Tender crossed his legs and closed his eyes.

"It is part of his training," she explained. "He will not be his normal self until he receives permission from the head of the household. We will have to wait for your father to give him permission."

Her other children continued staring at Tender until their mother said, "Let's leave him be. We'll just have to be patient. Go back to what you were doing. Our food will be ready soon."

Her other children reluctantly left the kitchen area, sneaking glances at their brother.

"May I be of assistance, Mistress?" Tender asked.

"No, Tender, thank you. You may unpack your bag in your room and then return here."

"Yes, Mistress." Tender bowed and disappeared. He returned after a few minutes and sat with his legs crossed in the same spot dutifully. He remained unnaturally still and only moved when he had to with his mother's permission.

For the next few days it was as if the family had lost a child but gained a perfectly obedient slave. Tender replied to every inquiry with extreme politeness and gentle, subservient obedience.

"No, Mistress."

"Yes, sister."

"I am well, brother."

Even his mother grew frustrated by the fourth day after she offered him some of the perfumed melon that she had just materialized. It was one of Tender's favorite foods but he responded with, "If it will please you, Mistress."

"What would please me is to have my son back," she cried, slamming her bowl onto the table.

He bowed to the floor with his arms stretched forward and cried, "Please forgive me, Mistress, if I have offended you in any way,"

"Get up. Get up!"

He sat up and she hugged him, knowing that he would not reciprocate.

Suddenly, on the cloth that hung on the wall, an image of her husband appeared. "Darling."

"Kind," she quickly tried to discreetly wipe away her tears.

"Hello, my wife. I will be away for at least another week as long as my master requires my presence. Tender!"

Tender bowed, formally. Kind recognized Tender's behavior immediately and painfully.

"Greetings, master of the house. I thank you for allowing me to stay in your home. I hope you are well."

"Yes, son, I am well." Kind looked at Darling, "He is in the middle of his test of strict obedience. It is difficult to maintain; I hope he's been doing well. Tender, you may be who you truly are, my son."

His words had an immediate effect, as every aspect of Tender now relaxed. "Papa?"

"There you are, Tender. I will return home as soon as I can."

He and his wife nodded at each other and his image disappeared.

Tender looked up at his mother and said, "Mama?"

"Tender!" They hugged and she cried out, "Children, our Tender is back!"

They rushed in and all melted into each other, hugging Tender so much that he could barely breathe. It was such a relief to feel him hug back that they didn't want to stop. But when they did, he finally looked directly at them, embarrassed.

"I'm sorry for scaring all of you."

"It's alright, Tender. It's part of your training, we understand." Darling replied.

"You were so weird and obedient," Dearest said.

"I know. I had to be," Tender said. "My teachers said that some djinn, when they return home, never get permission to be who they truly are. They have to stay obedient for the whole time."

"I'm glad you got permission," Sweet added.

"Me too," Tender replied.

"I was about to ask you to clean my clothes," Strong joked.

"I would have done it, too. But not now," he grinned.

With Tender free to be himself, he fell into his family's usual routines though he was much quieter than before and played less freely. He seemed to be monitoring everything that he did as if he had to decide how his teachers would respond to his actions once he returned. Every time his family noticed and asked if he was alright, he'd respond that he was fine, though it was clear that he wasn't. Tender felt as if he couldn't really relax. He wasn't sure exactly how closely he was being watched by his teachers or what they would do about all his behavior at home.

After another week, Kind returned home. "I'm back," he said, quietly. He was quickly surrounded by his wife and children, who hugged and welcomed him. All except Tender, who stood back with his head bowed, worried about what to do.

Kind noticed and went to Tender and hugged him. "It's alright, my son, it's alright," he reassured Tender, "your teachers will not judge you on your behavior after you have been released to be yourself. I was afraid of that too when I came home the first time. But it's alright, you can relax now."

Tears filled Tender's eyes as he hugged his father fully. Then he pulled back. "But am I supposed to treat you a certain way."

"No, Tender, not now. Not until you take the oath. Right now, I'm just your father."

Tender hugged his father again, "Thank you, Papa."

After this, Tender stopped monitoring his actions and was fully himself again. Relaxed and comforted by the understanding presence of his father, Tender began to behave as he did before his training.

During a quiet moment with his sister, Dearest, she asked, "What's it like?"

"It's hard, it's really hard. Right now, we're in the obedience part and you have to get everything right, or else."

"What do they do to you if you get it wrong?"

"Sometimes they make you do things that wear you out physically. Other times, they make you stand in one spot or stay in one position for a really long time. And sometimes, they don't feed us."

"That's not right. What do you have to do?"

"Sometimes it's simple stuff like fetching water. Other times, it's stuff like building something, or memorizing something, or completing some task. If you want to know the first laws of the djinn, I can tell you. I had to memorize them."

"For real?"

"For real. And at the middle of the year, they give us this bowing test. They make all of us get in line, kneel, and bow. If we don't do it at exactly the same time, in exactly the same way, we're not ready yet. It's their test to tell when we're done with our training."

"And are you ready?"

"No. Not at all. But that doesn't stop them. It's as if they want us to fail so they can teach us how to deal with it. I don't like it."

"No one would! I hope it gets easier for you."

"Me too. After another two years of obedience training comes more training in magic. Maybe I will enjoy that more, or at least, I hope I will."

"What do you miss the most?"

"Home. And all of you. And freedom."

"Freedom? Already?"

"Yes. It's not like we can do whatever we want at home but you do get to do more of what you want. You get to be yourself. The one thing they keep saying over and over is that we don't have any free will."

"Free will?"

"Yes. Our will is not our own. It belongs to them. We have to remember that all our decisions belong to them."

"So, like, you have to ask them permission for everything?"

"Yes."

"When to eat, what to eat, what to wear, and so on?"

"Yes."

"Even when you go to the bathroom?"

"Even when we go to the bathroom. They want control over every part of our lives. Most of the time we don't even get to ask. They just tell us what to do."

"Tender, I am so sorry."

"Why? You don't have anything to do with the rules and laws that I must follow."

"No, but I hate that you have to follow them at all. Doesn't it make you mad, aren't you angry about how ridiculous it is?"

"I can't be angry about it or I'd be upset all the time. And then they'd really get mad."

"Well, I can be mad at them and nothing will happen to me." Dearest was suddenly uncertain. "Right?"

"Right, they don't hurt family members. You can be mad at them for me."

The next twenty-eight days raced by, with Kind and his family happy to be together again. Saying good-bye was easier too, because they knew that things could return to normal, even when two members of the family were gone.

WHEN ALL THE young djinn reappeared at their school, they returned to the exact positions they were in when they had left, in the ready position in front of their beds with their green bags.

"You have done very well during your holiday, my young ones. Not one mistake from any of you whatsoever. Good." The First Teacher took a deep breath. "Now, you may unpack, change into your uniforms, and prepare for the evening meal."

Chapter 55
Tender's Story: The Tailor, Part Three

Jewel waited for two days before she went to the tailor's shop again. She asked Rose to go with her.

"Why?" asked Rose.

"Propriety. I don't want it to look like I'm visiting some strange man by myself."

"You talk with a genie once a week and now you're worried about propriety?"

"Please, Rose, I just want to get a new wardrobe. We can get a new one for you too if you like."

"Oh no. My clothes are just fine, but I will go with you while you choose some new clothes."

When they entered the tailor's shop, they went into one of the private sitting rooms and Rose made herself comfortable while watching the tailor present Jewel with an extremely wide variety of fabrics, or so Rose thought. What really happened after Rose sat down on the settee was the genie waved two fingers and put Rose in a trance.

"She thinks I'm showing you every type of fabric that exists," he explained.

"Does it hurt?"

"Oh no. It's actually a rather pleasant experience for her. Easier than this will be for you. Have a seat."

Jewel sat down while the tailor made a chalkboard on a stand appear besides him.

"Now first, let me begin with the actual translation of what you'll both be saying. Beginning with you."

He wrote her first line on the board in her language by magically waving at it with the chalk.

"'Djinn, hear me now.' And then he'll say, 'yes, oh, brave one, what do you wish of me.' Any mortal correctly speaking the djinn language is automatically labeled a brave one because of the whole threat of death thing."

"The whole threat of death thing. Right."

"Don't worry, Jewel. I wouldn't teach you any of this if I didn't think that you could do it."

She took a deep breath and nodded, "Okay."

He continued the lesson for about thirty minutes until he knew that she would be missed.

The tailor made the chalkboard disappear, unfroze Rose, who woke up as if nothing had happened, and left the shop smiling with Jewel. She even commented, "I never knew there were so many different fabrics in my life!"

Jewel smiled and nodded, feeling more than a little guilty about the deception. She loved Rose and didn't like including her in the scheme at all. And yet, due to the tailor's magical abilities, Rose had an easier time in the shop than she did, though Jewel always loved learning. She was glad she only had to memorize a few words and not an entire language.

For the next three weeks, Jewel and Rose visited the tailor almost every other day. The tailor and Jewel intensely rehearsed and studied the exact words that she would say to the genie so that she spoke the djinn language as if she were a native speaker. The tailor would also conjure a few new clothes for her as a cover for their meetings.

The king was reassured by this whole turn of events because it meant that Jewel spent less time with the genie, even if it was on something as trivial as clothes. At least it proved that she had other interests she could obsess over. And maybe then, she would have no more questions for the genie. His genie.

The genie, however, was worried. His best friend and his new friend were spending time together. What could it possibly mean? His friend had shielded all the conversations he had with Jewel from prying mind readers, which the genie expected, but he was also shielding all her thoughts from everyone, including him.

When the genie tried to use his focus to break through the shield to hear Jewel's thoughts, his friend issued him a warning, *"Oh no, my friend. It's best that you do not know what is going on."*

The second time he tried to break the shield, his friend gave him this thought, *"Trust me, Genie, you shouldn't know anything about this. Not yet."*

And the third time, *"My, aren't we persistent! I've always liked that about you. But trust me my friend, this will be worth the wait. Trust me. Please."*

The genie stopped trying after that, feeling a little more reassured. What could they be doing? She is not that into clothes, she never was before, she was not the type. He was also feeling a bit jealous. He missed Jewel and their time together. She had skipped their weekly meeting times just to go to the tailor's shop. Though the genie initially thought that he would eventually grow weary with Jewel's questions and hearing her constantly call him, he did not. It was the only way they could meet. He missed her and her endless inquiries.

THE TAILOR FOUND that a great deal of his time was spent making sure that Jewel thought the words exactly as she spoke them. A seemingly easy task that was made difficult because of how easy it was.

"No, no, I didn't hear you think the last three words. Remember to focus and to stay focused."

Jewel repeated the entire sentence.

"That was much better. We'll try the entire sequence again and work on your phrasing. You have a lot of the pronunciations right but the emphasis is a little off. Remember to always emphasize the second syllable, all throughout."

She repeated the sentence.

"That was better, much better. We'll try it again later to see if you remember it."

During this natural break in the lesson, Jewel decided to ask the tailor a few questions. "What happens afterwards, after the three days are over?"

"He goes back to being a good little genie, completely enslaved again," he answered with more bitterness than Jewel ever heard from him. "If I remember it correctly, you both will return to the same positions you were in when you made your wish, even to the exact day and time. It will appear as if nothing happened at all."

"Will he remember any of it?"

"Yes. He will remember all of it. Not only that, but he will also treasure those moments forever. He will not be able to speak of it though, or refer to it in any way. He must act as if it never happened."

"Will I remember it?"

"Yes, of course. Why wouldn't you remember any of it?"

"I don't know. Maybe because of some weird genie rule or something."

"You will also remember it, but you would be wise to also never speak or refer to it ever again. Those three days should remain a quiet memory that you both share. Otherwise, he will be forced to reveal it all to his master, which I assume you do not want to happen."

"No, of course not."

"Bringing it up would only cause problems for both of you."

"Will it change him?"

"Probably. Who knows?" He leaned back in his chair. "It changed me."

"You also had three days of freedom?"

"No. My first taste of freedom, I'll always remember. It was if I could breathe, fully and deeply for the first time since my oath. As if all my senses had been muffled and the wool was finally removed from my eyes. I felt alive, truly alive. But the experience is different for every djinn. Some djinn go mad, especially when their thoughts are released."

"What do you mean by that?"

"Part of being an enslaved genie, at least of our sect, means having your thoughts monitored and restricted."

Jewel drew back a little, suddenly flooded with memories of her accusations against the genie and of his reaction. "Yes, I've heard about that."

"Yes, I know about that," he said, mimicking her voice. "I looked into your past interactions with your genie friend. You weren't very kind or understanding to him at the time, were you?"

"You looked into my past interactions with him?"

"Yes, of course. I had to make sure your motivations were pure. That you had no hidden agendas, hidden even from yourself. You mortals are very good at hiding things from yourselves, you know."

"We are?"

"Yes, especially when you get all mixed up psychologically. You can be a real puzzle."

"So are my motivations pure?"

"Yes. Love. One of the easiest motivations to detect. And in your case, it's not complicated or weighed down by junk from your past. That's a good thing."

Jewel inhaled deeply and responded, "Good to know."

"Anyway, immediately after your genie friend becomes free, I would suggest that you back off a little and give him some space."

"Why? What is he going to do?"

"Well, that's just it, we don't really know what he's going to do. When a genie becomes free, particularly from this type of total enslavement, the first thing that happens is that their repressed thoughts are released, all at once. Every hidden thought, every quick comment to yourself, everything that you would have naturally thought to yourself becomes unleashed."

"So, he will be overwhelmed by every thought that he would have had since becoming enslaved?"

"Yes. It can be quite an experience. I remember I thought I was suddenly reliving my past. Which, in a way, I was."

"Did you go mad?"

"A tad. I was in a safe place so I didn't hurt anyone. But I can't guarantee that I wouldn't have, if I had the opportunity. This is why some genies kill the mortals who free them. The madness is temporary but lasts long enough for them to do that. It lasts only a few minutes, but it can happen. I doubt that your genie will be a threat to you, but it can be very dangerous."

Jewel felt the weight of his last statement hang in the air, so she had to break the heavy mood.

"What are your motivations in helping me? Are they pure? Do you have any hidden agendas that I should know about?"

He grinned, then said emphatically, "No."

"So why are you doing this?"

"He is my friend. He saved me from myself quite often when we were younger. It's too long a story to get into now and I sense that you will find out on your own anyway." His eyes briefly turned white. "Later, definitely later. But in many ways, I owe him. And I finally get the opportunity to do something nice for him too, for a change."

He glanced at Rose, sitting in a trance.

"Okay, let's try that last sentence again now and see if you can remember it."

Jewel repeated the sentence in the djinn language, remembering to think the words as well as speak them.

"Good." Suddenly, a new garment appeared in the tailor's arms and he handed it to her. "Here's your cover story for today. Say your line once more before you leave."

Jewel repeated the sentence she had been practicing.

"Much better. You're improving. I'll see you tomorrow, hopefully at the same time."

"Good and once again, thank you."

"You are most welcome, Miss." He winked at her as she looked at him.

They continued their lessons for another week without any problems, but the last time she visited, his tailor shop was in complete disarray. The tailor let Jewel and Rose inside but put Rose in a trance as soon as she walked in. He continued frantically searching for things around his shop.

"Sir, what's happened?"

"I'm afraid we'll have to end our little language lessons for now, as I must make a hasty exit from this kingdom. Your friend there will snap out of it ten minutes after you leave this room. She will follow you back to your rooms and wake up when you get there."

"But I still need to know..."

"You will be fine. You already have the words inside of you, you just need to focus on thinking them as you say them during the entire conversation. But you will be fine."

"Are you going to be okay?"

He found something under a pile of fabric, a tiny little box. "There! Now, I will."

He waved his right hand in a circle and the entire contents of the shop swirled around them and shrank until they were drawn into the little box in his hand. He put the box into his left pocket.

"It's good to leave a place exactly as I find it." He put his hand on her shoulder. "You will do very well, I feel it. Just take your time and don't rush the words, keep practicing, and it will come more naturally to you. I know that all will go well with you."

His eyes briefly glowed white as he looked at her. "Eventually. Enjoy yourself. Goodbye." With that, the tailor vanished.

"Goodbye," Jewel whispered to the air. She heard the tailor's fading laughter in response.

The genie also heard Ally's laughter from his lamp. And his voice. *"Goodbye, my friend. And please, try to have some fun!"*

The genie wondered exactly what Ally meant.

Chapter 56
Tender's Story: Free

It was early in the morning on the third day of the week, an hour before Jewel's morning lessons, when she decided to take a chance. Her uncle had new guests to entertain, ambassadors from somewhere, and would be preoccupied with them during and after a long morning meal.

She knew that the genie would probably still be in the Crystal Court Room, monitoring the thoughts of the guests for any signs of treachery, as he had often been required to do before.

Sure enough, she saw him as she reached the court. He was in his usual position, kneeling by the throne. Everyone else was gone, even the guards had moved into the banquet room. The genie was already bowing to her as she entered and walked towards him.

"Good morning, Miss." The genie sensed that something unusual was about to happen. "How may I serve you today?"

Instead of answering with her usual, casual, and cheerful conversation, she spoke with formal authority in the djinn language. "Djinn, hear me now."

She spoke and thought the words just as she had been taught. Immediately, the genie looked up and drew straight to attention, his eyes beginning to glow. He began to speak, as if in a trance, the words that she had been told to expect, which were, "Yes, oh brave one. What do you wish of me?"

He spoke slowly and mechanically, his language rhythmically fading in and out because of his telepathy.

She answered in his language, mimicking his rhythm. Careful to think the words as she said them, "I wish for your freedom for the maximum time."

"That would be three days, oh brave one."

"I wish for your freedom for three days."

"Your wish is granted oh brave one."

He closed his eyes and clapped his hands together, though it made more of a loud boom than a clapping sound and they were both suddenly enveloped in a huge whirlwind. The genie bent his arms towards his chest. The shackles around his wrists and ankles unlocked themselves and disappeared.

As the winds began to die down, she saw they had been transported to a green, hilly area near a forest. It was also morning and sunny. The tailor hadn't mentioned anything about being magically moved somewhere else.

She looked toward the genie and he was still kneeling with his hands together, but something was somehow different. Then she saw that he was not kneeling perfectly, as before, but was leaning to his right side, with his eyes still closed. He was also breathing heavily.

He tried to stand up but fell on all fours. Suddenly, his face began to contort as if he was experiencing great pain, and he fell back on his heels.

Every forbidden thought that he had ever had since his oath suddenly rushed through his head. He was being bombarded with every random thought, every suppressed emotion, every image and idea that he would have felt without any restrictions or monitoring.

It was painful, overwhelming, and disorienting; it was as if his brain were overheating. He grimaced even more, causing Jewel to gasp. But at the sound of her gasp, the bombardment stopped, and the genie turned his face towards her.

She took a step back but his features began to relax and his breathing returned to normal. He opened his eyes and focused on her. She took another step back, not quite knowing what to expect. After hearing of the tales of the newly freed and crazed djinn, she was prepared to run if she had to, even though she knew it would be completely ineffective.

The genie began to tremble but managed to stand to his full height. She had only seen him standing once before but did not remember how much he towered over her. He approached her, still shaking from his recent change. She stepped back, afraid, but then he knelt before her, taking her right hand and kissing it.

"I do not know how to thank you, Miss, or if I will ever be able to thank you enough," he tenderly kissed the back of her hand again as if it was the most precious thing in the world, and placed his forehead against it.

"No, Genie, it was the least I could do. I only wish it was longer than three days."

"No, Miss. Your most valuable gift, if only for an hour, would be worth more to me than you could ever know. For you have given me something that I have never known, Miss. Freedom." He involuntarily vibrated violently for a few seconds as he said that last word.

"Forgive me, Miss, I am still changing. That was the first time I have ever said that word out loud in this realm without any pain since my oath. I can say it now, freely, thanks to you." He kissed her hand reverently again.

"So many times I have wanted to say or just think that word. So many times, I wanted to tell you what I truly thought, what I really believed, but I could not. My oath and the djinn laws prevented me and my words were not always my own."

"Oh, Genie," she felt a familiar twinge of guilt.

"I must thank you for realizing that no matter what I said, or how often I denied it, the heart of every djinn longs for, yearns for, begs to be free."

"But it is only for three days."

"Enough for a lifetime." He kissed her hand again and slowly placed it back by her side, gently letting it go. He stood up, looked straight up, closed his eyes, and smiled. "The sun and wind on my face! Rare treasures for enslaved djinn."

He just stood there, enjoying the feeling. She smiled at the simplicity of his pleasure and only reluctantly asked, "So, tell me, Genie, what are you going to do now?"

He blinked and looked around. "I don't know, really. I suppose I can do all the things I've always wanted to do, but I am enjoying this right now."

He stood still in the light wind. Then, fully realizing that his shackles were gone, Tender looked down at his wrists and began touching them. The markings were also gone. As he examined the blank spaces, he asked almost absentmindedly, "Are you hungry, Miss? We could have a meal right here."

As he said this, a table full of food appeared beside them along with two cushions. She gasped at the sudden sight. "We could both eat something while I decide what to do."

"Of course, thank you." They sat down and slowly began to eat. They were too excited and filled with anticipation to focus on food.

"There are so many things that I've always wanted to see, and so many places I've always wanted to go. And so many eras I've wanted to experience."

"Eras? You can go anywhere in time?"

"Yes, Miss, I can go anywhere I like. I've always wanted to see Julius Caesar, or witness Napoleon's loss at Waterloo, or see Versailles in its full splendor, or the Eiffel Tower!"

"Who are those people? And are those places?"

"Famous historical figures and yes, truly fantastic places. There are so many wonderful things to see in this world! I would like to see them for myself and, if you don't mind my asking, Miss, with you."

"That was very direct of you, Genie."

"I have three days to enjoy. I do not have time to be coy, but I do have time to share. Since you are responsible for my newfound freedom, it seems only fair that you share the pleasure of it as well."

"I am not your only friend responsible for this freedom, Genie."

"I know. Hopefully, one day I will be able to repay him also. But for now," he stood up from the table and held out his hand. "Will you please join me in my adventures, Miss?"

"Yes, but only if you call me by my name."

"Will you join me, Jewel?"

"Yes. With great pleasure." His hand, still offered, she finally touched and held. "And what shall I call you? I can't continue to call you genie, especially in public."

"What name would you have me bear? For I am willing to be called almost any name that you find worthy."

"What do others call you?"

With some embarrassment, he replied, "My mother called me Tenderness, or most often, Tender, because of how sensitive I was."

"Then that's what I will call you. Tender."

Tender sighed. "It is good to hear that name out loud, it has been so long."

"Then I will use it as much as I can, Tender." She grinned as he blushed. "So, Tender, what do we do now?"

"Let's go to a place I have always wanted to see." Instantly they were at the top of Victoria Falls. It was loud, windy, and wet, but they appeared in a glass cube where Tender and Jewel could see everything but not feel it.

Jewel shrieked and instinctively looked for something solid to stand on, and then grabbed the genie's arm. Tender held onto her and kept her steady. "Don't worry, we're perfectly safe. I've got you."

She looked around, and then at him. "But how? How are you doing this?"

"My powers, of course. It's just that now, I'm doing what I want, instead of what someone else wants."

Their glass cube hovered over the top of the falls for a while, then gently descended over the falls to view the water.

"They say that over two-hundred and fifty gallons of water rushes over every second."

"It is beautiful and we're so close." They descended further until the cube nearly hit the base of the water, but it stopped and lightly floated over the furiously churning water.

"I've always wanted to see this; I just never got the chance. I hope it's not too much for you," Tender admitted.

"No, no, it's different, and a little scary, but it's not too much."

They watch the rushing water under their feet. "Most of my life I have been trained to be passive, submissive, and obedient. Trained to be a slave and to obey my master's slightest whim. I am still adjusting to following my own will, responding to my own mind - it is so very different."

"I think you're doing very well so far."

Tender shook his head and leaned on the side of the cube. "I'm not sure I know how to do this, miss-Jewel. To follow my own desires, to grant my own wishes, it is all so new to me. And so very strange."

"I can help you, Tender. What do you want to do? What do you feel right now?"

"I am happy but a little afraid also. That makes me anxious."

"I would think that's normal. It's always difficult to face an endless world of choices. Yet, choose we must. Would you like to relax?"

"Yes, miss. Jewel."

"Where is the most relaxing place you can imagine?"

"A beautiful beach. Deserted, except for us. An umbrella for shade, two reclining beach chairs with a table between us, with refreshing drinks."

"That's really good. Now, take us there."

Tender and Jewel reappeared on a deserted beach under an umbrella on two reclining beach chairs. A table sat between them holding refreshing drinks, exactly as Tender described it.

Jewel, who had been reclining on the chair, sat up and looked around. "This is perfect, Tender."

He smiled reluctantly and stretched while he reclined. They rested for about fifteen minutes until Tender suddenly sat up. "I know what I want to do."

"What?" Jewel asked.

"Watch a Shakespeare play while he's alive! Go shopping in New York during the 1980s. Witness the actual Trojan wars. See the very first djinn slave bow down to the very first mortal master. I want to see everything that we possibly can!"

"I hope we have time for everything."

"We do. We will. Come. Let's go." He took her hand, and they disappeared.

Chapter 57
Tender's Story: Shakespeare, a Pyramid, Enslavement, and the Eiffel Tower

In the Globe Theater during 1599, Tender and Jewel reappeared in period appropriate clothes. They sat in the balcony seats watching the performance begin.

Tender leaned over to Jewel and whispered, "Don't worry, you'll be able to understand every word."

They smiled and watched the performance. Afterwards, as they left, Jewel remarked, "That was really good."

"I was wondering if you would like it."

"It was funny, I liked it."

"Hungry?"

"Definitely."

"Good. But first, I must make a little stop and then we'll eat."

Tender and Jewel disappeared, unnoticed by anyone. They reappeared in very ancient times in their regular clothes. It was a cloudy night and extremely dark and difficult to see. They were behind some trees looking at a scene at a clearing near a campfire. Jewel was about to ask where they were but the unnatural quiet of the forest silenced her.

A man, dressed in fine clothes surrounded by other men in fine clothes, bent down and picked up a bottle with a cork. The man pulled the cork out and brown and dark blue smoke streaked with red poured out of the bottle, reforming into a genie.

The genie's clothes were dirty, bloodied rags, and he looked as if he had just come from an intense battle. He saw the man standing in front of him, then reluctantly, kneeled and bowed his head to him. The man held out his right hand and the genie kissed his ring. He then bowed to him again.

The man pointed to the bottle, said something in a language Jewel didn't understand, and the genie dissolved into red-streaked, brown and blue smoke again, returning to the bottle.

Tender turned away, looking extremely affected by what he just saw. Jewel started to say something, but he shook his head and they dissolved again.

Tender and Jewel reappeared on the side of a mountain in a small cave. Jewel gasped at how close they were to the edge and stepped back. Tender stepped back also but he was still recovering from what they just saw.

"Tender, what was that?"

"We just saw the very first genie be captured by a man and surrender as a slave to the very first mortal owner."

He thought about it some more and added, "I had to see it. I had to see the moment my people lost their freedom. It's still resonating within me, how quickly it happened, and how devastating the results."

"I'm sorry, Tender," Jewel thought for a second. "Why didn't you stop it? We were right there."

"Because I couldn't. All I could do is watch. The djinn cannot alter that history, as much as we may want to." He stared out at the mountain range and sighed. "I'm sorry, I shouldn't have brought you there. But I had to see it, I had to."

"It's okay, I think I understand."

He smiled at her and asked, "Are you still hungry?"

"Yes."

"Then let's go somewhere to eat, shall we?"

"Of course, but where-"

They disappeared instantly.

"-are we going?"

Suddenly, Tender and Jewel were at the Eiffel Tower in 1889 at the second story restaurant sitting at a table. They easily blended in with the other diners.

Jewel gasped when she noticed how high up they were. She reached for Tender's hand again. "Where are we? Is it safe?"

"We're in Paris and don't worry, it's very safe." Tender squeezed her hand and let it go.

Jewel looked around some more until she noticed the long-sleeved dress and gloves she had on. "What am I wearing?"

"Clothes suitable for this era. I'm wearing them too, see?" He pointed out his top hat, cane, and gloves. "This tower has just opened. We're part of the first group of people to eat here. I've always wanted to see it; I thought you might like it too." But Tender's expression contradicted his words.

"You're still thinking about what we just saw," Jewel posited.

"I'm sorry, I didn't mean to ruin the mood. It's just a moment, but it means so much to my people."

"It was the beginning of the enslavement of your people. Of course you're still thinking about it."

At that moment, they were interrupted by a waiter handing them their menus. Tender thanked the waiter and noticed the confusion on Jewel's face. He explained, "This is a menu, a list of the items available to order and eat today."

"So, I can ask for anything on this list?"

"Yes," Tender affirmed.

"That would be great if I had any idea what this stuff is or tastes like."

"I can make sure it will be food that you'll like. Let me order for you." Tender looked at the menu again, though this time, his eyes glowed brighter for a bit. He caught the waiter's attention and ordered in perfect French.

"What did you do?"

"I used my powers to show me the food that you will like," Tender answered, a little embarrassed.

"I am still amazed at the things you can do. Time travel. Automatically knowing what clothes we should be wearing and how we should look. And how is it that we understand anything here at all - aren't we in a foreign country? How can you speak to them?"

"My people understand and speak all mortal languages. I temporarily extended some of those abilities to you. I hope you don't mind," Tender blushed. "You know all those scrolls and books in my lamp? What I could not tell you at that time was that many of them were from the future. I like to read, not only past history, but future history as well. While most genies sleep between masters, I read."

"So that's how you knew about all of this. That's how you knew that this place, this structure."

"The Eiffel Tower," Tender filled in the name.

"The Eiffel Tower, you knew that this would come to exist."

"Yes. That was one of the many things that I wanted to tell you, but I couldn't. I hope you're not frightened by any of this."

"No, Tender. As usual, when it comes to you and your people, I am merely amazed. Astounded. Awed. Appreciative. And any other positive word that I can think of."

The waiter brought their first course, and they began to eat. "So, genies can travel to the past and the future? With no restrictions?"

"Well, specifically, we aren't allowed to transfer any items through time unless we keep them hidden from mortals. And we can't tell those of a past era about a future era."

"Then, you're breaking all of the rules with me?"

"In a manner of speaking, yes. But technically, right now, I'm free," he grinned mischievously, "so I can do whatever I want."

When they finished their meal, Tender ordered both of their

drinks. He added cream and sugar to each cup. "It's called coffee. I think you might like it but be careful, it's very hot."

Jewel sipped it. "Mm, not bad. You're right, I like this."

"Good. I always have."

"Where do we go after this?"

"I've got an idea."

They dissolved instantly again. This time they reappeared in a small room in an ancient building. They were wearing their regular clothes but still sitting at the French table with their coffees. There were many workers milling about and the one who appeared to be in charge barked orders and instructions to the others.

Jewel jumped at their proximity, but Tender quickly said, "Don't worry, they can't see or hear us." He thought for a moment and then added, "Or feel us."

"Where are we now?"

"Egypt. I wanted to change our view. Look," he tilted his head to the open wall on his left. Outside, a short distance away, one of the ancient pyramids was being built. "I admit, I've always wanted to see them being built. I've heard rumors that some of my Brethren assisted them."

Jewel, still somewhat shocked by all their traveling, gazed at the builders. She watched Tender as he also watched and calmly sipped his coffee.

"Is Tender your real name?"

"No, it's just a name my mother and other djinn call me. Like most djinn mothers, she came up with special names for all her children, names that she thought described our personalities when we were very young. Because of the danger to my people, our real names are known only by us, our parents, our spouses, and the Leader of all the Djinn."

He paused and suddenly looked up as if he just noticed something. "The Leader of all the Djinn." He paused again and looked around, surprised. "I said it twice and I didn't bow! I didn't even feel anything all. The book of djinn law."

Tender looked as if he was expecting a reaction, but nothing happened. "I didn't bow again. I have absolutely no desire at all to show the proper level of respect because I don't want to. Wow. Free will."

He instinctively looked at his wrists where the shackles and slave symbols were. Jewel didn't want his temporary freedom to remind him of his permanent enslavement, so she changed the subject. "How do you know what people want all the time?"

"I don't. I see what you see, and I make it with magic. Most of the time, I really don't know what people are asking for but if they can picture and imagine it, then so can I. I can make it exactly to their specifications according to the images and ideas in their heads.

"As a matter of fact, that's how you can tell a trained genie from a regular one. Trained genies are taught how to read the minds of mortals in order to know exactly what they're wishing for. Untrained genies can't read mortal minds but can only guess, or just try to figure out exactly what a mortal wants."

"I thought you heard the thoughts of mortals."

"Trained genies hear the thoughts of mortals. Untrained genies only hear the thoughts as noise." He glanced up. "Oh, look. They're about to put the top on now."

Jewel and Tender watched as the workmen put the final piece of the pyramid in place. Though a few of the slaves there managed to celebrate a little, the one in charged barked out more orders and they quickly got back to work.

"It's getting late," Tender said out of the blue.

"It is?" Jewel yawned.

He nodded, adding, "It's been about eight hours since you made your wish. I need to find you some place safe for the night."

He thought for a moment then looked up. "I know."

They appeared on the top of an enormous tabletop mountain in South America right as the sun began to set.

"Tender, this is beautiful," Jewel looked around. They were still sitting at the table and chairs from the Eiffel Tower.

"I can lead you to the perfect spot to watch the sunset." Tender showed her the same two lounge chairs that were on the beach, now facing the sunset. There was also a large tent behind them and next to it, a small campfire.

"This is wonderful," Jewel gushed as they watched the sunset.

When night settled in, Tender changed the angle of the chairs with a flick of his finger so that they could look up at the unfamiliar stars. "It's fun doing what I really want for a change." Tender marveled. "I've had to submerge myself so deeply and hide my personality that I feel like I am myself for the first time. Everything I did was always buried under so many rules and laws. I think they do that so that you forget who you are."

"I saw who you are. And I remember hoping that you were like the way I thought you were, and that I didn't just imagine it."

"Am I like you thought?"

"Yes."

They stared at each other for a moment. Then Tender lifted a finger and the backs of their chairs slowly moved so that they were both sitting up.

"I created a perimeter around this area that nothing can penetrate, except us. If you get hungry, sit at the table and think of whatever you want to eat and it will appear."

"You're not staying," Jewel began to worry a little.

"You are safe here. Get some sleep, we have a busy day tomorrow."

"You're leaving," she said as she looked around the area.

Tender looked at her for a second and flicked his finger again. Two palace guards suddenly appeared, standing on either side of the door to her tent.

"That should make you feel safer."

"Where are you going?"

"To see a few things that you may find unpleasant, but don't worry, I will be back before you wake up."

He led her to the door of the tent. "Just call my name if you need anything and I'll return instantly. But don't worry, Jewel, you are safe here."

Jewel still looked a little worried, but Tender kissed her hand. "Now get some sleep."

She went inside and was amazed at the setup. Not only was there a full-sized bed, but also fresh night clothes, water, and toiletries familiar to her. Some were identical to the items she had in the palace. There was even some fruit for her to snack on.

"Fantastic."

She sat down on the bed and laughed. This whole day was just so amazing. She was so excited; she didn't know if she could go to sleep. But her excitement also caused exhaustion and after freshening up and changing clothes, she settled in the extremely comfortable bed where she quickly drifted off to sleep.

Tender could not spend the rest of the night staring into her eyes. Feeling so much love for her, he knew that the temptation to act would be too great. He respected and loved her too much for that, even if no one else could ever find out. He would know what happened and that was not fair to her.

So now, to see some of the famous military battles that he'd always wanted to see. Onto Waterloo, Gettysburg, and to see if there really was a Trojan War, especially since it hadn't happened yet, in his own time.

Chapter 58
Tender's Story: World Tourists

Well, that was disappointing. The real Trojan War was much smaller than Tender imagined, though he surmised that it was often described by people who weren't actually there, so that was probably the reason for their less than accurate descriptions. He also thought that all the wars contained way too much raw slaughter than he really wanted to see.

Tender was more interested in the strategies and logistics rather than just watching mortals kill each other, so he found that the best views were from above where he could see the battle lines better.

When he had his fill of conflict, he returned to the camp that he made for Jewel. It was still early, and some clouds were rolling in, but the camp was exactly as he had left it, with the two guards standing outside. Tender was still invisible and lighter than air, so he walked into her tent through the wall.

Jewel was sleeping soundly. She was so vulnerable and peaceful that he watched her sleep for almost an hour. Seeing that she was beginning to stir, he went to his lounge chair, changed into the corporeal version of himself, and waited for her to wake up.

A gentle rain began but Tender stood up and waved his finger so that the tent, the lounge chairs, the Parisian table set, and the guards weren't touched by it. But he let the rain fall on him, turning his face to the sky and closing his eyes. He stood there long enough to thoroughly get wet.

Jewel, now dressed and ready for the day, peeked outside the tent's opening curtains. "Good morning."

"Good morning," the genie answered, turning to look at her.

"Tender, it's raining!"

"Yes, Jewel, it is."

"Don't you want to get inside?"

"No, I don't. I have never been rained on. It feels wonderful." He turned his face to the sky, stretched out his arms, and smiled.

"Well, I think I'll enjoy it from inside the tent," Jewel was about to go back inside but then she noticed that she wasn't getting wet. She went to the border of the dry area and tried to stick her hand into the rain section. Instead of getting wet, the dry area just extended to include her hand.

Tender remarked, "You wanted to stay dry."

"Amazing." Jewel sat down at the table and continued to experiment with the dry area border. Would her foot get wet? No. What if she held something in her hand, would it get wet? No.

After a few minutes, Tender joined her in the dry area, dripping with rainwater, but he waved his finger and was instantly dry. "That was fun," he said, grinning as he sat down. "We should eat our morning meal. We have a busy day ahead." Food appeared on the table.

"Where to now?"

"Well, I would like to see a few more wonders of nature and of man first. That is, if you don't mind."

"Tender, this is your trip, we're following your itinerary. I am just happy to be included and I'm willing to go wherever you want to take me."

When they finished their meal, the genie stood up and held out his arm, "Shall we go?"

"Of course."

After spending time in their tourist cube at the Grand Canyon, Parícutin, the Taj Mahal, Rio di Janeiro, the Great Barrier Reef, and watching the Aurora borealis, they paused at the Great Library of Alexandria.

This time, they stepped outside of the cube and into the local clothes and hairstyles of the era.

"I've never seen so much knowledge gathered in one place in my life," Jewel said while looking around in wonder.

"It's one of the greatest collections in the world, for now."

"For now? What happens to it?"

"Diminished reputation, a small fire, and eventually, neglect," the genie answered. "But there are many other libraries. Here, I want to show you something."

Tender delicately pulled one of the scrolls from the walls and placed it on one of the tables without unrolling it.

"This is a popular scroll. Put your hand on it," he instructed and Jewel did. He put his hand over hers, "Now close your eyes."

Almost instantly, she began receiving information and images about the grammar of the Greek language. She saw its written language appear as images in her mind, heard the voice of the author, and began to understand exactly what he was explaining. Whatever was happening to her was happening quickly as she absorbed all the knowledge from the book. She suddenly knew and understood everything in the scroll, from start to finish.

The genie removed his hand from hers and waited for her reaction.

"I don't believe it, but now I think I know almost everything this author says there is to know about the grammar of the Greek language. And I don't even know Greek!"

"That is how my people can learn so quickly, by absorbing the knowledge from scrolls and books."

"Can you do that with any scroll?"

"Yes, though some information is easier to absorb than others. I wouldn't try it with the higher sciences; you have to go through so many other books in order to truly understand the concepts. But it works wonderfully well with history."

"Tender, that is amazing. You could have really helped me with my studies."

"Unfortunately, it is a skill available only to my people."

"I think it's wonderful, Tender," and she just stared at him, still amazed.

Embarrassed, he replied, "We should probably go, now. Are you hungry?"

"Yes."

"I know a good place to eat," the genie replied.

"Oh, good. Where-"

They disappeared.

"-are we going?"

Tender and Jewel reappeared in China, sometime during the Song dynasty. Jewel and the genie blended in with the locals, dressed in local attire, and were outdoors at a small noodle shop.

"I've read this is where and when noodles were perfected. We're in China."

They were seated at the same table and chairs from the Eiffel Tower, which distinctly did not fit in with the local furniture.

"Tender, this is the same table."

"Yes, it is. Don't worry, no one will notice. To them we fit right in." He smiled as they were served a very fragrant noodle dish. Just as he said, Jewel looked around and saw that no one seemed to notice or care that they were sitting at a table and chair set from a completely different time period and place.

"Thank you," Tender said to the server and then to Jewel, "I've always wanted to try these."

He picked up the chop sticks and began to eat. Jewel tried to hold hers the correct way but had difficulty.

"Oh, don't worry." He waved a finger towards her and suddenly she became as proficient as he was.

"I hope you don't mind my using my powers to help you."

"No, of course not, Tender, it saves us a lot of time."

"I don't like to be presumptuous."

"Tender, it's fine. I'll just add it to my list of new skills along with Greek grammar."

He chuckled and they continued eating. A few minutes later they heard a loud slap. They looked in the direction of the sound and saw a servant being berated by his master, outside of the shop. The servant was pushed, hit, and even shoved to the ground and kicked until his master walked away, his anger satiated. The servant picked up his bundle and followed.

Jewel looked at the genie, worried about how he was affected by what they just saw, but Tender just looked down, staring at nothing. Eventually, he spoke. "'I am happy to be in the service of my master.' Tell me, do mortals really believe us when we say that?" he asked, incredulous.

"To a certain extent, yes, I think."

"Extraordinary. And tragic."

"People believe what they need to believe, I suppose," Jewel looked off in the distance. "Or what they have to believe in order to justify their behavior."

"I spend most of my time on my knees, bowing and obeying as if my life depends on it because to some degree, it does. But I cannot lie to myself. I realize what I am worth. I know what I'm worth to most mortals. I know what the ownership of my lamp means to your people-a source of unlimited wishes. Even I don't know if I would turn that down if I was mortal."

"I thought you preferred to be a djinn."

"I do. I must admit, though, I have wondered at times what it must be like, being mortal. Free will may be worth the cost of mortality, I suppose. But no. I prefer this state as I am right now. To be a djinn with free will."

"When you first changed from slave to free, I was afraid because of what I had heard from our mutual friend. I was afraid that you, becoming overwhelmed in your thoughts, would turn and attack me."

"No, no, never. It was the sight of you that brought me back to myself. The rush of my thoughts was painful and overwhelming, but then I saw you. I immediately thought of all that you had done for me and it brought me right back to the present. I had to thank you and show you my gratitude. And I am still, so very grateful." He took her hand and kissed it. "To experience freedom is wonderful. And so very valuable to me." He kissed her hand again and then looked at her and smiled.

"And now, let's try something totally different." He looked at Jewel earnestly. "Are you ready?"

"Yes," she answered, ready for anything.

"Okay, let's go." They dissolved and reappeared on a crowded sidewalk in Times Square in New York in 1987. They wore different clothes and had different hair styles but blended in with everyone around them.

"Here we are."

"Where?" Jewel cried, overwhelmed by the noise and the people.

"We're far in the future. In a place called New York. During a time of outrageous, conspicuous, consumer consumption."

"What? When?"

"They call it 1987. It's in the middle of a strange period of opulence. Let's enjoy it."

Jewel, still bewildered, agreed. Tender took her hand and led her along a busy street, full of shops and shoppers.

"Oh look," Tender pointed. "A real department store! I've seen them in my visions from books. Let's go see." They walked inside Macy's, looking around among many other tourists.

"Is this a market?"

"Yes. All this stuff is for sale," he picked up the nearest item, a shoe, and showed her the price tag, "See? This is how much it costs."

Next to the shoes were a selection of leather handbags. They wandered around, looking at all the other strange items. When they walked through the perfume section, the genie paused as the different fragrances surrounded him. He took a deep breath and sighed.

"Jasmine and musk. Some artificial, some real. Tea and rose," he inhaled again. "Mint, aloe, vanilla, lemon, lime, orange, cinnamon, lavender, rosemary, balsam, ginger, and more."

"Let's move on, I want you sober," Jewel grabbed his hand and led him out of the perfume section. He inhaled again, but Jewel kept them moving.

Tender wound up buying Jewel a large leather purse and a few other things while he bought himself a wallet. Neither of them knew exactly what they were going to do with their new purchases, but they planned on keeping them as souvenirs, if nothing else.

They shopped in a few more stores and then went to a small pizza restaurant. "Pizza is supposed to be very good though I've never had it," Tender explained to Jewel as they sat at their table. It was the same table from the Eiffel Tower, but again, no one noticed.

"What is pepperoni?" Jewel asked as she read the menu.

He closed his eyes, then opened them. "It's a type of sliced sausage. Do you want to try it?"

"Sure."

Soon enough, a pepperoni pizza and two plates were in front of them.

Jewel wondered, "How do we eat this? There's so much!"

Tender watched some of the other patrons and copied them by removing a slice. "I think we eat it like this." He picked up one slice and bit into it. Jewel copied him.

"What do you think?" he asked.

"I'm not sure. It's good, but now I wonder what the sausage tastes like," she answered honestly.

Tender quickly waved two fingers over the pizza and it changed from pepperoni to sausage, including the slices that they were holding. Jewel smiled and took another bite.

"I think I like the pepperoni better."

He waved two fingers again and the pizza changed back to pepperoni. Jewel laughed and they enjoyed the rest of their meal. By the time they were finished they had tried every type and combination of pizza on the menu but had only eaten two slices each.

When they left, Jewel remembered suddenly, "Oh, I left my bags!"

"I don't want to cause a scene with magic, I'll go get them," Tender volunteered and quickly went back inside.

It was twilight but the streets were still busy and crowded with people, some shopping, others hurrying home.

Three teenaged boys noticed Jewel and one of them bumped into her on purpose while the other grabbed her hand and yanked, spinning her around so that she faced the other way. Then they walked away.

"Oh," she exclaimed more out of surprise than anything else. Tender, having just come out of the pizza place with their shopping bags, saw the whole thing and ran up to her.

"Are you alright?"

"Yes, I'm fine, it's okay," she said, but Tender focused on the three, grabbed her hand, and followed them. The teenagers turned down an alley and so did he, pulling Jewel after him.

"What did you do to her?" Tender demanded, quietly.

The three teens, surprised, turned around and stopped walking. "What?" the closest one of them said.

"What did you do to her?" Tender calmly repeated.

The three boys smiled and the talking one laughed. "Nothing, we just took her for a spin."

Tender nodded and replied, "I see. You like spinning."

Tender waved his finger and the three teenagers suddenly jerked away from each other. Tender then made a circling motion with his finger and each teenager began to spin slowly at first, but then faster, as if on their own axis, from the top of their heads to their feet. The teenagers were just about to reach dangerous speeds.

Jewel cried, "No, Tender, no! Please, stop!"

Tender's concentration was broken by Jewel and he stopped spinning the teenagers slowly. He then waved his finger again and they were released from his power. They staggered and one vomited. Tender waved his finger again and he and Jewel vanished.

Tender and Jewel reappeared on a quiet plateau on the side of a mountain with a beautiful view of a hill-filled valley and sunset. They were wearing their regular clothes at a camp site with the earlier tent and provisions around small fire. The two palace guards were also there guarding the door to Jewel's tent. It was dusk and warm, as night was just beginning to fall and the stars were appearing, slowly.

Tender was struck by his own acts of violence as he sat down heavily in front of the campfire and sighed, "I would have killed them if you hadn't stopped me."

"But you didn't. They were just being obnoxious, silly, and terribly rude."

"No one should treat you like that, ever."

"You did scare them. I don't think they'll do that to any girl again."

"I thought they had hurt you and I was going to kill them in return."

"But you didn't, you didn't kill them and I don't think that you would have." She tried comforting him, putting her hand on his arm, but he shook his head.

"Maybe my people belong in lamps and rings and bottles. Maybe we're just too powerful to be around your people."

"No." Jewel said as she pulled back, determined. "Permanent slavery is not a solution. It can't be. There must be another way."

"I don't know if we can coexist. My people, we're too dangerous for mortals to be around. We can kill you with a thought over the slightest provocation," he looked at her earnestly.

"Is that what it's like in the djinn dimension? Do your people go around killing each other with their thoughts all the time?"

Tender chuckled softly, "No."

"Then there is another way. We just have to find it."

Tender nodded, realizing that he loved Jewel even more. So much hope and optimism. It was so enticing and extremely attractive. "It's getting late. You should get some sleep. We're safe here."

"Are you going exploring again?"

"Maybe, I don't know yet."

"Can you make it so that I don't need sleep? Like you?"

Tender answered, "Yes, but it will become obvious later. I can get twenty-four hours' worth of sleep in half a second in my lamp. You cannot, so you should rest now. I've placed all your shopping in a small box in my pocket. It will expand in your room when we get back."

Jewel entered the tent, "Good night."

"Good night," he responded. She closed the tent's curtains.

"There must be something that I can do for her," Tender thought to himself, feeling a surge of gratitude for his freedom, however temporary. He came up with an idea and pulled off one of the rings on his fingers. He studied it for a second then kneeled. Holding the ring in his left hand and covering it with his right hand, he closed his eyes and focused.

Chapter 59
Tender's Story: The Third Day

The ring began to glow white until it became like a light inside Tender's hands, causing them to glow. The light became brighter and brighter, then it went out.

Satisfied, Tender put the ring back on his finger. Then he was off to visit a few more places that he thought Jewel may not want to see, some of the most debased and debauched in the world, such as Las Vegas, Corinth, Nineveh, and Sodom and Gomorrah. He wasn't planning on participating, but observing to see if they lived up, or rather, down, to their reputations.

The short answer was, yes. He found the worst state of humankind exactly as he expected it until he could take no more. It was tragic, really, and it disgusted him so much that he watched a volcano erupt in the Pacific just to clear his mind and cleanse himself from the stains of the images he witnessed.

The eruption was a harmless one on an uninhabited island that had already been through several eruptions. It was extremely destructive, but beautiful in its own way. He sped through time while staying suspended in one place and watched as the island reinvented itself after its final eruption. Life was rejuvenated until the island was over-flowing with nature. It was truly refreshing.

He watched the sun rise repeatedly from several places around the world and then decided to see the view of earth from the moon and a few other planets. By then, he sensed that Jewel would soon be waking up, so he transported himself back to their camp. Her kindness was a soothing balm to the horrors of the world. He sat down on one of the lounge chairs and watched another sunrise.

Jewel came out of her tent, dressed and ready for another day. "Good morning, Tender. What do you have planned for us today?"

"Well, let's eat a light meal first at the Palace of Versailles." He waved two fingers and he and Jewel were instantly transported to the Grand Trianon at the Palace of Versailles at a truly grand table.

He and Jewel were dressed for 1688 and blended in well with the grandiosity of the other guests. They sat next to each other and were conspicuously ignored so much so that Jewel eventually asked Tender quietly, "Why isn't anyone talking to us?"

"They don't want to offend us. We are in the guise of the king's particularly favorite guests, two of the most easily offended people in all of Paris."

Jewel hid a laugh behind her hand and Tender replied, "Now for a tour of the palace proper."

"You mean there's more?"

"Yes, a lot more," he grinned as he stood up and held out his arm to her.

She began to stand but hesitated. "Shouldn't we wait at least until the king has finished eating?"

"They can't see us anymore, anyway." She looked and saw that the two people whose identities they had assumed were still seated at the table, calmly eating.

She looked down at herself, now dressed in regular clothes along with the genie. He took her hand and led her on a floating tour of the palace. When they reached the Hall of Mirrors, they paused.

"I've never seen such opulence," Jewel noted.

"I have, unfortunately. But on to our next destination, and a bit of a rest." He waved two fingers and they vanished.

Appearing again in the Colosseum in Rome, they went inside the Flavian Amphitheater. They were seated in the section for wealthy citizens with cushions, food, and servants. The spectacle being performed in front of them was a re-enactment of a famous battle that included extremely skilled archers and men on horses.

"A colosseum! I've always wanted to see one." Jewel cried, barely containing her excitement.

"I thought you would enjoy this."

"Oh, thank you, Tender," she resisted the urge to hug him in gratitude, settling for squeezing his hand instead. They had become quite accustomed to holding hands, having only each other in all their new surroundings.

As Jewel looked around in wonder, Tender also surveyed his surroundings but was much more wary. One of the servants looked at Tender knowingly and smiled and nodded. The servant was also a djinn.

Tender nodded back since it was extremely rude not to acknowledge a fellow djinn in the mortal world, but he did not like the feeling of being recognized for what he was.

When one of the guards of a different rich family also nodded without smiling, Tender nodded back, then said to Jewel softly, "We cannot linger here too long, Jewel, for I am already being recognized for what I am. I'm sorry, but there are too many of my people here."

"That's fine, Tender. The gladiators are about to fight and I don't think I want to watch people hurting each other."

"Thank you," Tender replied, then he waved two fingers and they vanished and reappeared in an amusement park in 2019 that was filled with roller coasters and other rides.

"Tender, what is this place?"

"A place called Cedar Point. In the future they will have these places called 'amusement parks.' Inside of them are what they call rides and various other forms of entertainment. I read about them and wanted to try it."

Jewel looked around and watched roller coaster cars rush by them with the people screaming and yelling and asked, "Is it safe?"

"Yes, and don't worry. Even if it wasn't, you're safe with me," he looked around. "Maybe we should try an easy one first to see if we like it."

"Definitely."

He laughed and still holding hands, they looked around to find an easier ride to try out.

Tender put them directly on the rides, avoiding the lines, and so they went on three rides back-to-back. After the third one, a roller coaster, Tender said, "I think that's enough for me."

"Me too."

He waved two fingers and they reappeared in their lounge chairs at a different deserted beach an hour before sunset. They were in their regular clothes and lying in the lounge chairs from earlier.

"Tender, it's sunset already?"

"I admit I've been playing around with time a bit. Putting us in different places at different times just so we'd be able to enjoy certain things."

"Like how the sun is about to set again?"

"Yes. I can't change the total amount of time that we have, but I can change our places within the time limit. I have an hour and a half left."

"Then let's just relax and enjoy it."

They both were extremely sorrowful at the prospect of their time together ending. But Tender didn't let himself think of his return just yet. Instead, he focused only on where they were now. Jewel also tried to be, if not cheerful, at least grateful for the time that they had left.

After an hour, Tender softly said, "This has been wonderful, Miss. I could not have imagined a better experience than I've had in the last three days. I must thank you again for it, Miss."

"You're calling me miss again." She wanted to plead with him to call her Jewel, but she knew that would be futile.

"I have already begun to change back, Miss. It seems to be an internal transformation as much as an external one. The slave symbols have reappeared on my wrists." He showed her the insides of his wrists and then looked out over the water again. "But I am still really enjoying this, Miss."

"Tender, I meant to ask you. What does the slave symbol mean? Is it the djinn word for 'slave'?"

"No, Miss. It is the djinn symbol for the word, 'under.'"

"Oh."

They watched the waves in silence for a few more minutes.

"I have a present for you, Miss. A small way to thank you for these few days of," he paused and quietly said, "freedom."

It was painful for him to say the word. Jewel saw him wince as he said it and she tried to keep from crying.

Tender removed a ring from a finger on his left hand and held it up. "This ring, Miss, when you wear it, will look like any other. But when you turn it around your finger it will allow you to see and hear as a trained djinn sees and hears. You will be able to see and interpret emotions to hear and understand the thoughts concerning any requests made of you, Miss, and occasionally see glimpses of the future.

"Turn the ring again, Miss, and the djinn abilities will disappear and you will return to your normal human state. The ring is yours and you may give it to whomever you will, whenever you will. Miss, you admired the abilities of my people so much that I had to share them with you in some small way." He placed it in her hand and she put it on her left forefinger. The ring was too big at first, but it resized itself to fit perfectly.

"All I ask, Miss, is that you try not to use it on me."

"Oh Genie, thank you. I hope it was not too much trouble for you to get," but the significance of his gift was lost to her being upset about his re-enslavement.

"I created it last night, Miss. It was nothing, really, I only had to focus on it for a few minutes. A gift from a djinn is usually considered a rare and precious thing for a mortal, but it is nothing compared to what you have given me, Miss."

"Thank you, Tender. I will treasure it, always."

"And I will treasure these few days with you, always, Miss."

They looked out at the water again for the remaining fifteen minutes. Then, out of nowhere, a giant whirlwind began to surround them. It affected nothing else around them except the items created by Tender's magic, which began to disappear. First the tent, then the guards, then the Parisian table and chairs. They all dissolved into nothingness.

Tender and Jewel stood up facing each other as the lounge chairs and umbrellas began to disintegrate. They looked at each other and held hands. The whirlwind continued closing in on them.

Slowly, they began to lean towards each other, almost involuntarily. Inevitably, they kissed each other, tentatively and gently, pulling away as the whirlwind began to overwhelm them.

The genie let go of her hand, closed his eyes, and began to float slightly off the ground. He lifted his arms up until his wrists were in front of his chest and four open shackles appeared before him, one for each wrist and ankle. They clamped slowly in place, locking with a loud metallic sound.

She watched his face as he appeared to rush through several emotions as the shackles magically took hold of him. Anger, then fear, and finally sadness, as he lost the struggle and his enslavement reclaimed him.

Then his face turned blank as he showed no emotion at all, and he appeared unnaturally calm. Or maybe, Jewel finally noticed how unnatural his calmness really was.

He clapped his hands together and they were instantly returned to her uncle's palace in their side room. He was back in his submissive position, kneeling before her while floating, as usual, and tilting his head, listening for his master's call, while she stood, silently, in front of him.

For the first time, she saw how abnormal this state of enslavement was. The genie was completely subdued, submitted to the oath and shackles that controlled him, suitable only for serving his master.

But Jewel had seen him as he truly was and could not bear to see him this way. Not now, the contrast was painful. He wasn't even allowed to look at her anymore. She ran off to her room while the genie lowered his head, ashamed of his lowly status.

<h1 style="text-align:center">Chapter 60
Tender's Story: Re-Enslavement</h1>

J ewel told Rose that she wasn't feeling well and wasn't up to continue her studies that day. Rose took one look at her pale face and red eyes and asked, "Should I fetch the doctor, Miss?"

"No, there's no need," Jewel replied. "I think it was just something I ate. I should be fine in a day or two, I just need to lie down. Thank you, Rose."

Jewel managed to interrupt her regular schedule with peaceful solitude, except for her raging and conflicting emotions. She could not immediately act as if nothing happened, as if she hadn't just spent three days with the love of her life. With Tender. Even thinking of his name almost caused her to cry. Three brief days. It was the only real time that they had together with his true personality out in the open. When they were free to kiss each other.

THE GENIE HAD to continue on as before, so he did. As far as anyone could tell from his behavior, absolutely nothing had happened. The genie was exactly as he was before, calm, deferential, submissive, and obedient, all signs of his complete enslavement.

Only in the silence of his lamp could he recall the excitement of the last three days and the pleasure of hearing his mother's name for him out loud. It was extremely satisfying to be known for who he was and not just what he was. Especially when it came to hearing Jewel call him Tender, which filled a need he didn't even know that he had.

His love for her only grew stronger, as did his desire to care for her. But he had to protect her at all costs so he could not dare to show any emotions towards her of any sort, even though his very being cried out for her presence.

Outside of his lamp, the demands and expectations did not subside, and his life continued to be at the mercy of his master, even at his next scheduled appointment with Jewel and their monitor.

He was next to the throne of the king in his regular place waiting for Jewel to appear, but he saw in his mind that she was moving slower than usual. He heard her governess ask if she was still ill, but Jewel told her that she was well enough to go on with her day, including her appointment with the genie.

In response, the genie bowed to his master, disappeared into smoke, and reappeared in their designated space, bowing to the captain.

"Greetings, Genie."

"Greetings, sir."

Then Jewel arrived in the court, bowed to the king, and went directly to their little area of the court. He could sense her strain immediately. He bowed to her.

"Good afternoon, sir," she spoke to the captain and he nodded. "Good afternoon, Genie."

"Good afternoon, Miss."

She didn't say anything for such a long time that the genie asked her, "Forgive me, Miss, but are you unwell?"

"Yes, thanks for noticing, Genie. I have been a bit ill lately but I believe I'm getting better, thank you." There was another long pause. "How are you, Genie?"

"I am very well, Miss, and thank you, Miss, for asking," he replied with a small bow.

There was another long pause. "Forgive me please, Genie, but perhaps I'm not as well as I thought. I will have to see you next week."

"As you wish, Miss. I hope that you feel better soon," he bowed his goodbye.

"Thank you, Genie."

He dissolved into smoke and reappeared by the king as she left. Their interaction was so brief that the king noticed.

"That was a really short conversation today, Genie."

"Yes, Master. Your niece is unwell."

"Really? Then I'd better go see her. Back to your lamp, Genie."

"Yes, Master." The genie dissolved into smoke and reappeared inside of his lamp. He could tell immediately what was wrong. He sat, closed his eyes, and focused on the king entering Jewel's bedroom. She was laying down again, attended by Rose.

"Jewel, are you alright?"

"Yes, Uncle, my stomach has been a little upset lately."

"Get the doctor," the king ordered Rose, who left the room.

"I'm sure it's nothing serious," Jewel added. This time, her stomach really was bothering her along with a few other major emotional upheavals.

"Well, let's just be certain alright, my dear?"

"Yes, sir."

The genie watched as the physician examined her, gave her some medicine to drink, and told her, "This will help you sleep. I want you to get plenty of rest for the next few days."

The doctor privately told the king, but mostly Rose, "She has an upset stomach. She should eat very lightly, if at all, for the next two days. Make sure she keeps drinking water and weak tea and gets plenty of rest. Let me know when her appetite fully returns."

"Yes, sir," Rose bowed and left to make Jewel more comfortable.

"Has she been under any kind of stress, lately?" the doctor inquired of the king.

"The strain of an upcoming marriage. We have scheduled a meeting with her first potential suitor next week."

"Then that's probably the cause. A few days of calm should quiet her nerves."

"As a child, Jewel would usually get an upset stomach when she was distressed."

"Then this is just more of the same. When do you plan on holding the wedding?"

"Next spring, I hope."

"Congratulations, sire."

The genie stopped listening to them after that and watched Jewel fall asleep instead.

Jewel continued with her routine after a few days of rest. She even met with the first prospective husband without a single incident. They were the royal family of a neighboring kingdom, so a certain amount of formality and ceremony dictated their first meeting.

Jewel was calm and demure, and the meeting was uneventful. She managed not to challenge the young man in any way, which was completely unlike her. Their few minutes together were pleasant, peaceful, and boring. Of course, that meant that the royal young man and his royal parents absolutely loved her.

After the king and Jewel bid the nice young man and his nice parents goodbye, the king turned to her and asked, "Alright, Jewel, what's going on?"

"Nothing, sir."

"'Nothing, sir?' Now I know something wrong. Why are you acting this way, Jewel? I've known you since you were three years old. I can tell when your heart is in something and when it is not."

"I'm sorry, Uncle. It's just that, it's so difficult to pretend to be interested in someone when I'm not. At all."

"Is it the young man? Is he not to your liking?"

"I don't know. Maybe that's just it. Maybe I'm finally realizing that what I'm looking for may not be available in any young man."

"Really?"

"Why marry someone who's just as young and ignorant of the world as me? Is it wrong to desire someone who knows more than I do? And is more experienced than I am?"

The king paused and said after a sigh, "Jewel, that is one of the wisest and most astute statements you've ever made. I have never known or even heard of any woman near your age, or older, demonstrate such good judge of character."

"Thank you, Uncle."

"I will keep that in mind when searching for a husband for you."

"Thank you, sir." Though that's not what she had meant. She was describing the genie, of course.

"And who knows, maybe I won't have to search so far and wide for the best husband for you. Maybe your best match has been in view the whole time."

"Sir?"

"I've got to go to court. I'll see you later, Jewel."

She wondered who he had in mind. She knew it couldn't be the genie. If only she could marry him then all would be well. She nervously twisted her new ring as she watched her uncle leave.

Suddenly, she heard her uncle's thoughts, "Maybe I should marry her. She is perfect for me and I could use a companion. Maybe not. I know her too well."

"Oh no," she said out loud as she hoped that her uncle's thought was just a fleeting one.

The next day, she was looking forward to seeing the genie since they hadn't spoken since that last fifth day of the week.

He bowed to her, as usual, as she entered the Crystal Court Room.

"Good afternoon, Genie. Captain."

The captain nodded and the genie spoke, "Good afternoon, Miss."

"Genie, I was wondering, how many wishes do I have left? The ones that I never used?"

"Five, Miss."

"Really? That many?"

"Yes, Miss. One each for your own birthday, and one for my master's for the past three years, Miss. Only one of which you used."

"I guess I'm just not that big on wishes."

"Perhaps you haven't found exactly what you want to wish for, Miss."

"Yes, Genie. Perhaps not."

The captain began looking around nervously.

"Sir?" the genie asked.

"What's wrong?" Jewel joined in. "What's missing?"

"My medal from the king, Miss. Would you mind terribly if I go and get it, or at least send for someone else to get it?"

"Do you wish me to get it for you, sir? It would take less than a second," the genie offered.

"Genie, would you?" He was obviously apprehensive.

"Yes, sir." A small silver medallion appeared in the genie's hand and he handed it over. "Here you are, sir."

"Thank you." He looked at the back of the medallion.

"Excuse me, please, Miss. I will return shortly." The captain left the crystal court, almost running away.

"What happened?" Jewel asked.

"He's going to get someone to repair it, Miss."

"You could have fixed it, Genie."

"He is reluctant to take advantage of my abilities, Miss."

"Well, your powers are truly remarkable, though it does take some time for us mere mortals to get used to them."

"Yes, Miss."

She paused. "Genie?"

"Yes, Miss?"

"I don't know if I can do this anymore. I just don't know if I can be around you like this."

"Forgive me, Miss, if I have offended you in any way." He bowed low.

"No, Genie. You have not offended me. It's just that, I don't know if I can keep doing this."

"I apologize, Miss. We may discontinue our conversations if they no longer please you."

"No, Genie, you always please me. I am not pleased with myself. Excuse me. Please." She ran off to her room, threw herself onto the cushions lining her bedroom, and began to cry again.

To see the genie, her gentle, sweet Tender, enslaved and so degraded, she couldn't pretend to blindly accept it anymore. The lively, inquisitive, fun, and highly intelligent genie that she had come to know even more over the last three days was gone.

To watch him kneel at her feet, begging for forgiveness after causing no offense, bowing to those he was clearly superior to, and groveling just to receive the basic necessities of life was too much to witness.

"It's not right, it's not right," she said to herself. "If only I could marry him."

"Perhaps we should not have kissed," Tender repeated to himself, trying to soothe the ache in his heart. His three days with Jewel were a dream, a perfect fantasy. The entire world was at his disposal and he had the perfect companion. It was so wonderful that he could hardly believe that it really happened.

But it did. And they *did* kiss. He unconsciously touched his own lips while remembering it and felt crushed at the prospect that he may never enjoy her companionship again. Jewel was the perfect partner for him. She eagerly allowed him to lead, was willing to try exotic new foods, and go to unusual places. She trusted and looked to him for answers. She even helped him through his brief emotional crisis.

Jewel was wonderful, a true gift, and he was deeply in love with her. She was already cherished by him. For several lifetimes. And a day.

He almost laughed at his own excessively romantic thoughts. *I suppose I was not meant for happiness or love,* he thought and tried to resign himself to losing her company. He could just resort to watching her whenever her presence was required in court. He was lonely before and he could be lonely again. The Leader of all the Djinn was right. He could not have her.

Chapter 61
Training: Fighting and Obedience

After all the boys returned from home, they were told to unpack immediately and join their teacher for their midday meal. Their excitement from being at home carried over into their conversation. Only Alley didn't speak as much.

"I got to play with my little brother; he can walk now," Clever said while munching on bread.

"I think my oldest sister might be getting married," Joy added.

"Mine too. It's going to be weird coming back home and she's not there," Tender said.

"I know. But we must wait a whole year. That's a long time," Joy replied.

"What did you do, Alley, while we were away?" Peaceful asked and all the boys became quiet to listen to his answer.

"Nothing much. I just stayed around the teachers, mostly."

"Did you get to go anywhere or do anything?" Bold asked.

"No. Not really." Alley glanced at the First Teacher, who winked at him. Alley smiled in return. "I just hung around the training building."

"Did you have fun?" Tender asked Alley, who nodded his answer.

"When I got home they had this big wedding for my cousin. I didn't want to go but I had too," Thoughtful volunteered.

TENDER APPROACHED Alley during their unstructured dorm room time.

"Do you want to try some of my perfumed melon? My mother made me bring some back from home with me," Tender said. "I have to eat it before it goes bad."

"No. That smells funny," Alley answered.

"You can change the smell to whatever you want. That's why I like it. Or it can have no smell at all." Tender thought to himself that he shouldn't have mentioned his mother.

"Why do you have to always be so nice all of the time?" he asked Tender. "I don't want your stupid melon."

"What's wrong?" Tender asked.

"Sometimes I just want you all to leave me alone. Just leave me alone!"

Alley began using magic to push Tender away with his right hand. Tender did what he saw his older brothers and sisters do, he used his powers to push back. They pushed each other to the opposite walls of the dorm room until the First Teacher appeared in the room. He quickly waved his hand and Tender and Alley's magic fight stopped.

"Stop it, both of you!"

Then the First Teacher, Tender, and Alley disappeared. The Second Teacher appeared at the desk, reading a scroll.

In the Teacher's Lounge, the three appeared. The First Teacher pushed Alley and Tender into chairs opposite his. "Alley. You've got to stop getting upset every time someone mentions a family member. Other genies have families. You should not be insulted by this. Tender was just being nice to you."

"I'm sorry," Alley replied with a tear streaming down his face.

"And neither one of you should ever use your powers against the other. Members of the Brethren don't attack each other."

"I'm sorry," Alley responded again. "I didn't even know that I could do that."

"I'm sorry too. I didn't know that I could do that either." Tender replied, smiling.

"It's an emotional response. Whenever you feel upset or threatened you can create bursts of energy that can literally push others away. If you had tried that on a mortal it could have destroyed them."

"Really?" Alley asked, intrigued.

"Yes. I should punish you both, but it is your first day back. Instead, I have something else in mind."

The First Teacher caused them to disappear and reappear in the Magic Room, a very large all white room.

"Since you both used your powers emotionally, you might as well learn how to focus and control it better." The First Teacher raised the index finger on his right hand and two targets consisting of large mounds of solid rock appeared at the other side of the room. "Tender, yours is on the left. Alley, yours is on the right. Now, with just as much anger and focus that you used before, shoot the targets."

Tender held up his right hand and Alley his left. They aimed at their respective targets and used their powers to push the solid rock back. The two mounds of rock moved slightly and reluctantly back just a few centimeters.

"That's good, but I want you to use all of the emotions that you showed before. Alley, use your anger. Tender, use your natural desire to defend yourself. Imagine the target as something coming to attack you and your family. Try again."

Alley's target moved back a meter, as did Tender's target. "Good! I knew you boys could do it. This Magic Room is a great place to go and work out your anger and to practice using your powers. You both have similar power levels and I knew that you could do it. Normally, we show the young Brethren how to do this near the end of your first year. But in this case, I thought that you both needed to learn how to do it at this present time. Now let's try to move the targets all the way to the wall."

Chapter 62
Tender's Story: Love, Part 1

Over the next few weeks, the situation worsened. Not only did Jewel lose interest in meeting with the genie, she also appeared to lose interest in everything else. Her participation in her daily routine dropped and she seemed more and more despondent and depressed.

While the genie's behavior seemed to be the same, some of his enthusiasm was definitely lacking. It was subtle, but noticeable to the one who spent the most time with him. It was at that point that his master began to suspect something else. "Genie?"

"Yes, Master?"

"Do you know what's bothering Jewel lately?"

"No, Master, I do not."

"Was her behavior towards you any different?"

"The last time we spoke she seemed to be reluctant to talk, Master. She didn't say much and she left very quickly."

"Did she seem hurt or angry?"

"No, Master. Just depressed and upset."

"And you haven't seen her since? She hasn't tried to communicate with you recently, in any other way, has she?"

"No, Master."

"Are you in love with her, Genie?"

"Yes, Master. Very much so."

The king slapped the genie so hard that he fell to the floor. He slowly returned to his submissive position while his master glared at him. "How dare you."

"Forgive me, Master, I could not help it."

"And what am I to do with you?"

"Forgive me, Master, please, I beg you."

"What use are you to me now?"

"Master, if I may, it matters not who I love, why I love, or even if I love anyone, Master. I am still enslaved to you, the owner of my lamp, and I must fulfill your wishes. My loves and desires are meaningless, especially when it comes to my service to you, Master. In order to fulfill my oath, I must serve you well and be pleasing to you. That is my only desire, Master. The concerns of my heart matter very little, if at all."

"That sounds more like a frustrated lover than a slave, Genie."

"My service towards you is my only concern, Master. All else matters not."

"So, nothing else matters, Genie? Let us put this to the test, then, since you only exist to please me. Guards!"

Four palace guards entered the Crystal Court Room.

"Bring Jewel and the slave master here at once. We will see what truly matters."

The genie started at the thoughts of what his master was planning, but he couldn't see any clear way to avoid it. Yet.

The slave master entered.

"Give the genie your whip," the king yelled to the slave master while pointing at the genie. Thoroughly confused, the slave master handed his whip to the genie, who took it reluctantly. Holding the instrument of his own torture felt very odd.

The guards returned with Jewel between them.

"Uncle?"

"Tie her up."

"Uncle, what-"

"My goodness, girl! Do you not know when it is best to be silent?"

She cowered but remained bewildered by her uncle's actions. The slave master brought out the rack and tied her to it.

"Now, Genie, punish her for allowing you to fall in love with her. Give Jewel three lashes."

"Master, I beg you, punish me and not her."

"That is not what I told you to do, Genie. I wish you to give her three lashes. Obey me. Now!"

The genie stood up, got into position, and raised the whip. But as soon as he looked towards Jewel, he froze, dropped the whip, and fell to his knees. "Forgive me, Master, but I cannot." Tender said quietly. He was suddenly struck with extreme pain all over his entire body. "She has done nothing wrong," he managed to say. "Punish me and not her, Master. Please, I beg you."

Tender fell to the ground, half bowing to his master, half reacting to the pain.

"Tie him up, too," the king barked. The slave master asked his assistant to bring in another rack.

"Please, Master, I beg you, do not harm her," the genie pleaded.

"Uncle, what is wrong? What have I done wrong?" Jewel asked, too shocked to be upset.

"Nothing, Jewel, nothing. Except to cause this magical creature to fall in love with you. This genie, who declares that his love for you has no effect on his service to me. Well, I believe I have just proven him wrong, haven't I?"

A second rack was brought in and Tender, once again, helped the slave master tie himself to it as his shackles formed loopholes again. His pain had subsided somewhat, but not entirely.

"Oh no, Uncle."

"And you." Her uncle turned towards her. "You're in love with him, aren't you? Aren't you!"

"Yes," she replied in anger.

Her uncle just shook his head. "I had great plans for you, girl. Great plans! You were being groomed to be a consort for a king, a companion to an emperor. And yet you fall in love with this, this slave?"

The king picked up the whip and prepared to strike her.

"No," Tender, still in pain, cried out, "No! Please, Master, I beg you, please do not harm her. Punish me instead, please, punish me, for I am guilty of falling in love with a mortal."

"Very well, Genie. Ten lashes for you and then ten lashes for her."

The king gave the whip to the slave master, who quickly began to whip Tender. Jewel, tears streaming, was determined to remain silent to not upset her uncle even more. Tender accepted his punishment stoically, barely reacting to the whip. The physical pain that he was already experiencing from his disobedience was far greater.

But as soon as the slave master turned to lash Jewel, the genie cried out again, "No! Please no, Master. Punish me again instead of her."

"No, ten lashes for her too! But only three if you do it yourself."

"Please Master, I beg you, do not harm her, for it was all my fault."

"No! The fault was mine! I should not have spent so much time with him," Jewel cried. "Please don't blame him alone."

The king stared at her and then at him, becoming more enraged at their defense of each other. "Bring me the Eye of The Djinn. It will make you both change your minds."

"Please, uncle-"

"Quiet! Both of you."

Within seconds, the djinn relic was brought to the king, who handled it with extreme care. The Eye of The Djinn was a strange white, round, glowing pearl on a red cushion encased in a silver box. The Eye emitted a strong, bright, green light like a spotlight. The king opened the box slightly and it projected a beam of light. He aimed the light directly at the djinn.

Tender cried out in pain. It was if his entire body and soul were on fire, leaving him writhing. The king closed the box after five seconds and Tender went limp with exhaustion. "Will that change your mind, Genie? Will you punish her now?"

Drained, Tender answered him, breathing hard and nearly whispering, "Have I not served you faithfully, Master? Have I not served you well? I have obeyed your every whim and yet, you show me no mercy."

"You deserve no mercy when it comes to my niece. If you will not punish her, then I will do it myself."

"No, please, Master," Tender cried, finding his voice again. "I pledge you my line, the entire line of my descendants to your entire line of descendants if you will please not harm her in any way. Please, Master."

The king, furious, only lifted the whip and was about to strike Jewel when he was interrupted by the sudden appearance of the Leader of all the Djinn in their midst with an extra flourish of white smoke.

He looked at the three of them, in turn. Tender bowed his head to him as much as he was able from the rack. The Leader returned his greeting with a small nod.

"Well, isn't this interesting. A djinn who might die is pledging his line of descendants. A young woman in love, being punished for an impossible relationship. And a king, about to destroy his most valuable possession because of a tantrum. A tantrum!"

The king wasn't remorseful but was subdued. The Leader of all the Djinn approached the genie. "I warned you, djinn, that this would not end well. I cannot protect you because you have broken one of our most important laws by defying your master. But I will stop you from pledging something that you have absolutely no control over. Especially now."

He turned to the king. "And you. Will your anger ever subside? Will you destroy your position, your palace, and all your property as well? None of which you would even have if not for this djinn, the one you so eagerly wish to punish."

The Leader of all the Djinn moved closer so that only the king could hear him. "'A consort to a king? A companion to an emperor?' Really? What king, exactly? Which emperor? Do not dare pretend to be so altruistic with me or I will demand, in front of your entire kingdom, that you name the nonexistent brother or sister that this niece of yours came from. If you wanted to groom another wife, why not just say so and be done with it?"

Finally, he turned to Jewel. "And you, my dear. Though you were wise enough to hide your acts of love and kindness in your daily routine, you could not prevent all the results of that love. You had no idea that it would be so destructive to the object of your affection because you were only following your heart. And before you even had your own wishes fulfilled."

He then faced all three of them. "I cannot interfere with these dismal and disastrous events. I can only ensure the fairness of these proceedings and make sure that no one oversteps their boundaries or promises too much. And, as always, clean up the aftermath. However. No one will die here today. I can ensure that."

"Then I can punish him with the Eye of The Djinn?"

"Yes. It will not kill him, but it will destroy his soul."

"Good." The king opened the silver box wide, again aiming it at Tender, who began to cry out and writhe in pain again.

"Wait!" Jewel cried. "My wishes!"

The king closed the box and the genie fell limp on the rack. "What?"

"My five wishes that I never made! The wishes that you said I could have! You promised me."

"You want to make your wishes now?" the king asked, incredulously.

"I want to make them while he's able to fulfill them, not when his soul is gone," Jewel said, recovering somewhat. "Please, Uncle, you promised me."

"Well. Hurry, before I destroy this creature."

Jewel paused, thinking for a second before she answered. "Genie," she turned to look directly at him, though he still hung his head. "I wish to marry you as a djinn and to live with you happily as your wife among your people."

"No," the king murmured, but it was too late.

"Your wishes are granted," Tender whispered and then lost consciousness.

Instantly, Jewel began to transform. The bonds of the rack dissolved and she walked forward. She blinked a few times as her eyes began to glow with the magic inside of her. She closed her eyes and became translucent and ethereal, floating in the air.

"No," the king whispered in vain as she gradually turned into white smoke. The unconscious genie also began to turn into smoke but it was a sickly greenish brown color with streaks of red. Both clouds of smoke quickly vanished.

The Leader of all the Djinn stared at the king. "You will never see her again and it will take some time for your genie to recover. You may decide what you want to do with him afterwards." Then he disappeared in a great cloud of white smoke.

Untitled

About Vibes: We are an independent publishing company that believes writers should only have to worry about writing. Meaning, you write your book, we'll do the rest.

To learn more about us, our authors, and their books, please visit us at

Writeandvibe.com | Fb & IG @writeandvibe

9 781953 430267